DEPRAVED SINNERS

SHERIDAN ANNE

Sheridan Anne
PSYCHOS: Depraved Sinners #1

Copyright © 2021 Sheridan Anne
All rights reserved
First Published in 2021
Anne, Sheridan
PSYCHOS: Depraved Sinners #1

This book is a work of fiction. Names, characters, places, and incidents are products of the author's imagination. Any resemblance to actual events or persons, living or dead, is entirely coincidental.

No part of this book may be reproduced, stored in a retrieval system or transmitted in any form or by any means, without prior permission in writing of the publisher, nor be otherwise circulated in any form of the binding or cover other than in which it is published, and without a similar condition, including this condition, being imposed on the subsequent purchaser.

Cover Design: Sheridan Anne
Photographer: Korabkova
Editing: Heather Fox
Formatting: Sheridan Anne

PSYCHOS

For the girls who need a little psycho in their life!!!
Restock those batteries!

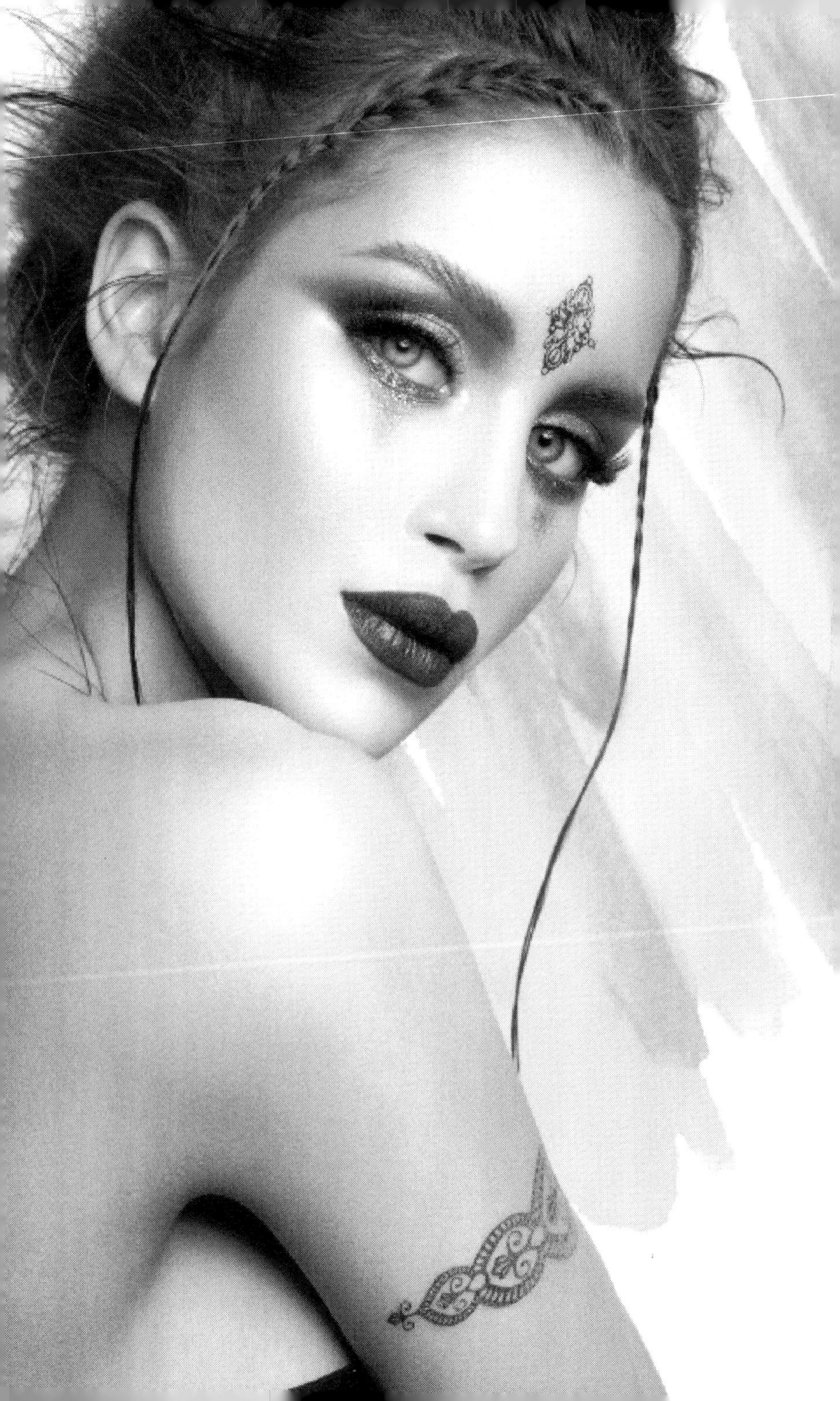

ONE

Fuck homelessness and fuck turd-tastic landlords. They can shove a stick of dynamite up their bitch asses and play with a box of fireworks while hoping to God they don't blow themselves up. We shall call it dynamite roulette and it will be the game of the century.

Letting out a sigh, I stumble to the fridge and I glare at the stupid piece of paper pinned beneath a magnet. 'Notice to Vacate' is printed in bold red lettering across the top and I can't help but feel as though it was printed this way just to mock me. "Fuck you too," I sneer, ripping the freezer door open and scowling at the contents.

My fridge is supposed to be my happy place, but the barren wire shelves are just a reminder of how awful the last six months have been. A single tub of half-eaten ice cream stares back at me, and with the week I've had, I'm shocked there's any left at all.

It's been one of those extra shitty days, and having my landlord shove the eviction notice under my door was the cherry on top of my shit sundae. I am royally fucked, and I have absolutely no idea what I'm going to do once these thirty days are up.

In all seriousness, I should probably lay off my landlord. It's not his fault that my rent hasn't been paid. I knew the eviction was coming, and to be honest, my landlord gave me longer than expected. Though he doesn't exactly deserve an award for his patience. The man's been trying to get between my legs since the day I moved in here. He doesn't give a shit about me being homeless, the asshole is just trying to see how far my desperation will get him. He should know by now that no amount of money, not even a roof over my head, is going to have me bending over for him.

My fingers curl around the tub of Oreo ice cream and I let out a heavy sigh before closing the freezer door with a little too much enthusiasm. It's just after four in the morning and I'm freaking exhausted. I've spent an entire shift at the club dodging assholes and straining to hear customer's orders over thumping music.

My head aches. The club has recently hired a new DJ who's a little more techno than he has the right to be, and every shift that I share with him has been nothing short of a nightmare. Not to mention, having to deal with my asshole boss who thinks it's acceptable to treat his female employees like a piece of meat is always such a special treat.

I need to get out of there, but for now, it's my only income, and I can't quit until I've got something else lined up. Though, no high school GED and no other qualifications means that it's either bartending, stripping, or selling myself to pricks on the street. I don't have great options.

Digging around in the kitchen sink, I search for the cleanest spoon I can find before dragging my feet down the short hallway to my bedroom. Kicking my shoes off at the door, I push my black ripped jeans over my hips and thighs until I'm awkwardly stepping out of them. My dirty black tank sails over my head in one quick motion, and I toss it into my ever-growing laundry pile near the closet. Setting my ice cream on my bedside table, I find a face wipe and begin scrubbing off the fake version of myself, more than ready to call it quits on this day from hell.

My mattress sags beneath my weight as I plop down and cross my legs, tucking my mismatched bra and panties beneath the blankets. Pushing the power button on the TV remote, an old rerun of *Game of Thrones* appears on the small screen. With a sigh, I peel the lid from my ice cream and dig the spoon deep into the yummy goodness.

There's nothing quite like unwinding with a tub of ice cream after a shitty night … hell, a shitty six months.

The Oreo ice cream melts against my tongue as I twist the spoon in my mouth. I swallow hard watching Daenerys take control of her big-ass beast of a man, and damn, the scene has me reaching toward my bedside drawer. I take my hat off to her. She's a fucking boss ass bitch living the freaking dream. Who wouldn't want to fuck Khal

Drogo? Just the thought has goosebumps spreading over my skin.

Shoving the ice cream back onto my bedside table, my hand falls right to the bottom drawer. I dump its contents on the floor beside my bed and start digging through the endless options. Majority of these little guys don't even work anymore. Their batteries are either fucked or I've lost their chargers, but there's one special guy who will weather all storms and always come through for me. I call him Tarzan, but not the animated version, the Alexander Skarsgård version. We've had some really amazing times together while watching that beast of a man swinging through the jungle.

My fingers curl around Tarzan's smooth body, and he looks me right in the eye, silently promising to turn my sour mood right around. I can't help the delicious smile that cracks across my lips. It's been far too long since I've screwed a guy, but for now, Tarzan will have to do.

I lean back into my pillows, scooching down the mattress and dropping Tarzan on the bed beside me. I raise my hips and slide my panties down my legs until they're a jumbled mess in the bottom of my sheets.

My knees spread wide and I close my eyes, feeling around on my bed for Tarzan. I find him right where I left him, and as my hand slips back under the blanket, a heavy excitement settles into the pit of my stomach.

I've been needing this more than I even realized. I've been so wound up today, that after a quick—or maybe not so quick—explosive orgasm, I should be able to rest my stressed mind and finally allow myself to sleep. I can deal with the bullshit fallout of the eviction notice tomorrow and figure out a game plan, but until the sun comes up, it's just me and Tarzan.

My finger hovers over the power button and I sink deeper into my pillows as Tarzan rests right over my clit. I press down gently until the first vibration rocks through my body like an earthquake. "Mmm, fuck," I whisper into my darkened bedroom, feeling the elation and pleasure pulsing through my veins, helping me relax.

All thoughts of eviction notices and stupid bar assholes are wiped from my mind, leaving me nothing but thoughts of Khal Drogo hovering over me. As my finger shuffles up Tarzan's curvaceous body to increase power, Khal Drogo's wicked grin widens as his eyes flame with a promise of a dangerous night.

Fuck, this is going to be a good one. I can feel it.

My body flinches with the powerful vibrations as a soft moan escapes my lips. My free hand drops to my ribcage and brushes over my skin, sending a wave of goosebumps spreading over me and pebbling my nipples. I tilt my head back, trying to remember to breathe as my back arches up off my mattress.

I bust it up a few more levels and the intensity shocks my system. "Oh, fuck yes," I grunt, clenching my eyes and going to town on myself as my whole body squirms. My breath comes in sharp, hard pants, but I'm not even close to finishing. If I can make this last until the sun is streaming through my bedroom window, I'll be one very happy girl.

Game of Thrones continues to play in the background, and it changes scenes, but screw Khal Drogo. This is now between me, myself, and I.

"Oh, shiiiiiiit," I groan through a clenched jaw, spreading my legs wider, and desperately wishing that I could flip onto my knees and feel a rock-hard cock slamming deep inside me. I mean, I could probably take this shit to the shower and suction cup one of my many silicone friends to the wall, but it's not the same. Besides, stopping now to get that all sorted out is only going to ruin what I've got going on and I'm not about ruining a good thing.

I feel that sweet pull deep inside me and groan as the intensity grows. It won't be long until my orgasm pulses through me, but I'm going to make it drag on as long as I can. I'm not ready to see the end of this.

My fingers brush over my tits, gently squeezing them as my clit is vigorously massaged, teased, and worshipped by Tarzan. Ready for more, I power up Tarzan just a little higher and squirm beneath his relentless vibration. My eyes fly open and I stare up at the white ceiling as my hand reaches back over my head, gripping the headboard and squeezing it hard. I dig my nails into the soft material and pant. "Fuck, fuck, fuck, fuck," I grunt as Tarzan's wicked power quickly starts to get the best of me.

My orgasm builds, intensifying with each vibration tearing through Tarzan. Everything tightens inside me, and I clench my eyes, preparing for the inevitable. So damn close. "Yes," I hiss, knowing that it's going to rock my world. Just a few more seconds and I'll be changing my name to Mrs. Tarzan.

It creeps in closer and closer. I'm right on the fucking edge, more than ready for Tarzan to throw me off into the abyss below. "Awww, fuck," I grunt, ready to lose myself. "Fuck, fuck, fuck."

My back arches just a little bit more and my chin raises higher as I tilt my head further into the pillow. My tits crave attention that I can't give them, just as my ass and pussy scream for a thorough pounding, but tonight, the pressure is all on Tarzan, and damn it, I know he's going to pull through—he already is.

I'm right there, ready to throw myself off the highest cliff when Tarzan begins to smoke and burn against my skin. "AHH. FUCK," I squeal, tearing Tarzan away from my clit and throwing him across the room. He crashes against the wall and my orgasm dwindles down to shameful ache, leaving my body even more wound up than it was before.

Tarzan bursts into flames on my bedroom floor and I panic, throwing myself out of bed and racing toward him with the bottle of water from my bedside table.

I dump the water over him and stare at his charred remains, feeling my whole world crumbling around me. Is it so much to ask just to get off without threatening to burn my clit right off my body? For fuck's sake. How do I have such bad luck?

I sink to my knees, wanting nothing more than to cry as I stare down at what used to be my best friend. "Nooooooo," I sigh as he smokes, telling me that my love affair with Tarzan has finally come to its devastating end and I'm left with nothing but the broken and overused toys that remain in my bedside drawer. I guess I'll be stopping at the store to figure out which batteries they need, though can I really afford a small fortune on batteries when I have overdue rent that needs to be paid?

Fuck. I'm screwed and not in a good way.

The soft sound of the TV plays as I scoop Tarzan's remains off the floor. I suppose the landlord will just add the destroyed carpet and the burn marks trailing up the wall to my growing amount of debt for this shithole.

Certain that Tarzan isn't about to spontaneously combust again, I dump him into my trashcan and crash down onto my bed, keeping my head slumped in my hands.

Welcome to my fucking life. It's a shit storm. Something is always going wrong.

There was a time that I was doing really well. It's not like I was ahead in my rent or anything like that, but I had enough saved up so that I could afford to take a break for a week or two. Working nights at the club downtown isn't exactly what I want to be doing with my life, but the tips are good—just not good enough. I had to slave every single night, working double shifts just to get that extra bit of cash. I had just enough to give myself a well-needed break when my scumbag father finally tracked me down and came bursting through my door with the determination to take everything he thought he was owed.

I thought I was safe here. I left his sorry, drunk ass in the dust four years ago and never looked back. He took everything I had saved, my rent, my food, even my fucking TV. I was lucky that Mrs. Brown down the hallway offered me her old one in exchange for a little help doing things around her home that aren't so simple for her anymore.

My father left me with nothing, tired and exhausted, with no way to fight him off. I give it only a few more months before that asshole finds himself in trouble again and he'll come storming back into my life. Maybe the eviction notice is a blessing in disguise. Maybe the opportunity to start over is exactly what I need to never see him again. But he'll just track me down like he always does.

I've been trying to get back on my feet ever since, but there's only so many double shifts I can take before the exhaustion claims me. Besides, I've learned the hard way that the tips don't come rolling in when you're practically asleep with your head squished against the bar.

My rent has been late every month since my father's visit, and even though I've explained my situation to my landlord, I don't fault him for wanting to get me out of here. Hell, if the situation were reversed, I'd probably be doing the same thing.

I love my home, though it's nothing special. The cabinet doors are falling off and there are more than enough marks on the walls from the previous tenants, but it's mine. I worked for this, and in a hard time where I didn't know what was going to happen, this was my salvation. And now, I have thirty days before it's all taken away from me.

My landlord is an ass. Shit, maybe that's not fair. He's only an ass when his eyes inevitably start to wander. Majority of the time, his inspections aren't so bad. The leering only comes at the end when his job is done. There have been a few marriage proposals over the years and a few drunken visits asking if I'm down to fuck, but he's always respected my space when I've asked him to leave. I know that's really not ideal qualities for a landlord, but it could be worse. Despite the eviction notice, I consider myself lucky.

My pity party is only just getting started when I go to lay back onto my pillow and sulk into the tub of half-melted ice cream, but as I attempt to forget about my horrendous night, my small apartment drowns into complete, utter darkness.

The TV cuts off, taking Khal Drogo away with it as the light above my bed shuts off. "WHAT THE EVER-LOVING FUCK?" I groan, more than ready to throw a goddamn tantrum, even if it means waking my neighbors in the surrounding apartments.

How is one person so fucking unlucky? What did I do to deserve this bullshit?

Feeling blindly for the bedside table, I shove the melting ice cream back onto it. A long sigh slips out as my head falls into my hands, feeling the weight of the world resting on my shoulders. Even though my landlord is usually on the ball with paying the utility bills, I can imagine he's seething over what I owe him. Shutting the power off must be his fucked-up way of telling me to go to hell.

I stifle a cry as I fumble through the dark bed to find my panties and once I've got them pulled into place, I rip the blanket off me and scramble around my bedside table for an old scrunchie. After twisting my light brown hair up into a messy bun and failing to find my slippers, I grab the tub of ice cream and trudge out into the hallway.

I'm too fucking tired for this. I'd do anything to be able to just close my eyes and forget that my life is as shitty as they come, but here, I am, stuck in this horrendous downfall. Taking my phone in my other hand, I light up the screen and use it to see my way as I get out of bed and wander back to the kitchen, determined to double-check if my neighbors have power or if it really is just me.

A cool burst of air fans my face as I shove the tub of ice cream back into the freezer with a scoff. Not sure if it's going to do much good without power, but a girl can only hope.

Trudging through the dark apartment, I make my way to the front door and undo the three bolts before pulling it open and peering out into the hallway. It's pitch-black, except for the small flashlight at the opposite end coming from Mrs. Brown's small apartment. "Are you alright, Shayne?" she asks in that old, croaky voice usually reserved for the elderly.

"I'm okay," I call back. "Do you need anything? Have you got some candles?"

"All I need is a nice strapping young man to make me feel like a woman again."

"You and me both," I mutter under my breath before giving her a wide smile. "If you need me, just knock on the door."

"Thank you, dear. Now go off to sleep. I'm sure the power will be back up and running by morning."

She closes her door and the light from her flashlight disappears, leaving the hallway in complete darkness again. I press the home button on my phone, lighting it up again as I close my door and bolt it. I double-check all three bolts until I'm certain that my small home is safe and start trudging back to my room.

The light on my phone keeps going out and I have to repeatedly press the button to see where I'm going. I'm not one to sleep in complete silence and darkness. I've always slept with the TV on to drown out the noise of the loud city outside my window, but tonight

I'm just going to have to bear it.

As I make my way down the short hallway, movement in the soft light catches my attention. My head flicks up to find a shadowy, hooded figure stepping out of my bedroom. I suck in a gasp, my eyes going wide as my heart begins to race.

I stare for a moment, certain that my mind is playing tricks on me in the darkness. I blink three times, trying to make the dark shadow disappear, but when a sickening laughter fills the small hallway, I turn on my fucking heels and make a goddamn run for it.

This is no fucking mind-trick. Someone is in my apartment.

A loud piercing cry tears from my throat as I reach the top of my hallway and look back over my shoulder to find the large, hooded figure slowly making his way toward me, stalking me as though he has all night to catch me.

I break out of the hallway and aim the light from my phone straight at my front door, knowing that I somehow have to get all three of the locks undone before the hooded man gets to me, but there's no fucking chance.

My feet pound against the old shitty floorboards as I struggle to catch my breath and move at the same time. The light from my phone jumps around my apartment with jarring movements, and as I get a few feet away from the door, the hooded figure slides in front of it.

Panic tears through me as I come to a screeching halt. "No," I breathe, backing up from the hooded figure. He was just behind me. How did he get there?

"How … how …" I stumble out before cutting myself off, only

that same sickening laugh sounds from behind me. I whip my head around to find the guy still in the opening and my stomach sinks. There's two of them, and I'm as fucked as fucked can be.

Backing up in the opposite direction, I move into my cramped living room so that I can see them both at the same time, but my back quickly presses up against a hard body. I spin around and look up into the horrifying, scarred face of Roman DeAngelis.

A terrified gasp tears from deep within me, too fucking scared to even scream.

If this is Roman DeAngelis, then I can guarantee that the two other hooded figures in my home are his brothers Levi and Marcus, the most feared brothers in town. They're notorious. Everyone knows of them and every fucking soul is terrified to get caught in the crosshairs of one of their twisted games. They're the things that nightmares are made of, they're slaughterers, executioners, and they fucking live for it.

I attempt to tear away from Roman, but his steel grip quickly encloses around my upper arms like a vice, his deadly scent wrapping around me. Trapped within his fierce grasp, I watch as his brothers slowly stalk closer, their dead eyes focused on their prey in a terrifying silence.

I shake my head, knowing that this is the fucking end. Where the DeAngelis brothers are involved, no one has ever lived to tell the story.

TWO

Levi and Marcus DeAngelis move in close enough so that I can see their faces beneath the shadows of their dark hoods, and the closer they get, the more my fear begins to cripple me.

These are not the kind of men a girl like me should be fucking with.

I have to get out of here, but they have me surrounded. I have no chance of survival. I was considered dead the second they broke into my apartment.

"She really is pretty," Marcus mutters darkly, his rich tone like a dagger straight through my chest. "It's a shame what happened to her."

My heart thunders, as the fear pulses relentlessly through my veins.

What does he mean '*It's a shame what happened to her?*' What are they going to do to me?

Their dark gazes flick between one another and a wicked grin pulls at the corner of Levi's lips, dropping his chin to look at me through his thick row of lashes. "Her picture was splashed all over the national news, her mutilated body with those lifeless big blue eyes. What kind of callous monster would have left her body in a shallow grave like that? It's a shame that bear got his claws into her fragile little body like that. There was nothing but ribbons of flesh. Nearly impossible to identify her in the morgue. If it wasn't for those blue eyes …"

FUCK. Fuck, fuck, fuck. The mental image is crippling.

They're going to kill me. They're psychopaths. Fucking monsters.

I just wish I knew why, only when it comes to the DeAngelis brothers, they don't need a rhyme or reason, this is just who they are. All they need is a pretty face and a warm body and their Saturday night slumber party has commenced.

"They're … they're going to know it was you," I stumble out, my words raw in my throat as the fear weighs me down. "They'll come for you. The police … they'll—"

Marcus laughs, cutting me off, and I quickly realize just how wrong I am. The news only ever tells us horror stories, shows images of victims with horrendous descriptions of how they met their end, but we never see an outcome, never see justice for the mourning families of our city. They get away with it every damn time.

The police are useless. No one can help me now.

These monsters murder for sport. It's a little adrenaline kick to get their blood pumping. Screams are their elixir of life. They need to feel someone else's fear just to keep themselves breathing. They should be locked up in straitjackets and denied every basic human right possible.

They are the grim reapers, and they will make sure that every last fucker who gets in their way knows it.

I'm going to be another statistic to them, another notch on their belts. Hell, maybe they're practiced enough that it'll be quick, but then, maybe they're also skilled enough to make it last hours on end. Either way, I need to make peace with it real fast because I won't be living to see another day.

Tonight, I will die.

Laughter floods my apartment and the sound sends chills down my spine as I shrink away, feeling so damn small around these beasts. They're almost larger than life, but not in the heroic, idolizing kind of way. They're demons who've stepped straight out of hell.

Never in my wildest imagination did I ever think I'd be so close to any of them, let alone be the object of their twisted attention. I'm a good girl. Sure, I curse a bit too much, but who doesn't? I don't take drugs, I don't whore around, I don't even get involved with bad boys because they'll break my heart and I won't be able to handle it. My life revolves around going to work, hoping I have enough to cover rent, and purchasing batteries for my friends like Tarzan. I'm as clean as it gets, I shouldn't be on their radar.

The light on my phone goes out and my world crumbles as it slips from between my fingers. I tug and pull on Roman's tight hold, hell that's assuming the guy behind me really is Roman. I've only ever seen their faces on the news, and they always use the same old pictures from when they were teenagers.

They got smarter as they grew and have managed to keep out of the public eye, but from what I'm seeing, they're fucking men now, and damn, they've grown up in the most deliciously wicked way.

They're fucking gorgeous with their dark, deadly eyes and the tattoos that creep up their necks and sharp jawlines, but that's exactly what they want. They'll happily lure willing girls like me into their traps, promising them a good night, only to take them home and see how quickly they can drain their blood.

These aren't just regular bad boys with a chip on their shoulders; these men are serial killers through and through. There is no other way to put it. Most mothers warn their babies against rapists and men slipping them pills in bars, but mothers around here don't even bother mentioning the rapists—they warn them about the DeAngelis brothers, telling of the horrors and stories that spread far and wide through our town.

And now those very brothers are in my living room, stalking me like they already own me.

The darkness overwhelms me as a sliver of moonlight filters through the kitchen window. There's enough light to see the coarse faces of the men surrounding me, but not nearly enough to guide me out of here. There's no escape.

I shake my head, nervously glancing between the two men in front of me, trying to get some kind of read on them, but it's useless. Their faces are like masks, completely concealing their every thought and desire. The need to spin around and try to get a read on Roman pulses through me, but I won't dare turn my back on the other two. Are they here to simply kill me, or do they have something a little more sinister planned?

"What do you want?" I demand, shrinking back against Roman's chest to try and get further away from his looming brothers, only all that does is allow them more room to move even closer.

Their faces don't change, not even a spark of life hitting their dark eyes as I demand an explanation. I've never crossed paths with a serial killer on the hunt before, but my gut tells me that a question like that would garner some kind of twisted smirk, but I get nothing.

My gaze flicks through the gaps between their shoulders, trying to see my apartment around them. My kitchen is only a few feet away. If I can get there, I could grab a knife from the sink and attempt to poorly defend myself. Hell, I could even throw myself out the kitchen window. I'd drop four floors, but I'd have a higher chance of survival than if I were to stay here.

I shuffle my gaze in the opposite direction and notice how the door is still bolted. My brows furrow and my eyes snap right up to Levi's hard stare—at least, I think it's Levi. To be honest, I have no fucking idea. "How did you get in here?" I demand.

The doors were locked when I got home, and I locked them behind me immediately after I walked through it. I spent two minutes trying to find my laptop to plug it into the charger and then got the ice cream from my freezer. There wasn't a single chance for them to have broken in without me knowing about it. Unless …

I suck in a sharp breath, my eyes widening in horror. "You were already here."

None of them smile or snicker, but the deadliness in Levi's eyes seem to shine a bit brighter. When I attempted to go back down to my room, he stepped out of it. This fucker saw exactly what just went down in there with Tarzan, and fuck me, he almost got to see me come.

"You're sick," I spit at him before looking across at Marcus. "You're all fucking sick."

Roman leans down beside me and I feel his lips at the base of my neck. A haunting laugh pulls from deep within his throat and that wicked grin that I've been expecting to play on his brothers' lips finally starts to spread. "Welcome to the family, Empress."

Oh, fuck no.

Roman releases my arm and I don't wait around to see what he has in store for me. My hand slams back against his junk and he groans low, so fucking low that I feel the vibrations through his chest, hitting my back.

Not wanting to waste the opportunity, I stoop low, knowing I won't be strong enough to barge through their shoulders. I hit Levi in the junk, trying to take him down too, and cry out as Roman's hand flies out and curls around my wrists. I scream, tugging harder as the desperation pulses through me. I try to barge through them as they struggle to compose themselves, but Roman's grip is relentless.

I kick up at him, narrowly avoiding breaking his nose as my long hair falls from its scrunchie. Levi starts to recover and Marcus casually steps around his brother and comes to a stop right before me. There's absolutely no way out.

Roman releases his hold on me, but only because his brother has me exactly where he wants me. A sick smile twists over Marcus' lips and his eyes flame with the slightest hint of what he has in store for me.

I shake my head, the fear well and truly sinking into my gut as my heart races, realizing that this is the end. He shuffles just a little closer until I can smell his sweet breath brushing over my skin. I gasp loud, knowing that Mrs. Brown down the hall would never be able to get to me in time, nor would I ever put her in this position. I have no choice but to accept my fate. This is it. I'll never get a chance to tell my landlord to go to hell, and I'll never get a chance to screw my father over just as he did to me.

This is it for me. This is all I'll ever be.

I'm going to die here in my mismatched panties and bra with Tarzan still smoking in my bedroom trash can.

Marcus tilts his head just a fraction to the side, and while it was a small movement, it was enough to show me just how dark and twisted he really is. I hold my breath, too afraid to move as his fingers come up and brush over the side of my face in a gentle caress. He leans in slowly as if he were going to kiss me, but his mouth pauses near the edge of my lips. His fingers trail down my neck until they're curling around the base of my throat. He squeezes tight. "Say your prayers, baby."

And just like that, his other hand comes down over my temple and I crumble to the ground, my world quickly fading to nothing.

My hip slams against the cold, hard ground and my eyes fly open as a pained cry tears out of me. It takes less than a second for reality to come crashing down over me, and the fear settles straight back into my chest with a harrowing relentlessness.

My stare sails toward the three men hovering in the narrow doorway, and I barely get a chance to get to my knees before their pitying gazes disappear and the heavy door slams shut between us, the loud *BANG* of the door echoing through my tiny room.

The first rays of morning sunlight shine through the small window high in the corner, but it does nothing to brighten the barren cell walls that surround me.

A loud echoey sound bounces through the room and I realize far too late that it was the sound of a heavy lock sliding into place.

"FUCK," I cry, racing to the door and grabbing hold of the handle, violently twisting and yanking on it as the desperation courses through my veins. This damn room is locked down like a fortress.

I can guarantee that I'm not the first person the psychos have had locked in here. They would have already made all the mistakes there were to make, leaving me to deal with nothing less than experts in their field. Every loose brick would have been cemented in. Every object in the room would have been carefully placed to ensure I couldn't find a weapon. Every possible way out of here has already been found and dealt with.

I'm their prisoner and the only way out is death.

Fuck, they should have just killed me back at my apartment. Anything is better than being forced to stay here to play the role of their special little pet.

What the hell do they plan on doing with me? I've never heard of them taking a hostage, but then, how the fuck would I know what they have or haven't done before? They don't let people walk, so even if they have been plucking random girls off the street to keep as their personal sex slaves, I doubt any of them are available for a little chit-chat to discuss the ins and outs of their stay.

How are these guys not already locked up?

I try to concentrate on my breathing, desperate to calm myself so I can try and figure out what the hell I'm supposed to do. My room is a little box with a small sink, an old toilet, and a hard looking bed in the corner. A change of clothes sits on the end and it has my lips pulling up into a disgusted sneer. Where the hell did they get these clothes and who did they once belong to?

The ground is made out of stone like you'd expect to see in an old castle from a million years ago, and damn, it's cold as fuck against the soles of my feet. I'm just lucky that it's the middle of one of the hottest summers we've ever had, otherwise I'd be shivering as well.

This is definitely some kind of twisted cell, but from what I can tell, it's built in the lower portions of a huge home. Who knows, when it comes to the DeAngelis brothers, this really could be some old-century gothic castle. They're made of money. At least, their rich as fuck father is.

Giovanni DeAngelis. The most powerful man in the country.

He's the leader of the most notorious mafia family—the DeAngelis Family—and from what I hear, they're not a family to be messed with. They're solid belief is shoot first, ask questions later, so I can only imagine how Giovanni's three sons ended up so screwed in the head.

They're heavily into manufacturing all those fucked-up little pills that I see floating around the nightclub. They're weapon dealers, smugglers, and I'm pretty fucking sure that they have every cop, judge, and prosecutor in the country on their payroll. That's probably why the three fucklords who just locked me up haven't been locked up themselves.

Anyone who stands in the way of a DeAngelis is guaranteed a shallow, unmarked grave. They're nothing but dangerous criminals, definitely not my cup of tea, yet here I am.

Fuck this. What the hell am I supposed to do?

I don't understand any of this. I have nothing to do with the DeAngelis brothers, the DeAngelis mafia family, or anyone in it. Hell, I don't even flirt with the guys at the club, let alone allow them to know who I am or where to find me.

How do these guys know who I am? How did I get on their radar? Was I targeted or is this completely random? It doesn't make any fucking sense.

My breath comes in a little faster and I quickly realize that if I don't get myself under control, I'm going to end up having a panic attack. I stop pacing the cramped cell and move over to the bed before standing on it and trying to peer out the little window, but it's too high up. I can barely reach the windowsill with my fingertips.

Glancing around the room, I realize there's absolutely nothing that I can dislodge to use as a step up. The only information this window is giving me is if it's day or night, other than that, absolutely nothing. Hell, I can't even see the tops of trees swaying in the distance.

Throwing myself out my kitchen window and dropping four floors is looking pretty fucking good right about now.

With nothing to do, I drop down onto the ratchet little bed and scan over the clothes laying on the end. It's a black tank and a pair of soft-looking sweatpants, but that doesn't change the fact that there's no way in hell that I'll be wearing them. They probably belonged to some poor girl who was gutted for sport. Though, the way they've been pressed and folded suggests that a maid has tended to these clothes. I shouldn't be surprised. They're spoiled little rich boys.

Even if we are in some kind of old, abandoned castle, I'm almost positive that these assholes would still have a full roster of staff tending to their every need. After all, psycho little serial killers still need to eat.

My face drops into my hands and I close my eyes. The exhaustion of my night has more than gotten to me. I'd give anything to just lay my head down on the shitty little pillow beside me and try and forget everything that's gone down, but I'm not about to allow myself that kind of vulnerability in a place like this. So instead, I listen.

I try to decipher every little sound that comes through the cell, wondering what each noise could be or how far away it is. I don't know if mentally trying to map this place out will help me, but my only priority is to escape this hell hole any way I can. It's a long shot, but it's the only one I've got.

Minutes turn into hours, and when a bright light shines directly into my eyes, I glance up through the small window to see the sun high in the sky. It's already midday and I haven't had any interaction with the psychos upstairs, but I know they're still here. I can hear them wandering around.

A low growl ripples through my stomach and my hands clamp down around my waist to silence it. Although I haven't eaten properly in six months, the hollow ache in my stomach reminds me of my last pitiful spoon of ice cream for dinner last night. I've already lost more weight than what's comfortable since my dad turned my shit upside down, but it's been a good twenty-four hours since I've eaten anything substantial. I need a real meal if I'm going to sustain even an ounce of energy to stay alive, but something tells me that a meal is something that I won't be coming by anytime soon.

They want me weak. What's the point of having a prisoner and then giving them the resources to help keep them from falling apart? These guys know what they're doing, and while this is certainly my first rodeo, it's not theirs.

I let out a heavy sigh. I was friends with the weird kid obsessed with death during my first years of high school, and she would always tell me strange and wonderful facts about death. I never thought her odd little facts would ever be something I would think of again, but sitting here in my little cell, I'm remembering it all. Starvation isn't the way I want to go. I need my food. I need my energy. I need to get the fuck out of here.

A soft thumping sounds through the ceiling and my back straightens as I listen. It's repetitive and almost … rhythmic, yet there's something so hollow and broken about it. It continues, getting faster and faster, but as I listen closely, I realize that the sound isn't moving. It's coming from one spot rather than traveling through the building.

I strain a little harder, moving toward the door of my crappy little dungeon cell and pressing my ear up against it. I hear the familiar sound of a bass drum mixed in with the rhythmic tones of a high-hat and snare. I quickly realize that it's not someone being murdered with a jackhammer but one of the brothers playing the drums.

I pull back from the door, shaking my head. The last thing I need is to be picturing these psychopaths as normal people and giving them human qualities. The DeAngelis brothers are monsters through and through, and the exact moment I start humanizing them is the moment that I lose the game I never wanted to play.

THREE

Drip. Drip. Drip. Drip.

"Fucking hell," I groan, slapping my hands over my ears as I lay back on my hard bed. "Make it stop."

The dripping started a little over an hour ago and it's been grinding on my nerves ever since. I've searched my cell like a maniac trying to find the source of the drip, but it's useless. There's no puddle on the ground, no water in the small sink, even the plumbing pipes are as dry as my pussy has been over the last few months. You know, besides those lonely nights with Tarzan, but now even that's been taken away from me.

I'm more than convinced that this dripping sound is some bullshit form of torture done by the DeAngelis brothers, it has to be. There's probably some hidden speaker in here and they're intent to drive me insane with it. The small sink probably isn't even hooked up to a water source.

Fuck this and fuck the DeAngelis brothers.

Drip. Drip. Drip. Drip.

"FUUUUUCK."

I clench my jaw and press my hands over my ears. I'm not cut out for a life of torture. I was created for the sole purpose of getting my rocks off in the privacy of my bedroom and scowling at assholes. That's where my skills lie. This bullshit right here is way out of my realm of capabilities.

The drip doesn't ease up and I throw myself off the shitty bed, ignoring the dull ache in my stomach and the way that my eyeballs seem to hang out of my head. I've been trapped in this little dungeon for well over twelve hours now, and I'm quickly reaching the end of my patience. I'm hungry, tired, and pissed off.

I haven't seen or heard from the brothers since they dumped me in here, and while that's probably the best thing to happen to me all day, I'm also at the point where I wish they'd just come and get their bullshit over and done with so they can either let me go or put me out of my misery.

I don't handle the unknown well. Waiting for the inevitable is what's going to kill me, but somehow, I think they already know that.

I bet those assholes are sitting up there in their bitch-ass castle, sipping on poison while resting back in their twisted thrones made from the bones of the men, women, and children they've slaughtered. Fuck, these assholes should have been born a million years ago. They would have been hailed as ruthless gods, but instead, they're just known as being fucked in the head.

The cold metal from the door stings my waist as I press myself against it, slamming my hands onto the doorframe and listening to the echoes reverberating off the walls of a long as fuck hallway. "GET ME THE FUCK OUT OF HERE, ASSHOLES," I scream, my throat burning from the raw intensity of my tone. "WHAT DO YOU WANT WITH ME?"

A harrowing laugh sounds through the small cell, the noise bouncing off the walls in every direction. I spin around, pressing my back against the cell door and flicking my gaze from corner to corner. The laugh was so loud, so real. It sounded as though it came from right behind me, but there's not another soul in here, just me and my racing heart.

"Who's there?" I demand, my voice breaking as my knees grow weaker by the second. A loud sob tears from the back of my throat and I slowly begin to sink, my back sliding down the cell door and catching against my bare skin. "Who's there?"

The laugh sounds again, but this time louder, and I can't help but feel as though someone is watching me. I've searched the cell for hours. There are no cameras, no speakers, no wires, cords, or cables. I'm as alone as can be in this fucked-up little dungeon, but I have to believe that I'm not because the only other alternative is that I'm being haunted by the ghosts of past dungeon guests. Honestly, I'd prefer to deal with the brothers than have that twisted thought confirmed.

Tears well in my eyes and I bury my face into my knees, desperately trying to block out the sounds flying around the room, but when a metallic dragging sound pierces through the dungeon, my back straightens and I fly up off the ground.

I turn, spinning to face the door as my eyes widen with fear.

They're back.

My heart thunders, my pulse beating loudly in my ears, drowning out the other sounds in the cell. My hunger is completely forgotten and my tired eyes remain locked on the door as my breath hitches.

I instantly start backing up, terrified of what or who is about to come striding through the door. It creaks open and I watch as though it's happening in slow motion, but I don't dare stop. I keep moving until my back is flush with the wall behind me, the sharp crevices from the bricks digging into my skin.

The heavy door pushes wider, and where I expect to see light pouring in, there's nothing but shadows.

I see a haunting darkness moving from behind the door, and as the heavy metal drags against the old stones of the ground, a chill sweeps through me. The door gets wider and wider and with each passing second, I feel the weight of the situation bearing down on me, pressing against my chest and making me wish for sweet relief.

My sharp breaths increase until I'm on the verge of hyperventilating, but I do my best to mask it, not wanting them to know just how fucking scared I really am. Though my tear-stained face and the way I cower in the corner is bound to give me away.

As the door fully opens, the shadow gains more shape and I quickly recognize one of the brothers, though his face is masked in heavy darkness and it's impossible to tell which one he is. That is until he steps deeper into the room and I can make out the distinctive tattoos winding up his neck.

Levi DeAngelis. The youngest brother and questionably the most impulsive. At least, that's what the news has always alluded to. I guess it's all that egotistical, needing to prove something to his older brothers bullshit. Or maybe he just got dropped on his head a few too many times as a baby. Either way, he's not somebody that I want standing this close to me, but I guess none of the brothers are a great option.

His dark eyes bore into mine, and as he takes another step toward me, I shrink further back into the brick wall until I feel blood trailing down my back. His eyes only seem to get darker as I drop my gaze down his body, searching for some kind of clue about how this is going to go down.

Is he just going to snap my neck with his bare hands or is there a gun hidden in his pants? Maybe he's a dagger kind of guy. Shit, that's too easy for him. After all, the DeAngelis brothers have a reputation to uphold. I bet I'll be slaughtered in the most spectacular fashion, but nobody will ever know about it. I'll never get avenged. I'll never see justice. The brothers will just continue getting away with this because no one will fucking miss me.

He's fucking stunning though, just like his two big brothers, and that makes him even more dangerous than any man has the right to be. His hair is black as night and cropped short, while his perfectly symmetrical face dares me to try and find a flaw.

I can't help but notice that he's wearing a three-piece suit and damn, he wears it well, but that's the least of my problems. He's probably planning some fancy date with a poor unsuspecting girl and waiting for his opportunity to strike. I'm the pathetic pre-game warm-up.

Levi gets nice and close, so fucking close that I smell the small touch of cologne that's been sprayed by his neck, mixed with the sweet, natural manly smell that's all him. I can feel the warmth coming from his tanned skin and I swallow hard, but he just keeps getting closer until his chest is pressed right up against mine.

He towers over me. He must be at least 6'3 and built like a fucking bull. He's easily three times the size of me. A man like this could snap my bones with just a flick of his wrist.

I have no doubt that he can feel my rapid pulse, hell, my heart is beating so damn loud that he can probably hear its terrified thumping too. He leans into me and I catch my breath, silently willing myself to think of a sweeter time in my life and not the horrendous things that he's about to do to me.

Levi drops his head and his nose grazes along my skin, tormenting me with his silence. "What do you want?" I ask, clenching my jaw and desperately trying to block him out, but he's already inside my head without even saying a single word.

The tip of his nose trails up from the bottom of my jaw right to my temple which is where it comes to a stop. He breathes me in and I close my eyes, trying to calm my terrified tremors.

A low, animalistic growl sounds in the back of his throat, and

I hold back tears, preparing myself for death. But when nothing happens, I open my eyes again and swallow hard before slowly tilting my chin to meet his dark, horrifying gaze.

Letting out a shaky breath, I try to find what little strength I possess. "What. Do. You. Want?" I demand, not ready to stand here all night playing his twisted games.

The corners of his mouth flinch with the makings of a wicked grin but he holds it back as something presses against my stomach. My gaze drops to his hand to find a black silk gown scrunched up between his fingers.

His deep, growly voice floods the cell and my gaze snaps right back up to his. "Put it on."

My brows furrow as I instinctively take the gown from him, my knees shaking as I feel the sound of his deep tone vibrating right through my hollow chest. Realizing that he still has plans for me tonight, I raise my chin and narrow my gaze. "Why?" I snap, not about to make this easy for him as my eyes flicker toward the open cell door. He's left me the perfect opportunity to escape, assuming I can get past him.

"Because I said so," he growls, not appreciating my reluctance. I'm sure a man like him doesn't hear the word no unless it's his victim's last plea for mercy. "You're our guest and you will join us for dinner."

My brow arches. "Guest?" I laugh. "More like a fucking prisoner. Tell me, how many other 'guests' are you keeping down here?"

Levi doesn't respond, just keeps staring at me with that dead gaze until my patience gets the best of me. "You're fucking kidding me,"

I scoff, immediately regretting my tone as his eyes flash with anger. I shove my hand against his solid stomach and force him back a step. "You want to dress me up in some bullshit gown that probably belongs to some dead woman, parade me around for your psychotic brothers, and treat me to dinner? You really are fucked in the head."

Levi's head tilts to the side, the same way his brother's had moved right before he knocked me out cold. "The gown belonged to my mother," he tells me in a flat, emotionless tone. "And you're right. She is fucking dead. Now put the gown on before I do it myself, and trust me when I tell you, you won't like it."

My jaw clenches and I refuse to tear my gaze away from his, but even if I wanted to, it's not possible. He holds me hostage with his stare alone, but now that stare seems so much more than just anger.

"Now," he orders, his tone dropping even lower, probably pissed that my question brought up the memory of his dead mother, but seriously, how was I supposed to know?

"You want to dress me up like a fucking Barbie doll in your dead mother's clothes? You don't see how messed-up that is?"

His jaw clenches and the thick muscles of his neck flinch, making his winding tattoos almost seem real. His fingers ball into fists at his side and my gaze settles onto them, knowing that with just one punch, I could be dead.

I let out a shaky breath and slowly drag my gaze back up his wide body to meet his stare, knowing that I've already pushed him too far, but I can't figure out what game we're playing. Do I sit quietly and do what I'm asked in hopes of delaying the inevitable, or do I go all out, balls to the wall and make their time with me just as hellish as my time with them?

My fingers scrunch into the soft silk and I struggle to take a deep breath, wanting to get down to business. "Why me?" I ask in a small voice, already exhausted by his bullshit.

His gaze hardens and I realize all too quickly that he's not about to start explaining anything. I'm going to be left in the dark for as long as the boys deem necessary.

Levi doesn't budge, just remains before me with his intimidating size, more than ready to take action if I don't hurry up and do what he's asking. So with no other choice, I release the fabric between my fingers and pull it over my head, letting it slide into place, momentarily hating those few short moments that the silk masks my sight.

The gothic gown fits me like a glove, sailing down my body until the hem is gently grazing the stone beneath my feet. The neckline plunges down between my breasts with a flimsy piece of material holding it together and keeping my tits from spilling out, but the plunging neckline has nothing on the back … or lack thereof. It sails right down to my ass, and if I were any shorter, I'm positive that my whole ass would be hanging out.

My gaze flicks back to Levi's and he takes a step back, his dead eyes scanning over the subtle curve of my body and taking me in, but his face doesn't change. He gives absolutely nothing away, and just like that, he turns on his heel and stalks toward the cell door.

"Move," he demands, not bothering to look back, assuming that I will follow him blindly, but what choice has he really given me? I can either stay here in a fucking haunted cell, or I can follow him, getting a brief understanding of the property's layout and hopefully learning a little something about why the fuck I'm here. So without another second of hesitation, my bare feet drag along the cold stone and I move my fucking ass.

Levi's strides are wide, making it nearly impossible to keep up with him, but I do my best while keeping myself far enough away to make a run for it if I see an opportunity, but something tells me that an opportunity like that isn't going to fall into my lap. Besides, judging by the size of him, he'd be able to catch me within moments.

If I'm going to try and escape, then I have to be smart about it, and running rampant around their home, having absolutely no idea where I'm going doesn't exactly classify me as the sharpest tool in the shed.

Levi leads me through a dark tunnel-like hallway, dimly lit by small pendant lamps that send waves of yellow light flowing around them, but it doesn't go far. The walkway looks like it comes straight out of some twisted medieval torture chamber. It's fucking creepy as shit. Maybe this really is an old castle that they've got me in.

Just fucking perfect. A castle is exactly what I need. This place probably comes fully equipped with a million different rooms, a hundred kitchens, a thousand bathrooms, and the perfect murder chamber laid out to each of their specifications. Even if I did decide to run, I'd be lost within seconds.

We come to a big wooden door with thick, black hinges keeping it locked, and I watch as Levi grabs hold of it and gives it a hard tug, his muscles rolling through his suit, telling me just how fucking heavy this door is. If a guy like Levi struggles with it, then I have no chance in hell.

He glances back at me before nodding through the open door, silently telling me to get a move on. Holding my head high, I walk past him and a chill sails right down my spine. He closes the heavy door behind us and indicates for me to walk ahead of him.

The tunnel is dark enough as it is but having him behind me where I can't watch his every single move? It's the most nerve-racking thing I've ever experienced.

We approach a narrow set of concrete stairs and I slowly make my way up them, being careful with each steep step. Levi quickly catches up to me and his hand presses against my lower back. If he were a gentleman, I'd assume he was trying to keep me from falling, but the way he presses against my back tells me that he just wants me to hurry the fuck up.

Natural light shines at the top of the stairs and it has me moving a little faster. Natural light means that I'm almost on the main floor of the building, and surely there's a million different options to escape. Hell, I'll even throw myself out a window or scale my way up the chimney of an old fireplace if that's what it takes. Knowing my luck, the bastards would probably just light the fucker and laugh as the flames licked closer and closer to my ass.

I reach the top step and I don't miss the way that Levi begins to hover closer. His hand doesn't move from my back as we walk through a wide opening with magnificent marble floors. It looks fucking expensive, and my gaze instantly begins shuffling through the wide space.

There's huge floor to ceiling windows built into what looks like some kind of fancy sandstone walls, and I find myself wondering again if this really is an old castle. The space is empty and I can almost imagine it being filled with hundreds of people. Women in fancy ball gowns with fake smiles, struggling to breathe in their corsets gowns while men in ridiculous penguin suits court them around the room. It could be like a scene out of *Pride and Prejudice,* but my reality is anything but.

Levi pushes me discreetly through the property with one hand, and as we exit the giant ballroom, we move on to yet another hallway paved in the same exquisite marble floor. Haunting windows create enough light that even the hall glows brightly despite the late hour.

We bypass a number of rooms, some that look lived in and others cluttered with old furniture covered in white, dusty sheets. "What the hell is this place?" I murmur, unsure if I'm just musing to myself or actually seeking out a response, though it doesn't matter because he doesn't offer me one anyway.

We walk and wind through random rooms and I can't help the feeling that he's leading me on a wild goose chase, trying to get me lost so that I don't learn my way around. But the second I smell a delicious roast wafting through the old building, every last direction falls from my mind.

I'm starving. I'd do just about anything for a meal, but that doesn't mean that I'm about to trust any food given to me by the DeAngelis brothers.

I'm doomed to starve.

"Through here," Levi mutters behind me, indicating to his right.

I turn to face the large double doors, and as I step toward them, they open wide, revealing the final two DeAngelis brothers leaning back in their chairs around a massive dining table. Wicked grins stretch across their faces, more than ready to fuck with my fragile mind.

FOUR

The dining room is as grand as they come, and as my gaze quickly sails around, I come to the conclusion that we're definitely in an old castle. There's no other way to describe this place. It's like something out of a Halloween movie designed to fit their every whim.

Low hanging chandeliers hover above the massive oak dining table that's big enough to seat at least thirty people. Gorgeous, gold-trimmed chairs line the big table and I stare in shock, feeling as though I've just walked into a scene from a movie. These are the sons of the most powerful mafia boss in the country. They probably wipe their asses with gold sheets.

Oversized windows line the room, showcasing the magnificently manicured gardens lit with strategically placed spotlights as the evening sun drifts lower in the sky.

Levi strides past me as I hover awkwardly in the open doorway. The need to turn on my heels and run sparks low in my nervous stomach, but I think about the maze of halls we've been wandering through with hesitation. "Don't even think about it, Empress," a low, rumbling tone comes from across the room.

I follow the sound to meet Roman's hard stare. He's fucking gorgeous. They all are. There's no other way to put it.

Roman leans back in his seat in an impeccable suit, exuding the cocky confidence that comes with wealth. When I first saw them in my dingy apartment, they hid in the shadows, covered by black hoodies and their cryptic silence. It was nearly impossible to see the sharp edges of their jawlines or just how defined their massive bodies really are. But here, standing before their judgmental stares, they can't hide from me anymore. Though the same could be said for me.

I narrow my gaze on Roman, slowly trailing over the rough stubble covering his jaw, wondering if he's the one running this show. Strands of thick, dark hair hang unkempt from the tied-back mess on top of his head. He's a fucking masterpiece, but deadly from every angle. Add the rough stubble around his jaw and he's the very definition of the man of my dreams. Too bad he's a fucking psychopath.

His obsidian eyes are locked on me as I notice the angry scar slicing through one thick brow and over the top of his eyelid. It trails down to the very tip of his cheekbone, and I can't help but wonder what happened to him. The scar sits on a perfect angle, but it's just rugged enough to have everything clenching inside me. While the brothers all look freakishly similar, Roman's scar sets him apart. I can't explain why I feel a sudden connection to him without a single exchange of words, but his hard expression speaks to me on a different level. I've had one strange conversation with Levi, but so far, Roman is the one I feel I know the most about.

"What happened to you?" I ask, folding my arms over my chest and popping out my hip. "Fuck the wrong man's wife?"

A dagger spins in his hand, the pad of his fingertip pressed right against the sharp tip of the blade and seeing the lethality in his eyes, I wish he'd just throw it and pierce my heart, putting a premature end to the shit storm I know I'm about to endure. "Sit."

I keep staring, refusing to abide by his orders as my gaze continues down, sailing over the relaxed way he leans back in his ridiculous gold-trimmed chair. He flinches, adjusting himself slightly to hang his arm over the backrest of the chair beside him, and as he does, my whole body jumps. For just a brief moment, I really expected him to throw the knife.

His muscles roll with his movements and the way the corner of his lips twist up into a crooked grin tells me that he knew exactly how I was going to react to his sudden movement. He's fucking with me and he loves it.

My back straightens and I clench my jaw, not appreciating his bullshit in the slightest. Despite how brave I'm trying to appear to be, he knows just how scared I really am.

Fearing that he truly loves my attention on him, I turn away, not wanting to give him what he craves. Glancing down the long table to his brother, I find him sitting at the very end, acting like he belongs at the head of the table when we all know that spot belongs to the eldest of the bunch.

My gaze drags over his hard demeanor. I didn't think it was possible but he somehow looks even more pissed to have me here than his brothers do.

Marcus Fucking DeAngelis.

Just looking at him sends waves of rage pulsing through me, remembering the way his hand curled around my throat and the heavy blow that knocked me out. My head has been hurting all day because of his shit. I mean, I'm five foot nothing and weigh less than a freaking bug. They could have easily subdued me, taped my mouth shut and disappeared. There was no reason to knock me out cold.

Fucking asshole, but a freaking gorgeous one.

Why couldn't I have been abducted by ugly dudes? The last thing I need is to be sexually confused by these guys. If only Tarzan didn't give out on me the way he did. He's been the only consistent man in my life. I trusted him and he didn't come through for me, but then, I'm more than pleased that Levi didn't get to see me come while watching me through my closet door. Fucking creep. Who does that? He was probably rocking a semi while he watched me.

Marcus leans right back in his chair looking completely unfazed by my appearance in his big-ass dining hall, but why should it bother him? I'm certainly no threat to him. I'm like an irritating cockroach who he could trample at any given time. His feet are propped up on the edge of the dining table as he watches me through his long lashes. When he tilted his head to the side in my apartment, he looked fucking crazy, but bringing his chin down and staring up at me like this turns my blood cold.

This is my first real meeting with these guys, and while nothing has really been said yet, it's clear that whatever time I spend here with them is going to be the most horrifying thing I'll ever endure.

Determined not to fret under his deadly stare, I let out a shaky breath and call on my middle school acting classes. I raise my chin and slap a bored expression over my face. I scoff to myself, keeping my gaze on Marcus as I stride toward the big table. "Can't say that I'm impressed," I sigh. "For such a reputation, you guys are really dropping the ball. Dinner parties and gowns? Fuck, sounds like you're losing your edge."

Marcus flies to his feet and I pause, my foot hovering off the ground as I blanch, watching just how fast he can move his tall frame. I suck in a breath, one that I'm sure all three of them can hear from their respective corners of the room. My act isn't fooling anyone.

Judging by the determination and pure hatred swirling within his eyes, I expect him to come after me. But Marcus remains still, glaring at me from the opposite end of the table. It's painfully clear which one of these boys has anger issues in the family.

His hands clench into tight fists as I watch his sharp jaw become so much more defined. He's on the edge and I don't doubt that one more snide comment from me would have him breaking loose and putting an end to this twisted game.

I bite my tongue, knowing when to push and when to reel it in. After all, I lived with my father for eighteen years before finally finding freedom. That was more practice in restraint than any young girl should ever have to put up with. I should consider it a warm-up for this exact moment of my life. I bet the other girls these assholes have plucked off the street didn't come fully equipped with years of abuse training.

Keeping still, I refuse to break eye contact with Marcus, ready to see this through, but I don't have to when Levi stands and glares across the wide table to his brother. Not a word is said out loud, but their silent conversation has both their gazes flicking back to mine.

"Sit," Levi orders, his tone filled with authority as he repeats the one order his eldest brother had given only a few short moments ago.

Levi's deep voice somehow still seems to vibrate through my chest just like it did when he was pressed right up against me. I turn my head toward him and swallow hard, unable to avoid his authoritative demand. Taking a step toward the table, I slowly pull out the chair closest to the exit.

I feel both Marcus' and Roman's stare on me as well, but I keep mine trained on Levi as I slowly take my seat.

The table is filled with food and my stomach growls, but despite the brothers' full plates, I don't dare reach for any of it, not even the glass of water by my knife and fork.

None of them make a move to start on their dinner, far too intrigued with their shiny new toy. "You're going to want to eat," Levi explains, leaning back in his chair and picking up a dagger of his own, trailing his forefinger up and down the sharp blade and letting the chandelier light glisten off the shiny metal. "That's the last meal you're going to be offered."

I clench my jaw as my gaze drops to the array of food scattered around the table and it doesn't go unnoticed that food isn't the only thing here. There are bottles of booze spread from left to right, brands that my boss could only dream of affording in his nightclub, but it's the unlabeled pills and cocaine that hold my attention. I didn't take these guys for ones to mess with drugs. Their minds are already fucked up enough, but then, maybe they need something to help them forget just how monstrous they really are.

I've never been one to indulge in drugs and alcohol, but I'm certainly no prude. I had my experimental years right after high school. I got smart after watching a friend overdose at a party and I haven't touched them since—the drugs, that is. I'm more than happy to have a glass of cheap wine to wash down my dinner. Not tonight though. I want a clear mind while dealing with these guys.

Sitting back in my chair, I make a point of not eating, though I know they've been hearing my stomach growling since the second I walked in here. "What is this?" I question, waving my hand around the table. "You think you can try to win my cooperation with a fancy meal and some wine? You're fucking psychopaths. I'd be a moron to willingly accept any food from you. Who knows what you've done to it."

Roman sits up straighter and slams the tip of his dagger down into the hard oak table. "Do not question our generosity," he spits, his words filled with venom. "Eat or don't. It doesn't mean shit to me. It just means that you'll starve faster. And trust me, it's a long, painful way to go."

Marcus laughs, relaxing into his seat and propping his feet back up on the table, acting as though he didn't just fall into a rage induced episode not two seconds ago. His laugh is hollow and lacks any kind of humanity, just like the dark depths of his eyes. "I do wish that you would eat, Shayne. You're going to need your energy for what we have in store for you," he tells me, shocking me with the casual use of my name, though it's not so casual. It comes out as more of a haunting torment. I hadn't realized that they knew who I was. I figured I was a random hit, but that only goes to prove that they targeted me, which means there has to be a reason why.

My eyes flash back to Levi, seeing him as the least psychotic of the bunch. "What's that supposed to mean?"

He just grins, the thought of what they plan to do with me exciting him in a way that reminds me that these guys lack every quality that makes them human. They're the grim reapers. Why do I keep expecting them to respond and react in a normal way? They're not normal, far from it.

Seeing his brother's excitement, Roman decides to take pity on me and offer me just a snippet of information. "You will earn food and water, Empress. Nothing will come to you for free, so consider the dress, accommodation, and your final meal as gifts."

"Kill me now," I mutter to myself before repeating his words. "I have to earn food and water? Look around you. It's more than clear that you assholes already have enough hired help to keep your big-ass house running. You don't need me slaving over you. What's your game here?"

"You will not cook and clean," Marcus spits, looking at me as though I'm stupid for clearly not reading their twisted minds.

I pull back, my chin raising as realization dawns. "You want me to be your little sex slave?" I screech. "Over my dead fucking body. You're insane if you think I'm about to go spreading my legs for you sick murderers. What the hell is wrong with you? There would be plenty of willing chicks out there who would be down for your kinky asses. What's the deal? You like it when they scream for you to stop?"

Roman's eyes narrow. "We don't rape women to get what we want from them."

"Well you sure as shit ain't getting me on my knees."

His lips pull up into a smug grin, almost as though he knows something that I don't, and damn it, that smile is as lethal as they come. I can only imagine what a real one would look like, but I'm not down to wait and figure it out.

I shake my head and stand, hating the feel of the cold marble beneath my bare feet. "I'm out," I tell them, glancing around the table, still unable to believe that we're in the middle of some bullshit dinner party. I mean, I expected a number of things to happen tonight, but this? Hell to the freaking no. "I'm not down for your twisted mind games and bullshit threats. Either kill me now or let me go."

All three of them just stare at me, and I can only imagine the things going through their minds. When none of them decide to grace me with a response, I make my move, knowing that it could land me in a world of trouble.

I turn and walk for the door, holding my chin up with pride and foolishly hoping that they've had enough fun to allow me to walk straight out the door.

The sound of a chair scraping against the ground echoes through the room, but I don't dare turn back. Instead, I pick up my pace, certain that someone is coming for me. My feet move faster as my heart pounds in my chest, and just as I reach the massive double doors, Roman's dagger plunges deep into the wood of the frame, mere inches from my face.

I come to an immediate standstill.

A sharp gasp tears from my lungs as my eyes widen with fear. "I DID NOT GIVE YOU PERMISSION TO LEAVE MY DINING HALL," Roman's booming tone tears through the room. "YOU WILL SIT AND YOU WILL ENJOY YOUR LAST FULL MEAL."

I slowly turn, crippled with fear and unable to put one foot in front of the other. My gaze comes straight back to Roman's and I stare at him as though his brothers aren't even in the room.

He steps out from his chair and walks around the table, taking painfully slow strides toward me, stalking me like his pathetic prey as though he has all night to inflict his devilish torture. He doesn't stop moving until he stands right before me, and I'm all too aware of his thick fingers hanging by his sides, knowing just how quickly they could snap my neck. "Poor behavior will get you nowhere," he promises me with a deathly whisper, his breath brushing against my skin as he towers over me. "Don't be fooled. If you make threats and offer us the chance to take your life, we will take it willingly, but here we are offering you the gift of life by allowing you to continue breathing. You are new here and do not yet know our rules, so for tonight, we will be lenient with you, but pull that shit again, and you will suffer the very real consequences. Is that clear, Empress?"

I swallow hard and nod, absolutely positive that he means every damn word, and while I put on a brave face, I'm not ready to die, not even close. I haven't even had a chance to live yet.

Roman hovers over me, his eyes not budging from mine as his brothers watch on with interest. A lump forms in the back of my throat and I find myself starting to break. "Why me?" I murmur, asking the same question I'd asked of Levi, the very one he'd refused to answer. "There are so many other girls. I'm not who you need for … for whatever this is, and I … I'm not ready to die."

Roman's head tilts with that same psychotic expression that both of his brothers possess. His fingers come up and trail down the side of my face making me flinch with his contact. "Sit and eat," he demands, his tone not matching his gentle touch. "Do as you are told and I will consider giving you the insight in which you seek."

"You mean that?" I question, not prepared to trust his response.

"Do not question me in my home," he growls, his fingers dropping away from my face. "I have told you that tonight you will be given leniency. How far that leniency goes is up to you. Now sit and eat."

His hand reaches up again, this time moving around me, and I hold my breath as his skin brushes past my unkempt hair. He pauses for only a second, his eyes boring into mine, and without warning, he flinches, yanking the knife out of the door beside my head.

I suck in a gasp, hating how obvious I am about my fear. He takes a step back and indicates for me to move back to my seat.

Not ready to push boundaries again, I hastily move back to the table, glancing up just in time to watch as Marcus washes down a pill with a clear liquid that I assume is anything but water. Taking my seat, I glance around the table again, going over the options and hesitating with the foods before me, not educated enough to know what half of it is. "When you say that I'll need energy," I question, glancing back at Levi. "How much are we talking?"

"You better fill that plate," he tells me. "And make it fast. My patience is growing thin."

FIVE

My plate is all but licked clean and I stare down at it in astonishment. That was one of the best meals I've ever had, despite the possibility that it could have been laced with drugs, poison, or who the hell knows what. It was the expensive kind of meal that I imagine a fancy restaurant would serve. People like me don't eat like this, but I guess the DeAngelis brothers are living in luxury every freaking night. Though, I'm sure they probably have a professional chef chained to the stove. I'll have to check that out at some point.

I slide the plate in front of me, unsure if that's proper table etiquette, but honestly, I don't give a fuck if it's not. All I want to do is make a point that I've been a good little girl and abided by their ridiculous rules. So now, maybe they can offer me what I want to know in return.

Realizing that Roman is the one calling the shots here, I turn my gaze to him. "Why me?" I ask, the burst of energy from dinner making me brave, but the same fear still pulses through my veins. "Earlier, Marcus called me by name. You know who I am, which means that I wasn't some random girl you chose to abduct for your wicked games. You targeted me."

Roman leans forward onto his elbows and rubs his thumb and forefingers over his chin, his eyes narrowing in thought. "Yes," he finally says, giving it to me straight. "We know exactly who you are. We know every last thing there is to know about you, but you were not targeted. We were simply collecting what we were owed."

I shake my head, my brows furrowing in confusion. "You mean … me?"

Roman nods. "Correct."

"No," I rush out. "That's insane. You've got the wrong girl. Owed? What does that even mean? Are you under some fucked-up illusion that you *own* me? Because that doesn't make any sense. I haven't made any weird deals with anyone. I don't owe anyone any money. I haven't stolen anything. I mean, I owe my landlord this month's rent, but he's not about to go and sell me to you to get even. He'd shit his pants at just the thought of making a deal with you. No," I repeat, vigorously shaking my head again. "You've got the wrong girl. I don't even have any friends."

Levi sighs, bored with the conversation. "Is your name Shayne Mariano?" he questions. "Do you go by the name of Shay? Twenty-two years old. Your birthday was in March."

"I … I mean, yes, that's me, but you've got your wires crossed. There's been some serious fuck up with the paperwork. So please, drop me back at my apartment so I can go back to my miserable life. Hell, just kick me out the front door. I can find my own way back and you can sort out whatever mix up there was on your end. I won't even say anything about it, just please, let me go home."

Marcus laughs, standing from the table and slowly walking toward me, his sickening gaze locked on mine. He walks around the back of my chair and I slowly suck in a deep breath, not trusting him behind me for one second. He leans forward, his chest arching over my seat as his hand comes down on the armrests of the gold-trimmed dining chair.

He reaches around me, and I watch with caution as he takes the knife from my dinner plate, admiring the sparkles of the chandelier's light dancing across its dull blade. Before I can react, he's pressing it against the base of my throat.

"Is your father Maxwell Mariano?" he questions, that name sending dread sailing through my veins. There is no mix up here. I'm exactly where I'm supposed to be, no thanks to my father. I slowly nod, letting out a sigh and not even bothering to fear the knife at my throat as I come to grips with my new reality. "Then we have the right girl."

Marcus laughs and pulls away from me, grabbing a bottle of scotch before making his way back down the long table. Dropping into his seat, he hooks one leg over the armrest and leans back to get comfortable. "Like I said," he grins, holding the bottle of scotch up in cheers. "Welcome to the family."

My heart races as I look back at Roman. "Okay, so … what? He's broke again but instead of stealing from me, he stole from you, and now I'm supposed to repay his debt?"

Roman nods. "Something like that."

I let out a shaky breath and stand, making all three of them flinch as I begin to pace the floor behind the chair. "So what now? You just … own me? I become part of the furniture, and live down in that torture chamber until you inevitably decide to kill me? I'm just supposed to be your toy to fuck with?"

None of them respond. They just keep watching as I drive myself insane with questions. "Couldn't you just … Why did you have to ruin *my* life? He's the one who fucked up and stole from you. Fuck up his life. He's a worthless piece of shit. I didn't … I don't …"

"Sit. Down," Roman's voice flows through the large dining hall.

Needing to calm myself, I sit back down and reach for my drink, and as I take a sip of water and close my eyes, I realize that I'm more fucked than any girl has the right to be.

I'm theirs.

The DeAngelis brothers own me.

I'm their property and there's nothing I can do to fix this. Death seems to be the only way out of here, and it's my fucking scumbag father that condemned me to such a fate. His gambling addiction should have been the end of him, but instead, it's the end of me.

Fucking hell.

My elbows hit the table and I drop my head into my hands, needing to scream, but something tells me that the three psychos in the room have already had enough of my outbursts today. Roman said they've been lenient, and I have to agree, but that's only going to last so long.

My tongue rolls over my bottom lip and I let out a shaky breath, wanting to know every bit of information that they're willing to offer me before this little grace period is over. "You mentioned rules," I ask, not aiming my question at a specific brother. "What rules?"

Levi takes the reins. "As we mentioned, you will earn your meals. Behave and you will be rewarded. Try to run from us, and you will suffer the consequences as you learned before. However, we do not make a habit of missing. Do not be fooled," he says, allowing his knife to glisten in the light and shine right into my eyes. "I have no issue stabbing this knife right through your back."

I swallow hard. I'm certainly not fooled. These guys have earned their reputation for a reason.

I nod, starting to feel the heaviness of the situation weighing down on me. "What else?"

"It's quite simple," Marcus says, filling in for his brother as his voice drops to a tone so sinister that chills spread through my body and send goosebumps rising on my skin. "When it's time to play, you better be ready. Girls who refuse us don't often enjoy what comes next."

"Play?" I question, a lump forming in my throat all over again. "You mean … sex?"

Roman chuckles, the sound so innocent yet filled with so much danger. "You're intrigued by the idea of fucking us," he states as though it's a cold-hard fact.

I shake my head. "No, I just … What else could you mean by *play*?"

He leans forward, his eyes focusing on mine and holding me captive. "When was the last time you were fucked so hard that you couldn't walk in the morning?"

I straighten against the backrest of my chair as though that could magically help me put space between us. "How is that any of your business?"

"We own you," he reminds me. "Your body belongs to us. Every freckle, every scar, every time it's been touched is my fucking business. Answer the question."

"I … uhh." My cheeks flush and I find myself glancing away, too ashamed to admit that no man has ever fucked me quite like that. I mean, I've had plenty of good ones, a few alright ones, and far too many guys who could barely get it in before they were finishing on the side of my leg. But a real, honest to God, deep and thorough fucking? Yeah … that's not something I've ever experienced.

Roman leans back, more intrigued than ever. "You haven't. Are you a virgin?"

My eyes nervously flick around the room, not loving the topic of conversation. First off, how is that any of his goddamn business? And second, what does it matter if I am or not? I won't be spreading my legs for him. "I thought you weren't into raping girls," I spit, wanting the topic off my sex life.

His eyes harden and the anger pulsing within them has me shrinking in my seat, wishing I could slide under the table and completely disappear. "WHAT DID I TELL YOU ABOUT QUESTIONING ME?"

Fuck.

"I—"

"ANSWER THE FUCKING QUESTION."

"NO," I yell back at him. "I'M NOT A FUCKING VIRGIN. I just—"

Levi narrows his gaze. "Haven't been fucked properly." I glance away, unsure why I feel so ashamed of my shitty, limited experience, but he takes pity on me and changes the topic. "When is your period due?"

My eyes bug out of my head. "Excuse me?"

"Your period," he repeats, in frustration. "When is it due? Or would you prefer to sit on your bed and soil your sheets with blood? It doesn't bother me either way. Though, if I'm honest, the sight of blood smeared across a pretty girl's bed gets me fucking hard."

I raise my brow, more than done with this inquisition into my life as I try to ignore his murderous comments and focus on the topic at hand. "I have irregular periods. It comes when it wants, but I'm surprised you don't know that. It would be mentioned in my medical files."

"We do know that," Marcus throws right back. "You've been seeing the same doctor since you were nine. You were prescribed birth control at sixteen to help regulate your period, but it just turned you into a raging bitch, so you stopped using it. Risky fucking game, don't you think?"

I glare down the table at him, more than ready to turn the tables and press a knife to his throat, but a fucked-up psycho like him would probably just get hard and come in his pants. Who does he think he is preaching to me about risky games? I'm not the one running around slaughtering half the town. I take a deep breath and let him see the rage in my eyes. "If you already know," I growl, "then why the hell are you asking?"

No one bothers with a response and that only infuriates me more, but I guess they don't need to. They were testing me and I failed. Though I have no idea what the fallout is going to be or why they chose the topic of my period to test me on.

Roman nods toward my plate. "Are you finished?"

"I was finished before I started."

His lips twitch just a fraction and he nods to Levi. "Get her out of here. I think we've endured enough."

I stand, clenching my jaw, not ready to be thrown back into that shitty little torture chamber. "No, please. Don't send me back down there. Please. I don't like it."

Roman just stands and strides out of the room as though he hadn't even heard me begging, and before I can call him out on his douchebag behaviors, his brother is at my back, his hand pressing against my skin and pushing me forward. "I'd suggest that you move that tight little ass a bit faster," he tells me. "I'd prefer to not have to drag you down the stairs."

A hollowness sits in my chest, and while I'm thrilled to be getting away from the three brothers, I'd also give anything to not have to go back to the dark, haunted dungeon.

As we move back through the house, I don't miss how he leads me through different rooms and different hallways, keeping me disoriented and confused about the layout of the big-ass castle. Only when we reach the big ballroom, my senses come back to me and I know exactly where we are.

I hit the top step and the pressure from Levi's hand against my back has me moving faster down the steep concrete staircase. As I go to take the next step, I slip and tumble, rolling forward and smacking the back of my ribs against the sharp edge of the step.

I cry out, the pain almost too much as I tumble down the steps and come to a devastating stop at the bottom, but before tears can fill my eyes from the pain, Levi is there, gripping my upper arm and yanking me to my feet, his hold like a steel vice, bruising and determined.

I pause, trying to catch my balance as I test my weight on my feet, mentally mapping out the damage from my fall, but as I look around myself, a dark shadow at the top of the stairs catches my attention.

Marcus is slowly following us through the big castle and a shiver sails down my spine. We've been walking for at least three whole minutes and I haven't noticed him once. What happened to women's intuition? If a man is following me on the street, I can feel it. I know to be cautious, but with the DeAngelis brothers, there is no warning. They'll stalk you until you're bleeding out in their hands.

"Move," Levi snaps, not thrilled about my fall or the few extra moments I've taken to check on myself. His hand comes back to my skin and he pushes me harder, forcing one foot in front of the other to keep up with his long strides, relentless in his mission to get me back inside my cell. I can't help but look back over my shoulder and watch how Marcus continues, even after being caught. He doesn't fucking care.

With each passing step that plunges us deeper and deeper into the darkness of the tunnel, the dread settles over me and I find my strides getting smaller as Levi's hand presses harder. "Please, no," I whisper into the darkness as the cell door approaches. "Please, I swear. I'll behave. Not there. I'll play whatever fucked-up game you want me to play. I don't—"

My whines are cut off when Levi tugs hard on my arm again, pulling me into him until I'm stumbling. He catches me with his strong arm around my waist and throws me over his shoulder like a ragdoll. He picks up his pace, moving at a speed that I would never be able to keep up with, and before he allows me a chance to plead my case, he's already at my door, opening it wide and tossing me in.

My body crashes against the bed at a weird angle, and before I can catch myself, I fall straight down to the cold stone beneath, hitting the same hip that I'd landed on when they threw me in here the first time.

The cell door slams shut and the noise of the heavy lock sliding into place haunts me. The familiar callous laugh echoes down the long hallway, and somehow I know that it's Marcus. I guess being taunted and stalked is something I'll have to get used to if I'm going to survive this, but I already know I'm not cut out for these conditions.

This is where I'll die, haunted and stalked by the grim reapers.

I break.

Heavy sobs tear from my chest as tears sail down my face at the speed of light, relentless as they fall and stain the black silk gown of my captors' dead mother. My head falls to my knees as I wrap my arms around my body, desperate to find even the smallest bit of comfort.

And just when the exhaustion of the past few days creeps up to claim me, the soft *drip, drip, drip* begins to sail through my small torture chamber, getting louder and louder with every drip.

White noise joins the incessant drips and I press my hands against my ears to block it out, only with every passing minute, the relentless sound gets louder and more infuriating. Doors begin slamming as strange white lights flash through the dungeon, blinding me like a bolt of lightning through the dark night.

The sound drills against my head as my eyes burn with the blinding lights, and I finally get a true understanding of the term 'play' that Marcus had alluded to. The boys don't intend to play with my body, they want to play with my mind, and fuck, they're not holding back.

I tear the silk gown off my body and wrap the material around my head, pulling it tight over my ears and eyes and doing my best to block all of my senses. This is only the beginning. My gut tells me that it's just going to get worse from here.

I crash down onto the hard bed and pull the blanket right up over me, cocooning myself under it and riding out the storm the only way I know how.

SIX

The heavy metal door drags along the old stone flooring of my torture chamber, breaking through the haunting silence of the night. My head shoots up off my pillow, my eyes wide as my heart races with fear.

It's the middle of the night and I can't see a damn thing. It's pitch-black, not even the dull glow of moonlight shines through my stupid little window. I'm on my own with absolutely no advantages in my corner.

The door keeps dragging, inch by inch, the sound getting louder by the second. I scurry around on my hard bed, ignoring the searing pain from my fall down the stairs and pressing my back right up against the brick wall. My arms pull around my legs and I feel the soft silk from that ridiculous dress laying across my small bed. It would have only been a few hours ago that I'd wrapped it tightly around my head to block out the white noise and infuriating dripping, but that seems so far away now, so insignificant and trivial compared to the thought of one of these psychos slipping into my room in the dead of night.

I keep as far away from the door as possible, willing myself to become a small ball at the end of my bed, hoping that whoever is walking into my little dungeon is just as blind as I am in here. If he tries to grab me, I'll at least be in a position to dart away, but the brothers are too fast, too skilled. I'll never get away, no matter how hard I try.

The loud, rapid thumping of my pulse sounds in my ears and I strain to hear over it. My senses are dulled. My vision is gone, and all I have is my hearing to keep myself alive, and right now, apart from the sound of the door dragging on the stone and the thumping inside my ears, I hear nothing. Not a single footfall, not the familiar rustling of clothes as someone moves throughout the room, not even the sound of their discreet breathing.

It's not possible. No one is *that* quiet, not even when they're trying to be. Every time I pace the room, stones shift beneath my feet. The grinding sound of loose concrete is unmistakable, yet my cell is strangely quiet despite the open door.

There has to be someone in here.

I can feel it. Their bullshit grace period is over. No more leniency, no more getting away with shit. Their rules have been set and explained and now their fucked-up, twisted little games have begun. Hell, the night of torturous white noise and relentless dripping is proof of that.

But which one is it? My chest sinks at the thought of it being Marcus. He's sick in the fucking head. From what I've learned of him so far, he'll brutally take whatever the fuck he wants from me without a second thought. I knew he was bad, but seeing him at the dinner table so void of humanity only proves just how far gone he truly is. If it's him walking through this door, I don't stand a fucking chance.

Levi or Roman is the most I could hope for. If their plans are to kill me, I feel that Levi would at least do it quickly. He'd probably love it and it'd be ruthless, but it'd be simple. A slit throat or a bullet to the head maybe, unlike Marcus who would likely take his sweet ass time.

Roman on the other hand, he strikes me as the type to torture me mentally and have me begging for sweet death before he's even laid a finger on me. He would be the worst yet somehow inflict the least pain. He'd be savage and twisted in his own fucked-up way and it's absolutely terrifying. Both he and Levi come off as calculated, whereas Marcus is unpredictable.

Though, I can only imagine what the three of them would be like if they were working together.

My chest constricts, squeezing with fear and tormenting me like never before. What the hell am I supposed to do? How am I supposed to save myself? I'm at a disadvantage. Nowhere to run. Nowhere to hide. I'm theirs to do whatever they please and there's not a damn thing I can do to stop them.

I'm like the piñata at a kid's birthday party, hanging from a tree with a massive target on my back, just begging to be beaten and broken.

Shivers spread over my clammy skin. How could my father submit me to this? I know we don't speak and haven't for years, but surely I mean more to him than this?

Fuck him. I hope he rots in the deepest pits of hell.

The silence in the room weighs heavily on my shoulders, just as the lack of sight does. I let out a shaky breath and keep my stare focused on the door despite not being able to see a damn thing, and just as I try to convince myself that it's all in my head, a feral growl rumbles through my torture chamber.

My back straightens as my eyes widen in fear. There really is something in here with me, but fuck, that growl was anything but human. It was almost … animal, but that couldn't be right. No animal is stalking this twisted old castle and pushing open heavy dungeon doors, right? Because that shit would be insane.

The growl sounds again, this time just a little bit closer and a thick lump forms in my throat.

Oh fuck. Oh fuck. Oh fuck.

I'm going to get mauled. I can just imagine the sharp talon-like claws slicing through my skin like butter. At least this shit show can finally be over. Whatever the fuck this thing is can kill me, and hopefully, it'll make it fast. If it really is an animal, then at least I'd die humanely, rather than being tortured by one of the brothers. There won't be any twisted mind games, no calculated slicing, no tormenting and making me watch, just an animal tearing me to shreds.

Fuck.

I close my eyes and breathe as I wait for the inevitable. Slowly in.

Slowly out. And repeat.

The animal moves in a little closer and I feel its hot breath against my legs before that same ferocious growl rocks through me again. Whatever the fuck this is, it's angry, and my presence here has clearly pissed it off.

A moment passes and I feel the hot breath moving toward my knee and I hold as still as possible while it tries to get a good read on me, but in a flash, the breath is gone. I hear the sound of rustling shooting past the open door before padded footfalls are bounding up the long hallway.

I keep still, my eyes refusing to move from the big door as my heart thunders in my chest.

What the fuck was that?

Confusion settles into my veins as that horrified feeling in my gut slowly seems to fade. I don't feel eyes on me, and I sure as hell don't feel a presence in the room anymore, yet the door remains wide open.

Surely this little game isn't over. They wouldn't just leave like that. They're smarter than this, but then, maybe this is another one of their ridiculous tests. Marcus' twisted words from the dinner table come back to me, haunting me with their devilish undertones. *'When it's time to play, you better be ready. Girls who refuse us don't often enjoy what comes next.'*

Dread sits heavily against my chest. If the door has been left open, then this must be exactly what he was talking about. They want me to play their game. They want my curiosity to get the best of me. They want me to try and run, but on the other hand, they also made it pretty fucking clear what would happen to me if I was to try and run. No matter what I do, it won't end well for me.

Staying here means not abiding by their rules. It means not playing their games and landing myself in a world of shit. But by walking out this door, I submit myself to whatever fresh hell they have in store for me.

Fuck.

Maybe it's best if I get this over and done with, no matter how badly I don't want to participate in their games. I value my life too much, and if there's a way that I can get through this, then I'm going to take it.

My hands uncurl from around my legs and my body begins to unwind from the tight ball I've been holding it in. Yet no matter how much I move, the rigidness of my muscles refuses to relax.

Grabbing hold of the silk gown, I pull it back over my head, not wanting to leave my fucked-up little torture chamber without any clothes. It's still impossible to see as I slowly shuffle toward the end of the bed, hoping that my gut feeling is right about the animal being gone.

My feet hit the uneven stone ground and my body aches as I push myself up. I ignore the pain from my fall. Something tells me that pain is one of those things I'm about to become all too familiar with.

If only I was strong enough for this.

I stretch my hand out in front of me, feeling for the door, then wrap my fingers around the handle to help guide me through. I come to a standstill in the open doorway, my gut telling me to step back into my room and slam the door closed. Perhaps I could detach the bed from the far wall and somehow jam it in front of it. The brothers won't be able to get in, but then I sure as fuck won't ever be able to get out.

Shit. I have no choice. I have to play their fucked-up little game.

Tears well in my eyes as I lean out the open doorway and scan up and down the long hallway. There's a dull light at either end of the hall, neither of them giving me a clue about what I may find.

My hands shake by my sides as I weigh my options.

Left or right?

Turning to the left takes me toward the unknown. When Levi had dragged me out of here yesterday, we went to the right. There's a long hallway, another heavy door, and some stairs that lead up into the ballroom. I know for certain that I wouldn't have the strength to open that other door. Going to the left means that I'll be exploring the unknown, and in a place like this, the unknown could hold all sorts of secrets that I'm not prepared to uncover.

That only leaves me one choice.

Stepping out into the long tunnel-like hallway, I turn to the right and hate every single moment of it. Slowly pacing, one foot in front of the other, I start making my way up toward the big heavy door at the end, though it's so fucking dark that I can't even see it. Hell, I was so aware of Levi beside me last time that I can't even remember just how far the door should be.

I keep myself glued to the wall as I walk, though who the fuck knows why. Maybe it's a survival instinct or something like that. All I know is that this wall is the only thing offering me any sort of comfort right now.

Every few steps I take, my head whips around, constantly checking the hallway behind me, more so when that same feeling of being watched pulses through my veins. Something or someone is here with me, I just wish I knew what it was.

My steps slow, knowing that at some point something is bound to happen, but I keep myself moving, terrified of what would happen if I were to stop. It's a fucking dead-end game for me. There's no way for me to win, but the brothers already know that. They carefully construct their bullshit tactics in the hopes of driving me insane. They're nothing if not professional, always going the extra mile.

As I creep closer toward the dim light at the end of the hallway, I start to make out the door up ahead. It's already open and I don't know what to make of that, but if I think too hard on what it could mean, I'll probably burst a brain cell. I just have to keep moving, keep putting one foot in front of the other and hope for the best.

The door comes and goes, and by the time I reach the concrete steps that lead up to the main part of the house, my whole body is covered in sweat.

This is too much.

My heart pounds and I hear the heavy thumping in my ears as my gaze shifts up to the top of the stairs. I shakily put one foot up on the bottom step and slowly transfer my weight, and as I go to raise my next foot to the second step, a loud *BANG* sounds behind me and echoes up the hallway like a haunting song.

A terrified gasp tears from my throat as my head whips around. I scan down the long hallway that I'd just walked through, but I see nothing but the dark, hollow tunnel. The door behind me is still open and there's nothing blocking my view of the dim light at the opposite end. The only other door that could have made that noise is my cell door but it's halfway up the hall. I would see a shadow if someone were there.

I stare a moment longer, my gaze sharpening as I scan from left to right, desperate to find what caused the loud bang, but there's nothing. Not a damn thing unless he—or it—is inside my cell.

Fuck me dead. How is this happening to me? I'm a good girl. I don't deserve this type of torture. Fuck my father. Why did they have to accept his deal? Why couldn't they have just taken him instead?

My whole body trembles with fear and, realizing that whatever game is being played is happening behind me, I whip my head back around and start racing up the high concrete steps, only as my gaze snaps to the top of the stairs, I find a large dark hooded figure looming before me, his presence the most haunting sight I've ever seen.

A loud screech tears from my throat and I fall back, dropping down the bottom step and catching myself against the wall. My eyes widen in horror and as the dark, hooded figure begins stalking me down the steep stairs, another horrendous scream tears from the very back of my throat.

Turning on my heel, I bolt through the long tunnel-like hallway, my feet pounding against the hard stone beneath. My breath comes in hard, sharp gasps as tears stream down my face, but I don't dare relent. One foot in front of the other just like before, only now it comes with a whole new desperation.

I look back over my shoulder to find the hooded figure gaining on me, yet somehow, despite his speed, I don't hear a single noise coming from him. It's not possible. The way he is hurtling toward me, there should be thunderous footfalls echoing my own, but there's nothing.

I pass straight by my locked cell and race toward the other end of the hallway, trying to ignore the fact that I'd left it wide open, meaning there's either someone inside of it, or someone very close by in the long tunnel.

The dim light gives away absolutely nothing, and as I reach the end and follow it around a narrow corner, I come to a fork—two separate pathways, each one daring me to take it.

I pull up short and quickly glance over my shoulder again, but the hooded figure is gone, which only seems to rattle me more.

"The fuck?" I whimper, the terror making my knees tremble as I try to figure out where the fuck to go.

My wide eyes flick between the three directions. Left, right, or back the way I came.

Fuck that. I can't go back there, but what does it matter? Regardless of which direction I choose, they're going to stalk me through the long, daunting hallways. I'm fucked no matter what decision I make, but what I do know is that I can't stop.

I break off to the left, my feet slamming against the ground as I keep my stare up ahead. This hallway is wider than the last and judging by the old-school fire lanterns braced against the wall, it's much shorter as well.

My gaze shifts from side to side, trying desperately to get a feel for the space and find wherever the hell these bitch-ass fuck knuckles are. There's nothing blocking my way up ahead so I forge through, needing to put more space between me and the fresh hell behind me.

The lanterns flicker from the dim fire within them, stretching my shadow far across the hallway and distorting it with every step I take, but when that same loud BANG echoes from behind me again, my shadow is the last thing on my mind.

Picking up my pace, I run as fast as I can, bolting toward the end of the hallway. I break out into an open space that's about as big as my fucked-up little dungeon. My eyes widen in panic. It's small and round with five different pathways leading away from here.

"Fuck," I pant, trying to catch my breath as I spin around, scanning over each of the pathways and trying to figure out which is the best one to take. I hear a faint dripping coming from my right and a ferocious growl from my left, but the growl sounds as though it's coming from a million miles away. It's probably the same animal from earlier begging me to race toward it so it can finally sink its teeth into me.

What the fuck am I supposed to do?

In an instant, the dim light coming from the lanterns behind me goes out and I'm left in nothing but darkness. My heart races and my eyes widen in fear, but nothing is worse than the sound of heavy footsteps in the hallway as something metallic drags against the stone ground, not even the sound of the ferocious animal.

"No, no, no, no," I breathe as I start backing up, too fucking petrified to concentrate on a game plan.

The sound gets louder as his wide strides bring him closer and closer, and I can only imagine the smug as fuck look on his damn face, knowing exactly what this bullshit is doing to me.

My back hits the wall of the small round space, just missing the entrance of the pathway directly opposite to the looming figure, but that small touch on my back is all I need to jolt me back into action.

Spinning on my heel, I launch myself down the long, dark corridor, having absolutely no idea where it leads or what's waiting for me at the end. All I know is that anything is better than the bullshit behind me. My heart thunders in my chest to the point of pain, but I push through it, determined to somehow save my life despite the fact that everything about this night has proven over and over again that I'm nothing but a pawn in their fucked-up games.

With one hand dragging along the wall, I run until my toes slam against a hard step, sending me tumbling against a set of stairs that were invisible in the dark.

I scramble up them, forcing myself to not look back, fearful of what I might see. There's a wicked ache against the front of my chest from where the edge of the concrete step broke against my skin. It sure as hell is going to bruise, but what does it even matter right now?

My knees shake with fear, making each clumsy stride up the stairs feel impossible. The metallic sound following me down the hallway whines over my ragged panting, fueling each step forward. All of this is getting more fucked up by the second.

I reach the top step and feel in front of me, finding another hard door blocking my way. "FUCK," I cry as my hands roam over the splintered wood, desperately seeking freedom.

Cold metal skims across my fingertips and I latch onto it with everything that I have. The door is heavy as fuck. I press the weight of my whole body against it to bust it open and it creaks loudly, the sound a testament to just how rarely this door has been used.

A dim light shines through the small crack and I push just a little harder, feeling the sweet relief of light. The door opens just enough that I can finally slip through the narrow gap, and as I break out into an old wine cellar, complete with antique wooden barrels, I come to a screeching standstill, finding Roman DeAngelis standing right before me with a giant fucking dog at his side, growling like he's about to get dinner, dessert, and a fucking show.

I scramble back, my spine slamming against the sharp edge of the open door as he seems to loom over me, his wicked scar peeking out from under his dark hoodie. His eyes are filled with fire, a raging storm brewing beneath them. I can't tell if this sick little game is getting him off or if he's pissed as all hell that I broke their stupid little rules about making a run for it. Either way, I don't want to find out.

Roman moves toward me, his big-ass dog moving with him as his sharp teeth seem to glisten in the dim light. A growl sounds through the room, but I can't tell if it's coming from Roman or the dog. All I can focus on is the way he continues to move toward me, almost as though he's floating across the floor.

My back presses harder against the door and I hear the footsteps in the hallway behind me finally reaching the stairs. I shake my head. "No. No, please don't," I cry as tears flow down my cheeks, dropping onto my chest and staining my already filthy skin.

A second growl comes from behind the door and I quickly realize that there must be another dog, but all that matters is Roman and the way his hand moves by his side.

My gaze drops, desperate to know what he has planned for me, but the lighting is too low, I can barely make out his face, let alone what's in his hand. All I can see is that it's some kind of dark material and … fuck, what's that smell?

The corner of his full lips twitch as his eyes seem to flare. "Boo," he mutters, the single word lingering in the air between us, and then all too soon, his hand whips out and covers my face, instantly sending me into a dark abyss of haunting nothingness.

SEVEN

Loud drumming seems to shake the walls as I peel my eyes open to find the window above my bed flooding the room with sunshine. I groan as the glaring light instantly makes my head pound. I've been trapped in the darkness for so long that the blinding sunshine is almost painful, add the fact that Roman De-Fucking-Angelis decided to drug me with something last night, and today is already shaping up to be one of my worst.

I drop my hand over my eyes and press down, trying to relieve the dull ache that's booming inside my skull. Who the fuck is even playing the drums? And why now? Those assholes stalked me through the night. Surely, they'd still be asleep, but I guess there's no rest for the wicked.

What even was last night and how the hell am I still breathing? I thought for sure that Roman was going to end me. I was about to become a chew toy for one of his big-ass dogs, or one of his fucked-up brothers. So why the fuck am I still here now? This doesn't make sense. All I know is that coming face to face with Roman like that was the most terrifying thing I've ever experienced.

Disappointment floods me, and for just a brief second, I wish that he had killed me. I just want this over with. I can handle being held in this twisted little torture chamber and the weird as fuck dinner parties, but their games are where I draw the line. They're fucked in the head and I'm simply not strong enough to go on like this. I've never felt this level of torment and fear pulsing through my veins before last night's games. But something tells me that they're only just getting started.

I'm not going to make it through this.

My bed creaks as I roll to face the dirty wall, desperate to block out the blinding sunshine. If I were smart, I'd be soaking up every moment of the light because once the darkness comes around again, I'm sure the brothers will be coming right along with it.

"Don't," comes the devilish growl of Marcus' low tone through my cell, "turn away from me."

A loud, fearful gasp tears through me and I scramble back on my bed, forcing myself closer to the wall as I flip over to find Marcus hovering in the furthest corner of my cell, shadows covering his face. He leans against the wall, his hands buried deep in his pocket with his foot propped up like he's more than prepared to spend hours in this very spot.

My eyes widen as my back stiffens with fear, watching the way he takes me in with interest. Anger pours through me as I slowly adjust my position, pulling myself into a low crouch on the bed, more than ready to lash out if I have to.

Marcus doesn't miss a damn thing. His eyes are sharp, and though he hasn't taken his hard stare off mine, something tells me that he can read my every thought and intention as if it were written across my face.

My heart races with dread and I quickly realize that these three brothers are never going to tire of tormenting me. They'll never tire of sneaking into my cell, and they'll never tire of watching me fear for my life.

I'm their play toy. I'm their bullshit entertainment and there's no way out.

They're never going to give up the game, especially when my reaction to their bullshit torture makes it so damn worth it for them. If only I was capable of not reacting, of being so okay with their shit that it didn't even phase me. Then perhaps they'd get bored of trying and leave me alone. I doubt they'll ever let me go, so my choices are to be so boring that they forget I'm even here or to be ended quickly and quietly.

This is my life now. This isn't just a game of fucking with my head, this is a game of survival and my sanity is the prize.

Maybe my life has always been a game of survival. I struggled long before my father ransacked my home and sold me to these animals.

I'm not missing out on some big adventure in my old life, and no one is mourning my sudden absence. But at least I knew how to survive in that meager life I'd carved from nothing, keeping my head down and working my ass off. But here? How does anyone know how to live in a world like this? I'm barely breathing.

Marcus pushes off the wall and strides toward me like a lion stalking its prey until his shins are pressing against the edge of my mattress. He reaches out, and before I get the chance to flinch, his thumb and forefinger are gripping my chin and forcing my eyes up to his. "Much better," he growls, his tone like a knife straight through my chest.

The anger works its way through my body, and completely forgetting that my new plan of attack is to act bored with their bullshit, my hand flies out and slaps his wrist away from my chin. "Don't fucking touch me," I snap, flying to my feet on top of the mattress and putting us eye to eye.

His head tilts in that strange fucked-up little way that makes him and his brothers seem even more deranged than usual, and he watches as I peel myself off the wall and step in even closer. I narrow my eyes in rage, flooded with the painful realization that I've always been a fucking prisoner. First to my father, then to an isolated life hiding in my one-bedroom apartment, and now to these three men.

"You don't get to touch me," I growl, adopting that same darkness that seems to swim in the depths of his eyes. "You don't get to fucking touch me. Is that clear? You're a pig, a fucking animal."

His eyes flare, and for a moment, I fear that I've pushed him too far. "On the contrary," he tells me, that deep brassy tone bouncing off the walls. "You're mine to do whatever the fuck I please."

I swallow hard and press my hand against his chest before shoving and forcing him back. I drop down off the mattress and stand before him, feeling like a fucking kitten standing up against the fearless lion and trying to roar. "Like hell I am," I tell him. "You have two fucking seconds to get your ass out of here before I bust it wide open. I'm not spreading my legs for you or your fucked-up brothers, so you better get used to the idea now because you sure as fuck won't like the consequences if you attempt to put your hands on me again."

Marcus' lips twitch and his eyes narrow in irritation before his hand snaps up and curls around my throat, his big fingers practically touching at the back of my neck, yet somehow still allowing me to breathe. My whole body is jostled around as he lifts me right off the fucking ground and presses my back against the cold stone wall.

He leans into me and I suck in a breath, smelling him all around me. His eyes linger on mine before slowly dropping down my body and scanning over my subtle curves, still in his dead mother's black silk gown.

He gets closer and closer and the little hairs on my arms stand to attention as chills sweep over me. "That's a mighty bark for such a little pup," he mutters just before his tongue sweeps out and curves over his full bottom lip. "Tell me, what's your bite like?"

I fight against his deathly hold, desperate to get away, or at the very least to put just a bit of distance between us, but it's no use. I might as well be in chains; his hold is just that strong. "Fuck you," I snarl, clenching my jaw as anger and frustration get the best of me.

His eyes come back to mine and the interest within them has my stomach swirling with unease. "Are you done?"

His bullshit tone suggests that I'm having some kind of tantrum and I gape at him in confusion. "Am I done?" I snap back at him, bringing my hands up and latching onto his tight vice-like grip around my throat. I dig my nails in as hard as I can, trying to pull him away, and for a slight moment, I could swear that the filthiest type of pleasure rocks through him. "As long as you assholes are keeping me locked up in your fucked-up little torture chamber, I'll never be done."

Finally catching on, he releases his hold on me and drops his hand, but he doesn't dare move out of my way, keeping me trapped with his large, toned body. He doesn't say a damn word, only tilts his head in that weird way and watches me like he's imagining just how fun it'll be to drain the life right out of me.

I swallow over the lump in my throat and sink back closer to the wall, desperate for space between us as his wickedly intoxicating scent is starting to fuck with my head. I mean, damnnnnnn. On top of looking like a devious little treat, why does he have to smell so freaking good?

"What's your deal?" I question, desperate to keep him talking rather than eyeing my body like his next meal. "Why can't you just let me go? I played your stupid little game. You stalked me through the fucking castle with your goddamn dogs. You've already humiliated me. You kidnapped me and forced me through some bullshit dinner party. Haven't I done enough? I don't deserve this shit. Just let me go already."

"Wolves," he clarifies. "We stalked you with our wolves, not dogs."

I give him a blank stare. "Are you kidding me? That's the part of my comment that you choose to clarify? Wolves, not dogs? Are you in-fucking-sane? What is wrong with you?"

His lips twist into a sick smirk just moments before his tone drops low, the thick, deep, vibrations instantly reminding me that Tarzan is a little bitch who left me with the worst case of blue bean imaginable. "Baby, you couldn't even begin to imagine the fucked-up things that are wrong with me."

I swallow hard as my heart races, matching the rapid beat of drums coming from upstairs and causing all sorts of havoc inside my chest. My hands ball into fists at my sides. I should be utterly repulsed by this psycho, not turned on. Screwing a guy like Marcus DeAngelis would surely earn me a one-way ticket to hell. Besides, he's that fucked in the head that he'd probably kill me first and then fuck me.

I shake the thought from my head. Why am I even thinking about that? What is wrong with me? I shouldn't be considering sleeping with one of my three inevitable murderers. I should be thinking about survival or figuring out a way to delay my untimely death because let's face it, once they're done with me, they're going to go straight back out there and pick up some other poor girl to destroy.

The realization that I can't just give up shoots through me. I have to endure this for as long as possible because the alternative simply isn't okay with me. A fierce hopelessness fills my soul, and as I meet Marcus' hard stare once again, I know he senses it.

"Why haven't you killed me yet?" I blurt out as the fight leaves my body and I resign myself to my new fucked-up future, somehow convincing myself that I have to be okay with it. "That's what you want, right? You want to watch the life drain out of me. You want to strangle me or slice me open. That's what gets you off, so what are you waiting for?"

He grins back at me, a real deranged and twisted grin, and my chest sinks as the weight of the situation sits heavily on my shoulders. His dark eyes flare as he leans in even closer, so close that the tip of his nose skims over my cheekbone. "Because I haven't had my fun with you yet."

My blood runs cold. He doesn't even try to deny my claims of him wanting to kill me. We both know it's true, so what's the point in even pretending?

My gaze shifts down as his hand slips inside his pocket and I catch my breath when he pulls out a thick piece of black material, eerily similar to the one Roman had used to knock me out last night. Fear pulses through me and my heart kicks into gear all over again. "No," I whisper, violently shaking my head, fearing what a guy like Marcus could do to me while I'm out cold on my torture chamber floor. "Please don't."

He presses harder into me, capturing both my wrists in just one of his big hands and wrapping the black material around them, binding them together. His gaze remains locked on mine as a soft breath of relief pours out of me, realizing that this isn't a repeat of last night. But that could only mean that he's got something else planned for me.

Marcus steps back, dragging me along with him and pulling me away from the wall. "I'm going to fuck you," he tells me, his tone leaving no room for argument or question. "You're not going to scream. You're not going to fight. I'm going to fuck that tight little pussy until you come on my dick. It's going to be hard and fast and I'm not going to stop until your fucking knees are shaking. Is that understood?"

I swallow hard, staring at him as though he was speaking another language.

He wants to fuck me, and shit, why does the very thought of me convulsing around his hard cock get me so damn hot?

I start shaking my head. "No," I say, trying to pull back as shame washes through me. I shouldn't want this. I shouldn't be flooding with need, but fuck, a guy like Marcus DeAngelis could destroy me in all the right ways.

He's a fucking murderer, they all are. He's dark and deadly and the last thing I should want is to allow myself to be vulnerable around him, to allow him to take my body and make me feel more alive than I have in days. Am I that fucked up in the head to want this? Because since the second those words slipped from between his full lips my pussy has been clenching with anticipation.

I'm going to fuck Marcus DeAngelis, and though shame pulses heavily through my veins, I can't wait. It's going to be raw, hard, and fast, exactly what my body has been craving. So why the hell not? If I'm going to die anyway, I might as well reap the rewards and join the dark side before I do.

EIGHT

Marcus' tight grip keeps me from pulling away as my body shakes with nerves. I can't stand the thought of him being so close to me, the thought of his fingers touching my body, but how else is this supposed to happen? He's going to have me whether I'm pulling away or not, so I might as well come to terms with it and try to find pleasure in his touch.

His hand falls to my waist and he forces me back until I'm standing directly in the center of my small room. My tough girl act falls away and I'm left with nothing but the shy girl who hasn't truly been touched by a man in months. I have no idea how this is going to go. He's already promised that it'll be hard and fast, and he sure as fuck made it clear that he won't stop until I'm coming undone beneath his touch. The question remains—is a psycho like Marcus DeAngelis even capable of giving a woman what she needs without slicing her throat in the process?

Fuck. What the hell have I gotten myself into?

My breath is shaky and despite the bright sunshine streaming in through the small window, the room has never seemed so dark. I'm determined though. If I make it out of this alive, I want to know that it wasn't all for nothing. Besides, how many other girls get to say that they've been thoroughly fucked by one of the notorious DeAngelis brothers? Actually … probably a lot.

His eyes remain locked on mine, so deep yet somehow so dead at the same time. It's impossible to look away. It's as though he's daring me to try and run, daring me to fear him and fear what he's about to do to me, but that little twisted feeling inside my gut has me standing here in silence, waiting to see just how good this is really going to be.

The shame is thick and I don't doubt that once he's done with me and I'm left as a helpless heap on the dirty floor that I'm going to regret my decision to not fight him on this, but my curiosity and need is thicker.

My knees buckle under me and I barely keep myself standing as he raises my bound wrists above my head. A fearful whimper escapes my lips and I don't doubt that he can see just how scared I am to explore this with him.

I keep my eyes locked on his as he continues raising my hands high, and for a moment, I wonder what the fuck he's attempting to do, but that curiosity doesn't last long as the thick material keeping my wrists bound is slipped over a large hook.

My loud gasp pierces the tension-filled silence and my gaze snaps up in confusion. I've searched this room a million times over the last few days and I could swear until I was blue in the face that there was no hook dangling in this room. He must have brought it with him and attached it to something in the ceiling while I was out cold, no thanks to his douchebag brother.

I tug hard on my wrists and the loud clanging of chain links fills the room. "What the fuck is this?" I demand, my gaze shifting back to Marcus, my heart racing as I realize that maybe he has a little more in mind than a simple hard and fast fucking.

His already dead gaze darkens and drops down my body, looking over my curves in the black silk gown like a snake taking in his next meal. "You didn't think I was about to lay you down and seduce you like some kind of love-sick fool, did you?"

I swallow hard and suck in a deep breath, clenching my jaw as the reality of just how screwed I am starts pulsing through my veins. He steps across the room and I watch as he reaches out and curls his wrist around a low hanging chain. My gaze shifts over it and just as I realize that it's the same chain connected to the hook around my bound wrists, he pulls hard and I'm lifted right off the ground, my tiptoes barely skimming across the hard stone beneath my feet.

"PUT ME DOWN," I yell, the panic tearing through me, certain that he's about to kill me.

I'm a fucking idiot. I should have fought against him, screamed for help, or done something, but what good would it have done? No one is coming to save me.

Marcus moves the chains around, locking them in place and making sure that I won't be able to get away, and as he looks back at me, I see nothing but pure lust and desire pulsing through his dark eyes. He moves back toward me, and as he does, his hand slips into his pocket and pulls out a dark red pocketknife, flipping the black blade out as he goes.

My whimpers come in hard and fast as his gaze continues skimming over my body. "No," I murmur into the horrifying room. "Please no."

Marcus steps toward me and the way he looks at me is as though he can't even hear me speaking. I'm just an object, here to deliver his darkest desires. He's in-fucking-sane and I just played right into his twisted little game.

His head tilts as he studies me, and though I attempt to pull away, hanging from a fucking thick ass chain makes it almost impossible to put any distance between us. He steps in even closer, so close that I feel his warm breath against my skin, and when the tip of his black blade presses against the hollow at the base of my throat, I know this is the end.

I don't move an inch as I draw in a shaky breath. His eyes seem to pulsate with his twisted needs as my body trembles in fear. "No," I whisper again, begging for him to hear me while knowing that there's no use, not with a guy as fucked up as Marcus. "Please. I don't want to die."

The sharp blade starts trailing down my chest, leaving a stinging pain in its wake but he doesn't cut me deep enough to draw blood. The blade sails right down between my tits until it hits the top of the silk gown and slices through it like butter.

His big hand falls to my thigh and I flinch at his touch before he bunches up the rest of the gown and brings the blade down in a precise arc, tearing through the flimsy material with ease. I suck in a gasp and just like that, he releases the soft silk, letting it fall open and exposing everything beneath it.

The black silk falls to either side of my full tits and the way his sharp gaze travels over them has the excitement returning deep in my gut. My nipples harden under his intense stare and I can't help but want him more. The blade slips into the side of my underwear and with one quick flick, the cotton is torn and falls to the ground, making a rush of intense desire pulse through me.

What the fuck is wrong with me? What girl in her right mind would crave someone like this? Surely after allowing a serial killer to take me, I'll be going straight to hell.

His tongue rolls over his bottom lip as his eyes flame with desire, and despite their intensity, I can't possibly look away. He takes me in as though he's still deciding exactly how he plans to do it, skimming his gaze over my toned stomach and down past my bare pussy.

If I could shrink back, I would. No woman likes to be judged, and right now, I feel as though I'm standing in a store window while he considers if what I have is good enough for his pristine tastes. I'm not a thick girl. I've always been told that a little more meat and a few extra squats could go a long way. The last six months of eating cheap food also hasn't helped, but I've never really cared too much. I'm healthy and that's all that counts, but damn, his scrutiny is killing me.

I *need* to know what he thinks, *need* to hear those fucked-up thoughts streaming through his twisted little mind. Though, I'm not stupid enough to hold my breath waiting for an answer that I know will never come. Marcus and his brothers are professionals at mind games and they wouldn't dare miss out on an opportunity to fuck with me even more.

Marcus presses the tip of his blade back to my skin, right in the middle of my sternum and slowly sails it over my body, though the stinging pain from earlier is gone. The tip gently brushes over my chest and it's almost like a caress. The tip curves over my breast, pushing the silk further out of the way before dropping down past my waist and sending a wave of goosebumps scattering across my body.

He brings his hand away and I watch as he effortlessly flips the knife, the blade catching in the sunlight before Marcus catches it, the sharp tip resting against his palm. He moves into me and places his other hand on my waist, his calloused fingers rough against my body. He tilts his head down and I feel his breath against my shoulder as his fresh, manly scent intoxicates me. Before I get a chance to question what he's doing, his arm flinches and the smooth handle of the pocketknife skims right between my legs.

I gasp, my pussy flinching with the sudden touch as the cool metal brushes over my aching clit, slowly moving further down. My pussy clenches, even more so when he starts moving in the opposite direction, teasing me as he drags the smooth handle back past my clit and away from my body.

He holds up the knife and I see my arousal glistening on the metal handle, but along with that, the small trickle of blood from the tip of the blade that rests in his palm. Marcus raises his hand until the glistening handle sits right between our faces, and just when he has my complete and undivided attention, his tongue slips out and rolls up the long edge of the handle, tasting everything I've got on offer.

"You say no," he rumbles, his deep tone bouncing off the walls as he carelessly tosses the knife across the room. It clatters against the stone wall and falls to a soundless stop on my bed, sending a wave of relief pulsing through my veins. "But your body is screaming yes."

There's absolutely no denying it now. He's seen the evidence for himself. So, knowing that I could be making one hell of a big mistake, I nod, feeling my gut twist with unease.

His fingers trail up my thigh and sail over my waist before finally coming to a stop at my shoulder. He takes the remaining black silk that hangs by my side and effortlessly tears it before doing the same on the other side and letting the silk fall away, leaving me vulnerable and scared. Though something tells me that he truly is here just to fuck. My sex-deprived little soul is screaming in elation, but my head is still warning me to be cautious.

He steps around me, slowly circling me as his fingers sail over my skin. I feel his sharp stare on my body, watching me closely and studying every inch of me while my heart races, not liking him out of my sight as he stands directly behind me.

My body trembles as he moves in close and I feel his hard cock straining against his pants as he presses his body up against mine. His hand softens against the curve of my ass and a breathy moan slips from between my lips.

My eyes widen.

Fuck. That was a bad move. It's one thing letting him know that I'm down for a bit of senseless fucking but showing just how badly I need it is a mistake, one I'm positive that I will pay for.

His hand draws back and I brace myself, knowing exactly what's coming next.

SLAP.

A loud, breathy gasp tears from my chest as the sharp sting sails through my body. My ass burns from the spank, but before I can focus on the throbbing, his hand curls around my body and slides down around my thigh.

Marcus raises it high and pulls my knee out to the side, opening me wide as his other hand curls under my ass and cups my pussy. He adjusts his fingers, capturing my clit between his pointer and middle finger before giving it a firm squeeze. "This is mine," he tells me. "I own you. You're not to give this up for anybody. Not Roman or Levi, or any sorry fucker who comes looking for you. Is that understood?"

Instinctively, I grind against his hold, desperate to feel his pleasure while fighting my inner thoughts, telling me that I should be bawling like a fucking baby in the corner of the room. "And if I say no?" I ask, the words leaving my mouth before I can stop them.

The heat of his breath skims my neck, sending a wave of electricity straight to my core. "Are you asking me to stop?" he questions as his hard stare hits my fragile one.

"No," I whimper, shaking my head, the desperation pulsing through me. I'd give anything for him to release my clit and give me what I need. "Please don't stop."

"Then tell me you understand." His fingers squeeze just a little bit harder and I gasp, sucking in a shaky breath as I nod adamantly. "Say it," he breathes into my ear.

"Only for you."

Marcus responds by releasing my clit and rubbing slow circles over it, finally relieving the dull ache, but not nearly enough. I'm just getting used to his rhythm when his hands fall away and a whimper slips from between my lips, but before the disappointment pulses through me, he takes my waist and spins me, the chain effortlessly turning and whipping me around.

I come face to face with Marcus and see his deadly eyes focus on mine and remember who the fuck I'm dealing with. I shouldn't be allowing this but now my body is far too worked up. On some level, I know this has to be a twisted joke and that he's bound to leave me high and dry. Nothing is ever this simple with the DeAngelis brothers.

He moves into me and trails the back of his knuckles down the side of my face as I feel his hard chest pressing up against mine. His head tilts in that creepy way, and for a moment, the fear starts to overtake me again.

Without warning, his lips drop to the curve of my neck and my body freezes as his tongue teases my sensitive skin, but when his hand comes back to my waist and caresses my skin, I find myself relaxing again.

In any other situation, I'd be reaching out and staking my claim, but not here and definitely not now. I'm obviously stupid, but I'm not suicidal. Though something tells me that Marcus isn't the type of man to appreciate a bold woman.

His hands roam over my body, rough, strong, and determined. His fingers dig into the curve of my ass, hard enough to leave marks as he sucks and nips at my neck and shoulder. It's intoxicating and freeing, something I never thought I'd feel while locked up in this hell hole.

He teases my body, slipping his fingers down between my legs and exploring every single inch of me, bringing me to the edge only to pull back and deprive me of what I truly need. Another soft moan slips from between my lips and then all too soon, he pulls away again.

The harsh sunlight streaming through the small window plays in his dark hair as I watch his gaze shift over my body, taking in the subtle red marks from his fingers and soft bruising that will fade by the end of the day. Excitement glistens in his eyes, but it's nothing compared to the fierce desire reflected in my own as he drags his black shirt over his head and shows off his incredible, sculptured body.

Tattoos cover his skin like a haunting masterpiece, sailing over his broad shoulders and winding down his muscled arms, all the way to his knuckles. There's a beautiful girl across his ribs, and fuck, she looks as though she's been through the worst kind of hell, but the way he grips my chin and forces my gaze off his body tells me that lingering is not a good idea. Though, I don't miss the subtle sparkle of the diamond piercing that sits right where the dimple in the girl's cheek should be.

"Eyes on mine," he growls, the sound vibrating right through my chest.

I swallow hard and nod. He waits a long moment, his jaw clenched as fury pulses in his gaze, and for a minute, I fear that he's about to walk out and leave me hanging in the middle of the room, but finally, he releases his vise-like grip.

His hands drop to his pants, effortlessly releasing the button and undoing the fly as my every need and desire tells me to look down, but I don't dare. I keep my eyes on his, hoping that at some point he'll be far too distracted and that I'll finally get a good look at what he's packing inside those pants.

The heavy material drops to the ground and I watch in my peripheral as his big hand strokes up and down his impressive cock, making my pussy flood with need. I'd give anything for him to fill me right now. To drop to my knees and take him in my mouth. Fuck, to make one of the DeAngelis brothers come undone beneath my touch would be one of those moments that I'd never forget.

He comes back toward me and I suck in a breath, having absolutely no idea how this is going to go. I'm hanging from the fucking ceiling and can barely touch the ground. Though it's damn clear that he's done it this way to rob me of any control. I can't use my hands and I can't move myself around. I'm at his mercy, and I have to hope that he doesn't take things too far.

The look in his eyes tells me that this is going to be just as he promised—hard and fast.

Without warning, he grabs me and a squeal tears out of me as I rock against the thick chains, having no choice but to hang my weight into them. His hands slip between my legs and push them wide open as his gaze shifts down to my pussy, taking in every fucking angle as he steps into me and curls my legs around his narrow waist.

Marcus grips my waist, holding me still and with devastating precision, lines himself up with my aching cunt and slams his cock deep inside of me.

I cry out at the sudden intrusion as I throw my head back and get used to the feel of him inside me. He stretches me wide and I groan low, dangling against the chains. I could tell that he was big, but nothing could have prepared me for that, not even any of the broken and over-used toys in my bedside drawer.

His fingers dig into my waist, his nails bound to draw blood, but nothing else matters except for my pussy getting its next hit.

Marcus slowly drags back out of me and I prop my head back up, needing to see the way that his body rolls as he moves inside of me, and fuck, it's worth every damn second. His strong body is perfect, like an Adonis created out of rock-hard muscle. His muscles tense and relax as his sharp, clenched jaw screams for me to drag my nails through his stubble.

He's fucking everything. It's a damn shame that he's a murderer.

Marcus slams back into me and spits through his clenched jaw. "Fucking take it," he says with a fierce desperation, telling me that he's been needing this release just as much as I have.

He works my body over and over again as my pussy gets used to his deliciously wicked ways. He starts slow and rapidly increases his speed, giving me everything he's got as his thick cock slams deep inside of me.

My wetness spreads between us and I all but cry when he adjusts his hold on me and brings his fingers down against my clit. He rubs it in slow, torturous circles between two fingers and I throw my head back again, the intense pleasure more than I can handle.

My pussy aches, clenches, and trembles, but I hold on, not ready for this to end.

I'd give anything to free my hands. To wrap my fingers around his cock, to feel where we connect and the way my arousal coats his thick length and helps him to slide back inside my tight pussy. Fuck, just to knot my fingers into his hair and pull as fucking hard as I could, but damn it, giving him complete control also has its advantages.

"FUCK," I cry out, clenching my eyes as the overwhelming pleasure takes over me. "More."

His fingers pinch down on my clit and I cry out again, a sharp, howling sound that I didn't even know I was capable of, but the pain instantly fades as his fingers press down again, rubbing those same torturous little circles. "You'll get what I give and nothing more," he growls, the deep grumble vibrating right through my chest and sending a jolt of electricity firing through me.

Fuck, I need to come and I need to do it now.

My pussy clenches around his big cock and I squeeze tight as he draws out of me, his low groan making my deprived little soul scream in elation. His fingers tighten on my waist, and just as I open my eyes to meet his shallow, dead ones, he slams deep inside of me and my orgasm violently tears through me.

My whole body spasms as I scream out, the sudden ferocity of it completely overwhelming my system as my pussy convulses around his hard cock. "Holy fuck," I breathe, throwing my head back and clenching my eyes as I ride out the big, heavy waves tearing through me.

My body trembles as Marcus keeps moving, relentless, fast thrusts deep inside my pussy while his fingers keep circling my clit. When my body finally comes down from its epic high, he picks up his pace, fucking me just how he needs as I groan and cry out with his delicious movements.

Without warning, my legs drop from around his waist just as he reaches up and pulls on the black fabric around my wrist. It comes undone, and as he pulls out of my pussy, my body falls to the ground, my knees too weak to hold myself up.

Marcus lets me fall, grazing my knees as I come to a hard stop with his impressive cock right in front of my face. His hands wind into my hair and he tears my head back just in time to push his cock between my lips. I open wide for him, and despite him kidnapping me right out of my fucking apartment, I still want to impress him.

I taste my arousal on his cock as I take him deep, but I'm not surprised when he grips my hair tighter, holding me still and taking over control. He fucks my mouth and I feel him right in the back of my throat. I choke way more than I'm prepared to admit, but he doesn't seem to mind. Don't get me wrong, I've done this more than the next girl, but I can't say that I've ever had a guy so demanding, rough, and forceful.

Anyone would think that I'd hate it, but that need to satisfy him and make him feel just as good as he made me feel won't go away. I need to see this through, even if it means choking on his big fucking dick until the sun goes down.

He gives it to me hard and I have no choice but to stabilize myself against his thick thighs, and despite knowing that I shouldn't, I can't help but wind my hands up his tight body, digging my nails in and leaving marks everywhere they go.

I grab his strong, defined ass and feel the sharp ridges of his abs, loving the way he seems to relax into my needy touch, and then all too soon, he pulls my chin up just a little higher, and with a deep, guttural groan, he sends hot spurts of delicious cum sailing right down my throat.

I don't dare move, taking everything that he's got for me and swallowing hard. He pulls out of my mouth, releases my hair in the same instance and I sink down deeper onto my knees, feeling the throbbing of my thoroughly well-fucked pussy.

I can't help but watch Marcus as he pulls his pants on and tucks himself back inside. He doesn't look at me and I'm grateful, needing that short moment just to breathe. He doesn't bother with his shirt, leaving it forgotten in the corner of the room as he steps back toward me.

My eyes snap up to meet his just as his hand tangles into my hair again. He tears my head back, forcing my chin up as he bears down on me, that same fearless psychopath instantly returning. "Next time," he growls with a furious anger. "You come when I say you come."

And just like that, he releases me and walks out of my cell, leaving me sitting on the dirty ground, wondering what the fuck just happened.

NINE

I fucked a psychopath and I loved it.

Fuck, I didn't just love it, it was the best damn fuck that I've ever had. It's as though he could read my body like he was reading a book. He knew exactly what I needed and he didn't hold back. It was rough, it was fast, and it was fucking dangerous. Just as he promised.

Fuck, I love a man who can keep his word.

Most guys talk a big game, saying how they're going to give it to you hard and be the best screw of your life. They make all these exciting promises only to get you home, fuck you with a half-soft cock after drinking too much, rub your left labia until it's red-raw, and then pass out after you told them that they couldn't stay.

Not Marcus DeAngelis. He held up his end of the bargain. He did exactly what he said he was going to do, took what he needed without wasting my time, and then he fucked right off afterward. What more could a girl need? *If only he wasn't him.*

Searching around the room, I pick up the discarded silk gown and sigh as it falls to pieces between my fingers. My underwear is useless and I'm sure as fuck not about to remain naked in this room. Marcus' black shirt lays haphazardly in the corner of the room, completely forgotten and while I hate the thought of being naked, I hate the thought of wearing his shirt even more.

Having no choice, I pick up the old tank and sweatpants off the floor that had been left here from my first night in this hell hole, cringing as I pull them on. A million thoughts go through my mind, all focusing on the woman who these might have belonged to before me.

Bile rises in my throat and I try to swallow it down as the soft material hugs my body and brings me my first ounce of comfort in days. I hate this. I hate everything about this, but more so, I hate myself for letting Marcus Fucking DeAngelis screw me like there was no tomorrow.

I shouldn't have enjoyed it. I should have been repulsed by his calloused touch, and I sure as fuck shouldn't be wanting to do it all over again, but I do. Does that make me just as sick as he is? What the hell is wrong with me? What woman would allow that to happen, to allow her kidnapper to take pleasure in her body, to come in her fucking mouth and then swallow it down like a horny bitch?

Fuck. There's a special place reserved in hell for girls like me.

There's no doubt about it. Marcus made my body come alive for the first time in years, well, apart from when Tarzan did, but that hardly counts. But I'm no fool, I know this isn't going to change anything. One good fuck isn't going to suddenly have the guy fixing a halo over his head. When he gets his chance to finally kill me, he'll take it no matter what. It'll be brutal, twisted, and sick. That's a guarantee.

He's a monster who knows exactly what I taste like. If anything, that'll only make things worse.

The reminder of his tongue sliding up the handle of the knife sits in the forefront of my mind and I find myself glancing toward my small bed. The black blade sits just below my pillow and I can't help but wonder if he left it here on purpose.

Why, though? It doesn't make sense.

Someone like Marcus DeAngelis doesn't make mistakes, especially ones like leaving a fucking knife for his kidnappee. I mean, it's not like I'll be able to use it properly or inflict any real harm. I have no training, and even if I did, I've seen the brothers in action. Their reflexes are way too fast. I'd be a joke to them, but I'm not going to lie, its presence in this fucked-up little torture chamber goes a long way in giving me just a sliver of hope. More than that, the remaining blood that lingers on the blade from Marcus' palm, only fuels my need to make him bleed. No matter what I have to do, this knife will spill more of his blood.

I drop down onto the bed and my pussy throbs, reminding me that I'm going to be feeling Marcus for days to come, but that's to be expected after being so thoroughly fucked. Marcus is the most unhinged out of the three and if that's how he fucks, I can only imagine what Roman or Levi would be like.

Roman would be put together. His plan for how he takes me would be carefully thought out. He'll know exactly what position he wants me in and exactly how to work my body to get me off as proficiently as possible. Though, he's probably screwed so bad in the head that he'd be all about just getting himself off and leaving me feeling used and abused with the worst case of blue bean known to womankind. Levi though, he'd be the 'go with the flow' type. He'd fuck me every which way until we were both spent on the fucking floor and forgetting that I'm supposed to be kidnapped. It'd be hard and angry, there's no denying it.

All three of them would be magical in their own unique way, but there's no doubt about it that all of them would come with a fierce, relentless passion, not stopping until the job is thoroughly done, which thanks to Marcus, I'm only now realizing how damn good that can be. God, their depraved little dark souls could take me on the ride of a lifetime.

Fuck. Don't go there. That's murky waters, and a bitch like me will likely drown. Assuming one of the brothers' hands aren't already wrapped around my throat and holding me under.

My knees come right up into my chest as I lean back against the stone wall of my torture chamber, though I suppose I have to stop calling it that now. What I just experienced was anything but torture. Well, kinda. I don't really know what that was. It's not like he was sweet and compassionate about the whole thing. He was going to fuck me whether I was screaming or moaning and he wasn't going to relent until I shattered around his thick cock.

The knife rests between my fingers and I carefully spin it, studying its sleek curve and the impressive matte blade. I've never seen anything like it. I haven't really seen many regular ones either, but this one ... there's just something so sleek about it. It's almost like it was a gift from Marcus, but that couldn't be right. Thinking like that is only going to get me in trouble.

Minutes turn into hours and my back is just starting to ache against the hard stone wall when the heavy metal door is barged open. A loud gasp tears from deep within my throat as I throw my hand down beside me, quickly burying the knife within my sheets.

Roman DeAngelis stands before me and I find myself shrinking back against the wall. Every time I see him, it's like a slap in the face. He's larger than life in the worst possible way. Everything about him screams for me to run, and that scar that cuts straight through his brow and down over his cheekbone warns me that he's no quitter.

I hold my breath and watch as his gaze shifts over me with a calculated curiosity, the door hanging wide between us. His stare falls to my hand beside my thigh and without a damn word passing between us, I can tell that he knows.

He holds a silver tray and my stomach growls with hunger, hoping to whoever exists above that whatever is on that tray is some sort of food. It's been two days. My stomach is as empty as it comes and after racing through this fucked-up castle and having Marcus put me through an intense workout, food has been all I've been able to think about for hours.

Roman doesn't move away from the door and the more he seems to stare, the smaller I feel. His gaze shifts to the shredded silk on the floor, my torn panties, and the black shirt discarded in the corner of the room. Anger pulses in his dark eyes as they come back to meet mine. "Which one?" he demands.

I clench my jaw, unable to look away from his cold-hard stare as the anger in his eyes clearly lets me know that a scheduled fucking wasn't in the plan. I swallow over the lump in my throat and weigh up my options. There's a good chance that Marcus doesn't want his brothers to know what went down in here and if I give up his name, that'll put me at the very top of his shit list, but not giving up his name puts me at the top of Roman's.

Fuck, why are these brothers always putting me in impossible situations?

I guess the question is, which one do I fear more?

I narrow my gaze and slowly shake my head, trying to call on that fiery attitude that's buried deep down inside of me. "Go and interrogate your asshole brothers and leave me the hell alone. I didn't do shit, just following orders like a good little kidnappee. Now, why don't you hurry along and go fuck with someone else's day?"

The silver tray of barely recognizable food is thrown across the small room, sending what must be a pathetic excuse for scrap slamming into the wall and dropping to the ground with a sloppy thud. My heavy stare remains on Roman because I can guarantee that he's never had a damn person ever speak to him like that and for good reason.

He storms toward me and my eyes bug out of my head. The last time he was anywhere near me, I ended up out cold, and I sure as hell won't be allowing that bullshit to happen again.

He reaches for me in the same instant that my hand whips out from under my sheets and as his big hand curls around my throat, Marcus' forgotten knife presses against his.

He tears me up to my feet, so that I stand before him, reaching eye to eye, not even noticing—or caring—about the sharp blade pressed against his fragile, warm skin. It must take a big fucking man to be so careless with his own life, but then, he probably knows that I don't have the guts to see it through.

"You're in no fucking position to speak to me like that," he growls, his words vibrating right through my chest as his heavenly scent consumes me. "You need to watch yourself."

"What's the point? It's not like I've got anything to lose," I spit right back as his other hand curls around my wrist and squeezes so damn tight that I have no choice but to release the knife at his throat.

The metal drops down between us and clatters to a stop at Roman's feet and only then does his gaze shift down and take in the sleek curve of the red-handled knife and the pristine matte blade that glistens in the late afternoon light.

Recognition dawns in his eyes and just like that, he knows.

Roman releases me, dropping me back to my bed and kicking the knife into the corner of the room, but making absolutely no attempt at taking it away from me. "Stay away from Marcus," he grumbles, his eyes narrowed in distaste.

I laugh, straightening myself on my bed and slamming my back against the wall, keeping as far out of his reach as possible. "You think I asked for it? That somehow I broke out of this shithole and hunted him down like a fucking cat in heat? I've got news for you, it's not me who needs to stay away from Marcus. This is all on him."

I have a damn good point and he knows it.

His hard stare lingers a moment longer, still not appreciating my careless tone, and then all too soon, he turns his back and begins stalking for the door.

"Wait," I rush out, hurrying off my bed and clambering to my feet, having absolutely no idea what I need to say. All I know is that I can't be alone in this torture chamber for much longer. I'm going out of my mind. Hell, I'll even accept Roman's company over that of my own.

Roman stops and slowly spins to face me, his pissed-off stare speaking volumes. He doesn't say a word, just looks at me expectantly, annoyed that I dare to even try to ask anything of him.

"I … umm," my gaze flicks to the corner of the room to where my sloppy food scraps lay in a pile. "I'm hungry. I need proper food and water, not these disgusting scraps. I played your stupid games. You and your brothers tortured me with white noise and then had your freaking wolves stalk me through your dungeon hallways in the middle of the night. You said if I played along, I'd be rewarded."

Roman scoffs and steps toward me, his eyes softening and instantly putting me on edge. I flinch as he raises his hand and gently runs his fingers along my collarbone, brushing over the faint bruises that his brother left on my skin. "Did he make you come?"

I pull away, my brows furrowed as I stare back at him. "How is that any of your business?"

His hand shifts from my neck in a flash like lightning and wraps around my wrist. He yanks me into him and I barely keep upright with the momentum. "Did. You. Come?"

"Yes," I spit, my other hand coming up and shoving him hard in the chest, fruitlessly attempting to put some space between us.

"Then consider yourself rewarded," he tells me, his eyes flashing with a sinister darkness, and I realize that this is his version of a big ole 'fuck you.'

My jaw clenches and I do everything I can not to huff and groan like some delinquent child, but damn it, it's hard. "People are going to start looking for me soon," I warn. "You're not going to get away with this."

Roman laughs, pushing me away from him until I'm standing in the center of the room, looking back at him, completely helpless. "No one is coming for you, Shayne," he taunts, his tone low and full of venom as he begins stalking me again. "You think we just plucked you out of thin air? That absolutely no thought went into this? We've been planning this for months, watching you, learning your routine."

I start backing up, his words like a knife being stabbed straight through my chest. "No. You're wrong. Someone will come."

"You're kidding yourself," he mutters, his eyes sharp like daggers. "The only person who's visited your apartment in the past three months was your landlord and even he wants you gone. Your so-called friends at the club don't notice you as it is. They'll just be pissed that you didn't show for your shift and were made to cover you. You've got no one, not even Daddy Dearest is coming for you. You're as good as dead to them. Though, it probably doesn't help that we had your death certificate signed and news of your untimely demise splashed across every news outlet in the country. It was a particularly nasty death. Believe me, no one is holding out hope that a fragile little thing such as yourself could have survived that."

I shake my head as my back hits the far wall, that distant memory from when they invaded my apartment flooding back to me. Levi and Marcus laughed about the story that would be leaked to the news. It was horrendous. I would have been murdered and left in a shallow grave for a wild bear to come and tear my body apart. There would have been nothing but ribbons of flesh left. "You're not going to get away with this."

Roman steps into me, his big body flush with mine as his head tilts down. The tip of his nose skims across my cheek as his hand twines around my jaw, following the curve into the back of my head. "That's just the thing, Empress," he murmurs, his tone low and deadly as I feel his warm breath brushing against my skin. "We already have."

TEN

Darkness sweeps over my room and once again, I'm left to endure the long, fearful lonely night. Only this time, I won't be making such a stupid mistake like allowing myself to sleep.

Roman's words have circled my head all night. *We already have.* But he's right, they did get away with it. I'm screwed. Literally nobody is searching for me. Hell, this is the beginning of my third night and I bet not a damn person even realizes that I'm gone, though the news story that was put out about my death sure wouldn't help. The world already thinks I'm dead, so why would they even attempt to look for me? There's even a signed death certificate and everything.

I've already been forgotten.

It's got to be well past midnight and I find myself staring up at the ceiling. The heavy chain still hangs from the roof, however Roman had taken the hook that dangled from the bottom of it, though I have no freaking idea why. It's not like I could have done anything with it. He'd have been smarter to take the chain, but in reality, a chain that big would be too heavy for me to fuck around with anyway. So rather than spending my afternoon trying to figure out how to use it to my advantage, I spent my long, lonely hours using Marcus' knife to shred his discarded shirt into a million tiny pieces.

The knife has stayed in the palm of my hand since the very second Roman stormed out of here, and all I've been able to do is think about how I'd like to give him a matching scar for the other eye. Though, thinking like that is only going to turn these bastards on.

Fucking hell.

I throw myself to my feet and start pacing the small room as waves of uncontrollable anger surge through me. I have to get out of here. I have to … fuck. I don't even know. This is too much. That tiny slither of hope that burned brightly inside my chest has fizzled out and turned to ashes.

I've got nothing. I'm doomed to live out the remainder of what's bound to be a short life, suffering at the hands of the DeAngelis brothers.

Devastation rests heavily on my shoulders and I sink to my knees, feeling them graze against the uneven stone beneath me. My head falls into my hands as the tears start filling my eyes and pouring down my cheeks. Heavy sobs pull from deep within my chest and they barely get a chance to shine before the door is thrown open and the three brothers pour into the room.

My head snaps up as fear rockets through me, my watery eyes blurring everything around me.

They rush me as I take in their black hoodies and terrifying masks that completely cover their faces. My piercing scream wails through the room, bouncing off the walls and echoing down the long hallway. Hands grab at me and I try to make out who is who, but the darkness is too harsh, too unforgiving, and they use it to their advantage. Their distinct features are concealed, leaving nothing but their haunting eyes that beg for me to try and fight them off.

I try to pull away but their fingers on my skin are like tight vices, impossible to budge as they tear me up from the ground. Scuffles are heard all around me and it happens so damn fast. I barely get my feet down before a black bag falls over my face and a hand jams into my back, pushing me toward the door.

My feet scramble to keep up with their long strides as I try to scream, but what's the point? No one can hear me, and I'm sure as fuck that no one is coming. Fingers dig into my arms, and without warning, I'm lifted off the ground just enough that my toes drag along the stone as the brothers move up the stairs.

I'm released with a heavy thud, the only thing keeping me up is the hand shoved into my lower back. "WHERE ARE YOU TAKING ME?" I yell out, the panic in my tone clear as day.

The only response I get is a tightening of their fingers digging into my skin and a hard shove. The sound of their feet against the stone changes and suddenly a smooth, cool flooring hits the bottom of my feet. We must be in the space I declared as an old ballroom, assuming the boys are taking me in the same direction that Levi had taken me the night of the dinner party. Though I've quickly come to learn not to make any assumptions.

My heart races a million miles an hour, wondering what the fuck they plan on doing to me when I'm tugged violently to the left. I stumble into one of the boys who promptly pushes me back to my feet.

"Watch it," a deep tone rumbles through the room, the sound bouncing off the walls and letting me know that we must be in a big empty space, probably very similar to the ballroom. Though I have no idea if the comment was directed at me or one of the brothers.

The sound quickly fades as I keep stumbling through their home, terrified of what they have planned for me tonight. I'm pulled to the left again and after a few short steps, I go flying to the right, the hands barely keeping me up.

Disorientation swirls through my head and I quickly realize that the boys don't want me to know where I am in their home, but that's more than alright with me. I have absolutely no intention of learning anything about this place.

We walk in circles, going up and down stairs, through carpeted rooms and onto cold tile before moving through to old wooden flooring. Some rooms are cooler than others while some feel as though a toasty fireplace has been cranking all night, but then finally, I'm pulled to a stop.

Nerves race through my body and I get the overwhelming need to make a break for it and run for my life. I was cool with walking. When I'm walking, that means that I still have time, but stopping … that could only mean one thing. My time is up.

A loud squealing breaks through the silence and my knees tremble. It sounds like some kind of ancient door, but before I can figure it out, a rush of cold air slams into me and I'm pushed through an opening.

A harsh breeze flows through the air and the familiar sound of branches and leaves rustling in the wind tells me that I've just been thrown out of a door.

My back straightens as just the tiniest bit of hope flutters through my body. Have they listened to me? Are they finally letting me go?

I'm pushed hard just as the hands on my arms release me and I go crashing down to the hard ground. My hands fly out and I catch myself, cutting up my palms in the process, but that's the least of my worries.

I flip myself over, not liking the idea of the boys at my back and tear the black bag off my face. The three brothers loom over me, my position from the dirty ground making them look like fucking giants. Their hard stares are locked on me but with those creepy-as-fuck black masks, it's impossible to get a read on them.

The brother in the middle takes a step toward me and I scramble back, my heels pushing in the dirt as I quickly take note of my surroundings. I'm in some kind of overgrown garden, but it's not like anything I've ever seen before.

The brother keeps moving toward me as the other two flank his sides, moving as one. "Wha ... what are you doing?" I rush out, my eyes wide as I watch their creepy little act while desperately trying to scramble away.

They step up right in front of me and I swallow hard as the one in the middle crouches down. "You wanted to be free, right?" he questions, the darkness making it impossible to tell him apart by his eyes, but the harsh tone of his voice is unmistakable.

Roman.

I don't bother responding, knowing that this has to be some kind of game. There's no way that they're about to let me go. My gaze flicks between the brothers before coming back to Roman's. This is clearly his moment to shine, and something tells me that he's going to make it count.

"I like to think that we're the kind of guys to give a pretty woman what she wants, so we're prepared to make a deal with you."

My back stiffens, sitting up straighter.

"Look around you, Shayne. Do you see where you are?"

My brows furrow and I reluctantly tear my eyes off Roman's, glancing around the overgrown garden and quickly realizing that it's so much more than just overgrown bushes. It's a fucking maze. It's like a scene out of *Harry Potter and the Goblet of Fire* only creepier, and from memory, Cedric Diggory never made it out alive.

"What is this?" I demand, discreetly shuffling further away from him, though there's really nothing discreet about it. He tracks every single movement I make and adjusts himself to keep the advantage.

"My brothers and I have been talking," he says, his eyes brightening with a devilish laughter. "We understand that this little arrangement isn't for everybody and you've made it quite clear that you're not down to play our … games, so we're prepared to make a deal with you."

I narrow my eyes, not trusting a damn word that he says. This whole nice guy compromising act isn't right and it doesn't sit well with me. He's lying. They kidnapped me. They broke into my home and took me right out of my apartment. They're the most notorious killers in the country and certainly not known for how accommodating they can be. So why the hell would they go and offer me a deal? This has to be a trap, but what is their angle?

I cautiously pull my feet up under me and with my gaze locked on Roman's, I stand on shaky legs. He mimics my movements until we stand face to face, only his impressive height has him towering over me. "A deal?" I question.

He nods so slightly that I could be imagining it. "If you can find your way out of our maze, then you're free to go," he tells me as Levi and Marcus slowly move closer, their attempts at being discreet going to waste.

"Free to go?" I repeat, my heart rate rising higher by the second. "I just have to make my way out and you'll let me go? Alive?"

"Mmhmm," he says, his eyes darkening as he drops his chin, making him look like a fucking image right out of a horror movie. "That's what I said, isn't it?"

My stomach twists as I slowly take a step back. "What's the catch?" I ask, my voice shaky as I cautiously watch the way that all three of them start to move toward me, stalking me like prey. "I don't believe that you'll just let me go."

"The catch is," Roman says, his usually dead eyes coming alive as I hear the wicked smile in his tone, "you better run fast."

Fuck.

I turn on my heel and take off like a fucking rocket.

There's no doubt that it isn't as easy as it sounds. There's a trap, a nasty as fuck catch that I'm missing, but I'm not risking hanging around to figure it out. It's a maze garden after all, so all I have to do is be faster than them and I should be alright. I just have to find my way through it first.

The opening of the maze passes by me as my bare feet slam against the cold, hard ground. Overgrown branches scratch my arms and ankles but I force my way through them, determined to see this through. Hell, if I can't find the exit, I could at least find somewhere to hide and wait them out.

Hope rises in my chest and it pushes me faster. I could get out of here tonight. I could be free.

The maze is thick and twice my height, making it impossible to try and map out a path. I have to rely on my senses, and right now, they're not saying a lot, just to keep running and put as much distance between me and the brothers as possible.

Apart from my feet slamming against the hard ground and my rapid, sharp pants as I run, the maze is silent. There's no rustling of bushes, no familiar sound of the night, no owls or even a soft breeze, just dead silence.

The haunting thought of this being some kind of graveyard for the brothers' many kills filters through my mind, sending my blood cold as shivers trails down my spine. I push the thought aside, but with every step I take, the image of zombified hands shooting up through the dirty ground and capturing my ankles haunts my mind.

The small hope of freedom is like a beacon shining brightly inside me, keeping me going despite the lack of energy pulsing through my veins. I haven't eaten properly in so long that my energy is quickly draining, but my determination to find freedom keeps me going.

The silence consumes me, stealing every last ounce of sanity I have left as I try to navigate my way through the maze. I go left and right before coming to a dead end and doubling back, only to go down a path that I've already been.

I keep going, but this time I take the second right instead of waiting for the third, and as I make my turn, my gaze shifts up and I see the massive home in all its glory with the moonlight shining against it.

It's a haunting sight and I almost hate myself for being right … Well, mostly right. It's not technically a castle, but it's the closest thing to it. The boys' home looks like a gothic Tudor-style mansion from the 1500s, complete with the gargoyles at its peaks. Old vines wind up around the walls of the mansion and most of the windows are protected with bars. There must be hundreds of rooms inside.

I'm fucked. So damn fucked.

Ten minutes turn into twenty and before I know it, I'm positive that I've run down every possible path. Tears well in my eyes and as they fall down my face, I push myself on, but every passing second, that small beacon of hope inside me starts dwindling, its bright light burning out and telling me that I was a fool to allow myself to hope for a future.

I turn back for the millionth time and keep trying. My clothes are torn and my arms, face, and feet are cut up from the overgrown, stray branches, but I'm determined not to give up. I must have missed something.

I'm deep inside the maze and my brain is fried. I can't even remember which way I've turned or how to get back to where I started. My chest hurts from gasping for breath and my feet ache from the uneven ground. This is more running than I've ever done in my life. If I knew that running through creepy mazes barefoot in the middle of the night was in my future, I would have at least hit the gym a few times to prepare.

A rustle in the bushes beside me has me coming up short as a cold chill sweeps through me. Up until then, this maze was silent. A branch snapping to my right has me whipping around but another rustle in the hedges behind me has me spinning full circle.

They're here with me.

"Are you lost?" a haunting whisper asks from in front of me, the overwhelming darkness making it impossible to pinpoint exactly where they are. "I can help you."

I go to my right, creeping through the maze in the opposite direction to the noises I'd heard while desperately trying to mask my heavy breathing. If I can't see them, there's a good chance that they can't see me either, but I'd be a fool to be so naive.

"Don't be like that," another voice whispers through the thick bushes. "We won't bite ... much."

A comment like that has to have come from Marcus, but I'm not willing to hang around to find out.

I take off at another sprint, but this time, the silence no longer exists. The rustling of the leaves follows me, coming from all angles, branches breaking and feet slamming against the hard ground.

I turn a corner only to find a shadowy figure waiting for me at the end, forcing me to double back as fear rockets through me. Every step I take, every turn I make, they're there, waiting for me to fall right into their trap.

The familiar sound of padded paws slamming against the hard ground has my back straightening with fear. I should have known that they'd get their wolves involved in this bullshit, but while they're stalking me through the maze, something tells me that the brothers have these animals trained. They're not going to hurt me unless specifically asked to. In their little animal heads, they're probably just out for a run with their twisted masters.

The rustling continues, getting closer and closer as I hear my name whispered through the thick bushes, daring me to give up, daring me to come just a little bit closer. I feel them there, feel them close but they're hidden within the bushes, haunting it and turning my already fragile mind into a complete mess.

Disorientation claims me and I have absolutely no idea where to go, but when I take the next left and trip over a low riding branch, I go sprawling out on the ground, scratching the shit out of my elbows.

The exhaustion quickly catches up to me and within mere seconds, a massive wolf is hovering over me, his sharp, intimidating gaze locked on me, ready to attack at a moment's notice.

Terror rocks through me and I keep still as the sight of his sharp teeth has a million thoughts racing through my mind, all to do with just how quickly he could tear out my throat, but it's not enough to keep the heaving sobs at bay.

My head hangs into my hands as that little beacon of hope completely disappears, helping me to finally realize that no matter what I do or what the brothers promise, there will never be freedom for me.

I struggle to catch my breath as the wolf watches me with a cautious eye. He's as still as the gargoyles up on the roof of the mansion, that is until a hooded figure steps around the corner with the other wolf right by his side.

He strides toward me and with a simple flick of his wrist, the wolf hovering over me retreats to his master.

The wolves both sit and as the hooded brother keeps moving toward me, the other two brothers start moving in from different directions, not stopping until I'm completely surrounded.

The brother directly in front of me crouches down, slowly peeling his hood back and pushing the mask up over his face to reveal the devilish face below.

Roman. Why am I not surprised?

The two brothers on either side don't bother revealing their faces, but what's the point? It's not like I don't know who they are.

Roman shakes his head, his eyes flaming with fury. "You broke our number one rule," he says, his condescending tone itching at my skin.

Do not run.

"No," I rush out, the tears staining my face. "That's not fair. You told me to run. You told me that you would let me go if I found the end. I … I …" Realization dawns on me and my eyes widen in horror, the dread sinking heavily into my chest. "There is no end to this fucking maze, that's the damn catch, isn't it?"

Roman's eyes sparkle with laughter and just like that, I know I'm right. I played right into their hands. I allowed them to give me hope, only to have it thrown back in my face. I stupidly trusted his word and believed that if I just kept trying, I would find the end of the maze. Even after searching the whole thing, I never once stopped to think that he was lying. I guess that's what I get for allowing one of the DeAngelis brothers to give me hope.

"You're an asshole," I cry, the devastation quickly washing over me.

Roman just smiles, his eyes sparkling as though he just had the time of his life, not even a hint of guilt in his dark gaze.

Levi's familiar tone breaks through the silence to my right and my head whips in his direction. "Break our rules, little one, and you must be punished."

Marcus' harrowing laugh echoes through the maze as I scramble to my feet, the tears refusing to ease. "No," I cry, my helpless tone breaking my own damn heart as my head spins, the lack of water and energy quickly beginning to claim me. "I played your stupid game. He said that I could go. I … I did everything right."

"But did you?" Roman laughs, moving into me as my body sways. He leans in close, his warm breath brushing along my clammy skin. His voice drops down low, taking on a darkness that I've never experienced from any of them before. "Don't be fooled, Empress. You will never be free."

And just like that, I crumble back to the ground, not one of the stubborn, twisted psychos around me even daring to catch me.

ELEVEN

The soft pillow beneath my head is the first sign that something isn't right. The pillow in my torture chamber is notoriously hard. It's a piece of shit, but the one below my head is like a freaking dream, it's something that even after a million shifts at the club, I'd still not be able to afford.

My eyes fly open and I find myself in a large bedroom, the warm sunshine streaming through the room with birds chirping merrily outside the window.

Okay, maybe I died last night. Maybe the twisted, fucked-up maze was the end of my story because this doesn't make sense. Don't get me wrong, this alternate universe of waking up in a massive comfortable bed to warmth and sunshine is a million times better than the torture chamber, but it's screwing with my head. The only logical explanation is that they finally killed me, and now I'm here in this ... I don't know. Maybe this is some weird form of reincarnation or maybe my version of heaven is just living it up in style. Who knows. Though, if I am dead, I guess I should be thankful that they did it while I was passed out. I didn't feel a thing.

I sit up and the blanket falls to my waist, showing off the shallow cuts and bruises along my arms and sending a wave of disappointment through me. Surely if I were dead and living it up in heaven, the cuts and bruises would have magically vanished, right?

That only leaves one option and I don't fucking like it.

My gaze circles the big bedroom. It's modern and impersonal. There are no pictures, no artwork, nothing to indicate that anyone has ever lived here before. It's like walking into a clinical hotel room ... a fancy hotel room though, not one of those shitty ones that'll give you hives.

My feet cautiously hit the floor and I glance toward the door, eyeing it with disdain before lifting myself off the bed. My legs ache from the night of hell, but it sure doesn't stop me from bolting across the room and fumbling with the lock until I hear the sweet sound of it clicking into place.

I doubt something like a little lock is going to be enough to keep the DeAngelis brothers out, but for now, it's giving me enough peace of mind to make it just a little easier to breathe.

Terrified that they'll somehow know, I keep my eyes on the door as I slowly back up, taking me deeper into the room again. When I'm positive they're not about to come busting in here, I tear my gaze away from the door.

Looking around, I find myself moving toward the wide window. Resting my hands against the small ledge, I gaze out, a soft gasp pulling from deep within my chest. I'm up high—like really fucking high. It's a stark contrast to the view out of my torture chamber window—not that I'm actually tall enough to see out of that one. Though if I could, I doubt that I would see anything good.

I feel like a fucking princess locked up in the tower, just waiting for a prince to save me. Only in my story, there's no such thing as heroes. There's no hope for me here.

This window lets me see for miles. There's no maze below me so I'm assuming that's on the other half of the property that I can't see, but the bit that I can see only goes to prove just how screwed I really am. There are no other properties in sight, only massive open fields with manicured gardens. A winding driveway sprawls over mountains, and further in the distance, there is nothing but an overgrown forest. No wonder the DeAngelis brothers have never been caught; their home is so hidden that no one would even know this property exists. I'm further away from civilization than I could have possibly realized.

A soft howling has my gaze shifting down to the open field, and I watch in amazement as a big black wolf sprints across the manicured grass at speeds that I can barely comprehend. A second wolf joins him, and for a moment, I'm completely mesmerized by the sight.

There's no doubt about it—the wolves are incredible. They're gorgeous in the most fearless kind of way. They're terrifying, and just the thought of what they could do haunts me, but I can't lie, they're stunning creatures, just like their psycho owners. It's fitting, I guess.

The wolves cover miles in no time, and before I know it, they're disappearing into the thick forest, probably to spend their day hunting helpless creatures.

A shiver runs down my spine at the very thought and I peel myself away from the window. Looking out at the wide-open space isn't going to help me get out of here, it's only showcasing just how difficult my escape would be. Hell, maybe that's why the brothers have stashed me up here. Gotta love their dedication to the cause.

A soft drum beat echoes through the walls, much louder than the times I've heard it while in my little dungeon. The little drummer boy must be close. I still haven't figured out which one it is, but my gut tells me that it's Levi. Roman is too … assholish to spend his time perfecting something that doesn't result in decapitation, while Marcus is just … Marcus. Besides, he was down in my torture chamber while the drums were being played up here. I ruled him out ages ago.

With nothing to do, I go back to the window and stare out into the vast nothingness, desperately wishing that I could be stronger.

An hour turns into two before the joke gets old and my frustration claims me. I'm dirty, sore, tired, and pissed off. I'm over their bullshit, over their games, and over this stupid twisted castle. I'd give anything to go home, to smell the fresh air, hell just to smell the sweaty bodies grinding against one another in the club I work at—at least, I think I still work there. I've probably been fired by now for not showing up to my shifts. Assuming they haven't heard the news stories about my untimely death. I bet my landlord has been having a great time snooping through my bedside drawer and clearing out my things.

Maybe it's not in my best interest to get out of here. I'm probably already homeless, have no job, no money, and nowhere to go. At least I have a roof over my head in my torture chamber. Though knowing my luck, the brothers will probably start demanding that I somehow pay rent.

What the hell am I supposed to do?

I start pacing my room, only with every step I take, I find myself closer and closer to the door, up until my fingers are curling around the handle and I'm standing here wondering what the fuck I'm doing. I can't stay in here anymore, waiting for them to show up unannounced and play their twisted game.

When else might I get the opportunity to snoop around their stupid castle? It's the middle of the day, the drums are still playing loud and proud, and I haven't heard a peep from the other two. Now might be the only chance I get to figure out what kind of secrets this place holds.

Taking a shaky breath, I turn the handle and shove my head out into a long hallway. Sunlight pours in from a massive window at the end, picking up every little particle of dust in the old mansion, and if I weren't so damn scared, I might even take a moment to appreciate how truly hypnotic the sight is.

I pause for a moment, checking left and then right before padding out into the hallway. I make my way to the right, following the sound of the drums despite my gut telling me to go in the opposite direction. The drumming has to be coming from deeper in the castle, but it's almost impossible to tell, so instead, I start learning the layout of the property.

I take lefts and then rights, spying into as many open rooms as I can get my eyes on. The mansion is huge and twisty, and so far, I'm pretty sure that I've come across at least four secret tunnel openings and I haven't even hit the ground floor yet.

Each level is unique in its own way, some of it looking at least a million years old while other parts look as though they've been freshly remodeled. Hell, there are some rooms that are still in the in-between phases.

The brothers are clearly trying to make this place their own, but something tells me that they struggle between the castle's century-old gothic vibe and a modern clinical look. If it were up to me, I'd say that the old gothic thing suits them just fine.

I go past at least thirty bathrooms, some looking inviting and making me desperate for a hot shower, while others have me scrunching up my face in disgust. There are countless bedrooms, offices, kitchens, laundries, and living spaces. It's almost impossible to figure out which ones the boys actually use.

I get all the way down to the ground floor and pass the main dining room where the brothers had formally introduced themselves and their twisted rules. That's when it occurs to me that I haven't heard the familiar thumping of the drumming in a hot minute.

My back stiffens and I pause in the doorway, taking in what's around me, but not just the things I can actually see. My gaze shifts from left to right before trailing back over my shoulder and realizing that I'm not alone, and I haven't been for quite some time.

My back flattens against the wood as I turn to find them, searching in all the darkest corners and shadows of the room. Then as one, the three brothers step out, each from different corners of the room and each looking like my worst kind of nightmare.

They float toward me in complete silence, their shoes barely even touching the ground as they move. It's creepy as hell, and has me wishing that I could sink back into the wall and disappear for good. Levi is the closest and he doesn't hold back as he steps into me, his calloused fingers instantly curling around my throat as his thumb forces my chin up and jerks my head to meet his feral stare.

His head is tilted and those dark, creepy eyes seem to dive straight through my own to read every damn thought I've ever had. He towers over me, and although my stare is focused heavily on his, I'm still aware of exactly where his brothers stand in the room.

My heart races and I don't doubt that he can feel it through the pulse in my neck, though even if he couldn't, he would know. He's just that kind of guy. He gets off on the thought of fear. It's fucked up in every kind of way, but damn, it suits him.

"What do you think you're doing?" he growls slowly, his deep tone vibrating right through my chest as every word is spoken slowly and with intent, making sure that I don't miss just how out of line I am right now.

My gaze flicks toward Roman and Marcus who watch through

hard, narrowed stares, and I quickly realize that once again, I'm out in the wilderness fending for myself. Levi's tight grip pulls on my chin, forcing my stare back to his, and judging by the sharp growl in the back of his throat, he didn't appreciate me looking away in the first place.

"I … I …"

His grip tightens on my throat, making it impossible to get my words out, but something tells me that he's not interested in listening to me grovel for forgiveness. "We reward you by allowing you to stay in a room, giving you food and water, new clothes and access to a bathroom and this is how you repay us? You betrayed our trust."

My eyes bug out of my head and before I even know what I'm doing, my hands are slamming into his chest. I pull back, tearing my chin right out of his tight grip. "Betrayed?" I laugh, knowing that from here on out, I'm not going to be able to control a damn thing that comes flying out of my mouth. "You really are fucked in the head."

A pissed-off growl comes from over Levi's left shoulder and my gaze instantly flicks toward Marcus. "Watch yourself," he warns. "You're two seconds away from finding yourself in the lion's den, and trust me when I tell you, that's not somewhere you'll ever come back from."

I scoff at his remarks. "Oh wow, another death threat. Really? You've gotta find a little more originality with your bullshit. They're becoming laughable or at the very least, unimaginative and doubtful. Come on, you're the famous DeAngelis brothers. When are you actually going to act like it? You're letting the system down. The whole country is under the belief that you guys are these terrible monstrous serial killers and the best you can come up with is a lion's den that I'll never come back from? God! What have we all been so scared of?"

Marcus's eyes narrow in rage and I try with everything that I have not to imagine the way his sculpted body rolled as he fucked me into submission, so I turn my attention straight back to Levi before I start begging for more

"Tell me," I ask, clenching my jaw and raising my chin in defiance, more than ready to push all three of them right over the edge. I step a little closer, knowing just how dangerous this little game is but not willing to relent. "How the hell can someone betray you when you never had their loyalty to start with?"

Roman steps in closer as Levi just stares back at me, his jaw clenched as the fury rolls off him in waves. "Might I remind you that we *own* you? We don't earn loyalty; we're *entitled* to it. It's ours whether you want to give it or not."

I roll my eyes, knowing their patience is quickly running out, but fuck them. It's one thing being their little kidnappee, but I refuse to be their little pet as well. "Let's get one thing straight. I'm being held hostage here. I'm not your little friend who's come for a visit. *You kidnapped me,* and that sure as hell doesn't entitle you to claim ownership over me. I own me, nobody else. Fuck your little deal you made with my father, that's between you and him. It has nothing to do with me, and if you want to collect, then you can take something from him because I'm not it. So, let's be clear, no matter what you say to me, what sweet little nothings you and your brothers want to whisper in my ear, if I get a chance to fuck up your little game, I will take it. You. Do. Not.

Own. Me. And I sure as fuck don't owe you my loyalty."

With that, I turn on my heel and stalk deeper into the dining room as the three psycho assholes stand in the doorway wondering where the fuck I get off speaking to them like that, but damn, I'm not going to lie, it felt good.

I make my way over to the big dining table and drop my ass straight down into the seat that Roman had occupied the other night and instantly start helping myself to what I'm assuming is his lunch. It's not exactly my meal of choice, but after eating nothing good for the past few days, it'll do.

I don't bother looking up as their hard stares will surely terrify me, and as long as there's no knife being stabbed through my chest, then I'm considering myself safe. Besides, I could be hallucinating, but I'm pretty sure Levi said that they offered me food, water, and a bathroom for being such a good little maze survivor, and I know for a fact there was none of that in the big room upstairs. As far as I'm concerned, I'm entitled to Roman's lunch, just as he thinks that he's entitled to my life.

More than willing to rub salt in the wound, I pick up a whole chicken leg and lean back in my seat, propping my dirty, cut-up feet up on their dining table as I watch the three of them hovering in the doorway. "Is there something you need?" I question, liking this whole taking the reins thing. "You're disturbing my lunch."

Levi's hands ball into tight fists and the sudden movement has the muscles in his arm flinching, making his tattoos almost appear to be moving on top of his skin.

Roman's hand snaps out and presses against Levi's chest,

demanding his patience, and Marcus just narrows his wicked gaze, his head slowly tilting to the left and daring me to keep going down this dangerous path.

He steps into the dining room and I watch his every step, not trusting a single one of them. Silence spreads through the room until all that I can hear is the sound of my racing heart as he steps in behind me.

My feet are pushed off the table and in one quick motion, he pushes my chair in until the armrests are slamming against the hardwood and locking me in. I sit up straighter, breathing deeply through my nose as I fail to keep chewing the food in my mouth.

His hand floats down in front of me as he leans forward, hovering over the back of my seat as his other hand rests beside mine on the massive table. His fingers trail over my collarbone until he grips my chin and tears it up, forcing my stare to his in one sharp movement. I swallow hard, forcing the half-chewed chicken down my throat as I meet his wicked stare. "Are you telling us that you're not … *satisfied* with your stay?" he questions, that deep tone slicing straight through my chest. "Just say the word and I'll make sure that you get the complete DeAngelis experience."

I don't respond because what's the fucking point? I've said what needed to be said and how they handle that is completely up to them. From here on out, the ball is in their court, and something tells me that there's nothing I can do about that.

Both Roman and Levi slowly creep deeper into the room and my gaze quickly flicks their way before coming straight back to Marcus'.

When it was Levi hovering over me like this, I could trust him enough not to lose control and snap my neck from a few snide comments, but Marcus is different, and while I'm willing to give myself up to him when it comes to sex, that doesn't mean that I shouldn't watch my back around him.

"Marcus," Roman says, his voice low and full of authority as he and Levi take their seats at the table. "That's enough. Let the girl eat, and then tomorrow, she will pay for her little performance in the hallway."

In an instant, Marcus' fingers uncurl from around my chin, but as he goes, he leans in even closer, his lips brushing against my ear. "Better prepare yourself, baby, you just gave me the motivation I needed to make this my most exciting kill yet. Your sweet little pussy won't save you this time."

Fear races through my veins, and as he goes to pull away, my fingers curl around the steak knife beside my plate. A harsh laugh tears through him and before I even know what I'm doing, I bring the knife up and slam it down over his hand, slicing straight through his flesh until I feel the tip of the blade slamming into the hardwood of the table beneath.

Marcus' harsh laugh is cut off as a piercing scream is torn from deep inside my chest, the horror of what I've just done racing through my veins. "Oh, fuck," I shriek, scrambling back in my chair to try and get away but Marcus' big body has me trapped within the confines of my chair.

Levi and Roman just watch on with curiosity, wondering how all of this is going to play out, and damn it, I'm fucking curious too, but after what I said in the hallway, I'm fucking done for.

As if in slow motion, I watch as Marcus curls his fingers around the handle of the steak knife. His eyes bore into mine, and as he slowly pulls the serrated knife out of his skin, his eyes shimmer with excitement.

What. The. Actual. Fuck?

Blood pours from his hand, and just when I think the same blade is about to slice a deep arc across my throat, it's tossed into the center of the table. The clattering sound of the blade against wood is the only noise I hear in the whole room as I realize that he truly does get off on the pain.

He straightens, letting the blood fall to the ground as his lips pull up into a sick grin. "I'll be seeing you." And just like that, Marcus DeAngelis strides from the room, leaving both of his brothers watching after him.

I stare in horror, unable to believe that I just stabbed a fucking psycho in the hand, and damn it, the fucker liked it. I'm screwed in all the worst ways. He's not going to forget it and I'm going to pay the price. Shit, it's one thing mouthing off to them, but this? What the hell is wrong with me?

"The fuck was that?" Levi's deep tone cuts through the room, stealing my attention away from the empty doorway to find his confused stare on his brother. "Why didn't he kill her? Marcus doesn't play like that."

Roman's lips press into a tight line, and as his narrowed stare comes back to mine, he leans back in his seat as though he has all the answers in the world. "He's fucking her."

Levi throws himself to his feet, his fists leaning against the hardwood table as his sharp glare penetrates my own. "That true?" he demands, making me swallow hard and pull back in my seat as though I could somehow get further away from him. "Did you spread your legs hoping that he'll take it easy on you?"

"Fuck off," I snap back at him, deciding that I'm already in hot water and that it can't possibly get any worse. "How the hell do you think it went down? He came in to feed me sloppy leftovers and I got on my knees and begged him to fuck me? Screw you. You know damn well that fucking psycho was the one who came to me looking for a good fuck. He even brought his chains with him, but I'm not going to lie, it was damn good, and if he comes looking for more, I'm sure as fuck going to give it to him."

Levi's hand snakes out, smashing into a glass of water and sending it flying across the room, slamming into the wall and shattering into a million little pieces. "You'll do no such thing."

"Oh yeah?" I laugh. "And how do you plan on stopping me? Face it, you're going to sleep at some point, and when you do, he's going to come looking for more and I'm going to let him have it. You know it's true, don't you? He didn't kill me just now, and you and I both know that's because he's not done with me yet."

Levi growls, his anger filling the room like a toxic gas as he stalks to the door, surely to go and have a word with his brother, only he stops at the door and looks back at me. "Did you make him come?"

I scoff and lean back in my seat. "Do you really think he'd be looking for more if I couldn't make him come?"

"FUCK," Levi spits, rubbing his hands over his face before glaring at his brother. "He knew the fucking rules."

"Take it up with him," Roman says, not caring about who or what has taken possession of my pussy.

Levi's frustration gets the best of him as he turns back to me. "Where?"

"Huh?" I question, my face scrunching in confusion as I watch the frustration cross over Levi's, the tattoos winding up his arms and neck seeming to move across his skin again.

Levi steps back up to the table, standing directly opposite me as he leans forward, bracing himself against the table and looking at me as though he could kill me with just his stare alone. "Where. Did. He. Come?" Levi demands, clearly annoyed that he doesn't have an answer already.

I push my chair back and stand, slowly walking around the table and putting myself right in front of him. I reach forward and grab his junk, loving the way his eyes flame with rage. "Don't worry, soldier. He didn't come in my tight little cunt if that's what you're asking, but I'm not going to say no if you wanted to," I whisper, Marcus' demand for me to not play around with his brothers sitting at the forefront of my mind. "I don't mind sharing, but something tells me that Marcus isn't so inclined."

And just like that, I release his junk, grab another piece of chicken right off Roman's new plate, and stride out of the room, as I listen to the sweet sounds of Roman's low chuckles behind me while Levi berates him for not sharing the news earlier.

Taking myself straight back to my torture chamber, I eat what's left of my chicken leg, knowing for damn sure that I won't be getting another one of those for a while.

TWELVE

A hand curls around my arm and my eyes spring open to find the back of Roman's head in the early morning light as he drags me out of my tiny little bed. "Oh, thank fuck," I sigh as I scramble to get my feet down before my body falls, but just as my ass is pulled off the edge of the bed, Roman's strong hold pulls me up and keeps me from falling.

Roman immediately stops and my momentum has me running straight into his back, coming to a painful stop. He turns and shoves me back, his sharp glare snapping down to mine, bringing me to the realization that it's way too early for his broody assholery. "Oh, thank fuck?" he demands, spitting my words back at me and making me realize just how stupid they were, though nothing is as stupid as the bullshit that came flying out of my mouth last night. But when I'm on a roll, it's nearly impossible to bite my tongue.

My eyes widen as I stare up at him, only the longer it takes me to respond, the more perplexed he becomes. And damn, a man like Roman with that scary as fuck scar down his face, letting that arrogance and confidence fade away for just a second is the rawest emotion I've ever experienced from him. For just a moment, he seems almost human, and I'm not going to lie, it scares the shit out of me.

"I just …" I take a breath, trying to figure out how to explain my relief at him being the one to barge into my torture chamber, rather than his brothers. "I've been expecting Marcus. You know, after the whole knife through his hand thing. I figured that he had something particularly brutal in store for me."

He narrows his eyes and somehow seems to get closer, yet he doesn't move a single inch. "Trust me, Empress," he murmurs, his deep tone rumbling through the room. "He does, but I don't think he's the one you need to be afraid of."

His eyes shimmer with darkness and a cold chill sweeps through my bones at the thought of just how much worse it could get than that, but before it can become something more, Roman's grip returns to my arm and he tugs me toward the door.

"The fuck do you think you're doing?" I demand, my sleep-filled voice making my demand seem a little less threatening and more like a kitten screeching about a little bit of cold water.

Roman grunts and pulls hard, flinging me through the open door before jamming his hand against my lower back and giving me a shove. "Walk," he orders with that same authority he uses to order his dimwitted brothers around.

I roll my eyes and let my dumb-bitch flag fly free. "No shit, asshole," I snap, letting my attitude shine bright as I start moving my ass up the long hallway, but what can I say? I spent most of my night fretting about Marcus coming in after realizing I wasn't strong enough to close the door. It was left wide open all night, leaving me completely unprotected, which is exactly how Roman was able to get in without warning. "What did you think I was going to do? Crawl?"

Roman's hand presses a little harder into my back and I decide that now is probably the best time to shut my mouth and move a little faster.

We make our way through the long, dark corridor, and each step we take makes me even more aware of the man standing at my back. I don't know what's gotten into me over the last twelve hours. I played it smart up until I decided to go snooping through their home, well … mostly. Maybe the whole maze experience flipped a switch inside of me and I started fighting fire with fire. I honestly don't know. It's a dangerous game, but for some reason, Roman isn't handling it like I thought he would.

It's as though this fiery bullshit that I've been throwing at them has Roman intrigued, but not in a good way. I guess maybe he'd written me off as a lost cause, someone not worth the games, but all of a sudden, he's watching me closer and I don't like it.

Roman steps around me to open the heavy wooden door between

the corridors, and within moments, we walk up through the steep concrete steps and out into the open ballroom. I go to make my way to the right, only Roman's hand curls around my upper arm and tugs me to the left instead.

My brows furrow. The boys have never led me this way before. I came through this way yesterday but that was due to snooping, not because they intentionally wanted me to be there. "What's going on?" I demand as his hand falls straight back to that spot in the center of my back and nudges me along.

Roman doesn't bother with a response and my irritation grows. My jaw clenches and I find myself slowing as we approach a closed door. I shake my head, my gut telling me that the last thing I want is to walk through that door, but Roman's pressure on my back makes it impossible to stop.

We reach the door, and as he leans around me to twist the handle, I take off like a fucking rocket. My feet slam against the old tiles and I dodge around Roman's body before flying back the way we just came. I get three steps away from him when those fast reflexes have his fingers snapping around my wrist and yanking me back into his hard chest.

My body slams against his with a loud *oomph* and I don't miss the way his hands fall to my waist. His chest rises and falls against my back and goosebumps spread over my skin. His hand brushes up my body until his fingers are trailing over my cheek. Instinctively, my head tilts to the side, offering my neck for him as a wave of hunger surges through me. "Such a pretty face," he mutters, his soft whisper brushing over my shoulder. "It'd be a shame to have to mess it up."

I fly away from him, tearing myself out of his arms as the realization hits. I've been fucking with serial killers. What the hell is wrong with me?

I stare at him in horror. He means every damn word, and I know he'd come through on that if I were to step out of line again. So why am I pushing the boundaries? I should be keeping myself backed in a corner, not provoking the slayer squad. "What's inside that room?" I spit through my clenched jaw.

His eyes sparkle, just as they had in my torture chamber, and without another word, he reaches for the door and throws it open. "In."

"Over my—" I cut myself off, my eyes widening as I realize what I was just about to say and the smirk that stretches across his face tells me that he's more than happy for me to complete my threat.

"Please," he insists, a sickly-sweet tone filling the space between us. "Finish what you were about to say. I dare you."

I shrink back away from him as my gaze flicks toward the room. "What is it?"

Roman's patience gets the best of him and he reaches out for me, gripping the front of my tank and pulling me into him. My chin snaps up, my gaze remaining focused on his as I catch myself against his wide chest. This close up, his wicked scar reminds me that a man like Roman DeAngelis isn't one to be messed with. Levi though, that's another story. "Either get your ass inside that room, or I'll put it in there in pieces."

Well, fuck.

"Tell me," he continues. "Would you prefer that I slice and dice with a blade, or can I just get in there with my teeth? Though do be warned, the wolves won't be able to resist that kind of fun."

My hand falls to his on the front of my shirt and I pry the material from between his clenched fingers before begrudgingly stepping toward the open door. I don't take my eyes off him, too afraid of what he might do with my back turned, and as I step through the narrow doorway, I finally allow myself to peer through to what I assume will be my doom.

Only I find a man staring back at me, one who doesn't bear any resemblance to a DeAngelis brother. A gasp pulls from between my lips, and before I can ask what the hell is going on, Roman appears at my back, shoves me the rest of the way through the door and slams it shut behind me, leaving me trapped with this strange man.

I glance over him in caution as he does the same to me, but it only takes me a moment to spot the stethoscope dangling around his neck. "You're a doctor?" I ask, my back straightening as the smallest ray of hope rises from the ashes within me.

The man nods. "Yes," he says, glancing away, refusing to meet my eyes. "Please take a seat."

I shake my head, gaping at him as though he just pissed on a cactus. "No … no. What do you mean take a seat? You have to get me out of here. You have to help me. Please."

"Miss Mariano, please take your seat so that we may commence."

"Commence?" I demand. "Commence what?"

"Your appointment. I'm here to discuss your contraceptive

requirements and do a thorough health exam, nothing more."

I gape at him, hardly able to believe what I'm hearing. "What?" I rush out. "I'm not about to discuss contraception with you. These assholes are keeping me hostage. They kidnapped me right out of my apartment. Please, are you hearing me? I need help. I need your fucking help. You have to get me out of here. I swear, I'll do anything. Please. The things they make me do ... Fuck. I can't do this anymore. They're going to kill me. Do you have any idea what these guys are capable of? The things they've already done ..."

Tears fill my eyes as the doctor just glances back at me with pity. "Please, Miss Mariano. Take your seat. We don't need to make this any harder than it already needs to be. Believe me, if I could help you, I would. I'm about protecting and preserving lives, not destroying them, but right now, I'm more about protecting my family from these assholes. So, today, we're going to discuss your contraceptive needs and then we're going to give you a thorough health exam. Is that clear?"

That small ray of hope dies within me, and I realize that no matter how much I beg, no matter what I say or do, nothing is going to change his mind, and nor should it. Not when his family is at stake.

"Alright," he goes on compassionately. "Have you been on contraception before?"

"What does it matter?" I question, tears welling in my eyes. "I'm going to be dead soon. So what if they knock me up? It's not like I'll last long enough to see through a full term pregnancy."

The doctor leans forward, his eyes searching mine. "The point is that if you somehow survive all of this, you don't want to come out of it with one of their evil spawns inside of you. Protecting yourself is the least you can do. Besides, if you were pregnant, what do you think would happen? Do you have the means to care for a child, the financial support, or how about the father? Will he be in the child's life? I don't see these assholes playing nice when it comes to custody arrangements, nor do I see them releasing you while carrying their child."

"Okay," I rush out, cutting him off before he can paint any more of a clearer picture. "I get your point. Just ... do whatever. I don't care."

The doctor nods and moves back into his chair. "Are they using any form of protection when they ... touch you?"

I clench my jaw and glance away, unsure why I feel so ashamed of the moment I shared with Marcus, even more so because this guy automatically assumes that he had forced himself on me. So why the hell am I not doing my part in letting him know that it was consensual? But then, I guess it's really none of his business. It's not like he has any intention of actually helping me out of this.

"No," I finally tell him. "I've only been with one of them, but there was no condom."

"Aftercare?"

I shake my head.

"Right, I'm assuming that I don't need to warn you about the risks of practicing safe sex?"

"Are you kidding me right now?" I demand, staring at him in irritation. "Do you have any idea who you're talking about here? These are the DeAngelis brothers. They slit throats for sport. Do you really think they're the kind of guys to stop and put on a rubber first?"

"Don't make this harder than it needs to be, Miss Mariano. Do you foolishly assume that you are the first woman in this situation whom I've had to care for? The last girl those brothers got pregnant didn't fare well with their father."

I stare at him in horror. "Their father killed a pregnant girl?"

The doctor shrugs his shoulders. "I don't know, that is just my assumption, but what I do know is that she only got through three months of her pregnancy before the appointments stopped. So, please, just answer my questions so we can get you protected. Do you require any information about practicing safe sex?"

I let out a heavy sigh and shake my head. "No. I know what I need to know, but my … living conditions make cleanliness almost impossible. Practicing safe sex isn't something that I have the ability to do. I just have to cross my fingers and hope that they don't give me anything."

"Okay, I understand," the doctor says before pausing and truly considering my situation before grabbing his bag and rifling around. He pulls out a bunch of boxes, glances over their labels before finally placing a small box on the edge of the table. "Have you heard of a birth control implant?" he questions.

My gaze narrows on the small box and I shake my head. "Up until now, unplanned pregnancies have never really been something I've had to think about."

"Ideally, I would have started you on the pill. It's non-invasive and easy to manage. However, in your unique situation, I can't guarantee that you'll be allowed to take a pill every day, nor can I guarantee that your prescription will be filled."

I shake my head. "I was on the pill a few years back and it messed with my system. I was a raging bitch all the time and had to stop using it."

The doctor nods. "I could fit you with an IUD. However, that is invasive, and for some, it's an uncomfortable procedure. Your best option is an implant. It will be inserted into your arm and you may feel numb for a few hours afterward, possibly with slight bruising."

I swallow hard as nervousness washes over me. "Is … is it permanent?"

"No," he says, the fear in his eyes reflecting mine for very different reasons. "Removing the implant is as easy as making an appointment. It's a simple procedure which should only take a minute or two."

A single tear rolls down my cheek and I nod before moving toward the small exam table that's been set up in the center of the room. I've never been one to have to consider any of this before, but right now, I feel as though the decision to protect my own body has just been stripped from me. Despite knowing that this is in my best interest, I simply can't be happy about it.

"This is a good thing," the doctor tells me, seeing the distress stretched right across my face. "If you get yourself free of all of this and somehow manage to move past the trauma and want a family of your own, you're going to be happy that you did this. You're protecting your future, giving yourself a chance."

Another tear rolls down my face as a numbing agent is injected into my skin. I look away, unable to watch. My gaze locks on the black wall opposite me, and after a few long minutes, a small bandage is placed over my arm and I'm officially protected from the evil spawns of the DeAngelis brothers.

He pulls back and quickly cleans up his tools before changing out his gloves and looking back at me. "I need to do a thorough examination. This includes an internal pelvic exam," he tells me, the emotion completely drained from his voice knowing that even if I weren't to consent, that he'd still have to do it. "It will be quick and pain free. Do you have any questions or concerns before I get started?"

I close my eyes and shake my head. "Just get it over and done with," I tell him, my voice dropping to a near whisper.

The doctor gets started, and as his trained gaze travels over my body, I can't help but feel the humiliation washing over me. If I had needed a thorough examination, I would have taken myself to the doctor that I've learned to trust over the past few years, not some stranger who somehow got himself involved with the DeAngelis brothers.

He tells me about his family, his two young daughters who have only just started daycare, and while I appreciate his attempt to keep my mind off the way his gloved fingers brush against my inner thigh, it's not possible.

True to his word, he keeps his examination prompt and pain free, and after a short minute, he's pulling away from me and purposefully keeping his distance to ease my discomfort.

I slowly sit back up as the doctor grabs his bag and pulls out a smaller bag from inside. "I'm going to leave this here," he tells me, his eyes focused heavily on mine as though he's trying to send me some kind of silent message. "It's full of alcohol wipes and first aid supplies. If something were to happen to you and you were able to get away, this bag could save your life. Do you understand me?"

I nod and watch as he stands up and slides the bag into a high cupboard before softly closing the door and officially hiding it away. He takes his bag and pulls it over his shoulder before looking back at me. "Good luck, Miss Mariano. I truly hope that you find some way out of this to have a full and courageous life."

I don't bother nodding or even acknowledging his kind words because we both know that a dream of getting out of here is just that—a bullshit dream that's never going to come true.

My legs dangle off the edge of the table and I watch as the doctor walks to the door and raps twice against the wood. The door pulls open and all three of the brothers are looking straight past the doctor at me.

Marcus' gaze travels over my body, and despite the bandage around his hand, the knowledge that I just had to go through all of this because of his need to get his dick wet isn't lost on me. Before I let them have it, Marcus nods to the doctor and he steps out of the room.

Marcus disappears with him and I'm left with the two broody ones.

I jump down from the table and stare up at them, letting them see the anger in my eyes and not bothering to wipe the stray tears off my cheeks. "You're all fucking assholes," I spit.

Levi steps toward me. "This is on Marcus, not us," he tells me, his eyes darkening. "You want to take it out on someone, take it out on him, but let it be known that I do not approve of you spreading your legs for my brother."

I scoff. "Really? I could hardly tell."

He continues as though I didn't say a damn word. "You're a play toy. Nothing but a quick fuck to pass the time for him. Don't get yourself attached, and if you think that getting pregnant on purpose is going to save you, think again. Nothing will save you."

My chin raises, and for just a moment, I see a flicker of something real in his dead eyes. "You mean like the last girl you psychos had stashed down here?"

His jaw clenches and Roman's eyes blaze with fire as he pushes past his brother to get in my face. "What do you know of it?"

I push him out of my face and flick my gaze between the two. "I know that one of you bastards knocked the poor girl up and Daddy Dearest had her killed. So what the hell are you waiting for? Just kill me now. GET IT OVER AND DONE WITH."

Neither of them flinch at my sharp tone and it only has the anger soaring through my veins like poison. "DO IT," I demand. "NONE OF THIS SHIT IS WORTH IT. JUST DO IT. KILL ME ALREADY."

Levi grabs my wrist and pulls me into him. "Don't tempt me, little one," he tells me. "You're not ready for death. You have too much fight left in you."

Without warning, Levi releases me, and just like that, both he and Roman stride out of the room, leaving me behind with nothing but my torturous thoughts. Nobody bothers to take me back to my cell downstairs and I sure as hell don't make a move to go back down there. So instead, I just sit and hope that I don't turn out like that girl.

I get lost inside my thoughts when a loud *BANG* echoes right through the whole fucking mansion. My heart skips a beat and immediately kicks into gear. My sharp gaze flicks around the room, desperately searching for some kind of threat, but when nothing comes, I find myself standing and sneaking out of the room.

I follow the soft murmuring of voices coming from the ballroom, and as I turn the corner, I find Roman hovering over the doctor's lifeless body, a perfectly round bullet hole right between his wide-open eyes.

Roman slowly turns his sharp gaze to meet mine. As I slowly start to back up, knowing this is completely on me. My heart races a million miles an hour and fear rockets through my body.

This is his official warning for simply knowing about the girl who used to be me—I'm next.

THIRTEEN

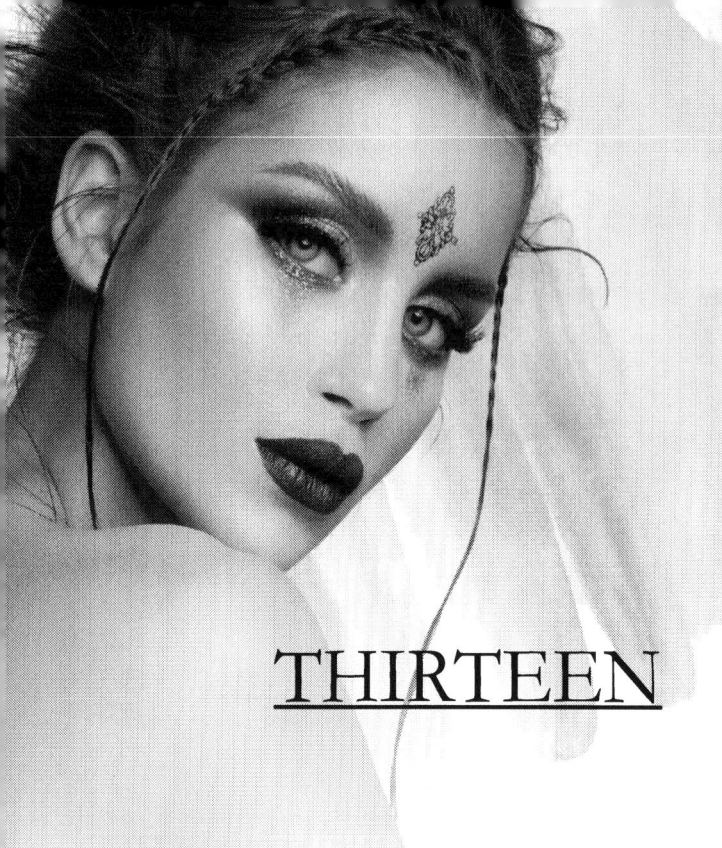

My feet slam against the steps as I fly up the grand staircase. Tears stream down my face while the image of the doctor lying in a pool of his own blood plays on repeat in my head, his haunted eyes staring right at me.

I've never seen a dead body, and fuck, it's not something that anyone should ever have to get used to. Fear was still pulsing through his wide-open eyes. Though, I know that's not possible because of the hole directly in the center of his forehead.

The brothers just stood there and watched as though murdering doctors is just a casual afternoon activity. Feed the gigantic wolves? Check. Prepare something for dinner? Check. Organize a doctor's appointment for the kidnappee? Check. Murder said doctor in cold blood? Double-check.

Fuck me. It was one thing being their little sex slave kept down in the dungeon, but murder? I knew they were more than capable, but I never considered that it was going to be something I would be so openly witness to. There was no remorse, no regret or guilt, just callous, cold-blooded murder. Roman's eyes, though. I've never seen him look so at ease, so peaceful or comfortable. It's sickening.

This world is so much worse than I could have imagined. I knew they were serial killers, heartless and cruel, but what I just witnessed … fuck. No words could describe the dread and horror that's sinking into my chest, the heaviness of what just went down, or the overwhelming fear that threatens to cripple me.

I'm next.

I bet the three of them don't even understand the weight of what they've just done. They probably just stepped over the body as though it's nothing and are now sitting down to a nice, refreshing whiskey, using the doctor's body as a footrest. Fucking bastards.

He had children, and now those children are going to grow up never knowing their father, all because I had to go and open my mouth about the girl they knocked up. How am I supposed to live with myself now? He was trying to warn me, trying to protect me from this vile evil and I couldn't help myself.

I was reckless. Foolish. What was I thinking? I could have waited until the doctor was safely out of here, but even if I had, they would have just tracked him down. I should have kept quiet. I should have protected him like he protected me, but I never imagined that it would come to this. How could I have known?

His blood is on my hands.

Bile rises in my throat and I slap a hand over my mouth as I hit the top step and race down the long hallway, desperately trying to remember which of these rooms was a bathroom.

I start kicking in doors, and by the time I hit the third one, I find what I'm looking for and immediately drop to my knees in front of the toilet. I heave, throwing up what little remains in the pit of my stomach. Over and over again until a cold sweat takes over and I'm left shivering on the bathroom floor.

Tears sting my eyes, and before I know it, I'm tearing off my clothes and crawling across the cold tiles to the shower. I reach up to turn on the taps and expect to have cold water, but there's nothing cold about it. I press my back against the wall and curl my knees into my chest as the water rushes down over me, drenching my hair and sailing over my skin like some kind of security blanket.

I see my reflection in the shower glass and I realize that it's the first time I've seen myself since being taken from my apartment. I look like a fucking mess. There are deep bags under my eyes and my long brunette hair is dry and uncared for, but it's the fear in my blue eyes that makes it nearly impossible to recognize myself.

My eyes are usually bright and full of life because no matter what, I'm a fighter. I've always searched for the positive, but now, I've never seen them so bleak, so unfamiliar and dull. I'm a stranger to myself.

What is this place doing to me?

It isn't until a shadow falls over me that I realize I never shut the bathroom door, but glancing up to see Roman standing over me, it dawns on me that I don't even care. What does it matter at this point? I'm dead inside, and it's not like he's not going to see my naked body at some point. Hell, he's been stalking me for the past few months, I wouldn't be surprised if he's already seen it.

My gaze shifts over his face and my stomach churns at the sight of the doctor's blood splattered all over his body, but what's worse is the way Roman seems to wear it like a trophy.

My eyes drop away and I go right back to staring at the marble pattern in the tiles, hoping that if I don't say a word, that he might just go away.

A silent moment passes before he lets out a sigh, and for a fleeting second, it almost seems as though he gives a shit, but I know that's not right. "We had no choice," he tells me, his tone factual and straight to the point. "Marcus went in unprotected. It was either that or meet just how brutal my father's gun can be, and we're not nearly done with you yet."

My head snaps up and I look him right in the eye. "What the fuck is wrong with you? You think I'm up here having a tantrum over the fact that you forced birth control on me, rather than what you just did to the doctor? You shot him. You just took his life like it was nothing."

His brows furrow and he glances to the side, deep thought crossing his face. "That's ... what your problem is? That I killed that little snitch?"

I gape at him. There's no saving them when they don't even

understand just how wrong they are. "You're fucking kidding me, right? You murdered him in cold blood. You stole his life because he tried to warn me about you three. You're a fucking monster. He didn't deserve that. He had family at home."

Roman shrugs his shoulders, his dark gaze glistening. "They're better off without him."

"How can you say that?"

Roman's face darkens as he steps around the glass wall of the shower and crouches down right in front of me. The hot water soaks his skin, washing away the stained blood as he reaches out and grips my chin, keeping my stare focused on his. "You don't know that man, Empress. You don't get an opinion. You had one forced conversation with him. I've had a lifetime. So when I tell you that his family is better off without him, you're to trust my word. Don't you dare question me."

I tear my chin out of his grip and look back at the marble tile, unable to keep looking at the blood that's slowly mixing with the water and rushing down the drain.

"Who was she?" I murmur, my throat raw from my performance over the toilet.

"She?" he questions, his stare boring into the side of my face.

"*She*. The girl you guys knocked up, the one the doctor warned me about. Who was she? What did you do to her?"

In the blink of an eye, Roman rises to his feet, taking me right along with him and slamming my back against the cold tiles. He presses into me, his face barely an inch from mine. "*She* is none of your damn business," he growls, his warm breath brushing against my skin. "*She* was twice the woman you will ever be and *she* met her downfall because she refused to follow instructions."

My hands curl into fists at my side and I clench my jaw, the anger pouring out of me in waves. "Your father murdered her because she got knocked up."

Roman presses into me harder. "You don't get to speak about something you know nothing about," he murmurs, the authority in his tone sending shivers through my spine. He pulls away, releasing me in an instant and moving out of the shower.

Water rushes off his body and I watch him, my jaw clenched and my nails digging into my palms. He stops just outside the shower and lets out a deep breath before turning back to face me. He peels his soaking shirt off and throws it in the corner of the bathroom, the wet material making a sharp slapping sound against the smooth tiles.

My gaze drops over his body, taking in the tight ridges of his defined abs and skimming over his wide chest, but as he watches me in return, a soft sigh of relief passes through my lips, realizing that there's absolutely nothing sexual about this, he's just simply getting rid of his wet shirt.

"Look," he finally says. "You … you're not the only one being held against your will here."

My brows drop as I watch him in horror. "How many are there? Do you have little sex slaves hidden all over your freaking castle? Do you just pick one each night to go and fuck with, or am I just extra lucky because I'm new?"

Roman groans, the sound so soft that if I wasn't paying attention, I would have missed it. "I'm talking about me and my brothers," he snaps. "Our father confined us here to this place because whenever we step out, too much attention is drawn to us. Every fucking murder in the city is pinned on us whether we did it or not, so here is where we stay. And you," he continues, "you were supposed to be a gift to entice us not to cross out into the real world."

"What?" I rush out. "That doesn't make sense. You said that I was here because my father made a deal and sold me to clear his debt."

"He did," Roman says, stepping closer to the shower glass again. "The debt wasn't with us. Your father borrowed from the DeAngelis family, and when our father collected, he saw it as the perfect opportunity to set things right with his sons. After all, he took her from us, so in his mind, it's as simple as replacing her with someone else."

My gaze shifts up to meet his. "Why does he try to keep you locked up here?"

Roman's eyes darken and a soft smile pulls at the corners of his full lips. "Because every time we leave the boundaries of this property, we make it count."

A chill sweeps through me, and despite the hot water raining down over me, I can't seem to make it go away. "You're sick, you know that? You and your brothers. You're callous, cold-blooded murderers."

"So what if we are? It's exciting, don't you think? Watching the life fade out of a man's eyes while he struggles and begs for another shot at freedom?" He smiles and his eyes sparkle wickedly, almost as though he means every damn word. "Don't worry, Empress. There's still a chance for you. Give me a reason to keep you around and I might just let you rule by my side."

My brows furrow and I pull back away from him. "What the hell is that supposed to mean?"

"Prove your worth, Shayne, and maybe I won't use you for target practice. After all, it would be a waste to have to break in another girl."

Understanding dawns and I shake my head. "I won't ever be like you."

Roman laughs. "We'll see."

And just like that, he turns on his heel and starts moving toward the bathroom door. "WAIT," I rush out, stepping into the glass as if to go after him. Roman stops in the doorway and looks back, his gaze dropping to the way my naked body presses up against the glass, perfectly framing it.

Impatience crosses his features as I gather up the nerve. "I'm not going back down to that dungeon. If you want me to stay and be chill about it, then I'm staying in that room upstairs. Otherwise I will bitch and moan every fucking chance I get."

His eyes narrow and I slowly pull away from the glass as he walks back toward me. "Where the fuck do you get off making demands?"

A sick grin of my own crosses my lips and I raise my chin, letting him know how damn serious I am about this. "When I realized that you're not the one pulling the strings."

Something sinister flashes in his eyes, and if looks could kill, I'd already be dead. He stares at me for a moment too long, the silence filling the room just long enough to make me squirm under his stare, but I quickly realize that this right here is his comfort zone.

"You remain down in the cells," he tells me, his tone filled with a deadly venom as the weight of my comment fills the air between us. "Be ready. We're having a party tonight, and you're our main attraction."

Then with those harrowing words, he walks out of the bathroom and pulls the door shut behind him, leaving me with nothing but an endless array of sick and twisted thoughts streaming through my head, each one of them telling me that being the main attraction at a DeAngelis party is not something any girl wants to be.

FOURTEEN

Darkness takes over the castle as humiliation swirls deep inside my bones. I was given a freaking uniform for tonight which consisted of skimpy black lingerie, thigh-high heeled stiletto boots and a fucking thick choker to sit around my throat. If I was going to some kind of skanky Halloween party, then I would have fit the dress-code perfectly, but this is too much.

I thought that I could handle it, that I'd just have to show off my body to their fucked-up friends and bare my teeth every time someone tried to touch the merchandise. But when Marcus showed up in my doorway and led me to where the party would be held, I quickly learned that things are not always as they appear to be, not where the

DeAngelis brothers are concerned.

I was distracted by Levi to the right of the room, sitting at an all-black drum set. He was banging on the drums so loud that each hit vibrated right through my chest. His eyes were closed and it was the first time that I ever saw him looking so at peace with himself. I couldn't tear my eyes away, which is exactly how I missed Marcus leading me right into the center of the fully-stocked bar and scooping up a heavy chain. Then in the blink of an eye, he hooked it to the back of the choker around my neck and chained me to the fucking bar.

It's been four hours and so far, the party is only just getting started. It's packed with the kind of people anyone would expect the DeAngelis brothers to be friends with—fucking ratchet-ass, drug-induced, dirty motherfuckers who should have been locked away the day they were born … or swallowed.

This is not the place I want to be, especially in lingerie, boots that I can barely move in, oh yeah … AND CHAINED TO THE FUCKING BAR!

Bodies are everywhere and it doesn't take me long to start recognizing faces from the 'MOST WANTED' news stories that are splashed all over the TV. Even some of the chicks around here look eerily similar to the 'MISSING GIRL' posters that appear on the back of the bathroom doors at the club, yet they don't seem to be too upset over their 'missing' status.

My hands are sweaty and my knees haven't stopped shaking. The DeAngelis brothers are the most dangerous in the room by far, but I like to think that I've developed some kind of a relationship with them—not a great one, but it's more than I can say for the other people here.

When the brothers approach the bar for a drink, I know they're coming to glare or make snide comments about how wonderful it is to see the fear their party has induced in my eyes, but when the other party-goers come up to me, I don't know what to expect.

The room is dark and gloomy, though to expect anything different would be foolish of me. The whole party is a vibe. It's sophisticated and clearly an invite-only type of thing, but it's also wild in ways that I've never experienced at the club.

Girls are dancing on tables, their bras falling to the ground as men linger and grab at their bodies. Their hands are encouraged whereas at the club, most girls would be pulling away from guys like this. Couples are fucking out in the open, rough and unforgiving, while others stand back and watch in appreciation, but what really gets me are the pills circling the room.

Cocaine is being used at nearly every table while I watch in horror as drinks are spiked all over the room. Hell, it's the reason why I'm going on the fourth hour of this party without even a sip of water.

A hard stare hits me from across the room and I can't resist glancing up to find Roman's eyes locked on mine. He's been watching me all night, along with his brothers, but Roman is the most focused. Levi has been so engrossed with his drums that he barely even notices the party around him, while Marcus is busy getting fucked up, making it clear whose idea this party really was. Though, the thought of Marcus losing control like this is just as horrifying as the idea of being alone with him, especially considering that his hand hasn't even begun to heal yet.

A woman sits beside Roman, too close for comfort, and I don't miss the way her gaze continuously sweeps over my body. She's been watching me all night while whispering in Roman's ear and running her taloned fingernails up and down his strong thigh, but it's the way he encourages it that has my blood turning cold.

Trying to ignore them, I focus my attention on the task at hand. Drink orders are coming at me left, right, and center, and damn, they're fucking pissed that I can barely keep up, but what were they expecting? There's one of me and hundreds of them. Sure, I'm used to this level of demand coming from the club, but there's usually a few girls working it with me, and I'm sure as hell not restricted to the bar by a fucking chain and choker. Though, not a single person has even looked twice at my choker, balked, or questioned it. It's just considered normal. I don't know if I should be comforted by that or if I should be scared shitless.

I guess by now, I should just start rolling with the punches.

The music is so loud that I barely even notice when the drumming stops from across the room, but when it does, it has my full attention. My gaze shifts as I scurry to fill a glass of the most expensive whiskey that I've ever come across, but what I find has my heart thundering in my chest.

A girl in nothing but a black diamanté thong steps around Levi, moving into the small space between him and the drums, effectively cutting off his music. She takes the drum sticks right out of his hands and balances them on his set.

The audacity of this woman has me in awe. What girl in her right mind would have the guts to do that? She must be suicidal.

She takes his hands and places them on her body, and I watch, completely captivated by the way he scans over her naked breasts. They're full and perky, exactly what every man is hoping to have thrust in his face, and I'm not going to lie, her confidence with him is pulling at something inside of me.

She drops to her knees and I watch as she reaches for the front of his pants. Surely, he's going to push her away and tell her to go and fuck some other sorry asshole, but when he allows her to continue, a fierce jealously cuts through me.

I tear my gaze away and quickly fill my order before taking another, but the compulsion is too strong, and I find myself looking back to find Levi's massive cock standing tall and proud. His fist hovers at the base of his cock but she quickly replaces it with her own, freeing his hands to grab his drum sticks once again.

Her tongue starts at his base and it works right up to his tip before she closes her mouth over him. His eyes close in pleasure for just a brief second and within moments, his drumsticks are coming down on his set, creating the most erotic sound I've ever heard.

Her head bobs up and down as her mouth barely fits around him. He's huge, just like his brother, though I'm not surprised. Guys that exude that kind of confidence simply don't come with small equipment. Hell, I can only imagine what Roman's would be like. But damn, right now, all I can seem to think about is Levi's.

The way she moves, the way she touches him … I know I could do him better, and damn it, he'd fucking love it. That should be me.

Fuck. No, it shouldn't.

Where the hell do I get off feeling all kinds of entitled to DeAngelis cock? They're not mine, and while they claim that they own me, I'm sure as hell not about to start spreading my legs for them and becoming their little whore … you know, apart from that one time with Marcus. That was just a moment of weakness that will never happen again, but fuck. This chick just ain't it. She's not working her tongue, she's not using her hands, she's not giving him anything that he needs, not like I could.

"Hey, bitch," comes a loud voice, cutting through my foggy mind. "I'm talking to you. Where's my fucking drink?"

My head whips around to find my pissed-off customer staring at me like he's picturing just how quickly he could skin me alive and my gaze drops to the empty glass in my hand.

Ahh, shit.

I never took myself as the kind to get so distracted by a big cock and a girl doing it wrong.

"It's coming," I snap back at the guy as I get busy filling the glass.

I place it up on the counter and try to remember what the skank next to him had ordered, and when I grab the bottle of vodka and start mixing her drink, a big hand snakes forward and snaps around my wrist, squeezing it so damn tight that I'm certain it will bruise.

A pained gasp pulls from between my lips as the big man yanks me forward, pulling my body toward him as my head snaps back against the tight chains. "You're fucking pathetic," he murmurs low, his sick, dark eyes staring into mine and giving everything he's got to try and intimidate me, but after spending the last few days with the DeAngelis brothers, very little can phase me right now.

Who would have thought that on a night like this, the one thing that has me triggered is not being the bitch down on her knees?

My fist tightens on the glass full of vodka and without thinking, my hand snaps out and I throw the contents at the man. "LET GO OF ME," I snarl, yanking my arm right back as he fumbles back a step, his eyes pulsating with rage as his woman shrieks beside him.

In one smooth motion, the man catapults himself over the bar and drops down beside me, his hand immediately going to the base of my throat before slamming me up against the back of the bar. Bottles smash and rattle behind me, rocking on the shelf and threatening to fall, and as he leans into me a knife is pressed to my throat, right above the fucked-up choker. "Any last words, bitch?" he snarls, spit spraying over my face.

Well, fuck. This isn't how I thought this was going to go.

I push against his rock-hard grip as it becomes harder to breathe, yet somehow, I find enough oxygen to mutter the sweet, sweet words of "Fuck you."

His grip tightens and I feel the blade of his knife digging into my fragile skin as my fingers slip into the top of my thigh-high boots.

A shadow appears at my side, and just as he's about to slit my throat open for the world to see, the shadow moves in closer and his ferocious gaze snaps to the terrifying man hovering over us. "She's mine," Marcus growls, his tone so low that it rumbles right through my chest.

The guy backs up a step, but the restrictive bar only allows him to go so far. "I … I … I'm sorry," he says, his eyes filled with a crippling fear. The knife drops and clatters to the ground as the unaware partiers continue around us, gyrating to the music and fucking up against tables as their partners pop pills into their mouths.

Fear rattles him, and for a fleeting moment, everything becomes clear.

I'm theirs.

In this room, among these people, I'm the one with the power. If they take DeAngelis property, they're fucked. If they hurt me, they're fucked. If they even look at me wrong, they're fucked.

They can't touch me, not without consequences.

I pull myself off the wall and the shattered glass of the bottles at my back fall around me, cutting my skin as it goes, but I put myself in front of Marcus, for the first time, stupidly trusting him at my back.

The man looks between us, unable to work out what the fuck is happening here, but honestly, same. This whole situation is fucked up, and for those who know the DeAngelis brothers well, they would know that they don't often get possessive over a toy.

"She … she …"

"Spit it out," Marcus growls, his hurt hand falling to my waist and gripping my skin tightly, a silent warning that I'm not innocent in all of this.

"Your bitch threw a drink in my face."

Marcus shrugs his shoulders. "So?" The guy gapes at him, unable to figure out why Marcus isn't appalled on his behalf, but when his eyes darken and his head tilts just a fraction to the side, I know his fun is only just getting started. "Apologize."

The guy's face scrunches in confusion. "The fuck?"

"You heard him," comes a familiar growl from behind him.

My gaze snaps up to find Roman standing on the opposite side of the bar, directly behind him and within arms distance to simply reach out and snap his neck.

The guy swallows hard, clearly seeing the situation that he's in, and a twisted grin stretches over my face. I quite like this little turn of events. It's exciting, raw, and thrilling, though it's not something I want to get used to. If Marcus hadn't shown up, I'd already be on the floor. Well, I'll be dangling near the floor, seeing as though the chain around my neck wouldn't reach that far.

The guy straightens and he looks at me. "Sorry," he mutters darkly before attempting to move away.

"For what?"

He looks back at me, shooting daggers through his venomous stare. "Huh?"

"Sorry for what?"

Roman narrows his eyes, meeting my heated stare as Marcus' fingers tighten on my waist. The guy looks between us before finally settling his stare back on me. "For hurting you."

"You see," I say with a heavy sigh as I step out of Marcus' hold and move right into the guy. I pull Marcus' black-bladed knife right out of the top of my boot and like lightning, I whip the blade up to his throat, just how he'd had his at mine. "The hurting me part I can deal with, but you called me a bitch, and you know what? I didn't really like that. So tell me, what do you have to say for yourself?"

Panic flickers in his eyes as he glances to Marcus over my shoulder, wondering what the fuck is going on, but that would make two of us, because damnnnnnn, I'm making this shit up as I go.

"I … I'm sorry," he rushes out as I begin trailing the tip of the knife over his throat and slowly down his body. "I said sorry. I take it back. I won't call you a fucking bitch."

My eyes widen and I lean in just a little more. "A what?"

"A BITCH. A FUCKING BITCH."

Roman's shallow nod in my peripheral sends a wave of venomous confidence sailing through me, and as his strong arm curls around his throat from behind, I shove the knife so deep into his gut that I feel the blood pouring out around my hand.

A pained howl comes from the man and I lean in just a little bit closer so that he can hear me over the thumping music, though I don't dare yank the blade out just yet, instead, I give it just the slightest wiggle. "Have we learned a lesson about how to treat a lady in a bar?"

He swallows hard and violently nods his head. "Yes, please just … let me go."

"Your wish is my command," I tell him before yanking the knife right out and smiling sweetly. "I hope you enjoyed your stay at the DeAngelis resort and spa. Please do consider leaving a review and don't forget to take your whore with you on your way to the door."

And with that, Roman's grip tightens around his throat and pulls his heavy body back over the bar, leaving a sickening trail of blood in its wake.

As I watch him go, the daunting realization of what I've just done begins to weigh down on me. Marcus steps into me again. His fingers trail down my arm, starting at my elbow and going all the way down until his big hand is circling around the knife in my hand.

He takes it from me, and I watch as he wipes either side of the blade onto the small sliver of skin showing on my thigh, making me wear his blood like a trophy.

Marcus doesn't take his eyes off mine, and when the blade is as clean as it's going to get, I watch as he skillfully presses the knife back inside my boot, keeping it safe for when I might need it next. "There might still be hope for you yet," he tells me, his rich tone dark and sinister, filled with promises that I want nothing to do with. His fingers curl around my chin and he raises it up, holding my stare a minute longer. "You have a job to do, if you're going to drool over Levi getting his dick sucked, make sure you're prepared to get on your knees first."

Then just like that, he walks away, leaving me staring after him, still completely horrified and confused by everything that just went down.

I could have sworn that Roman said something about Marcus getting payback for what I did to his hand, but that version of Marcus didn't even seem to remember.

FIFTEEN

As 3 am rolls around and the guests are starting to tire, I begin doing a quick clean of the bar out of habit, though something tells me that all the early hour has done is weed out the weak and left us with the ones who plan on staying for the long haul.

I pack away all the fruity bitch drinks and leave out the heavy shit as I listen in on a murmured conversation to my right. Marcus sits at the bar, a bottle of scotch in his hand as a naked girl lies on the bar in front of him. A line of coke rests right between her tits and just as he's about to take the hit, one of the wolves rushes through the bodies and sits its big ass right beside Marcus. The wolf nudges him with his nose and I watch in fascination as Marcus immediately stops what he's doing and offers the line to the chick who's been hanging off him for the past two hours.

How fucking peculiar. Do the brothers have the wolves trained to sense when one of them is going too far, or did Roman or Levi just send it over to tell Marcus to cut the shit? Either way, I'm impressed, not only that the wolf is so well trained, but because Marcus respected it and stopped.

The girl snorts the white powder off the chick's tits and as they meet each other's eyes and start laughing, I know exactly where this is going. The naked chick grabs the girl's head and they immediately start hooking up on top of my bar. Marcus leans back, watching as one girl does down on the other.

He meets my stare and raises his brow. "You want in?" he questions, his eyes lazily drifting over my body. "I bet a good girl like you has never run your tongue over a sweet cunt or felt another woman coming on your fingers. You wanna try? I bet you'd love it. After that first hit, you'll be a little whore for it. Do you know how good it feels to have a tight cunt convulsing around your fingers, only to pull them out and have them drenched with that sweet cum?"

I lean forward onto the bar, hovering over the girl and indicating for Marcus to come just a little closer. My tongue rolls over my bottom lip and he watches intently. "The only way you're going to watch me fucking another girl with my mouth, is if I already have that big cock of yours deep in my ass."

A low groan rumbles through his chest as desire spreads over his features, but before he can comment, I pull back. "Shame you have me here working like a fucking dog. As long as you see me as property, you'll never have me again."

With that, I turn my back and focus on the bar. Though, all that does is spin me to face Roman who sits across the room, watching me with that same girl possessively glued to his side while Levi sits a little further back, banging on his drums again.

All three of them have been drinking tonight, but Roman and Levi have been taking it slowly. Marcus is pretty buzzed, but the other two could probably still shoot me directly between the eyes from all the way across the room.

As I clean up the bar, I become mesmerized by Levi as he plays. This time, there are no girls blocking my view, just Levi looking more vulnerable than I've ever seen him. His eyes are on me, but mine are on his body, watching the way his muscles flex and roll with each hit of the drum, watching how his knee bounces as his foot slams down on the bass.

As he plays, the tension seems to leave his body, and pure bliss washes over his face. His warm skin is coated in the softest layer of sweat, and I quickly realize that this is his peace. Playing the drums is what eases the darkness that clouds him, just as Marcus abuses drugs and alcohol to clear his mind. Roman though, I have no fucking idea what his vices are yet, but something tells me that I won't find out easily.

I can't take my eyes off Levi. I've always been hot for drummers, but watching this broken man do his own thing, so completely clueless to the party around him, it's hypnotic. I'd give anything to go and climb onto his lap and feel my body moving against his as he beats the drums, his knees bouncing under me and feeling the vibration right between my legs.

Fuck. I have to have a taste. I can only imagine what it'd feel like to be fucked on his lap while he played.

Shit, there I go again, thinking up idiotic situations. I should just ask the brothers to go and fetch me one of those toys from my apartment to keep my mind out of the gutter. At least that way, I could stop having inappropriate thoughts about these psychotic serial killers. I bet they'd just love to fuck me to death. Is that even a thing? I guess the bigger question is, is that a good way to go? Would it be a good experience? Who knows? If they do come for me, I hope they come prepared. I have enough pent-up frustration to keep up with all three of them.

But all three of them at the same time? Now there's an intriguing thought.

A fight breaks out across the other side of the room and snaps me out of my trance. I glance over the two girls fucking on the bar to see the fight going down behind the brunette girl's head. A deep sigh pulls from within me. I'm so over this shit. It's the fifth fight of the night. The first two held my attention, and I'm not going to lie, they were all assholes so it was pretty thrilling to watch all of them hobble out of here with broken bones, but that shit gets boring quickly.

A loud squeal erupts from the other end of the room, and my head whips back to find a girl running through the bodies, desperately trying to find a way out. She holds bags of pills in her hands and I let out another sigh, already knowing what's about to happen.

I glance away just in time to see Marcus leaning back in his seat, pulling out his gun, and shooting straight across the party with one eye closed in concentration.

The loud *BANG* echoes through the room but the thumping music quickly drowns it out. Her body falls right into Levi on the drums and he doesn't skip a beat, pushing her off him as her blood seeps onto his kit.

Her body lies forgotten on the dirty ground, surrounded by the stolen bags of pills. Levi though, he just keeps playing as though not a damn thing happened, her blood ricocheting off the drums with every fucking hit.

Marcus laughs and I can't help but look back at him, only to meet his devilish stare. "That's just pills. Imagine what would happen if someone were to steal something actually important to us."

His eyes darken and a cold shiver runs straight down my spine, forcing me to look away from him. I can't handle him when he goes into this dark, twisted mood with his ridiculous comments that are filled with mysteries that I don't quite understand. But glancing back at Levi and seeing his unfazed reaction to the lifeless body on the ground, or the pool of blood growing at his feet, I wonder how he would have reacted had the dead girl been one of his brothers. How would any of the brothers react to that? Are they even capable of feeling that fierce protectiveness?

I can't help but drop my gaze to the girl as a heaviness rests against my chest. I can't understand why people would willingly throw their lives away for this shit. Sure, if she were stealing it to sell just to keep a roof over her head, then I get it, but where do you draw the line? Substance abuse just ain't for me. Seeing as though I just became roommates with the three biggest suppliers in the country, I guess it's a good thing the shit doesn't interest me.

At least, their father is the biggest supplier in the country, but seeing as though it's so widely available here tonight, my guess is that they've been dipping their fingers into the cookie jar and have learned exactly how to get away with it.

Hours tick by, and the first rays of morning sunlight shine against the massive windows, showcasing the mess that I'm positive I'll be left to clean. Levi steps into the bar and silently walks up to me.

Nerves flicker through my body. All I can seem to think about is how good it'd be to get railed on his drums. His hands raise and I suck in a breath as his fingers play at the back of my choker. Seconds pass before the choker loosens around my throat and quickly falls away, freeing me from the confines of the bar. "Come," he orders before silently turning and walking away.

I watch him cautiously as I scurry after him, leaving the bar to be scavenged by the masses. He leads me toward his two brothers who sit back in lounges, the woman still sitting by Roman's side with her long dark hair falling over her shoulder and her eyes clocking every step I take. The closer we get, the harder my nerves pulse through my body. What do they want with me?

The short walk across the room feels like the longest path I've ever taken. When we reach Roman and Marcus, Levi tells me to stop, putting me right in the center as Levi drops down into the opposite couch, boxing us into a private little area. "Do … you need something?" I ask, eyeing the way that little miss popular presses her body into Roman's side and rests her hand possessively against his knee.

The woman raises her chin, and as the light hits her face, I can't help but notice how damn beautiful she is. She must only be in her twenties. My guess would be that she's close to Roman's age, but the depth in her eyes tells me that she's been through some shit. "Do a turn," she purrs, captivating me with her dark painted lips. "Let me see you."

My brows furrow and my gaze flicks to Roman's. "Umm … what?"

"She asked you to turn for her," Roman says, his tone low and filled with the kind of authority that makes me want to throat punch him. "Turn."

I swallow hard and look back at the woman before slowly starting to turn. I feel her eyes dragging over my body, studying every curve and imperfection. "She's skinny," she murmurs like an insult. "Nice ass though. I want to see her bare."

I quickly finish spinning, turning the rest of the way. "Excuse me?" I rush out, my eyes bugging out of my head. "I'm not about to strip down for you. Who are you anyway?"

Her lips purse into a tight line as her taloned fingernail drags over her red lips. "I thought you'd have her trained better by now," she sighs. "Your father is going to be disappointed."

Roman scoffs. "She has an issue with authority," he tells me, eyeing me menacingly, a silent demand to shut the fuck up and do what I've been asked before he does it for me.

I let out a sigh and glance around the room. There are still people everywhere, not nearly as many as there were a few hours into the party, but the ones who remain are well and truly fucked up now. Besides, there's been enough nudity here tonight that no one is going to look twice at my body, especially when the other women in the room have so much more to offer.

The room is still dark enough, and that's about all the privacy I'm going to get, so I suck it up and reach behind me, feeling Marcus' gaze on my ass. I unclasp my bra and the black flimsy material drops to the ground at my feet, and before I allow myself the chance to feel humiliated by my nudity, I hook my thumbs into the sides of my thong and slowly drag it down my legs, knowing exactly what Marcus can see.

Looking back at the strange woman who somehow has her claws into these guys, I take a step toward the small coffee table between their couches. I prop my stilettoed boot up onto the table and my fingers fall to the zipper. Slowly, I begin unzipping the thigh-high boot, getting the zipper to my knee before the woman shakes her head. "No, leave them on," she tells me, her eyes becoming hooded as her gaze sweeps over my body in hunger.

"Mmmm, a damn good choice," Marcus says from his prime position behind me as I try with everything that I have not to meet Roman's eyes, though I feel his heavy stare on my body. If he likes what he sees, he sure as hell isn't showing it, but damn, his rejection would hurt.

The woman's hungry gaze remains on my body as she points to the coffee table. "Sit."

I swallow hard and step around the table, hating how much closer it puts me to her and Roman, but I do as I'm told and drop my ass onto the edge of the table, nervously keeping my gaze on her.

"Open." My back stiffens and my eyes widen, but her insistent nod has me slowly peeling my knees apart. "That's right. Lean back on your hands and show me what you have."

Her sultry confidence somehow puts me at ease, and although I feel Roman's gaze dropping right to my pussy, I kinda like it. Hunger settles into both of their eyes and the woman licks her lips. "Marcus tells me that you've never been with a woman."

My eyes bug out of my head, more than ready to nail Marcus in the junk. I shake my head. "No, that's not what I—"

The woman flinches, her sharp stare snapping straight back up to mine. "You're not calling Marcus a liar, are you?" she asks, her tone filled with the most dangerous kind of vindictive venom.

I pull up, slowly shaking my head. "I—"

"Did you or did you not tell Marcus that you would fuck another woman, only if his cock was buried deep in your ass?"

"I mean, I did, but—"

"Good," she says, cutting me off again. "There's no need to be embarrassed. Everybody starts somewhere, but luckily for you, you're going to get the best of both worlds."

My brow arches. "What's that supposed to mean?"

"Shhhhh," she hums, pushing up off the couch, using Roman's

strong thigh to give herself a boost. "You're going to love it. I can tell."

She slowly begins circling the coffee table until she's kneeling behind me, balancing herself on her knees with one hand on my shoulder. Her other rests at the base of my neck and as she slowly leans down and skims her red lips along the curve of my neck, her soft fingers brush along my skin, gently caressing my curves.

She trails her fingertips right over my breasts and my nipples pebble under her touch. "There," she whispers against my skin. "I knew you were going to like it."

But she couldn't be more wrong. While her touch is definitely something I've never experienced before, it's not what's getting me off. It's the way both Roman and Levi are watching my body as though they wish they could be the ones enjoying it. If only Marcus would move so I could see his eyes on me too. I'd love to see that raw, desperate hunger of his just one more time.

Marcus' words from the night he screwed me into oblivion come back to haunt me. *'You're not to give this up for anybody. Not Roman or Levi, or any sorry fucker who comes looking for you. Is that understood?'*

I'd agreed wholeheartedly for the sole purpose of him finishing me off, but if I were alone with either of his brothers, I'd pretend like it never happened. But right now, his eyes are on me. He knows that the second this woman touches me, those words will fail to hold any weight.

I glance back at him, and as I meet his narrowed stare, I realize that we're both on the same page. He's remembering those exact words just as I am, remembering how I promised I'd only be with him. He's fucking pissed, but at the same time, the desire pools in his eyes. He wants to watch, he wants to see her hands on my body, see the way I squirm beneath her gentle touch.

A private moment passes between us, and after a short pause, he finally nods, relenting to what he knows is bound to happen anyway. After all, he might as well sit and enjoy the show rather than be pissed and miss out on all the fun.

The woman's hand drops even lower, skimming over my stomach so softly that I suck in a breath as her fingers tickle my sensitive skin. I can't help but pull my gaze away from Marcus and focus on her touch as her long dark hair falls forward and brushes over my shoulder. It comes to a stop at the top of my thigh and a breathy groan slips from between my lips as her tongue grazes over my neck.

The boys watch closely, not missing a single flinch or exhale as her fingers drop between my spread thighs and start rubbing tight little circles over my clit.

I suck in a breath and my tits press harder against her arm. She smiles against my neck. "I knew you'd like it," she murmurs. "Just wait until I fuck you with my tongue. You're such a lucky little whore."

Roman's hard gaze rests against my pussy and from where he sits, I know that he can see just how wet I am. Fantasizing about his brother and drums earlier probably didn't help, but damn it, I can't lie, this small bit of relief is helping to ease the ache within.

The woman's fingers dip lower and she swirls them with my wetness before slowly pushing them deep inside me. My legs instantly open wider, wanting to take her deeper, but there's only so far fingers can go.

As if reading my body, her thumb works my clit as her fingers move in and out of me, and just when I start to forget that she's a complete stranger and probably someone I don't want to know in this world, she pulls away from me and a pained cry pulls from between my lips.

"Don't worry, sweet angel," she purrs, standing from the coffee table and moving around until she's directly in front of me. The morning light shines in behind her and creates a soft halo around her face, though something tells me that's the most deceiving thing I'll ever see. This woman is anything but an angel. "I've been watching you all night. You're feisty but innocent. I know exactly what you need and I won't stop until I've got your sweet taste on my tongue."

She drops to her knees in front of me and presses her hands against my thighs, spreading them wider and making Roman adjust his cock inside his pants. My eyes lock on his, and right now, I don't even care that he hates me, all that matters is having his eyes on my body and watching me as I get off.

The woman reaches up and gently caresses my tits before sliding her hand between them and pushing against my chest until I'm laying back on the coffee table, my brunette hair brushing up against Marcus' knees.

She wastes no time and closes her warm mouth over my pussy and my whole body flinches from her touch, but when her tongue starts working over my clit and her skilled lips suck and tease every inch of me, I know that I'm a goner.

She presses her fingers up into me and as I cry out in pleasure, I can't resist reaching up and cupping my tits. My fingers lightly pinch my nipple, and within moments, Marcus leans forward and does the same to the other. I can't help but wonder if this is his way of showing his brothers that he has me right where he wants me, displaying a show of dominance over me, showing that I'm all his to do as he pleases. Either way, if he wants to join in, I'm down.

With Marcus so close, I stretch my arm back over my head and grip the front of his pants. His cruel stare immediately drops to meet mine and without a damn word passing between us, he slides off the front of his armchair and releases his big cock from the confines of his pants.

Not one to hold back, I take him in my mouth, working him up and down as his brothers watch on. His fingers knot into my hair and I let loose. I give him everything I've got, proving to Levi that no matter how hard that other chick sucked his dick, nothing compares to me.

The woman between my legs comes at me with the same frame of mind, and damn it, I've got nothing to compare her to other than men, and so far, she's proving one hell of a good point.

Her tongue flicks over my clit, teasing and rubbing at the same time while her lips promise me everything sweet in the world. Her fingers move inside of me, massaging deep and rubbing up against my walls in all the right ways. I've heard girls in the club insisting that the best person to get a woman off, is a confident woman who has already mastered her own equipment. Though, I'm pretty sure they were trying to get me to join some kind of lesbian orgy, but they were right. This woman knows exactly where I like it and is reading my body as if it were her own.

Marcus' cock hits the back of my throat and as I work him, I look back at Levi who is watching me closely. His stare is hard, but the jealousy in his eyes tells me that I have him right where I want him. Roman though, he's still a long way off, but that doesn't mean that I don't still feel his hungry stare on my pussy, getting the best view in the house of the way his little girlfriend is eating my cunt.

She applies more pressure to my clit as her fingers work just a little faster, moving in every fucking direction. I moan against Marcus' cock, and in return, his fingers tighten in my hair. He doesn't steal control like he had before but instead, he lets me give it to him the way that I see fit, and damn, I don't see him complaining.

She flicks her tongue over my clit just as Marcus pinches my nipple, and it's like an electric current pulsing right through to my cunt. I groan, my whole body flinching under her as it almost becomes too much.

She's fucking right. I love it. The men I've been with before her were worthless in comparison, but something tells me that her skills won't compare to what the DeAngelis brothers could do with their tongues.

She hits my clit again and again and my eyes roll to the back of my head as my body prepares to explode. I feel it growing inside me, getting stronger with every pass of her tongue. She sucks my clit and I cry out, the sound muffled by Marcus' thick cock.

"Mmm," Levi grumbles, the raw excitement and desire in his tone enough to push me over the edge. "She's going to come."

"Damn right," Marcus says. "Just you wait. She goes off like a fucking rocket, and that tight little pussy … it's like heaven."

"Don't get used to it," Roman mutters darkly, his voice low and dangerous, the sound flowing straight through me as a low cry pulls deep within my throat and my eyes clench in anticipation. "There's no place for guys like us in heaven. We're going straight to hell and we're taking her with us."

Marcus looks back at his brother, venom in his tone. "You mean, there's no place for guys like you. *This one is all mine.*"

The woman's tongue flicks over my clit one more time and my world explodes, shattering into a million pieces. My toes curl inside my stilettoed boots as my eyes clench, the power of my orgasm rocking right through me. My pussy convulses around her fingers and I feel her soft breath against my clit as she laughs. "I knew you'd look like a fucking angel when you came."

Marcus groans low, his fingers tightening in my hair, and as the woman keeps moving her fingers deep inside of me, letting me ride out my high, Marcus comes hard, his warm seed hitting the back of my throat. I swallow him down and glance up to meet his heated stare.

"Like I said," he murmurs in a low whisper, only for me to hear as his fingers graze over my pebbled nipple. "A fucking rocket."

His stare remains locked on mine and I watch him as confusion sweeps over me. Isn't he supposed to be the unpredictably wild one? The one with a chip on his shoulder who will go insane with the flip of a switch? Sweet little nothings is not what I expected to come out of his mouth right now, especially after the little incident involving that steak knife and his hand. If anything, it's post orgasm gratitude. It'll go away soon. He'll be back to sneaking into my room with the intention of chasing me through a fucking graveyard before I know it.

Once my high has come down, the woman pulls away from me and makes a show of licking her lips as Marcus steps away and fixes himself inside his pants. Without another word, he walks away, and seeing that the show is over, Levi gets up and makes his way back toward his drum set.

Roman holds out his hand and helps the woman to her feet as I sit up on the coffee table. My knees close and I instantly feel my wetness soaking between my legs.

The woman glances down at me with a smug expression that I instantly hate. "I don't hand out favors," she tells me, flipping her dark hair back over her shoulder. "I'll be expecting the same in return when I see you next, and be warned, I don't forget when I'm owed a favor."

And with that, Roman walks her out of the room, leaving me sitting here, in a room full of rapists, murderers, and thieves in nothing but my birthday suit.

SIXTEEN

Three hours of sleep is all I get before there's an asshole barging down the door of my torture chamber. "For fuck's sake," I groan, pulling the old pillow right over my head as the sound of the heavy metal scrapping against stone pierces through my head. "Get lost. I'm sleeping."

"Get up," Levi's familiar growl echoes through the room and bounces off the walls right down the long hallway.

"Whatever bullshit you have planned for me today can wait. I'm not in the mood to be stalked through your stupid-ass castle. Let me sleep."

"Suit yourself," he mutters darkly, just moments before a bucket of ice water is tipped over my head.

A loud shriek pulls from deep within my chest as the sound of the water crashing over me and splashing against the old stone rocks through the room. I throw myself out of bed, the chill in the water instantly seeping into my bones as my teeth chatter. "What," pant, "the fuck," shiver, "is wrong with you?"

I curl my arms in on myself, the cold far too much for me to handle. I'm a summer girl through and through. It rarely snows where I'm from, but when it does, I'm in the worst kind of hell. My heating gave in on me for three days last winter and it was the worst three days of my life. That is until three brooding psychopaths broke into my apartment and decided to ruin everything.

"Good," Levi says, a bored expression resting on his face as he grips my wrist and starts pulling me toward the door. "You're up. Lunch is in ten minutes. You need to be dressed and ready, and fuck, Shayne, if you don't look like you're meeting the fucking queen, I will personally see to it that you sleep out in the woods with my wolves."

I swallow hard and attempt to pull back on my arm, determined to know what the hell is going on. "Where are you taking me? I don't want to go to some fucked-up lunch to listen to Roman talk about how much he wants to slaughter me in my sleep or get whiplash by Marcus' bullshit mood swings. Not to mention yours. I thought Marcus was the one who needed anger management, but turns out, you're just as screwed up as he is."

Without warning, Levi reaches back, grips my arm and pulls me hard. I fly up off the ground and within seconds, my stomach is coming down hard over his big shoulder as he storms up the hallway. "You're quickly running out of time," he growls, his arm coming down over my legs to keep me from squirming. "So, I suggest, that if you would like to make it through this lunch with your life still intact, you shut the fuck up and get yourself showered and ready."

"I hate to be the bearer of bad news," I mutter, hanging over his back. "But I have nothing to wear to a nice lunch, unless you'd prefer me to show up in the bullshit skimpy lingerie you gave me last night. And for the record, it's impossible to get ready in ten minutes, especially now that your bitch-ass dropped a bucket of freezing water over my head. It takes a minimum of ten minutes just to dry my hair. Not to mention that when you kidnapped me, I didn't exactly get a chance to pack my makeup or any of my nice clothes. So thanks for the offer, but I'll pass. Feel free to turn your caveman ass right around and throw me straight back in my torture chamber."

"Do you ever stop talking?" Levi grunts, moving up the concrete steps and out into the fancy ballroom that has me squinting in the light, despite it not even being all that bright in here. "Fuck, you're giving me a headache."

"Right back at ya, asshole. Maybe tomorrow morning, I'll wake you up with a pot of fucking ramen noodles over your head so you can see how fucking pleasant it is," I throw back at him. "But honestly, if you can't handle your own shit, then perhaps you should have called it quits before Roman's little girlfriend decided to put me on show. You know, gone to bed early like a good little boy."

Levi reaches back and grabs my waist before pulling me off him and throwing me hard against the wall. His body presses into mine as his vicious scowl bears down on me. "One word of advice," he mutters darkly. "The woman who ate your tight little cunt was my father's new wife. She's a whore with a fucking hard-on for Roman, but if Father Dearest finds out that you touched what's his, I promise you, your life won't be worth living."

My eyes bug out of my head as I feel my chest rising and falling with pained gasps. "That was Giovanni DeAngelis' new wife?"

"Ariana DeAngelis in the flesh," he tells me. "Don't worry, she won't be here for lunch, but lucky for you, my father will. Better hope that she didn't accidentally say something when she got home. Gotta wonder what prompted this unexpected little visit."

Levi walks away and I find myself gaping after him.

Giovanni DeAngelis is coming for lunch and he may or may not know that his new wife ate my pussy like she was digging for gold at an all-you-can-eat buffet.

Fuck my life!

My breath comes in short, sharp pants as I race after Levi. "Wait, wait. What am I supposed to do? What if he knows? He's going to kill me," I rush out as he stops and turns back, pulling me up short as his tall frame looms over me. "She ... she... surely he knows that it was all on her. I didn't ask for it. I swear."

"Oh, but you laid the groundwork for it, whispering those wicked little promises in Marcus' ear, knowing that he wouldn't be able to resist," he says. "You knew what you were doing. Though next time, cut the shit and just ask for what you want. If you're down to fuck a chick, then say so. If you're jealous over some slut sucking my dick, then say so. There's no need to play twisted little games."

"Right, because twisted little games aren't the go to around here," I mutter, narrowing my gaze on him. "And for the record, I wasn't jealous of anything. I just thought she was doing a fucking awful job."

"She was," he agrees as he watches me for a long drawn out moment. "But stop kidding yourself. I saw the way you were watching me. You wanted it to be you. You wanted to be the one drawing your tongue up and down my fucking cock. You got wet just watching me, picturing all the things I would do to your tight little cunt. It drove you insane with jealousy, but I'll let you in on a secret."

He pauses and I find myself leaning into him, far too mesmerized by the way his dark eyes bore into mine. My chest raises and I find my chin tilting up to meet his heated stare, the anticipation of his little secret burning me up inside. The silence just about kills me when he finally tells me what I've been waiting to hear. "You're down to four minutes."

With that, he stalks away, leaving me a shivering, horny mess behind him.

Four minutes. The fuck?

Giovanni DeAngelis will be here in four minutes to fucking kill me.

Shit.

I race up the stairs, trying my hardest to forget about Levi's drum cock and the way that my body seems to always come alive around him. He knows what I need, what I desperately want, but he refuses to give in and ease the ache that builds every time I see him. But as he said, he's not down for twisted games. If I want it, I have to ask for it, and that shit is never going to happen.

I race through the quickest shower of my life, scrubbing my hair with something that smells a little like shampoo, but I'm honestly not sure. I get halfway through my shower when the door barges open and Roman comes striding in with a handful of clothes and a makeup bag that looks all too familiar.

I stop what I'm doing and watch as he crosses the bathroom to place the clothes on the edge of the marble bath. He turns to face me and I see nothing but pure hatred in his eyes. "Hurry up," he tells me as his gaze shifts over my body. "I've experienced firsthand what it's like to be late for my father, and trust me when I tell you, you're not cut out for it."

I swallow hard and quickly rinse the shampoo out of my hair as he watches me a moment longer. Deciding that he's satisfied with my pace, he walks out the door and pulls it shut behind him, and the second I regain my privacy, I shut off the taps and step out of the shower.

I'm never going to get my hair properly dried, but if I can at least throw on a little makeup and get a nice dress to cover all the important parts, I might feel a little better about myself. Twisting my hair up into a towel, I quickly race through my makeup and pull a tight black dress over my head. Naturally, there's no underwear in my pile of clothes, but when the dress plunges deep between my breasts, I realize that underwear wouldn't have worked anyway.

Black liner and mascara line my blue eyes, and finally, I start to recognize myself again. Though remembering that I stabbed a guy last night has that dull, lifelessness quickly returning. Something tells me that blood, guts, and gore are the new normal for me and that I better get used to it—fast.

I slip my feet into a pair of heels that I can already tell are going to give me blisters, but after the night walking around in stiletto boots and spending the night before that racing barefoot through an overgrown maze, I couldn't possibly do any more damage than I already have.

Flipping my head forward, I catch the towel as it drops from my hair and I dry it as best I can before running a brush through my long, brunette strands. I search the cupboard and only just get the hair dryer plugged in before a fist bangs against the door. "Thirty seconds," Marcus hollers. "Be there on time or prepare yourself for hell."

Fuck.

I flick the hair dryer on and start counting back from thirty as I desperately try to get my hair to sit just right, but when I get to one, I realize that today is going to be one hell of an epic fail.

I haven't prepared for this, and honestly, I thought that I'd be dead before I actually got around to meeting the most senior member of the DeAngelis family. You know, the one who runs the most terrifying mafia group known to man. These people are cold-hard killers, they're unforgiving and relentless, and if I don't meet their ridiculously high standards, then I'm as good as dead. Though I don't understand why it matters. I'm the trash that was purchased as entertainment for the man's three wicked sons. I shouldn't have to meet anyone's fucked-up standards. Hell, I shouldn't even be included in this ridiculous little lunch.

Making my way out of the bathroom, I pull and twist my hair, trying to style it the best way I can, but I'm usually a hair down and out kinda girl. I don't know how to do fancy, but I guess it's too late now. My heels tap against the stairs as I make my way down to the dining room, but as I get closer and closer, I try not to make a sound.

My nerves are quickly getting the best of me, and as I reach the grand entrance of the dining room, I find myself hovering outside the door, too terrified to go in.

"No," I hear Roman's authoritative tone coming from inside the room. "We have to be patient. If we move too soon, we risk it all."

"I don't know about you, dear brother," Marcus mutters, his tone filled with something sinister that has a shiver sailing right down my spine. "But my patience is wearing thin. We need to do this now before she ends up like Flick."

My brows furrow. Who is the 'she' he's referring to and who the hell is Flick? Is that the pregnant chick who was killed by their father? Am I the 'she' he doesn't want that to happen to?

"Leave Felicity out of this," Roman says darkly. "You're getting too attached to this girl."

"Right," Marcus laughs. "*I'm* the one who has attachment issues. All I'm doing is enjoying what's on offer. Do I need to remind you about the ring you had stashed away for Flick? The ring that our father found which prompted him to slaughter her before our fucking eyes? Yeah, don't fucking preach to me about getting attached."

What the ever-loving fuck? My mouth drops as I try to unload the bomb that Marcus just dropped. Ring? What ring? That couldn't be right. In order to have a ring for someone, you have to first be in love, and Roman DeAngelis is simply not capable. But then … if it's true, if that really did happen, how callous and cruel must one man be to take his eldest son's pregnant girlfriend's life in front of his eyes.

What the hell have I got myself involved in?

"Don't talk about shit you don't understand, Marc. Felicity meant something to you too. Pretending that she didn't is a fucking insult. You and I were just as attached as he was," Levi says. "But Roman is right. You are getting attached to Shayne, and it's a dangerous little game you're playing, one that won't end well. You know what father says about attachments to women. It makes you weak, and the moment they start playing a role in the decisions you make, you're as good as dead. You need to watch yourself around her."

A low grumble sounds through the room. "You don't know what the fuck you're talking about," Marcus says. "She means nothing to me. So can we please just focus on the real issue at hand? We need to overthrow father before it's too fucking late."

An irritated scoff sounds through the room and I'm pretty sure it comes from Roman before Levi's curt tone steals my attention. "We can't," Levi snaps back. "It's too soon. He's got too many players on his side."

"We have Ariana."

"What good is she going to do?" Roman grunts, the words almost sounding somewhat pained as they're forced from between his lips.

"She's a whore. She only comes to us because she doesn't get good dick at home. Don't be fooled by those blood-red lips. She's not on our side."

There's a low murmur that I can't understand but I find myself zoning out. Are the brothers really talking about overthrowing their father and using his new wife to do it? That's insane. It's a suicide mission. But I mean, damnnnnn. I am so here for that showdown, but on the other hand, a game like that could only result in countless lives lost. It's not something I want to be anywhere near. Not if I value my life.

If Giovanni DeAngelis and the rest of the DeAngelis family got wind of this, the brothers would be slaughtered. It would mean war. But it leaves me with one hell of a decision. Do I go running my mouth to their father and have them killed for my freedom, or will it backfire on me and I'll just end up as one of the many casualties?

A loud bang comes from inside the dining room and I jump at the sound. "Where the fuck is this girl? I thought she was told ten minutes?" Roman growls.

Well, fuck.

SEVENTEEN

I reach forward and push my way through the massive double doors of the dining room only to have all three of the famous fucklords staring back at me.

Just great. This is going to be a shit storm.

Roman stands, his tight fists pressing against the dining table. "Where the fuck have you been?" he demands. "You were given ten minutes to get yourself presentable and you show up looking like this?"

I swallow hard and drop my gaze down my body. My hair is definitely a mess and slightly frizzy from the half-assed dry that I just put it through, while my dress is crooked and twisted at my waist. My makeup seems alright, at least, I thought it did.

"I—"

"No," Roman says, holding up a hand and cutting off my argument. "I don't want to hear it. Just go and stand in the corner of the room and try not to make a fucking sound. He'll be here any minute, and if you insist on making it through the next hour, you'll keep your damn mouth shut. Don't say a fucking word about what went down last night, and don't even think about acting like a brat."

"But—."

Levi stands, his harsh stare locked on me. "NOW," he hollers through the room, pointing toward the very corner that he wants me to stand in.

Fuck. They're big mad.

I get my ass moving across the room, keeping my head down as the nerves continue floating around my body, their harsh warnings making everything so much worse. Levi tracks my every step and only when I'm stationed as far from the table as possible does he finally sit back down. "You won't look at him. You won't speak to him unless spoken to. You won't even fucking breathe. Is that clear?"

I swallow hard and raise my head, my eyes narrowing on his. "I endured that bullshit party last night, working my ass off while getting touched, spat at, and abused by your guests. Then you let that whore take what she wanted from me. She put me on display for everyone to see and you assholes just let it happen. You forced me onto contraception and have tormented me every chance you've had. I've played by your rules for long enough, and I'm done. I'm changing the rules. So here's how this is going to go down. You're going to give me a nice room with a private bathroom, clothes, and everything a girl needs to get by comfortably, and in return, I'll be a good little slave girl and impress daddy for you."

Marcus leans back in his seat, sipping at what looks like bourbon as he watches Roman move out from behind his chair and saunter across the room. My stare locks on Roman's, and with each step he takes, the anger in his eyes only gets worse.

He puts himself right in front of me and leans in, his dead eyes locked right on mine. "You got to come with the eyes of the three DeAngelis brothers on your tight little pussy. I'd say you've been rewarded enough."

"Really?" I question, more than ready to play him at his old fucked-up little games. "It would be a shame if I just happened to let slip that you invited step-mother dearest to your party and allowed her to indulge in your little whore. I'm not sure your father would like that very much."

Roman laughs. "Go right ahead and tell him. Let him know that it was *your* pussy she ate last night. Let him know it was *you* she touched and enjoyed. I'm sure he would love to hear all about it."

I swallow hard. "Give me my fucking room, otherwise I'm telling him that the three of you assholes are planning to overthrow him. But then, if I told him that, I guess you'd all be dead and there wouldn't be anything for me to be running from. Damnnn, such big decisions for me to make."

Fear flashes in his eyes for just a moment before he masks it and steps into me. I'm forced right back against the wall behind me as his hand falls to my waist, his fingers painfully digging into my skin. "Utter a single word about what you just heard, and I will tear your fucking tongue out with my teeth."

My hand presses down on his wrist and I push hard, forcing his fingers away from my waist. I step forward, pushing against his chest and moving him back, both of us knowing that his threat is a useless one because the second those words come out of my mouth, the three of them would already be dead.

"When will you learn, Roman? I fight fire with fire and I'm loyal to no one but myself. Give me a goddamn bedroom with a personal bathroom, and you have my word, I won't say a damn thing."

His jaw clenches, and just as he goes to respond, the dining room door swings wide with Giovanni DeAngelis standing front and center.

Roman quickly pulls away from me and turns to face his father, his shoulders pulling back as his chin rises. I find myself stepping slightly to the right, almost hiding behind Roman's big shoulders as my stare lands on the man who has all but ruled over the dark side of the world for the past thirty years.

My eyes go wide and I bite down on my tongue to keep myself from gasping at the sheer horror of just being in the same room as him. His all-black suit perfectly matches his dead eyes. Gold jewelry hangs off every available piece of skin on his body while old scars don his face. This man has been through some shit, but now, it's clear that he's the cause of everyone's nightmares. He exudes power—cold, cruel, and relentless power that no man should ever possess.

And to think that I came on his new wife's tongue only a few short hours ago.

Marcus doesn't bother sitting up straight, just simply turns his head to face his father while Levi stands to welcome him into the room, though the fear reflected in his eyes tells me that something much deeper is going on with him.

Giovanni's men come pouring into the room around him, and I watch in fascination as they scatter themselves around as though Giovanni needs protection from his own damn sons. Though, I've heard the stories whispered in the club and censored on the news. If they were my sons, I'd be terrified of them too.

His men look just as terrifying as he does, black suits wrapped around lean muscle and an array of weapons hanging from their belts. They each have small radios and earpieces, making out like Giovanni is some kind of king who needs the best protection money can buy. Either that, or he uses them as a show of force against his sons to overpower them to do his bidding. I guess life would be pretty sweet when you have three relentless sons who don't fear death. They're the perfect hitmen for anyone's team.

Roman's hands ball into fists at his sides and I watch how he visibly tries to restrain himself. Marcus' comment about how his father had slaughtered the pregnant girl swirls through my mind, and I can't help but wonder just how fresh that memory is for the three of them.

Their father begins surveying the room, scanning over every inch of the place, but before his harsh, lifeless stare can land on me and Roman, Levi steals his attention. "Father," he says, his tone sharp and straight to the point. "What brings you here today?"

"Can I not visit my sons without an ulterior motive?" he questions, his deep tone unsettling me right to my core.

"Seriously?" Marcus asks, hooking his legs over the armrest of his chair. "You haven't stepped foot into our little prison since you slaughtered Flick five months ago. So, what's the deal? Come to check up on us now that we have a new little toy to play with?"

Giovanni's attention falls right to me.

Fuck.

I'll have to remember to thank him for this great honor.

"Come here," Giovanni's booming voice cuts right through my panic, searing me with his deadly stare.

My gaze flicks to Marcus and then back to Roman, who looks as though he's about to shove his heavy boot right up my ass to get me moving. "What's it going to be?" I murmur, my eyes brimming with the power of my threat while becoming all too aware that my pause means Giovanni is forced to wait on me, something I'm positive he simply just does not do.

Roman doesn't respond but I see the irritation deep within his gaze. I've got him right where I want him, and assuming I make it through this, I don't doubt that I'll be paying for this risky little game.

The longer I wait for his response, the worse things are going to be with their father, but a girl has gotta risk it for the biscuit.

Roman glances back at his father and the slightest nod of his tells me that my game has finally come to an end. Victory washes through me, but before I get a chance to bask in my win, Giovanni's fierce roar tears across the room. "HOW DARE YOU KEEP ME WAITING,

GIRL."

Fuck.

My eyes bug out of my head and I quickly get my ass moving, trying to remember everything the boys said to me before he walked in here. Don't say a word. Don't look at him. Don't even dare to breathe.

Well, shit. Judging by the shitty first impression I've just made, something tells me that all three of those helpful little hints are as useless as Tarzan's burned remains sitting back in my trash can at home.

I scurry around the big table, my heels clicking against the marble floor as I feel the nausea building deep in my gut. If at any point during all this shit that I was meant to die, this would probably be it.

I sense the three brothers discreetly moving around the room with me, which causes Giovanni's men to do the same, and damn it, if I'm aware of it, then I can guarantee Giovanni is too.

Situating myself in front of the most terrifying man I've ever met, I try to remember to breathe. My knees shake and my hands grow sweaty at my sides while I try my best not to fold in on myself.

His wicked gaze starts at the mess on top of my head and before he's even moved down to my face, a disgusted scowl settles over his lips. His lingering stare travels over my features, or lack thereof. "Turn," he demands, the scowl stretching further across his face.

"This is it?" he questions in disgust, glancing up at Roman as I finish my slow spin. "This is not at all what I thought she was going to be. She's a twig, barely enough to keep a man satisfied, let alone three."

Roman shrugs. "That's it."

I bite down on my tongue as I remind myself over and over again that his wife got more enjoyment out of tasting me on her tongue than what she would get for spending her long nights with this fat bastard flopping around on top of her. And no matter what he does to me, he will never be able to take that knowledge away. So who really holds the power here?

Giovanni's gaze sweeps over me again, inhumane, cruel, and callous, looking at me like an object rather than a human with a heart and soul. "Remove your dress."

Horror ripples through me, more so than it had last night when his whore of a wife had asked the same thing, but this time, I know better than to refuse an order. The nausea swirls through me as I reluctantly slip the straps of my dress down over my arms and let the flimsy fabric fall to the ground as tears fill my eyes, knowing that every security guard that lines the room is taking me in like a fucking object, like trash they get to walk through and use at their disposal.

Humiliation washes over me as I stand before him, my lacking body showing off my barely-there curves. Giovanni moves in closer, scanning over me from every angle like he was checking the engine on an old, run down car.

My gaze rests on the marble tiles between us until his fingers curve around my chin. He tears it up and forces my stare on his. "You're the daughter of Maxwell Mariano?" I swallow hard and nod, too afraid to speak up. "He promised a full figure, plump tits, and a nice ass. You're nothing at all like the photograph he supplied. You're weak, pathetic. There's not an attractive feature about you."

Anger pulses through my veins. "Guess that's what happens when two vile assholes get together and make a deal. You're both going to get screwed."

His hand whips back and slams hard against my face, so damn hard that my whole body spins from the momentum and I crash to the ground. A loud cry tears out of me and Giovanni crouches down. "You and your father will not get away with ripping me off. You're worthless. You barely scratch the surface off the debt he owes."

"Take it up with him," I spit, blood pooling inside my mouth as I yank my dress out from under his expensive leather shoes. "Send the bastard my regards."

Giovanni stares, fury rippling through his gaze as he slowly stands. A glint of silver catches my eye as he pulls a gun from the back of his pants. Knowing this is the end, I shrink away from him. He holds the gun out, the barrel pointing right between my eyes, and just as he's about to pull the trigger, Marcus sighs. "Really, father? And to think I was the dramatic one of the family. Sit down so we can eat. I'm bored of this."

Giovanni holds my stare before curiously glancing toward his son. "Why are you protecting her?"

Marcus shrugs his shoulders as a lazy grin flutters across his careless lips. "What can I say? The whore is a good fuck and has a skilled tongue. There's value in her still. I'll get rid of her once I bore of her tight cunt."

Giovanni glances back at me before finally holstering his gun and walking toward the table, leaving me an absolute mess on the ground. I hastily get to my feet and pull my dress back over my head as I wearily watch the leader of the DeAngelis family stride across the room and take his seat.

He starts with a sip of wine before scrunching his face in disgust and turning back to me, throwing the contents of his glass all over me. "This is horrendous. Go and fetch something worth my time."

My gaze flicks toward Levi directly across from me and he quickly nods, telling me to get a move on and I quickly turn on my heel before bolting toward the door.

"I'm disappointed," I hear muttered behind me. "I thought you would have trained her better than this. She's been here for four days and you've allowed her to run rampant in your home. The girl has a loose tongue and there's barely even a bruise on her. Get a handle on your whore or I'll be forced to step in. This is unacceptable."

Fucking hell. That was just perfect.

I step outside of the dining room, and the second the massive doors close behind me, I take a deep breath and sprint right up the stairs until the hardwood door of my new bedroom slams shut behind me.

The door rattles on its hinges and I quickly lock it before dropping my back against it and sinking to the ground.

What the fuck just happened? Screw the asshole and his fucking cheap ass wine. There's no way in hell that I'm about to go back down there. The boys be damned. They're on their own now.

EIGHTEEN

Watching Giovanni DeAngelis' entourage driving away from the big-ass gothic castle from the top level window is the highlight of my fucking life.

I don't think I've ever hated someone so fiercely, not even his cruel sons when they were chasing me through the maze garden and haunting me through the hallways of the dark cells with their fucking wolves.

Giovanni DeAngelis is pure evil, and I can't wait to be the one who gets to put him down like the fucking dog that he is. Well, at least that's the dream that's going to keep me going. Judging from his sons' reaction to his very presence in their home, I'd dare say that it'll be a race to the finish line.

Anger pulses through my veins, and the moment I know the coast is clear, I throw my new bedroom door wide open and march my ass downstairs, more than aware of the shit storm that's brewing inside of me.

I find the three fucklords standing in the foyer of their enormous castle. Marcus holds a whole bottle of bourbon in his hands while Levi is sophisticated enough to use a glass. Roman on the other hand holds nothing but a horrendous scowl, one that could rival his father's.

"Your father is a fucking asshole," I spit through a clenched jaw as I stare at the three brothers hovering in the foyer. "No wonder you three turned out so bad."

Each one of them glares at me, and for a moment, I'm frozen on the step. Their glares are sharp enough to cut glass and instantly remind me where my place in all of this is. Roman strides toward me, stopping right in front of me. "I asked you one simple thing," he growls. "Keep your fucking mouth shut."

I swallow hard. Maybe I should have given them a little more time before racing down here.

His stare is full of rage, but something tells me that it's directed at his father. "What the hell was I supposed to do? He insulted me, practically called me worthless trash after stripping me bare and humiliating me. He deserves a fucking bullet between his eyes for the way he treated me."

Roman narrows his stare, his jaw clenching as that nasty scar calls to me, daring me to push him just a little bit further. "You're lucky that you didn't get one between yours," he fires back at me, reaching toward Marcus and tearing the bottle of bourbon right out of his hands. "Next time you speak out of line and make me look incompetent in front of my father, there won't be anyone standing around to stop me from pulling the trigger."

He steps around me and stalks across the hall before turning into the informal living space. A loud grunt and the sound of shattering glass startles me.

Marcus groans. "Fuck, there goes the rest of my lunch."

"Why do you guys put up with that shit?" I ask.

Levi walks past me, sipping at his tumbler of brown liquid. "Don't worry about Roman. He gets like this after all of Father's visits. He'll calm down in a bit."

"I don't mean Roman," I say, turning on my heel and following him as Marcus steps in beside me. "I've heard all the stories, all the things that you guys are capable of, yet you allow your father to walk all over you. I just … I don't get it. Why haven't you done something about it yet? It's not like you guys have a moral compass or anything. What does he have on you?"

Marcus meets my gaze and shakes his head. "It ain't as easy as it sounds, princess."

"I'm no fucking princess."

"Don't I know it," he mutters darkly, his eyes flashing with the memory of my bound wrists and the heavy chain holding me up off the ground as he fucked me so hard that I could feel exactly where he'd been for days.

I swallow hard, averting my eyes as the reminder of the night has heat flooding deep inside of me, only his calloused hand gently pressing against my cheek pulls me up short.

I stop in the middle of the hallway, turning to meet his heavy stare, only he doesn't say a damn word, but he doesn't have to. It's all there in his eyes as a rare flicker of emotion pulses through him. Roman's comments in the dining room come rushing back to me—he's forming an attachment, and while the thought of a guy like him having any sort of feelings toward me is terrifying, that small attachment, whatever it may be, might just be the reason that I somehow live through this.

Marcus' gaze shifts over the red mark that his father left across my face, and I find myself freezing like one of the many statues scattered around the property. Anger swirls in the depths of his eyes, and it's clear that the idea of his father's brutal hit doesn't sit well with him, but where does he draw the line? Is it okay for him and his brothers to hurt me, but no one else?

"Why did you do it?" I question, more than aware of Levi stopping up ahead to listen in on our conversation. "He was going to kill me, but you stopped him. It doesn't make any sense. Isn't that what you guys have wanted all along? Your endgame is to see me in a shallow grave, so what's the point of delaying the inevitable? You've gifted me that black blade and now saved my life. I just ... I don't understand."

Marcus' hand drops away and that rare flicker of emotion falls away with it, bringing back the callous and cruel version of himself that I'm quickly becoming far too familiar with. For a moment, I fear that my comments have flipped that switch inside of him, but his silence speaks volumes.

My gaze flicks to Levi as he hovers in the entrance of the living room, his stare aimed right back at me. "That's not your intention, is it?" I question, my eyes widening with the realization. "You never wanted to kill me. You plan to keep me around."

Marcus' jaw clenches, his eyes hardening like stone, and I realize that this is so much more than just a 'treat 'em mean, keep 'em keen' kind of relationship. They stalked me for three months before making their move, they knew everything about me, they did their freaking homework. Why would guys like this dedicate their time to something like that, only to turn around and end my life? That's not what they want from me.

"When you said welcome to the family, you weren't just trying to fuck with my head. You really meant it," I say to Marcus. "What am I supposed to be to you guys? Am I supposed to be some kind of replacement for the last chick? Some whore you're all going to pass between yourselves to pass the time? All the threats and games, all the fear I've felt since the day you assholes took me, it's all been for nothing. You were never going to hurt me."

"No," Levi confirms, striding back down the hall toward me. "It's not our intention to end your life, but don't be so naive to assume that accidents won't happen. You saw the brutality of our world last night, and the cruelty of our father. We won't always be there to protect you, nor do I feel that you've earned that protection. You're here to play a part, but push us too far, and we'll be more than happy to put you in the ground and find someone else to fill the spot."

My stare lingers on his. "And what exactly is the spot that I'm supposed to be filling?"

His eyes narrow. "I guess that all depends on you."

Without another word, both Levi and Marcus continue back toward the living room and I cautiously trail behind them, my head a complete mess from all the bombs that have been dropped today. First, it's Roman's relationship with the dead pregnant chick, then Marcus' weird fascination with me which somehow morphed into the boys overthrowing their father. Though, I don't blame them. After meeting the guy for myself, I'd be doing exactly the same thing. But the latest revelations are messing with my head.

They don't intend to kill me.

This whole time, I've been under the impression that one step out of place would have seen me to a shallow grave. Hell, the brothers already have my death certificate signed and dated with news of my murder floating around the streets. The intention from the beginning is that I would never see my old life again, but I assumed that I wouldn't be able to see much of this new one either.

So, what the hell do they want with me? It sure as hell explains why I've been able to get away with my snappy attitude and why they bothered to put me on birth control. If I was just a toy, Giovanni wouldn't have had any interest in me either. Something more is going on here, and it grinds on my nerves that I don't have the answers I need.

I follow the brothers into the living room to find Roman sitting back on a three-seater couch, his feet propped up on a coffee table with a brand new bottle of bourbon in his hand. He's completely zoned out, staring out the front window as his big-ass wolf lays next to him, his enormous head resting in Roman's lap.

I stare for a long moment, still unable to come to terms with the fact that these guys have somehow managed to get their hands on these wolves. They're wild animals, and yet they're lying in their laps like they're part of the family. At this point, I wouldn't be surprised to find they had spiked collars with their names engraved on a tag.

Dragging my feet, I make my way across the room, more than aware of the way the big wolf tracks my every move. I'm not really an animal person, but if I were, I'd have a bunny or something small that doesn't require too much attention. Animals like this freak me out and, judging by the way he's watching me with his black eyes glistening in the light, he knows.

I bet he's dreaming about tearing my arm right off my body and spending the rest of his day happily gnawing on the bone.

Not having the chance to explore this room before, my gaze sweeps over every corner. It's got the guys' signature gothic feel to it, but it also looks like they've spent a shitload of money in here. There are high ceilings with beautiful trim. Massive windows frame the front of the room as a huge fireplace takes up the side wall, complete with beautiful white bookshelves around it. Really, it looks like a massive fire hazard, but who am I to judge their styling?

A cozy seating area has been built into the lower part of each massive bay window, and I find myself curling into a ball in the furthest window from the brothers. It's comfy as hell and gives me a perfect view of the front section of the property. Definitely worth the cash that Daddy Warbucks was probably forced to spend.

I can't help but follow the winding driveway far into the hills until I can't possibly see any further, but all that does is leave a heaviness settling inside my chest. I'm so far away from reality that I'll never see freedom, but I guess I don't have to fear the brothers as much as I have been, seeing as though their endgame doesn't revolve around dismembering me. But it still leaves me wondering why.

Their harsh stares focus on me as I stare out the window and I can't help but stare back. "What?" I demand, narrowing my eyes, not liking the way they so comfortably leer at me.

Levi shrugs his shoulders. "Nothing," he mutters as a teasing grin pulls at the corners of his lips. "Just odd seeing you sitting there in silence. I was getting used to your constant raging and bitching. It's peaceful."

I roll my eyes and look back out the window, curling my arms around my knees until I'm in a tight ball. "I know this might come as a shock to you, but when I feel that my life is being threatened or … I don't know, I feel that someone is being such an asshole that my pussy dries up, I feel that it's my civil duty to let it be known."

Roman mutters something under his breath and I make a point not to look his way. Instead, I glance right back over my shoulder to the section of the property which is mostly hidden away. My brow arches as I find the overgrown maze and a shiver travels right through my body.

That night wasn't one of my fondest memories of this place so far. The feeling of being stalked and chased, the fear of complete hopelessness, and of course, the horrifying terror of turning a corner to find one of the brothers standing there waiting for me. It wasn't my idea of fun, but it certainly was theirs.

"You guys are real assholes," I murmur, keeping my gaze locked on the maze. "That shit was next level fucked up, like … who even does that?"

A low rumble echoes through the room and it takes me a moment to realize they're laughing at me. A loud huff tears from within me as I fly to my feet and start storming to the door. "Fuck this," I mutter under my breath, intent to spend the rest of my day staring at the back of my bedroom door.

"Chill out," Roman says, reaching out and gripping my wrist as I pass him. "It was just a bit of harmless fun." Without warning, he pulls back on my wrist and all but throws me right into his brother.

Marcus catches me with ease, flipping me around like a ragdoll so that my back is pressed up against his wide chest, his hands tightly gripping my waist, but it's not in protection, there's something possessive about it.

Before I get a chance to pull myself out of his grasp, Roman's bottle of bourbon is thrust into my hands. "Have a drink, Empress. Fuck knows that temper of yours could use it."

I grip the bottle tighter, more than prepared to launch it at his head as his brother grips me tightly, refusing to allow me to move away. "Is this your version of an apology?" I growl, the rollercoaster of emotions becoming too much for me to handle.

Roman scoffs. "You need to remember who you're talking to. We don't apologize. We get even. Everything we do is done with purpose."

I stare at him blankly, his arrogance quickly making me wish for the knife I left down in my creeptastic dungeon. "So, chasing me through an overgrown, creepy-as-fuck maze in the middle of the night is your version of getting even?"

He doesn't respond, just simply raises a thick brow that has him looking nothing short of a nightmare.

"Pray tell," I grumble. "What the hell did I do that warranted your sick need to get even?"

Roman stands, hovering over me for just a moment as his wolf stands with him, the both of them appearing like a scene out of a movie that no woman should ever have to sit through. "What haven't you done?" he questions. "I'm only just getting started."

He turns and walks out of the room, his wolf practically strutting behind him and leaving me fearing what else he could possibly do to me. Though, something tells me that when a man like Roman DeAngelis plans on getting even, creativity is his greatest tool.

Just when I think Marcus will release his hold on me, Levi pushes off the couch directly opposite us and saunters across the room, his tumbler still in his hand. He takes a sip and by the time his glass is lowering from his mouth, he stands right in front of me, exactly where his eldest brother had been only a second ago.

"He's right. We don't apologize for shit. Everything we do is done for a reason," Levi rumbles, his dark, secretive eyes boring into mine as the tension quickly builds between us. As if sensing the change in the room, Marcus pulls back on me, dragging me back a step, already knowing exactly what his brother is coming for.

"So, the night you were hiding in my closet, watching me get off? There was a reason behind that?" I question, trying to push against Marcus' hold as his brother steps with us, keeping himself right in front of me.

Levi winks and everything south of the border clenches. I'm completely captivated.

Levi's fingers dip into his tumbler and he pulls out a perfectly round piece of ice and my gaze instantly drops to it. "Call it character building," he murmurs, his voice lower than I've ever heard it.

A possessive growl rumbles through Marcus' chest and I feel the vibrations deep in my back, but all that does is have Levi's hard stare flicking up to his brother. "You know the rules, brother," he mutters darkly. "Either share your toys, or I'll take them from you."

A short, tension-filled moment passes between them, and after a beat, Marcus' grip on my waist begins to ease, though something tells me that he's not going anywhere. The anticipation builds within me as I clench my thighs, too excited for my own good.

Any other girl would be running, but damn. If that night with Marcus is anything to go by, then I won't be going anywhere.

Levi's heated gaze sweeps over my body as Marcus' hands at my waist rise to the plunging neckline of my dress. He tears the fabric right down the center until I'm completely bare between them, and as Levi's stare meets mine, the tension in the room dissipates, and all that's left is his body moving in closer to mine, the ice slowly melting between his warm fingers.

The bottle of bourbon is taken from me and carelessly thrown to the couch as Marcus' fingers trail up and down my skin, leaving goosebumps in their wake. My nipples pebble, and as I take a deep breath in and my chest rises, the sensitive peaks brush against the front of Levi's shirt.

I track his every movement as I press my legs together, desperate to relieve the ache that's burning deep within me. Levi's hand raises and he holds the ice between his fingers, slowly letting the cold water drip onto my shoulder before gently pressing it to my skin.

Marcus' fingers tighten on my body and I sense the excitement radiating off him in waves as I quickly come to terms with the fact that, no matter what they want to do to me right now, I'm going to let them. Screw every last moral that was drilled into me as a kid, screw knowing the difference between right and wrong. I want this, and I'm not about to do anything to screw it up.

Levi trails the ice down over my shoulder and around the curve of my breast before slowly circling my sensitive nipple. I suck in a gasp and tip my head back to Marcus' shoulder as I raise my eyes, watching the way that Levi focuses on the small piece of ice that's causing havoc to my body.

A small drip of water begins trailing down past my breast and I suck in a breath as it makes its way over my waist and past my hip. It follows the curve from my hip around to my inner thigh and my knees go weak as it hits home.

Marcus holds onto me, his hand sailing up my body and gently closing in around my throat as his brother teases me with the ice, watching the smooth trail of cold water that he leaves behind.

Done tormenting my tits, the ice travels further down my body, teasing my waist and sending my eyes rolling to the back of my head as it slides down between my legs. Levi slowly massages the ice against my clit like the sweetest kind of torture, his eyes coming back to mine, flaming with desire. "I won't ever apologize to you," he murmurs darkly as he finds my entrance and pushes the piece of melting ice deep inside of me. I gasp, my eyes going wide as I reach forward and grip his shoulder tightly, my nails digging into his skin. "But that doesn't mean that I can't show appreciation."

"Holy fuck," I breathe as Marcus' arm winds around my waist, locking me against his hard body while his brother steps in even closer, his body pressing right against mine and sandwiching me between the two heathens.

Levi doesn't skip a beat, knowing that it won't be long until the ice completely melts, and moves two thick fingers to my clit. He rubs lazy, tight circles as my head drops forward to his chest, deep pants quickly overtaking me as I clench and squeeze the ice inside of me. It moves around and I groan low, never having experienced such a sweet burn in my life.

My hand moves from Levi's shoulder as his deep, manly scent overwhelms me and I slip it up under the expensive fabric of his shirt, needing to feel his warm skin beneath my fingers.

A low growl vibrates through his chest as Marcus' chuckle sounds from behind me. I grind down against Levi's hand, the pure pleasure rocking through my body and putting me on edge. It's not exactly the fantasy I had in mind when it came to Levi, but damn it, it's the next best thing.

Scrap that, it's better.

I feel Marcus' rock-hard cock against my ass as his brother's grinds against my hip, but when I go to reach for the front of Levi's pants, Marcus catches my wrist and pulls it up around the back of his neck.

Levi seems content to let this be the Shayne sandwich show, and I'm not going to lie, I'm more than happy to repay the favor another time. So rather than fight it, I dig my nails into the back of Marcus' neck and let the brothers treat me to a little well-earned appreciation.

My pussy clenches as Levi gently pinches my clit and rolls it between his fingers, and just when I thought that it couldn't get any better, I feel Marcus behind me. He reaches down below and pushes his thick fingers inside my pussy, drenching them with my wetness and pushing the ice even deeper inside of me. He draws his fingers out, spreading the wetness to my ass, teasing me before slowly pushing his fingers inside.

A low groan pulls from deep inside of me and I push back against his fingers, taking him deeper as I stretch around him. "Holy fuck," I breathe, my eyes closing as Levi rolls my clit between his fingers again. "Fuck, fuck, fuck. Yes. More."

The guys don't disappoint, picking up their pace and fucking me with their fingers. My eyes roll to the back of my head and I dig my nails deeper into Levi's chest, knowing that he can take it.

A deep growl vibrates through his chest and just the thought of him slamming his thick cock deep inside of me is my undoing. I come hard, a loud cry tearing from between my lips, but they don't dare stop. My pussy convulses around the dissolving piece of ice as I clench around Marcus' strong fingers.

Both the brothers keep moving, letting me ride it out. They're relentless with my body as my orgasm tears through me and it's more than I ever knew that I needed.

Who would have known that the DeAngelis brothers were even capable of making a woman feel so damn good? Had somebody asked, I would have said that hard, raw, and fast is the only speed they knew. I would have put them down as the selfish type, taking what they needed and leaving their woman high and dry.

But that? Fuck.

I've never felt so alive. My body is on edge, my pussy burning with the sweetest release, and damn it, they've only given me a taste of what I truly want. The two of them together … It's something that I never knew I wanted, but now, I won't stop until I have them both buried deep inside of me.

I finally come down from my high and Levi steps back away from me, his knowing eyes dropping to mine before that smug as fuck grin settles over his lips. Then still with his tumbler in his hand, he takes a well-deserved sip and walks away with his brother trailing behind him, neither of them saying a damn word as they leave me weak and panting for more.

Needing a moment to regain my energy as the last of the ice finally melts, I grab the edges of my torn dress and pull them tightly around me before dropping down on the very couch that Roman had been sitting on only a short moment ago.

I pull my legs up, feeling that delicious burn inside of me as I uncap the bottle of bourbon and take a quick hit, unsure of what the hell is going on, what their intentions are, or what the hell is going to happen to me.

My head drops back onto the soft cushion and as I stare out the massive window, both of the big black wolves come strutting into the room. One drops down in the space below me where my feet would have been as the other jumps up on the seat beside me, making himself comfortable as he drops his big head into my lap.

My heart races, the fear of their closeness fucking with my head, but what's new? I guess I'm officially part of the family now. Weirder things have happened over the past few days, so with another sip of bourbon, my hand drops to the big wolf's head and I relax back into the couch, more at ease in this gigantic castle than ever before.

NINETEEN

Water rains down over me as I tip my head back into the hot stream of the best shower I've ever had. My living situation isn't exactly ideal, but I can definitely get used to this kick ass shower. My room is a bit bland, but I'm not about to complain to the brothers about it. Knowing my luck, Roman would just crack the shits and send me straight back down to the torture chamber while Marcus would simply suggest painting the walls with blood to brighten it up.

I earned my new room fair and square. I played them at their own game, and for once, the risk paid off. Though Roman hasn't exactly cooled all the way down after his father's visit this afternoon, so there's still time for him to go back on his word. After all, the deal was that I kept my mouth shut, and I couldn't quite come through on my end.

The exhaustion of last night's party combined with the whiplash that I'm constantly getting from the brothers completely claimed me, and after sitting on the couch with the two ginormous wolves all afternoon, I woke in a daze to find myself alone on the couch with the sun nowhere to be seen.

Falling asleep out in the open like that probably wasn't my greatest moment. I left myself vulnerable in a place that I was unfamiliar with. Anyone could have walked in, and what if people from last night's party were still lingering in the castle?

Levi confirming their intentions were never to kill me has gone a long way in easing my constant fear. Don't get me wrong, it's still there and as consuming as ever, but I seem to have a better handle on it. After all, in the space of only a few days, I have been kidnapped, tortured, and stalked. Not to mention the fact that at least three people lost their lives during last night's party, and the doctor only hours before. Hell, I even stabbed a guy. But just because they don't intend to kill me, doesn't mean that I'm safe.

Waking up in the living room and not having any of the guys in sight, I used it to my full advantage, flying through the rooms and trying to find a way out of here. Every door was locked with an electronic keypad, and none of the windows were able to be opened. This castle is a fortress, but I guess that's just the way it has to be when you have so many enemies. It's the final defense for keeping them out of their home, but then, I guess the same could be said if someone were trying to keep them in.

I put it to the back of my mind as I take my time scrubbing my hair and attempting to wash off the horrendous memories I've collected over the past few days, but it's not that simple. The feeling of shoving a blade inside that man's body is going to haunt me for as long as I live. Hell, I stabbed Marcus too.

What the hell has gotten into me? These guys need to keep me away from knives, though to be fair, a girl needs every bit of protection she can get in a place like this.

During my shower, I take the time to scrub the dirt beneath my feet and trail a razor over my legs. Though, the chipped black polish on my nails seems like a lost cause at this point.

My body still aches from the abuse of the week, so after doing everything I possibly can to feel like a woman again, I stand with my head tilted back and eyes closed, enjoying the rare moment of calm.

That is until asshole number one kicks in my bathroom door and strides on in as though he has every right. He just stands there, his jaw clenched as I scurry to cover myself with the towel. "Have you ever heard of this magical thing called privacy?" I shriek. "Get the hell out."

Roman scoffs. "You've been naked in this hellhole more than you've been clothed."

He has a good fucking point, but I'm not about to go and applaud him on his quick comeback. "What do you want?" I demand, stepping out of the shower while still managing to keep my distance.

He throws a pair of old sweatpants and a cropped black tank at my chest and I barely manage to catch them without dropping my towel.

"Get dressed," he spits as he starts moving toward the door. "We're leaving in ten."

My eyes widen and I scurry after him. "Leaving? What do you mean? Where are we going?"

Roman stops after cutting through my bedroom and looks back at me with a deep scowl on his face. He doesn't say anything, but his silence is more than enough to remind me of my place in all of this. I don't get the right to answers, at least not yet, and definitely not where Roman is concerned. Though, I'm sure he believes I've already been rewarded enough for one day.

Roman holds my stare for a moment longer, and with each passing second, the need to shrink away from him rises in my chest until he finally turns away and leaves me gasping for air.

I seem to keep forgetting who these guys are. They're not my friends, not my people. They're my captors, murderers, and the very men who will ensure that I live in a constant state of fear.

The anticipation of leaving the castle has me rushing to get dressed, and before I know it, I'm down in the foyer, waiting impatiently for the boys to show. My hands shake at my sides, having no idea what I'm in for tonight. All I know is that we're probably not heading out for takeout, though that might be a possibility after the brothers have done whatever it is that they need to do.

Levi and Roman show up first, both of them wearing black pants with a black hoodie pushed back to show their faces. It's like some kind of unofficial uniform, but I'm not going to lie, every time I've seen them wearing this, I've ended up in a world of hell.

Roman's hair is pulled back into a tight bun as the bits underneath are cropped short and fade down to nothing. I find myself looking at it a moment too long. I've never been into the whole long hair on a guy thing before, but he's pulling off the *Jason Momoa* look like no man ever has before, not even *Jason* himself. His eyes are sharp and lethal, and I know without a doubt, what's going down tonight isn't something I want to be involved in.

Levi on the other hand, with his short-cropped hair and bored expression, looks as though he's ready to call it a night and spend the next few hours closed up in his room with his drumsticks.

Silence surrounds us as we wait for Marcus, and after a short moment, he steps out from the living room that I'd spent a good portion of my afternoon sleeping in. "Ready?" he rumbles, his gaze shifting over me while his question is directed at his brothers.

"Let's make it fast," Levi mutters as the three of them take off toward the dining room. "Can't risk Father catching us out of our prison, especially after his shit during lunch."

My brows furrow as I hurry behind them. "Prison?" I question, following them through the back of the dining room and through a narrow walkway that leads to the main kitchen, wondering if he's referring to what Roman had told me about their father keeping them locked up here.

My eyes widen and a sharp gasp pours out of me when I find the room filled with countless staff. They scatter around, busily cooking and clearing away used plates, and the moment the brothers' presence is known, they drop what they're doing, a heavy silence filling the room.

All eyes fall to me and I slow my pace, getting left behind as I gape at the people around me.

I knew there must have been staff working here with the type of food that's constantly presented at the table and how each bedroom looks pristine, but I didn't expect this. Apart from the boys, I never hear a damn thing. The castle is like a ghost town, and a part of me had wondered if the staff came and went during the middle of the night, but that couldn't be right. That's when the monsters come out to play.

The staff watch me with caution and it takes them no time at all to realize that I'm not exactly a willing guest here, just as I assume they're not either. Pitying looks are thrown my way and I stumble as I attempt to put one foot in front of another.

"MOVE," Roman's fierce growl cuts through the heavy silence.

My stare immediately falls to the ground as I hurry after the brothers, trying my best not to think the worst. We cut through the opposite end of the kitchen and wind our way down a steep spiral staircase. Trying to keep up with them has my breath coming in sharp, pained gasps. "Please tell me those people are staff and are not held here against their will?" I question, not really caring where the answer comes from as long as I get one.

"They're staff," Levi mutters, irritation in his deep tone. "They work a rotating shift and are paid accordingly. Most of them have been with us since we were kids. The fear you hold for them is offensive."

I attempt to wipe the horror off my face, but as we descend into a dark cellar and the boys lay their attention on an old bookcase, I realize that there's no need to even try. It's pushed aside and my brow arches as a narrow tunnel appears behind the shelving. "Come on," Marcus says, grabbing my wrist and giving me a tug to get moving. "Watch your step. The further we go through the tunnel, the darker it gets."

I try to look up ahead, but it's impossible to see where it leads. "What's wrong with the front door?" I mutter, realizing that I'm in for a long walk.

Marcus sighs. "I'm sure you noticed the electronic keypad on the door?" he questions as Roman sighs, realizing I'm about to get even more answers to the question he deems to be none of my damn business.

"Hard not to," I tell him.

"Put it this way," he says. "You're not the only one who's been locked away in this prison."

I quickly glance at Roman. He'd touched on this while I sobbed in the shower, but there are too many holes in his story, too many hard truths being held captive. "What's that supposed to mean?" I ask, wondering just how much I can push for information.

"We're our father's weapons," Levi cuts in, a strange darkness lacing his deep tone. "Trained to kill, pushed over our limits to ensure that nothing could break us."

Roman continues for him. "We're soldiers in an army of three and he's our leader, only this leader has lost his touch, and controlling his army isn't as easy as it once was."

I swallow hard, realizing just how far gone they are if not even their mafia boss father can keep them grounded. "Is that why you plan to overthrow him? You want your freedom back?"

Marcus grunts, that same darkness reflected in his own tone. "Freedom isn't the issue where our father is concerned," he says, leaving the topic hanging in the air and my curiosity brimming so high that it might just push me over the edge. "We have many scores to settle with that bastard."

We make our way through the rest of the tunnel until we're stepping out into a small private garage surrounded by thick woods.

"What the ever-loving hell is this?" I mutter as Marcus leads me toward the black Escalade that sits in the center of the garage. "I'm assuming that your father doesn't know about this little escape route?"

"Oh, he knows," Levi murmurs, climbing in the front passenger seat as Roman takes prime position behind the wheel. "The bastard just can't figure out where the fuck it is."

An image of their father attempting to discipline them and get answers filters through my mind and has a wicked grin pulling at my lips, not only surprising myself, but Marcus as well. "And you think we're fucked in the head," he murmurs, opening the back passenger door and practically throwing me across the backseat. "What are you picturing? The old man beating the shit out of us, trying to get an answer?"

My grin only widens as I straighten in my seat and keep my gaze locked out the window. "Something like that," I mutter under my breath, realizing that he's more than likely speaking one of his hard truths.

Marcus grunts and climbs into the Escalade beside me, and the moment the door closes behind him, Roman peels out of the secret garage, shooting out into the thick woods.

We drive for a few minutes before we clear the woods and I finally see the gothic castle in all its glory, and yet somehow, we're on the opposite side of the big security gates that line the property. "How did you guys find that tunnel?" I question, unable to look away from the haunting castle.

"Find?" Levi grunts. "We spent five fucking years digging that shit out."

My brows fly up as I turn my attention to the brothers sitting silently in the front seats. I've got to admit, I'm impressed. When the boys are committed to a cause, they sure as hell stick to it.

With the castle disappearing into the distance, we sit in complete silence for at least an hour. Cars pass us on the highway and my heart aches with every one of them. I'd give anything to wriggle through the big sunroof and catapult myself on top of one of those cars for just a slight chance at freedom.

Surely if I could somehow get out onto the road, one of these cars would pick me up. But just one look at my captors would have any rescuer bolting in the opposite direction.

Letting out a heavy sigh, I lean back into my seat, trying to figure out the dynamics of the boys being prisoners in their own home. They have staff who can come and go after their shift, staff who they have access to. So surely they would know how they get in and out. Though, I'm sure they would all have personal electronic codes for the gates and doors, but that almost seems too easy. Retinal scanners maybe? Then how do they leave when their father needs them to play the part of his perfect hitmen soldiers? Does he come to them or are they offered some kind of temporary code to be let out?

They stalked me for three months before finally making a move, so getting their freedom doesn't seem so hard. But then, I also haven't seen them leave their home since I arrived.

Another hour passes and the boys are discussing their plans to overthrow their father, though they talk in riddles so I can't follow along. They discuss names that I don't recognize, locations I've never heard of, and times that simply don't make any sense.

Their confusing conversation quickly gives me a headache, and just as I go to zone out, Roman turns off the highway and down a long dirt road. The conversation falls away, and I notice how the brothers sit a little straighter. They keep their attention focused out the window as though they're waiting or looking for something. Eventually the dirt road leads out into the backstreets of an old industrial area.

Worn down warehouses are barely visible by the dim streetlights. Most of them look as though they've been out of operation for hundreds of years, while others look like they've had the occasional slap of paint to keep them going.

Roman slows the car as we edge through the backstreets of the lonely area, and when he cuts his headlights, I find myself gripping the door handle nervously. It's nearly pitch-black inside the Escalade, and call me a wimp, but being alone in the dark with the DeAngelis brothers isn't exactly one of my favorite pastimes.

He drives the Escalade through an abandoned warehouse, cutting through the torn down opening and right to the back entrance. We come out into a dirt yard and he continues to the very back of the property before swerving around some aged trees and passing into the neighboring warehouse.

He drives slowly to not alert anyone that we're here, and after creeping closer to the warehouse, he brings the Escalade to a stop right in the perfect vantage point, giving us a complete view of the property. "Where are we?" I ask, staring out at the old building that's falling apart.

Dim lights are on inside and the front roller doors are wide open, shining light out onto a portion of the front driveway. A few banged up cars are sporadically parked inside, the doors left wide open as a small fire burns in a drum to the left.

"Just paying an old friend a visit," Marcus mutters darkly, the excitement in his tone reminding me that the three men who sit around me get off on savage murder.

I glance between the brothers before looking back at the warehouse. "Why did you bring me here?"

Levi glances back at me with a blank expression, his brows drawn as though I just asked the most ridiculous question he's ever heard. "Couldn't leave you back there all by yourself now, could we? Wouldn't want to risk you finding a way out."

I swallow hard, fearing this version of the man I enjoyed in the living room. That man doesn't exist right now, and I'm left with a callous, cruel asshole whose favorite hobbies include drowning the monsters inside his head, drumming over pools of blood, and probably a light Sunday afternoon decapitation.

Roman indicates toward the side entrance. "You two take the front and I'll get the drop on him out back."

Without another word, the feared DeAngelis brothers slide out of the car without making a damn sound, preparing themselves for a night of adrenaline-filled fun.

Not sure what I should be doing or where the hell they want me, I slip out behind them and keep close, only as my door closes behind me, three sets of obsidian eyes come back to mine. "The fuck do you think you're doing?" Roman grunts, but before I get a chance to respond, Marcus is leaning back into the car and pulls out a thick, black material.

My eyes widen, recognizing the bag that they shoved over my head only a few short nights ago, and as I pull away, more than ready to make a run for it, Roman catches me in his steel grip as Marcus shoves the black bag right over my head and presses his hand over my mouth, keeping me from screaming.

"You didn't think this was going to be fun, did you?" Marcus laughs, keeping his tone low as he wrestles me out of Roman's tight grip and drags my ass back to the car. I bite his hand through the bag and get a sick satisfaction out of the way he curses in pain.

He must be using the hand that I stabbed a steak knife through, but the menacing laughter reminds me that it's not just others' pain he gets off on, it's his own. "Mmmm," he moans, his face right up against mine as he captures my wrists in his big hands and forces them up. "What I would give to see the fear in your eyes right now, baby girl. But you have to promise, next time, you'll bite me harder."

Fucking hell. What kind of sick perverted asshole have I got myself mixed up with?

I'm thrown back into my seat and I pull hard against his hold, but it's no use, he's too strong. "Hurry up," I hear Levi outside the car. "She's drawing too much attention."

Marcus sighs, realizing that his fun is over. With one quick movement, I feel the familiar cool metal of handcuffs tightening around my wrists and hooking around the holy shit bar above my head. "NO, NO, NO," I cry out as Marcus moves away from me. But despite my objections, the car door slams in my face, followed by the soft click of the automatic locks. "ASSHOLES!"

I tug on my wrist but get absolutely nowhere as the fear of the unknown pulses through my veins. I have to do something. I have to get out of here, or at the very least, try. There were woods surrounding the industrial area. If I can get out of this car and somehow lose myself in the thick branches, then I might have a fighting chance.

With my new resolve, hope, and fear keeping my chin up, I pull my feet up under me on the leather chair. I try to stand, shoving my ass right up into the ceiling of the Escalade and lean forward just enough to shake the black bag off my head.

My hair goes staticky and falls over my face, but I quickly adjust myself to focus on my wrists. It's not exactly the first time I've been in cuffs, but I can't say that the ones I had before were real. I tug hard, the frustration of being trapped quickly sending me into a panic.

My gaze shifts out the window and I watch as Levi and Marcus walk in through the front of the warehouse with far too much confidence, but it's not like they haven't done this a million times before.

Someone is going to die here tonight, and I don't want to be anywhere near here when it happens. Though unfortunately for that guy, his fate has already been sealed. There's no saving him now.

Getting nowhere with the tugging, I let out a heavy breath and realize that to play with fire, I'm going to have to pull out all the stops.

I twist my hands around and grip onto the holy shit bar with everything I've got, and after taking another quick glance out the window and checking that I'm clear, I prop my feet on either side of the bar. With my back resting against the expensive leather, I pull as hard as I can. I push off my feet, putting my whole body weight behind it while gripping onto the bar with everything I've got.

I clench my jaw as I try and try again, and just when I think all hope is gone, the bar comes free and my body flies across the backseat. My ribs slam into the opposite door but I quickly shake it off, wanting to get out of here and put as much distance between me and the brothers before they realize that their new little dungeon mate is gone.

Without skipping a beat, I reach to the front seat and search for the little button to unlock the doors. But as my finger skims over the top of it, I pause, realizing that a move like this could potentially set off the car alarm.

The brothers are occupied in the warehouse and the Escalade is at least a hundred meters away. So if I do this, and the alarm goes off, I'll have one shot at freedom, one single chance to run for my life.

Taking a deep breath, I squish my nerves straight back down and I unlock the car.

TWENTY

My foot slams against the door of the Escalade as my fingers curl around the handle. I yank it open and I have a short moment of relief, realizing I'm safe. The alarm hasn't gone off, but the internal cab light sure as hell just lit up the whole damn street.

Fuck.

I scramble out of the car, hoping to God that the DeAngelis brothers are far too occupied to even look back at the Escalade. So as I get that first taste of freedom when my feet hit the hard earth below, I make it count.

My feet pound against the dirt, catapulting me forward and away from the Escalade. I don't dare look back, terrified that the brothers are already coming for me. I have no choice but to race across the road to get to the thick woods on the other side, and I do everything that I can to keep in the shadows.

My heart thunders in my chest and I briefly wonder how the hell I'm going to get away with this. If I somehow manage to make it through to morning, I'm going to have to hitch a ride and get my ass as far from here as possible. Hell, a fucking one-way ticket to anywhere but here will do.

My momentum has my feet slamming hard against the road, and my stomach drops as the noise echoes toward the warehouse. They have to know. They're too good at what they do to allow me even the chance to get away with this.

Nausea burns within me, and I promise myself that if I get out of this and am still alive come tomorrow morning, I'll spare a few extra seconds to throw up in a bush, but until then, I have to keep running. Soft music flows through the street, and it's my only hope that it's loud enough to drown out the sound of my escape.

Looking back over my shoulder, my gaze scans the front of the warehouse, but so far, I see nothing. The brothers are nowhere in sight and that could only mean one thing—they have no fucking idea.

My foot hits the edge of the road, and I launch myself toward the thick shadows of the woods when big fingers knot into the back of my hair. I'm yanked back and a loud, pained screech tears out of me as I'm knocked right off my feet.

My body crashes onto the road with a hard thud, and before I get a chance to fight off my attacker, he takes off, dragging me along the rough asphalt. My skin burns as the road rips it to shreds. I try desperately to get my feet under me as I reach up to the tight fist knotted in my hair, clawing at his skin.

"LET ME GO," I scream, digging in with everything that I have and feeling his blood pooling under my nails.

"FUCK," he roars, throwing me hard across the road and into the dim light splaying out from the old warehouse. It's not a voice I recognize and my heart pounds, the loud pulse like Levi's drums right in my ears.

My body skids across the road like a tumbleweed caught in the wind, and I do everything that I can to try and ease the momentum, only the man is there again. I look up, meeting his hard stare, and as he steps into the dim light, recognition has my chest sinking.

It's the guy from the party, the arrogant asshole with the bad attitude who jumped the bar in the hopes of strangling me right there in the middle of the room. Marcus had shown up just moments before he could slit my throat, and in return, I stabbed him right in the gut. Roman had disposed of him, and in my mind, I figured that meant he was already dead. If I knew he was the man they were coming for tonight, that they'd planned a nice little trip to properly see him off to the underworld, there's no way I would have allowed myself to be so vulnerable. Fuck, I guess that's what you get for playing with fire.

What the fuck was Roman thinking allowing him to walk away? That's not how the game is supposed to work. This should have already been dealt with.

I scramble away from him, knowing damn well that I won't be able to get up on my feet and away from him by the time he reaches down to end my life. I'm well and truly fucked.

"Well, well, this certainly is a nice surprise," the asshole says, a sick grin twisting across his face as he recognizes me from the party. "I'm going to enjoy this."

He reaches down and I let out an ear-shattering scream in the hopes that the brothers will somehow come through for me, but I haven't got a chance in hell. I put myself in this situation and they're not exactly the heroes whose sole dreams are to swoop in and save the damsel in distress.

His big hand curls around my wrist and he drags me back across the road, pulling me closer and closer to the big warehouse and into its dim lighting. "Hey boys," the guy hollers through his piece of shit warehouse. "The DeAngelis brothers left us a toy to play with."

Oh, fuck no.

"LET GO OF ME," I scream, tears stinging my eyes as he drags me past the random cars and into the center of the room. The guy laughs as he releases me on the ground of the filthy warehouse, and I watch in horror as he peels off his dirty jacket.

The place is a fucking mess. The same pills from the party are scattered all over the warehouse with white powder staining every available surface. There are empty beer bottles filled to the brim with cigarette butts and old pizza boxes strewn across the dirty floor. It makes me sick just being in it, but that's the least of my problems.

He looks down at me as men appear from the shadows, creeping in to get a front row seat to the main performance of the night. He crouches down, looking at me like a piece of meat that he's about to destroy. "Those sorry fuckers have finally screwed with the wrong guy," he spits, the scowl across his face having absolutely nothing on Roman's signature one. "They think they can disrespect me? I'll fucking destroy them for what they did, but not before I make you wish that you were never born. You're a fucking dead *bitch*. I'm gonna take it slow and you're going to feel it all, every slice of the blade, every tear of your skin. Your screams are going to echo through my warehouse for months, but not before I destroy your fucking soul first."

"Too late, asshole," I spit back at him, completely surrounded by his vile men. "You can't kill something that's already dead."

He laughs, standing as he reaches for his belt buckle. "Watch me."

Fuck. The one time I actually need the brothers, they're nowhere to be seen. Maybe this is their version of punishment for trying to slip away into the night. Fuck them and their twisted teaching moments.

The guy tears his belt straight out of its loopholes as he nods toward his henchmen. Two of them drop down on either side of me, holding me down as their boss rolls his tongue over his lips. I cry out as their fingers dig into my skin, their filthy body odor overwhelming my senses.

Boss man reaches for me, grabbing the waistband of my sweatpants as my heart races, the fear quickly becoming too much. It's one thing to let Levi and Marcus take me any way they want, but this is different on so many levels. I won't make it through this. I won't survive if they touch me. I'm not strong enough.

My sweatpants are torn right off my legs and fat tears stream down my face as I scream out for help, but I saw the area as we were driving in. This industrial estate is as abandoned as they come. That's probably the reason they chose here as their place of operation. They get away with all kinds of shit and I'm probably just one in a very long line of victims.

Desperate to try and save myself, I bring my knee up, slamming it right into the stab wound I'd given him last night. He flies back onto his hands as he lets out a pained cry. Rage settles over his face, and I fear that all I've done is anger the beast.

"YOU FUCKING BITCH," he roars, righting himself just moments before his heavy fist comes down over my face, splitting the fragile skin of my cheek as my head rebounds off the dirty concrete floor.

My vision spins and I crave the sweet peace of death, but I know it won't come, he won't let that happen until he's completely destroyed me first.

"Enjoying what's mine, I see," a familiar deep tone rumbles, cutting through the pain and sending the slightest sliver of hope coursing through my veins. "You know, I could have sworn that I warned you about touching what was mine just last night."

The guy spins around, his movement allowing me to see Marcus stepping out of the shadows, but he's not the only one. Roman comes from the back of the warehouse as Levi steps in from the left. The three grim reapers, coming to put my misery to an end. At least, that's how I'm assuming this is going to go. I can't imagine that they're thrilled with me right now.

The guy shakes his head as the men holding me down rush to get to their feet, recognizing the threat in the room, and knowing that despite their numbers, they don't stand a fucking chance. "The fucking bitch ain't worth it," he spits. "You left her wandering around my property. She's mine now. You know how this works."

Roman laughs and it almost sounds like he pities the man, but he is as good as dead, so I guess it doesn't matter what bullshit spurts from his mouth tonight. There's no changing the outcome of what's about to go down. Though it's a real shame he had to go and involve all his friends in this. All he's done here tonight is sign their death certificates too.

As the surrounding men keep their attention on the brothers, I scramble to my feet, grabbing my sweatpants before racing toward Roman. He's probably the least likely to care about keeping me safe, but he's also the least likely to allow anyone to slip past him. I see him as the brutal, unforgiving type. He'd be the type to get in and get the job done where the other two I fear would take their time, enjoy their kills to satisfy that wicked piece of their dark souls.

Being away from their circle allows me the chance to breathe and take it all in. As far as I can see, the boys aren't holding any weapons, but they're also wearing black hoodies that probably have a million places to stash blades or guns. Though something tells me that their greatest weapons are their hands.

They slowly start creeping in toward the men, and I watch as the cocky confidence quickly fades from each of their faces. They know better than most what kind of guys they're dealing with and running their mouths certainly didn't do them any favors.

There are six of them standing in the center of the warehouse, and as I glance across at Levi on the opposite side of the room, I take in the focused excitement brewing in his eyes. This is the kind of night that he dreams about.

One of the assholes who had been holding me down, cuts and bails. He turns on his heel and bolts for the open warehouse door, leaving his boys to face the DeAngelis wrath, knowing that he doesn't stand a chance if he were to stay.

I watch him go and the brothers allow him to get ahead just a few steps before Marcus' hand flies out with the force of a striking python. I watch with wide eyes as a silver blade sails through the air with lightning speed, and with a sickening crunch, plunges straight through the back of the runner's throat.

I suck in a loud gasp, shrinking back as the runner comes to an immediate standstill. He turns, the dim light of the warehouse barely shining upon him as his fingers claw at his throat. A gurgling sound fills the warehouse, and as blood pours out the corners of his mouth, the man falls to his knees, the dim light glistening against the tip of the blade that protrudes from the front of his throat.

A perfect shot.

My eyes widen in horror and I fall back, scrambling to get further away as I watch the man fall forward and quickly begin to bleed out. His men roar in fury, and before I can even let out a scream, the brothers descend.

Their speed is like nothing I've ever seen before, going from a standstill to a powerful sprint as they race in for what I'm sure they believe to be the sweetest kind of revenge. Marcus goes straight for the guy I'd stabbed as Roman aims for the two closest to him.

Levi is the quickest and reaches the guy closest to him before he even gets his gun pulled from the back of his stained jeans. I scream, a blood-curdling sound as I watch Levi violently snap the guy's neck with a ferocious twist. His head all but comes right off his fucking body with a loud crunch before Levi releases him, letting him crumble into a sorry pile at his feet.

I scurry back, unable to look away from the horrors as my heart races, the terror quickly pulsing through my veins. Marcus plays with his guy, dragging out his fun as Roman becomes surrounded by the three other men.

He holds them off with ease, pulling a blood-red dagger, and with a quick flick of his wrist, his blade severs a guy's hand clean off his body. He falls to his knees in agony and the loud grunt that tears from deep within him is one that will haunt me until my dying days. He throws his head back to scream, and not missing such a welcoming opportunity, Roman quickly finishes him off with his red blade searing straight down through the hollow at the base of his neck, not stopping until the tip of his blade pierces straight through his heart.

Roman leaves him drowning in his own blood, and as he turns to focus on the two remaining, Levi offers a helpful hand.

He steps in behind the chunkier one, leaving the easy kill for Roman, and politely taps on his shoulder as though he's about to discuss the man's extended warranty. Only as he turns, Levi whips his arm around in a low arc, slicing a thick blade from one hip to the other. Bile rises in my throat and I hold back a violent heave as his intestines tumble from his open wound like a string of sausages sploshing against the dirty ground with a sickening splash.

What the ever-loving fuck am I witnessing right now? They're brutal. Callous. Unforgiving. And fuck, they actually enjoy this shit.

Marcus' howling laughter only goes to prove that he's putting in the bare minimum to play with his guy so he can still watch the vile slaughtering going on around him like the sick fuck that he is. But why the hell not? They're down to two against the three brothers, and so far, only thirty seconds have passed. If this gets them off, they might as well take their time.

Roman quickly takes care of the other guy, leaving just the asshole from last night's party. I block out what's left of the five other bodies scattered around the dirty concrete floor and focus on the fear radiating out of the man's eyes.

His body is covered head to toe with shallow cuts, each one of them delivered swiftly by Marcus' blade. He trembles as both Roman and Levi surround him, and honestly, I don't blame him. I'd be a fucking mess too. Hell, it's not even me standing against them and I'm a mess.

Roman and Levi take the guy's arms and hold them out as Marcus steps into him and kicks his legs far apart. "It seems we've got ourselves a bit of a situation," Marcus mutters, his sick gaze trailing across to where I hide, trembling in a dark corner of the warehouse.

His attention turns back to the man. "But don't worry, we're going to make things right."

The guy tugs and pulls at the brothers' tight hold, but I've been on the other end of their strength. It's like nothing I've ever experienced before. They're machines—impenetrable and relentless. If they want to hold you down, then that's where you will stay, until they deem otherwise.

Marcus tosses a blade aside and it clatters against the ground before he pulls out a fresh one, twice the size and somehow even shinier. This is the kind of blade that means business.

As if reading each other's mind, Roman and Levi release their hold on him and kick out the back of his knees. He falls forward, catching himself against his hands, and before he can make a move, the boys' heavy boots come crashing down over his hands, keeping him pinned on his hands and knees.

Marcus crouches in front of him, his blade glistening in the light. "Do you know what happens to men who touch what's mine?" he questions as the guy stares up at him in horror. "They lose their ability to."

Without warning, the blade comes down over his hand, effortlessly slicing his four fingers straight off as he roars in agony. Marcus laughs, getting the worst kind of enjoyment out of this, but before even a drop of blood can even spill out on the ground, Roman grips his hair and yanks his head right back, forcing his stare back up to Marcus.

"Do you know what happens to a man who spits filthy words at my girl?" Marcus questions, sending dread flowing through my body. I shake my head, not wanting this to be true, but as I watch Levi grab a pair of pliers from his pocket and force the guy's mouth open, I know exactly where this is leading.

After a short struggle, Levi stands before the guy, his tongue held tightly between the pair of pliers as Marcus moves in beside his younger brother. "A man who talks down at what's mine, will never speak again." And with that, they take his tongue, letting it fall to the ground as blood spurts out of his mouth.

The violent heaves return and as the brothers force the man to his feet, I throw up, unable to handle the horrendous sight. The man sobs, the sound distorted by his missing tongue, and I look away, but the familiar sound of jeans hitting the ground has a newfound fire pulsing through my veins.

Knowing that what happens next will visit me in my dreams for nights on end, I focus my stare back on the man to find his jeans down around his ankles and Marcus' blade pressed firmly beneath his limp dick and balls. "Oh my," Marcus grins. "I might need a smaller blade for this one."

"Fuck you," the guy roars, spitting blood in Marcus' face as what's left of his tongue begins to swell in his mouth, slowly blocking his airway.

Marcus just laughs as Roman moves in behind the guy, holding a knife to his throat to force his cooperation. "I'm sure you've caught on to our little game by now," Marcus mutters darkly, his tone filled with a menacing promise to draw this out for as long as he can.

"I have one last question for you," Marcus continues, pausing as he applies just a little more pressure on the blade. "What do you think happens to a rapist who tries to steal the innocence out of what's mine?"

Rather than making a quick arc and slicing his dick right off, Marcus begins moving the knife slowly left and right like he was slicing a loaf of bread, tearing through the sensitive skin and painstakingly taking from him just as he had planned to take from me.

The bile in my throat rises as I frantically clamp one hand over my mouth. This man was going to rape me. He was going to torture and kill me in the vilest way. I want to look at anything but the carnage in front of me, but I can't bring myself to avert my eyes. His death is the sweetest revenge I'll ever get.

Once the blade has completed its mission of world domination, and the floppy torn appendage is lying in a pool of blood, the man falls to the ground where he slowly bleeds out.

Knowing that he won't be going anywhere, Marcus and Levi stride out of the warehouse as though they didn't just brutally murder six men.

Roman steps toward me. His hard glare meets my tear-stained face, and as he towers over me, I want nothing more than to shrink away. "Move," he growls, his single word filled with venom and a guarantee that I will surely be punished for my escape attempt.

Knowing better than to make things worse for myself, I get up on shaky legs and move my ass across the warehouse, stepping over discarded limbs and pools of intestines before hurrying back to the safety of the Escalade.

TWENTY-ONE

My stomach grumbles as I sit cross-legged on my bed. It's been twenty-four hours since the attack at the old warehouse and I've been grateful that the boys have left me in peace.

What I saw there … I just can't get the images out of my head.

The blood, the blades, the floppy appendage on the ground.

The DeAngelis brothers are so much worse than I thought they were. I knew they were dangerous, and I sure as hell knew they were brutal monsters, but what I witnessed was far beyond anything I could have even imagined.

Before I met them, when someone mentioned their names, the

first thought that came to mind was the callous way they would blindly shoot someone without rhyme or reason, just like I witnessed with that girl at their party. Though, she should have known better than to try and steal from the DeAngelis brothers.

News of their attacks were constantly splashed on my old television, but I'm only now just realizing how many details those news stories were leaving out. I have to give them credit, they certainly know a thing or two about creativity.

I mean … his fucking dick? Who cuts off a man's dick? Don't get me wrong, the asshole deserved it. He never got a chance to touch me, but I'm not so naive to think that I was the only one, and others might not have been so lucky. Though, perhaps the word *lucky* doesn't exactly fit the situation.

I am anything but lucky.

That shot Marcus made from across the warehouse, plunging the knife into the runner's throat, was perfect in all the wrong ways. The strength and precision that must have taken astounds me, while the way Levi gutted that man with such a practiced skill only goes to show how often they've done this.

Roman though, he didn't even think twice before slicing that man's hand right off his body and then plunging that dagger through his throat to pierce his heart.

My stomach twists with the thought and I find myself bolting across my room, slamming through the door of my private bathroom before my knees drop against the cool marble tiles. A violent heave tears through me as I hang my head over the rim of the toilet, only just like the million other times that I've been here, not a damn thing comes out.

I lean against the bathroom wall as a light sweat appears on my forehead. This world that I've somehow got myself caught up in is insane. But I have to be honest, while what I witnessed last night was the most terrifying thing any human should ever bear witness to, it could have been worse.

Up until that moment, I had foolishly convinced myself that there was something good in them. That they were just misunderstood, broken souls with daddy issues like the rest of us. Sure, they were brutal and cruel and dealt with their issues a little differently, but they were still human. I'd even allowed myself to get close enough to be vulnerable around them.

But despite their flaws, despite their unforgiving, brutal, and murderous ways, they've left me in peace to wrap my head around it. I could feel the anger coming off them in waves during the long car ride home. I could feel the tension boiling in the car, feel their overwhelming need to punish me for trying to escape them, but they've left me in peace. Left me to try and move past this, left me to grieve the old life that I will never get back.

They've shown me kindness and I'm grateful for that.

They don't want to hurt me, and though they probably look at the situation differently than I do, I see what lengths they'd go through to protect me.

I hear them around the castle, constantly walking by my door and stopping just outside to check on me, yet not one of them has forced their way in and demanded an explanation. Maybe there's hope for them after all, or maybe they're avoiding offering an explanation of their own.

My stomach growls again but this time more ferociously. I know I'm going to have to face them at some point. Eventually, they'll tire of my reluctance and come for me anyway. The best thing to do is take the reins and play their game.

Getting to my feet, I let out a shaky breath, fearing the thoughts that will haunt me when I see their faces. I make my way over to the sink and splash water over my face before glancing at myself in the mirror.

My lifeless blue eyes stare back at me, but I slap on a brave face, straightening my shoulders and raising my chin. I can do this. I can be brave, and I sure as fuck can survive.

Turning on my heel, I stride out of my bathroom and out into the main hall before I give myself the chance to change my mind. I hear Levi in the distance, his drums echoing through the castle as a muffled conversation comes from the opposite direction.

Trying to hold on to that courage, I start making my way down the stairs. There's no doubt that they already know I've emerged from my hideout. I'm barely making a noise, but where the DeAngelis brothers are concerned, they know everything that goes down in their home.

Hitting the bottom step, I make my way through the many twists and turns until I finally reach the dining room. Finding the table filled with everything delicious, I make my way right to it. My gaze skims over the endless options and finding a big juicy steak right in the center, I prop my ass on the edge of the table and reach.

Why the hell do they need such a big table?

I'm forced to kneel across the table just to get to it, and as I push other plates and cutlery out of my way, I hope to whoever exists above that one of the brothers had their heart set on this particular piece of meat. At least that way, I'll be able to take something, even though small, from one of them.

Not having the energy to climb off the table and find an appropriate chair, I drop my ass to the hardwood and drag the plate on top of my legs before dressing it with everything delicious. I add some baked potatoes, throw in a few steamed veggies and then saturate it with gravy.

My mouth waters. It's been far too long since I've eaten well. I know that I'll probably regret this meal once the images from last night come flooding back, but I need the energy to keep me going.

Scanning around the table, I search out a knife and fork, and as my gaze shifts over a steak knife, I can't help but remember that Marcus is supposed to be punishing me for what I did to his hand. But if I'm honest, I really don't think it's coming.

Just like everything else, I put it to the back of my mind and focus on the task at hand. Scooping up the knife and fork, I get busy, digging into the best parts as I sit with my legs dangling off the side of the table.

As I drop the first bite of juicy steak into my mouth, I roll it around and groan in satisfaction. I guess life can still be good, but as I'm chewing, I realize that I can no longer hear Levi's drumming and it only goes to remind me that from here on out, not all parts of life are going to be good.

I pause to listen, but just as my head snaps up, the three assholes appear in the open entryway of the massive dining room.

Dread flitters through me as I take them in. Marcus looks chill as fuck with a joint in his hand and a lighter in the other. Levi still grips his drumsticks and looks as though he's pissed that his brothers have called him away from his drums, while Roman just wears his signature scowl.

I swallow hard as I grab the plate from off my legs. "So," I say, lowering my tone as a forced, wicked grin stretches across my face. "How do you like your steak?"

A cockiness pulls at Marcus' lips as he strides deeper into the room, walking straight by me to his favorite position at the head of the table. "Fucking raw."

Roman scoffs to himself. "Right, you seem more like a medium done kinda guy to me."

A knife flies straight across the room, the tip skimming past my face and narrowly missing Roman's eye before plunging deep into the wall behind his head. Roman doesn't even look up and it leaves me wondering just how common flying knives are around here. Maybe that scar on his face was more of a 'serial killers will be serial killers' type of incident rather than a fucked the wrong man's wife one.

Levi is the last to take his seat. He's the closest to me with both of his brothers at opposite ends. His drumsticks rest in his hands, and as he leans back in his chair, he lightly drums them against the wooden table. "How do you want to do this?" he questions, getting straight to the point as I take in the way that his brothers cautiously eye me, waiting for me to freak out.

Nerves filter through my body as my gaze drops to his hands, remembering just how skilled they really are. "What do you mean?" I ask with a shaky breath, feeling completely surrounded.

"Last night," he confirms as if he didn't already know that we're more than on the same page. "Are we pretending that it didn't happen, or do you need to vent your frustrations?"

My eyes bug out of my head and I gape at him in horror. "Frustrations? That's what you're calling it? You guys slaughtered those men as though they didn't have family or friends. You're monsters."

"Great," Roman mutters darkly. "She wants to talk about it."

"I don't want to talk about shit," I throw back at him, more than prepared to throw a knife at him just like Marcus had. Though my aim wouldn't be nearly as great. "Trust me, I'm doing everything that I can to pretend I didn't see what you did last night, but it's not that easy. The images in my head … they won't go away."

Marcus sighs. "You do understand what they were going to do to you, right? They weren't preparing you for a fucking ping-pong show."

I give him a hard stare. "Of course I know what they wanted to do. I'm not fucking stupid. But slaughtering men isn't the way to go about it. There's something seriously not right with you guys. How can you just sit here and act like this isn't a big deal?"

"Because it's not," Levi says. "Would you have preferred that we just sat back and let it happen?"

"Of course not," I growl, the frustration quickly getting the best of me as my gaze drops back to my steak and I violently start cutting it into pieces, more than likely scratching the shit out of the expensive plate below.

"So, it's settled. We saved the girl," Marcus says proudly. "We're the fucking heroes that you never knew you needed."

My glare shoots straight down the table, boring into his with a ferociousness I wasn't aware I was capable of. I hold up my steak knife. "Bring me your other hand. Let me show you my latest party trick."

Excitement bubbles in his dark stare, and the longer he holds me hostage with it, the more heated it becomes. "Don't threaten me with a good time," he warns.

Fuck, for just a moment, I forgot how deranged this psychopath was.

My gaze narrows and I refuse to be the first to look away, but there's no way in hell that I have what it takes to win this round. A twisted grin edges across his face, and as he drops his chin and watches me through his thick row of lashes, I have no choice but to succumb.

I glance back down at my steak just as a shrill ringing cuts through the room. All three of the boys sigh as one as Roman pulls his phone from his pocket. He drops the phone onto the table and stares down at it with a heavy scowl before finally accepting the call and putting it on speaker. "Father," Roman says, his tone low and full of disdain.

"Do you have any idea of the trouble that I have gone through for you pitiful vermin over the past twelve hours?"

Marcus lets out a deep sigh. "Always a pleasure, Father. However, you're going to have to give us a little more than that. I'm positive that we haven't got a clue what you're talking about."

"Don't you dare play your fucked-up little games with me, boy," he spits, attempting to put his middle son in place, only the bored expression on Marcus' face says that he's accomplishing absolutely nothing. "The murders in the industrial area have your stench all over it."

"Oooooh, that," Marcus laughs as Roman shakes his head, probably knowing all too well the dangers of messing with his father. "That was just a little misunderstanding, but don't worry. We cleared it right up."

"A little misunderstanding?" he roars, the sound screeching through the room and making my ears hurt. "A misunderstanding isn't finding a limp cock on the ground next to a set of fucking intestines. What have I told you about leaving a scene like that? I've had the cops sniffing around me all fucking morning, asking questions and demanding answers. Do you have any idea what kind of heat you've put us under? Fucking hell. The whole family has to lie low."

"We have plenty of space here," Marcus suggests, sending a cold chill sweeping through my body as his obsidian eyes darken to a shade I've never seen before. "We'd be more than happy to host the entire family. I'm sure they'd love to see all the little surprises we have in store for them."

There's a short silence before Giovanni growls. "Explain yourselves. You're not to leave the confines of that property without my explicit say so. You had no kill orders."

"Ahhhh, shit," Marcus taunts, making the situation so much worse. "You see, I must have forgotten that my own father is callous enough to keep his three sons prisoner in their own home, only allowed out to perform the kind of tasks that he doesn't have the guts to do himself. Thanks for the reminder."

"You dare call me weak? I taught you everything you know."

"No, Father," he says, his tone dropping to a deadly challenge. "You taught me how to fire a gun. Everything else, I learned by imagining the kinds of things I would do to you. If only you weren't such a coward to show up here without your protection detail. I wonder how well you'd fare, though I also wonder what your precious family would think of you if they knew you were terrified of your own sons."

Shots fucking fired.

My eyes bug out of my head as my jaw practically drops right to the table. I stare across the room at Marcus, hardly able to believe what I'm hearing, though the bored expressions on Levi and Roman's faces suggests that this is a regular occurrence, but who fucking cares? This is prime time entertainment. Hell, I'm even willing to momentarily forget about the shit I saw last night just to be able to witness Giovanni DeAngelis get put in his place by his own damn son.

And here I thought the brothers overthrowing their father was some kind of big secret. If he hasn't worked it out by now, then he's not the fearless mafia leader that I always pictured him to be. Though, if anyone should be standing in his place, my guess would be Roman. He's got everything he needs to rule over the whole fucking country. But that begs the question—why are they really kept as prisoners here? Are they too dangerous to be allowed their freedom due to their relaxed views on murder, or does Giovanni fear how easily they could take everything away from him?

Levi grows bored of the conversation and stands. He makes his way around the table, his gaze focused heavily on the phone in front of his eldest brother. "Anyway, Father," he says in a lazy tone. "Like Marcus mentioned, it's been a fucking pleasure."

"DON'T YOU DARE HANG UP ON—"

Levi stretches out in front of Roman and drops his finger to the little red button on the front of the screen, cutting off his father with a sick satisfaction deep in his eyes. "Fuck, he's exhausting," he says as Roman leans back in his seat and turns his gaze on Marcus.

"Really?" he questions. "Why not go right ahead and tell him our whole fucking plan to overthrow him while you were at it? I bet he'd love to know exactly how we plan on doing this."

Marcus shrugs before reaching across the table with his fork, stabbing a piece of steak and dropping it onto his plate. "What can I say?" he mutters. "I was in the moment."

"Yeah, we know," Levi scoffs. "You're a fucking loose cannon when you're in the moment."

The brothers casually talk between themselves while annihilating the vast array of food around them, throwing meaningless threats at one another and bonding over their shared hatred of their father. I sit in silence, taking it all in. I can't help but feel at ease, something I never thought possible about being in their presence.

I'm safe here among these beautifully broken souls, but one thing is for sure, Levi was right. Marcus is a loose cannon; they all are. And while I may *feel* safe, that doesn't necessarily mean that I am. They're broken from a lifetime of abuse, and I guarantee that they've never been taught what it means to care, love, or even show true kindness. They're soldiers through and through. Weapons trained not to miss. Getting too close to them would be a mistake, one that would cost me dearly.

The brothers are only just getting started with me, and something tells me that I have one hell of a fight to survive.

TWENTY-TWO

*B*ANG!

My door rebounds against the drywall as scuffles quickly fill my room. My heart races as fear rocks through me. The scuffles get closer and hands are on me before I even get a chance to scream. They pull at me, dragging me to the foot of my bed as I wail, desperate to see through the darkness, desperate to get just a glimpse of their faces.

I kick out, connecting with something hard, but the pained grunt that tears through the room isn't familiar. "GET OFF ME," I scream so damn loud that the sound tears painfully up my throat.

The hands grip me tighter, effortlessly yanking me off my bed as

I struggle, shamelessly trying to free myself from the confines of their bruising grip. My body drops to the ground with a heavy thud and I cry out, but as I'm dragged across the floor and pass by the big window, the moonlight shines in, telling me my fears are right.

These guys aren't the DeAngelis brothers.

This is something much, much worse.

I cry out as I'm pulled off the ground and forced to my feet with a bruising jab under my ribs. A hand curls around my upper arm and propels me toward my bedroom door, sending me straight out into the hallway and slamming into the opposite wall.

Dim light shines through the hallway, but not nearly enough for me to make out their faces. I'm thrown straight back to that old warehouse with those filthy men touching me, holding me down and putting their hands on me.

Tears fill my eyes, but I don't dare give up, pulling and pushing, relentlessly trying to get free. "LET ME GO," I scream, my voice bouncing off the walls and echoing right down the hallway, but no one is coming. It's no use.

Where the fuck are the boys? Why are they allowing this to happen in their home? Have they run out of little games to play? Run out of mazes to stalk me through? Perhaps this is their punishment for escaping at the industrial estate.

They lead me through the massive castle, moving around the hallways as though they know exactly where they're going. We reach the top of the stairs and I'm pushed forward, barely managing to stay on my feet as I struggle the whole way to the bottom.

They release me just as we hit the last step and my weight drops right to the fucking marble tiles. My knees slam hard and I cry out, but they don't miss a step. Catching my arms once again, they drag me straight through the wide-open space.

I scramble behind them, desperately trying to get my feet back under myself, but they're too fast and way too fucking strong. I don't stand a chance. I try to glance up at them, hoping that I can recognize their faces from the boys' party, but I get nothing. These men are like soldiers, trained and heavily armed. They've been given a mission, and without a single word, have made it clear that they will see this through.

A dim light comes from one of the rooms and I'm not surprised when the men drag me in there. They pull me straight through the open doorway and I skid to a stop right at Levi's feet as they fall around the room, covering every damn exit.

My gaze snaps up as I desperately try to scurry away from Levi, only as I move closer to the center of the room, I quickly realize that this is something entirely different.

Levi stands with his brothers, all three of them with clenched jaws and murder in their eyes, looking like an impenetrable force. Not one of them even bother to look down at me as their heavy stares are locked across the room, staring at the man who holds the remote for the shock collars around their throats.

My eyes widen and I scramble right back toward Levi as I take in their father who stands with a wall of protection at his back, and despite the boys' wicked skills for eliminating targets, there's no way in hell they could stand against a force like this.

The way that he looks at his sons, it's clear that this is some type of retaliation for their little excursion into the old industrial area, and judging by the sweat coating Marcus' skin, this has been going on for quite some time while I peacefully slept upstairs.

My heart breaks as I desperately wish that I could somehow hide behind the boys, but something tells me that in a room like this, hiding is only going to see a bullet shot straight between my eyes.

I scramble to my sore, cut-up feet, disguising my cringe as my body aches from their rough hands. I stand before Levi, but as Giovanni steps around his security and fixes his stare on me, I pull back, pressing myself past Levi's shoulder until I stand between him and Marcus, my arms brushing up against theirs.

Giovanni doesn't stop, and as my instincts have me pulling further back, Marcus' hand discreetly presses against my back, keeping me still. "Why do my sons care for you?" he demands, stepping right into me and trailing his gaze up and down my body as though he didn't get enough of an eyeful of it over lunch.

I shake my head, my eyes wide as I feel my world coming to an end. "They … they don't care for me," I say, my words getting choked up in my throat, wishing that I could somehow find that courage I'd had when I'd faced him last.

"Is that so?" he questions, his chin raised as his eyes narrow on mine. "Because the way I understand it, Miss Mariano, is that after meeting Draven Miller and sliding your knife into his gut, my sons risked exposure to put him down. Tell me why they would do that?"

My back stiffens and I feel Marcus' hand tightening on my back, warning me to tread carefully. "Are you suggesting that I put the idea in their heads?"

"I'm not suggesting anything. Merely trying to get to the bottom of this."

"Then ask your sons," I fire back at him. "I have absolutely no influence over the things that occupy their time, and I highly doubt that they give a shit about what I think. Congratulations, you raised your sons to be the perfect little henchmen, only you seem to be having a little trouble keeping them in line. Though perhaps that has a little something more to do with you, than me."

A sharp slap stings my face and I let out a brief cry before biting my tongue, hating to show weakness in front of this vile man. "You watch your mouth, you filthy little whore," he growls at me. "I trained my sons to be soldiers. They don't step out of line."

"Really?" I question, narrowing my gaze, positive that I can take at least one more hit. "Because from where I'm looking in, your soldiers have been stepping out of line a lot longer than you care to admit, otherwise you wouldn't have them locked up here. Why is that? Are you scared of them? Do they make your knees shake? Send a cold chill sweeping through your body every time they look your way?"

His hand raises and I brace for another hit but just as it comes hurtling toward my face, Roman steps out, his strong arm snapping out in front of me and catching his father's wrist just moments before connecting with my face.

My eyes go wide as I watch the two of them struggle, locked in a motionless fight for dominance. Giovanni's men flinch, their hands hovering by their guns, more than prepared to put an immediate end to this.

"Leave her out of this," Roman spits through a clenched jaw. "She had nothing to do with it. Killing Miller was our decision. He disrespected our home and knowingly touched what was ours. Adding his friends to the scoreboard was purely a bonus."

The two of them stare each other down, strength against strength, and just as Roman begins to overpower his father, Giovanni presses a button that sends a fierce bolt of electricity shooting through Roman's collar, dropping him to his knees.

I suck in a loud gasp and shove my hands against Giovanni's chest, knocking him back a step. "STOP IT. LEAVE HIM ALONE," I yell, my eyes widening further as I realize that not only did I just yell at the man, I put my fucking hands on him as well.

I go to shrink back again but his hand snaps out and knots into a tangled mess in my hair. He throws me down with an impossible force as my heart hammers away in my chest. Giovanni steps toward me, his eyes narrowed in curiosity. "They do care for you," he muses as I clench my jaw, my breath coming in short, sharp pants.

My gaze flicks to Roman, still on his knees as his shock collar continues to keep him down. "Stop," I beg. "Why do they need to be punished? They've done nothing wrong. The guy and his asshole friends deserved it and you know it."

"Perhaps," Giovanni says as he draws a gun. My chest sinks as he slowly gazes over it, looking at it as though it were a long-lost friend. "What you're failing to understand is that my sons are my soldiers and they answer to me, and me alone. Despite my sons' ability to twist a story, they stepped out of line to protect some girl they barely even know. They ignored a direct order, they betrayed my trust and brought down a storm of hell over the DeAngelis family."

Giovanni glances back at his sons, his finger moving up and down the sleek metal of the gun as he releases Roman from his torture. "They must be punished," he says, crouching down as he looks back at me. Giovanni lowers his tone to a threatening whisper as Roman's deep breath sounds through the room. "Fortunately for you, Miss Mariano, I've learned that taking something they care about does not often pan out well for me, so I put the choice in your hands. Which one of them will die tonight?"

"What?" I breathe, positive that I didn't hear him correctly. My eyes widen in horror and I look back at the guys, all three of their ferocious stares locked on their father. "No, you can't make me. I won't."

He grins down at me before straightening up and turning to look at his sons. "On the contrary."

My heart thuds erratically and my body tenses as he steps back toward them. The three brothers are anything but angels, and while any court of law would gladly convict them with the death sentence, I simply can't get on board with it. I can't explain this weird feeling inside of me. They protected me in the old warehouse, they saved me from my attacker and despite the fucked-up situation we're in, I couldn't stand the thought of any of them getting hurt.

I shake my head, distantly noticing the way one of his men steps in closer to me, ready to finish me if I were to make a move.

Giovanni holds his gun up before slowly moving it between his sons. *"Eeny, meeny, miny, moe,"* he sings. *"Which of my sons has got to go?"*

The gun stops on Marcus and a sharp gasp tears from my throat, the very thought of him being shot right in front of me already haunting my every last thought. "NO," I rush out, the terror rich in my tone, my heart already squeezing with grief. "DON'T."

"No?" Giovanni questions, glancing back at me as he adjusts his position to aim the gun at Levi. "What about this one? I know he's got a pretty face, but it'd be a shame to waste those brains." I shake my head, tears welling in my eyes. Levi is intimidating as all hell. He's scary and ferocious, but there's still something good inside his heart.

Giovanni turns to his eldest son and steps right into him, pressing the gun to his temple, and there's no denying it, the excitement burning in his eyes tells me just how badly he wants to pull the trigger. "What about the mastermind?" he asks me, not taking his eyes off Roman's. "Tempting, isn't it?"

A loud sob tears from the back of my throat and I shake my head as the tears fall from my eyes. "No, if you want to murder your own sons, that's on you, but you will not put their blood on my hands," I demand, the overwhelming fear of not playing his game torments my mind. "I might have only known them for a few days, and while I can barely stand the sight of them, each one of them are better men than you will ever be. You want to give me a choice?" I spit. "Then turn that gun on yourself and pull the trigger. The world is better off without vile people like you."

Giovanni lets out a heavy sigh and looks back at me. "You see, that's not really how this works. You pick one, and I shoot. Otherwise, I'm left to make that decision for you, and trust me when I tell you that's not a decision that you want me to make."

I shake my head. "I'm not playing your fucking game."

"Very well then," he says, his gaze resting back on his three sons. "I guess the decision lies with me."

Silence falls across the room as he scans up and down the short row of his emotionless sons, softly singing *eeny, meeny miny, moe* on repeat. The way the boys stare right back, they fucking know that this could be the end, but they've made peace with it and are sure as hell prepared to haunt this motherfucker from the grave.

Giovanni narrows his gaze, and after a short pause, he drops his chin. As if on cue, another one of his henchmen comes striding in with a young girl held tightly in his impenetrable grasp. I get just a glimpse of her tear-streaked face and find her bound and gagged, covered head to toe in cuts and bruised with a face that I would recognize anywhere.

Abigail Henderson, one of the only girls from the club that I could have called a friend. "NOOOOO," I scream, my throat immediately aching as I rush forward. Two strong hands grip my arms, locking me in a vice-like hold.

Tears stream down her face and she watches me with fear, but before I even get a chance to plead for her life, Giovanni looks my way. "I've made my choice." And just like that, a perfectly round bullet plunges right between her eyes.

TWENTY-THREE

Abigail's lifeless body drops to the ground as a ferocious cry tears from the back of my throat. Blood splatters across the wall behind her and my hand shoots down to the hip of the guard who holds me. Without a second thought, my palm curls around the cool metal at his hip and I tear the gun right out of its holster.

My arm rises and I wildly shoot as a fucking battle cry tears out of my throat. The kickback has me falling back against the guard as the bullet strays through the small room, the sound of the gun ringing in my ears.

Men drop to the ground, terrified of death, but not the boys. Levi lashes out, socking his father right in the face as Roman and Marcus jump straight into action, more than ready to fight for their lives.

The three of them jump their father as the guards rush in, desperate to find some kind of peace. Marcus growls, a ferocious sound that tears at my chest, leaving him wide open.

I'm thrown on top of Abigail's lifeless body as the guard who held me races in to be the fucking hero of the hour. I crawl off her, unable to glance down in fear of what I might see. The pain is too fucking real, but right now, I can't think about it, I just need to get out.

A clatter sounds on the ground to my right and my head snaps up to find the small remote sliding across the marble tiles. I scurry after it, desperately trying to avoid the wild scuffle around me. I throw myself toward it, the gun forgotten on the ground beside me.

My hands shake as Marcus' pained groans echo through the room, but I get it in my hands, flipping it over to somehow try and make sense of the remote. There are buttons everywhere but I have to be fast. The boys don't stand a fucking chance with those shock collars around their throats, and I have no way to know if this is the only remote.

Guns sound through the room as the scuffle continues, pained grunts and curses flying from left to right. Blood splatters across the room as Giovanni's men work tireless to try and free their boss, but even with a man down, the brothers are un-fucking-stoppable.

Marcus drops to his knees as the pain becomes unbearable and I fret, not understanding a damn thing written across the front of the remote. This shit is written in German. "I … I don't know how to turn it off," I cry out, the panic quickly beginning to overwhelm me.

Marcus' head snaps up as he grips the sides of the shock collar, desperately trying to pry it from his charred skin. Relief sparks in his eyes as he sees the remote in my hands "THE BIG—ARGHHH—RED ONE."

I slam my thumb down over it and the electrifying shock crippling Marcus comes to an immediate stop. He doesn't allow himself even a moment to recover before he throws himself to his feet and races toward me.

He snatches the remote right out of my hands and hits a few more buttons, and in unison, the three shock collars around the boys' throats click open. Marcus pulls it free from his neck and I can't help but notice the raw skin beneath as he reaches down and grips my arm.

I'm pulled to my feet and shoved toward the door, but before I can even get a step away, one of Giovanni's men comes for me. Marcus spins with his jaw clenched, and as a piercing scream tears from my throat, he takes the metal collar and beats the living shit out of the guy.

He lays dead at my feet as Marcus grabs my shoulders and shoves me toward the door. "GO," he roars. "GO AND FUCKING HIDE."

I don't need to be told twice.

I race for the door, glancing back just in time to watch Marcus slam the remote against a heavy wooden desk, smashing it into a thousand pieces. Roman stands just over his shoulder, snapping the neck of one of the guards while Levi grabs a man's head in his big hands and digs his thumbs deep into his eye sockets.

My stomach churns just as a bullet lodges into the doorframe right beside my head, and I take that as my cue to fuck off out of here. The boys are holding their own just fine, but they simply don't have the numbers. It won't be long until Giovanni's men overpower them and they're put down, just as their father has always wanted. But the second that happens, he'll be coming for me.

Grabbing hold of the door frame, I propel myself out of the room, running as fast as I possibly can, tears streaming down my face for Abigail while the heaviness sits on my heart for the boys. They won't make it out of this, which is another three lives lost because of me.

I skip up the stairs with lightning speed, taking them two at a time, too fucking scared to look back in case I find one of Giovanni's henchmen right on my heels.

I hit the top of the stairs and I don't even think about where I'm going, I just run.

Gunshots sound on the floor below me and each one shatters something inside me that I didn't even know existed. I don't know how, and I sure as hell don't know when, but at some point, I started to care about these brothers. But I have to put that behind me now. They're as good as dead down there and now it's my turn to fight for my life.

I have to get out of here. It's one thing having the brothers wake me in the middle of the night with their sick and twisted games, but having Giovanni DeAngelis coming after me? Fuck no. This is too much.

I take turns that I've never explored before, twisting up the winding staircase and along narrow hallways. Tears stream down my face as all I can manage to do is think about the fear in Abigail's eyes as Giovanni pulled the trigger. He murdered her because of me. Because I refused to allow the blood of his sons to be on my hands. I thought I was doing the right thing, yet somehow I still got screwed.

Just like Felicity. She got too close and she paid the ultimate price. I guess Giovanni doesn't want history to repeat itself so he's just going to deal with the issue before it becomes one.

I keep going higher, sprinting up every staircase I can find, terrified of the noises coming from behind me. Dust fills every hallway and it's clear that this space hasn't seen the light of day in years. Curiosity pulls at me, and if I had the time or wasn't in the middle of running for my life, I'd be searching through each room, trying to discover every hidden secret this place holds. But right now, it means nothing to me because no matter what, I'm getting the fuck out of here tonight. I have no other choice.

Marcus said to go and hide, but I can't trust that he'll be here to find me. I want to put my faith in them, I want to believe that they're going to be alright, but the odds are stacked against them. There's no way they can make it out of this alive.

I come up one last staircase. It's small and only has five steps, and if it weren't for the moonlight shining in through the arched windows along the hallway, I wouldn't be able to see a damn thing.

One lone door sits at the end of the hallway. It has to be the oldest thing in this place. It's a huge piece of old oak with big black hinges and a matching handle that looks as though it weighs a ton.

I creep toward it and my stomach sinks. The rest of the castle looks somewhat newish, but not this. The stone walls and creepy arches are putting me straight back downstairs to the torture chambers below. I'm not going to lie, it's creepy as fuck. My choices are to forge forward or turn back, and turning back just isn't an option.

My fingers curl around the cold metal handle and I give it a hard shove, having to slam my hip into it to get it to budge. It opens with a loud creak, immediately sending chills sweeping down my spine.

The heavy oak door opens just enough for me to slip inside, and the second my gaze rests upon the room, I feel a deathly chill against my skin. This is a big fucking mistake. My back instantly slams up against the heavy door that I just stepped through as my eyes widen in horror.

A glass case coffin rests right in the center of the fucking room, a halo of light shining out from beneath it. "Oh, hell no," I breathe, shaking my head, too fucking terrified to take even a step away from the door as my heart pounds heavily in my chest.

The door slams shut under my weight and panic quickly overwhelms my system. I spin around, grabbing hold of the heavy metal handle and pulling as hard as I fucking can, but it doesn't budge. It's determined to keep me trapped inside this big-ass, twisted freezer.

I try and try again, my desperation quickly wearing me down as tears spring to my eyes. I can't be here. This is too much; it's too fucking weird.

I claw at the door until my fingers bleed, banging my fists against the hard oak as I scream for freedom, but I'm fucking trapped.

What in the motherfucking, messed up, Snow White bullshit

fuckery is going on in here? Who the fuck keeps a dead guy inside a glass coffin for them to come and watch over? What is this? Some old girlfriend that they're hoping to pucker up for and bring her back to life?

Fucking hell.

I thought being stalked through mazes and witnessing callous murders would be the worst part. I couldn't have been more wrong.

Realizing just how fucked I truly am, I turn back around, my mind taking me to a million places that I don't want to go. Though the one question that plagues my thoughts is who's in the box? And fuck me in the ass, please don't let it be an empty box that they're hoping to use for me.

My hands shake as my knees threaten to buckle beneath me, and despite my better judgment, I find myself creeping toward it. I get three steps in before I can make out what looks like long black hair, but shit, there's nothing even remotely pretty about it.

My stomach sinks. The glass is foggy and I realize that this is some kind of deep freezer, and from the looks of it, it's definitely a woman. My hand clenches at my side. All I would need to do is swipe my hand over the glass and I'd be able to see her face clearly, but how messed up does one person have to be to actually do it?

My curiosity gets the best of me, and my hand shakes as I gently brush my fingers across the glass, positive that something is about to jump out at me.

Before I can change my mind, I take a deep breath and peer inside.

A woman stares up at me and my loud squeal pierces through the room as I stumble back, my heart thundering with fear.

Short gasps force their way out of my throat, and after a long pause, I finally start to calm my racing heart. I creep back toward the woman and hesitantly peer down at her. This is the most fucked up thing I have ever seen. The woman looks uncomfortable and her skin is an off shade that could only be achieved with death.

Is this Felicity?

I study her decomposing features, trying to imagine what this woman could have looked like with life pulsing through her veins, with warm skin and a flirty smile, but I just don't see it. Her eyes are dark, so fucking dark that they somehow remind me of the three monsters downstairs. Is this their mother?

I don't know anything about the process of preserving a dead body or how long it can even be kept, but I was under the impression that the boys' mother died a long time ago. They haven't exactly opened up about her, but surely if men like this grew up with a mother by their side, they wouldn't be quite so messed up.

All I know is that whatever the guys are trying to achieve here, it's only partially working. I mean, surely they'd need some kind of epic deep freezer to make this work, but then, perhaps this isn't just a regular glass coffin. The room is cold as ice and the glass was freezing to touch, so perhaps they've put some thought into this.

Unable to keep looking, I pull myself away from the horrors inside the room and slam my back up against the door once again. My knees buckle and I sink to the ground, the tears flowing free and heavy down my face.

I thought things were finally starting to get a little bit better. The boys didn't want me dead, and while they have some fucked up ways of showing it, I thought I was going to survive. But their father … he's so much worse than I ever thought.

Abigail didn't deserve death; she was killed simply for knowing me. She was one of the only kind people in my life and while we weren't close friends, she was definitely one of the better people I knew. She covered my shifts when I was sick and I would do the same for her, though she had so much more of a life than I did. She was always calling and asking to switch things around, but I didn't mind because that meant at least one of us got to enjoy our lives.

Now she's gone and solely for the reason of showing kindness to a girl who she probably considered to be a lost cause.

I drop my head to my knees and prepare myself for one hell of a sob fest when a soft howling cuts through the room. My gaze snaps up and I hold my breath, realizing that I might not be alone in this fucked-up little room, you know, apart from Snow White in the glass coffin.

My gaze snaps from corner to corner, glancing past every dark shadow, but there's nowhere to hide in here. The room is practically a blank canvas with nothing but a glowing coffin in the center of the room.

The howling continues and I push to my feet, slowly trailing around the room and following the sound like a lion stalking its prey. It sounds almost like wind blowing through a small gap, but there's no windows in here, no holes in the walls to allow the breeze to flow in, nothing at all that could possibly allow such a noise to break through the structure of the room.

The walls are all dark and nearly impossible to make out their texture, but as I make my way around the room, studiously ignoring the body that seems to surround me with every step I take, I brush my fingers along the rough walls.

The castle is so old that a layer of dust builds up under my fingers, but on the third wall, I get nothing but a soft, smooth texture. It's newer than the rest, different in every possible way. My knuckles wrap against it and I quickly realize that it's a false wall, put in to deceive the true size of the room.

I push against it and it wobbles just a bit, but not enough to tear it down. The possibility that there could be something even worse on the other side weighs down on me, but I have to know, I have to find where that noise is coming from.

Looking back around the room, I find absolutely nothing that I could use to break through the false wall ... except for the glass coffin. But like ... where is a girl supposed to draw the line? Surely if this is their mother and I disrupt her decaying body in any way, they're not just going to shrug it off. They would be pissed.

The only option that leaves me with is, well ... me.

I let out a shaky breath. I've only seen this shit done in movies and they make it look so easy, but I have a feeling that it's really not. But what have I got to lose? My life? Because from where I am, I don't think that's even mine to lose anymore.

What the hell. I'm going for it.

I back up as far as the room will allow and shake my head,

knowing all too well just how fucking stupid this is, but if there's an open window on the other side, then I'm taking it. I can't risk being found by Giovanni.

I run full speed ahead, and as I approach the wall, I throw myself into the air, tucking my head under my arms and curling into the fetal position just in time for my body to slam against the drywall.

"Ahh, fuck," I groan as I tumble to the ground, adrenaline pulsing through my veins.

My body is bound to hate me for this reckless abuse, especially after the world of shit I've already put it through, but after I glance up and find a big crack in the drywall, it makes it all worthwhile. I have to keep trying. The howling gets a little bit louder and my determination only gets stronger.

Backing up again, I study the wall, looking over the big crack and trying to catch my breath. One more time should send me flying straight through the wall.

My hands pulse at my sides as I clench my jaw, knowing I have to run even faster, but I can do this. I've been through hell over the past few days. If I can endure that, then this is nothing.

Not giving myself another second to try and back out, I take off like a fucking rocket. My feet push off the dirty ground, propelling me toward the cracked wall, and at the very last moment, I throw myself forward with every last bit of momentum that I've got.

My body slams into the wall and my shoulder instantly burns, but the pain pays off as I crumble right through to the other side, the drywall falling in pieces around me.

I slam down against the dirty ground, my body tumbling with the force of my fall until I come to a brutal stop against the old stone wall of the castle.

I groan, gripping on to my shoulder, but as the howling tears through the room and I glance up, the pain is almost forgotten. A hole the size of a small window sits in the wall with loose stones around it, probably created after years of damaging winds and storms. It's most likely gone completely unnoticed.

I get to my feet, groaning with pain and quickly glancing through the small opening. I swallow hard, my heart pounding in my chest. If I'm going to get out of here, then now is my only shot.

I reach up, gripping on to the loose stone left in the wall and make the opening wider to slip through. It's pretty fucking dark outside. If I can somehow get down without dropping to my death, then I can run through the empty fields and get lost in the woods. Assuming Giovanni doesn't have the castle surrounded by his men.

The stones aren't easy to dislodge but after breaking a few nails, I finally get the hole big enough to slip through. My feet land on the old, tiled roof, and as my head slips out of the hole, I'm left standing on the roof with the howling wind threatening to knock me right off, realizing just how fucking crazy this is.

I should have run through the kitchen and into the long-ass tunnel that the boys spent five years digging instead of risking my luck with the glass coffin and falling off the roof. The boys were clear their father had never found their way out. What the hell was I thinking?

Keeping one hand on the side of the castle, I creep along the roof, desperately searching for the best place to try and get down. I'm at least four floors high and dropping from here is surely going to end my life.

I bypass three windows and drop down onto a small ledge before continuing, thankful for the millions of hidden walkways that these old castles were built with. Though, I'm sure they were built with the intention of fending off an enemy who dared come onto their land. Either that, or they liked to throw people from these heights to watch how they splattered on the ground below. Entertainment at its finest.

I come past another window before glancing over the edge to find the massive pool below. I let out a shaky breath, desperately trying to find that same adrenaline that was pulsing through my veins before.

It's just one jump into a big pool … four stories down.

What could possibly go wrong?

Tears spring from my eyes as I creep right toward the edge. All I have to do is jump and I'll be free. As long as the boys are alive and show affection for me, I will always be a target, no matter what. Whether it's Giovanni or the next asshole trying to take them down. There's no win in this life for me. If I want freedom, then I have to fight for it.

My heart thunders, the pulse in my ears making it nearly impossible to hear the other sounds of the night as the wind slams against my chest, rocking me back on my heels. If I miss … if I were to hit the bottom …

Fuck.

I can't think about that. All I have to do is close my eyes and jump.

TWENTY-FOUR

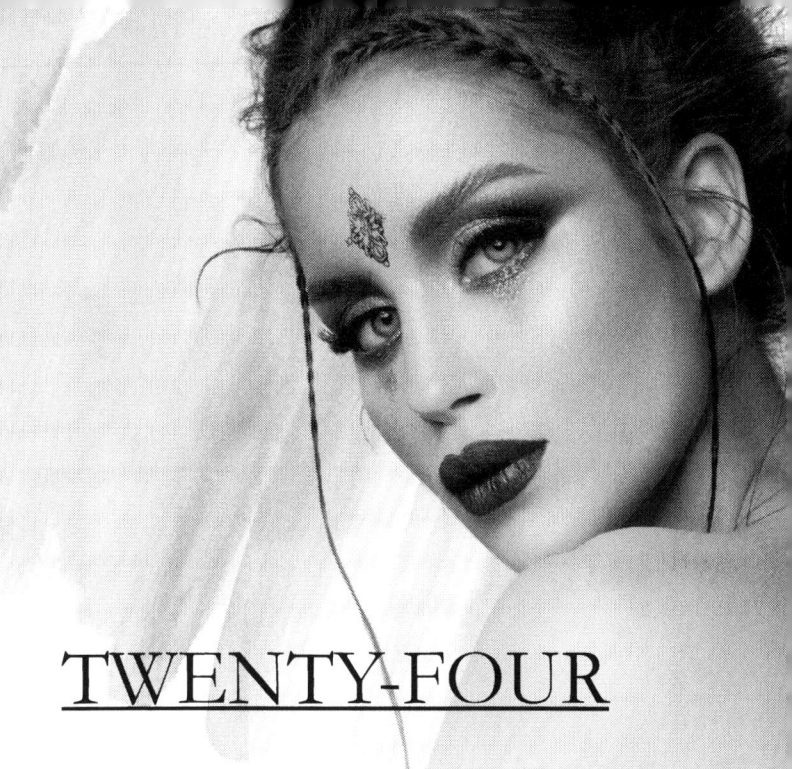

Vibrations travel through the roof and my eyes spring open. I wobble against the rough winds that blow me back a step and I glance back, desperately seeking out whoever is coming after me, but the night sky is like having a black mask pulled over my face. I can't see shit, but I can sure as hell hear the guy sprinting against the roof and feel the vibrations sailing through the soles of my dirty, cut-up feet.

He's close. Too fucking close.

Panic sets in.

It's now or fucking never.

I back up a few steps and without allowing myself to think this through anymore, I race toward the edge of the roof and fling myself off into the deep pits below.

A tight hold locks around my wrist, jolting me to a hard stop and leaving me dangling over the edge as a raw scream tears from deep inside my throat. I pull against the tight grip, desperate for freedom. "LET ME GO," I cry, my hopelessness shining through loud and clear as fear rockets through my veins.

I pull and claw at his hold, determined not to fall into Giovanni's trap. "STOP FUCKING FIGHTING ME," a familiar tone cuts through my wild panic.

My gaze snaps up and I stare into the dark eyes of Levi DeAngelis, confusion sweeping through me. He should be dead. There's no way that he made it out of that alive. There were too many of them. My heart races and my breath comes in heavy pants, making it impossible to even speak.

Veins protrude from his strong arm as he keeps me from falling. He's barely holding on himself. The majority of his body is hanging over the side, reaching down to have caught me before I fell. That couldn't be easy. I shake my head, tears stinging my eyes. "Just let me go," I cry, the desperation overwhelming me. "He'll never stop coming for me. As long as you guys keep protecting me, I'll be a target."

His jaw is clenched, effortlessly holding me up with just one arm as he grips onto the edge of the roof, keeping us both from falling to our gruesome deaths below. "Over my dead fucking body," Levi growls from above me. "I'm not nearly through with you yet. Especially not now."

Tears fall from my eyes as I squirm beneath his bruising grip. "Let me go," I beg, reaching up and attempting to claw at his impenetrable hold. "Please. I just want to go home."

"That pool below you," he growls between his clenched jaw, pulling hard on my arm and yanking me back up toward him, "is not a fucking pool. There's no water in it. You would have been dead the second you hit the ground."

My eyes widen in horror as I look down, desperately trying to see through the darkness, but it's too far down. I allowed my desperation to give me a false sense of hope and because of that, I threw myself off the goddamn roof. "THE FUCK?" I screech, panic settling deep inside my soul.

Levi hoists me up, and just as my body hits the edge of the roof, he gives me a hard shove, throwing me back a few steps until I'm sprawled out on the old tiles.

He pulls himself up and I stare at him in horror as his furious rage locks on me. I scramble back up the roof as he stalks me, slowly creeping closer and closer. "I thought we made ourselves quite clear about your attempts to escape us," he growls, the anger radiating through his tone.

I stare at him blankly. "Are you fucking kidding me?" I throw back at him, scurrying to my feet as rage pulses through my veins, the tears still staining my cheeks. "It's not you who I'm running from. Your father ... fuck. He killed Abigail for fucking sport, just because I refused to let him kill your stupid asses, and you know damn well that you shouldn't have made it out of that. Your brothers ..."

"My brothers are fine," Levi tells me before shaking his head. "My father was bluffing. He was never going to kill us. He needs us more than he fears us. It took him two seconds to call his men off and start retreating with the few who could make it out alive. He's gone."

"For now," I mutter darkly before I shove my hands against Levi's chest as the frustration gets the best of me. He doesn't move a damn inch, though a weaker man would have toppled back, straight over the edge. "HOW WAS I SUPPOSED TO KNOW THAT?" I yell into the dark night. "YOU ASSHOLES DON'T TELL ME SHIT AND NOW MY FRIEND IS DEAD."

"Your friend is dead because she was stealing pills from my father and dropping them into the drinks she made at your precious club," he spits. "Your friend wasn't a friend. She was fucking scum just like the rest of us. She spiked chicks' drinks and made easy prey for the assholes waiting out back for them. That's the bitch you're screaming about right now, that's the bitch you're out here mourning."

"That's … no," I demand, shaking my head, the weight sitting heavily against my chest. "I knew Abigail. You've got the wrong girl."

Levi steps into me, gripping my chin and forcing my stare up to his. "We don't ever get the wrong girl."

His words hold a double meaning and it's not lost on me, especially as I tear my chin out of his tight grip and glare up at him. "Well this time you did."

Without another word, I take off at a hard sprint across the roof, desperately searching for another way out. If the boys are alive and so is Giovanni, then nothing has changed. I'm still a target, still the girl who Giovanni will use to hold over his sons' heads. Only Levi has other plans. He's right there, bounding after me like a fucking tornado destroying everything in its path.

He captures me in no time and, rather than dragging me to a painful stop, he forces me forward, tumbling to my knees and pushing my chest right down to the roof tiles. I'm forced to capture the edge of the roof to keep from falling to my gruesome death below. "Is this what you want?" he spits, grabbing a chunk of my hair and forcing me further down until my chest is slipping right off the edge of the roof. "Do you want me to let go? Let you fall so you can paint the fucking asphalt red?"

"LET ME GO," I scream, feeling him on his knees behind me, my whole life literally in the palm of his hand. The adrenaline pulses through me, knowing that I won't be strong enough to hold myself up if he were to release me right now.

He pushes me a little further until I feel my rib cage rubbing against the edge of the roof. He has no choice but to adjust himself behind me to be able to keep holding onto me, but suddenly I don't fucking care because my ass is high in the air and the front of his pants are rubbing right against my pussy.

I couldn't seriously be this fucked in the head.

"What's it going to be, Shayne?" he questions, pulling back on my hair until my back is arched, forcing me up just a little from the edge and making the front of his pants skim past my pussy once again. "Do I let you go or would you prefer this to go another way?"

"You want to know what I want?" I spit, my fingers aching as they tightly grip the edge.

"I'm all fucking ears."

Knowing I could regret this, I let the words fly free before I give myself the chance to keep them to swallow them down. I let my true nature fly free and I don't hold back one fucking bit. "I want you to hold me over this fucking roof and pull my hair like it was the only thing keeping you breathing. I want you to spank my ass like it was one of your drums, then only when my ass is stinging from your handprint, I want you to slam that big fucking cock deep inside my pussy and fuck me until I forget why I hate you so goddamn much."

"Why?" he growls through a clenched jaw.

I shake my head, hardly knowing myself. "I need you to make me feel alive because your whole fucking family has slaughtered everything good inside of me."

"That's what you want?" he questions, his tone thick with suspicion.

"Fucking do it now or let me fall. It doesn't matter to me, not anymore."

Silence fills the air and just when I think he's about to let me go, I feel him shuffling behind me. His other hand grips the back of my sweatpants and he tears them right down to my knees, exposing my weeping pussy.

I feel the cool breeze against me but nothing else matters, not when I feel him releasing his thick cock against my ass. He pulls harder on my hair, ripping my head right back. "You sure this is what you want, little one?" he questions. "Once I bury myself in that tight cunt, I won't be stopping."

"Then you better make it worth my while."

Without even a shred of hesitation, he lines his thick cock up with my entrance and slams deep inside of me. I cry out, his delicious invasion stretching me wide and giving me exactly what I need to feel again. Levi draws back, his cock slick with my arousal before giving it to me again and again.

His fingers dig into my ass cheek, and just when I think that's all he's going to give me, his hand comes down in a bruising spank. I groan deep, clenching down around his thick, veiny cock. A deep guttural moan sounds from behind me, and knowing that he's enjoying me just as much as I'm enjoying him, nearly has me shattering around him.

Levi adjusts his hold on my hair, releasing it just enough to completely wrap his hand around it as he pushes deeper inside of me. I spread my knees wider and try to lower my chest even further over the edge, living on that adrenaline that pulses through my veins. I don't think I've ever done anything quite so stupid, but fuck it, this place has me doing things that I never in a million years would have expected of myself.

I release one of my hands off the edge, knowing that Levi won't let me fall, at least not until after he comes. I reach between my thighs and roll my clit between my fingers, groaning with the sweet pleasure rocking through me.

Levi's hand curves around my ass and just when I think he's going to spank me again, his thumb drops to my pussy and mixes with my arousal. He draws it back up to my hole and a shiver sails over my skin as he presses against it, slowly pushing his thumb inside me.

"Oh, fuck," I cry as he yanks back on my hair again, pulling me up higher from the edge. His thumb moves in my ass as I press down harder on my clit, rubbing tight, furious circles.

My pussy clenches and it's only a matter of time before I come undone, but not without him. I want to feel him emptying inside of me. I want to know that despite our fucked up little relationship and the way that he holds me over the edge, that I still hold the power.

His thrusts get harder and deeper and my eyes roll back as I feel myself burning from the inside out. I begged him to make me feel alive, and damn it, he's a man who sticks to his word. Hell, he even told me that he won't play games with me. If I want something from him, then I need to ask for it, and damn it, he's more than coming through for me.

His strong arm holds me up, keeping me from falling to my excruciating death below, while also bringing a whole new meaning to living on the edge. "Fuck, Levi, YES," I cry out, clenching my eyes as his thumb works my ass. I push back against him and he takes me deeper, hitting me at a whole new angle. I groan low, the sound vibrating right through my chest as I keep rubbing those tight little circles over my needy clit.

Levi wraps his hand around my hair one more time, keeping me still for his big finale, but he won't be getting it before I do. The walls of my pussy clench and I groan, squeezing down on him as he moves in and out of me, flooding me with arousal.

I love his strength. His raw need to give me exactly what I asked for. His determination to make it count. He doesn't dare hold back and that's exactly what I needed. I'm his freaking ragdoll to use as he pleases, and damn it, I need this to not be a one-time thing. But in order for that to happen, I need to be here. I can't keep pulling away from them. I have to accept that this is my life now. Besides, what has running ever got me? The first time I was nearly gang raped, and this time, I nearly flew off the fucking roof into a pit of concrete below.

Giovanni is never going to stop coming for me, but at some point, I have to trust that the brothers will protect me. They made it out alive tonight, and if they can do that, then there should be no reason for me to doubt them.

As I succumb to my new life, I clench harder around his thick cock, letting the weight of my fear sink away. I can't dangle from the edge of this roof without trusting the hand that keeps me safe, and that's exactly what I need to do. Trust that the boys have me, that they'll keep me from falling. That's all I can ask for.

The pressure builds deep in my pussy and I clench my eyes, feeling the power of his cock driving straight through me, massaging me deep within. His thumb circles in my ass as my fingers work my clit.

Levi shifts back and as he slams deep inside me at a whole new angle, it's all I need to shatter around him. "FUCK," I cry, my voice sailing across the night sky, my fingers digging into the edge of the roof as his pushes harder into my ass.

I clench around him, my walls convulsing as a low moan slips from between my lips. He doesn't stop, relentlessly taking what he needs from my body as I ride out my high. "Fuck, little one," he breathes, his jaw tight and his hold strong. "I can't wait to claim your fucking ass."

"It's all yours," I groan, more than ready to offer it up like a Thanksgiving turkey.

Levi groans and not a moment later, I feel his warm seed pouring into me. I push back against him, taking it all with a strangled cry. Keeping himself buried deep inside of me, he pulls his hand from my ass and curls his strong hold around my waist. He yanks me up so that I'm no longer falling off the edge of the roof and presses my back against his wide chest. "You're going to destroy us," he mutters in my ear, his comment holding the weight of the fucking world.

"Can't destroy something that's already broken," I tell him.

"Too fucking right."

Then just like that, he pulls out of me and rises to his feet, dragging me up with him. I barely get my sweatpants back up around my ass when I turn back to find both Marcus and Roman standing back on the roof. Marcus' arms are crossed over his chest looking more than pissed that I allowed his brother to indulge in my body while Roman just looks bored.

Then before I even get a chance to ask them how the hell they survived or how long they've been standing there, Roman narrows his hard stare. "Come," he says. "It's about time we talked."

Damn fucking right.

TWENTY-FIVE

The silence in the living room is almost brutal.

Each of the brothers are pissed for different reasons. Marcus is livid that I shared my body. Levi is furious that he just had to save me from flying off the roof. Roman is a harder case to figure out. He could be pissed about what just went down with his father or he could just be pissed at the world. It's hard to tell. Though one thing they have in common is that they're all furious with me.

I let out a heavy sigh as I lean back against the wall, watching as Roman drops down next to one of his sleeping wolves and pulls its big head into his lap. Marcus sits directly across from me, his harsh glare piercing mine like daggers while Levi stands, his hands clenching at his sides as he paces back and forth behind the long couch.

Nerves overwhelm my body as my gaze falls to the big wolves who seem to overtake the whole room. There's no reason for the nerves, but for some reason, I can't make them fade away. "What's wrong with them?" I ask Roman, not knowing much about the animal in his lap, but knowing that something isn't right for them to not even stir when we walked in.

"Tranquilized," Roman mutters, his hand knotting into the fur on the big wolf's head. "It's the only way my father was able to get in without detection. They like to hunt along the perimeter of the property at night so no one gets in unless they come prepared. They'll be fine. It's not the first time. They'll come around soon, but when they do, they'll be out for blood."

I swallow hard, my gaze shifting up from the wolf to meet Roman's. "What are their names?" I ask, knowing that on some level I should fear these animals, but when they're with their masters, they're obedient and kind, perfectly controlled.

"Names?" he questions, his brows furrowed in confusion. "They don't have any. They're weapons, not pets."

I roll my eyes and shake my head. "You're kidding me, right?" I laugh, pointing toward the beast who's tongue lolls by his thigh. "That right there is as pettish as a pet can get. They have food bowls in the kitchen, water in nearly every room. You let them out to run in the fields and I bet you even snuggle them at night. Look at the way you're scratching his head. They're pets. You care for them. Are you so far gone that you don't see that?"

"You have no fucking idea what you're talking about."

"You know I do and that scares the shit out of you."

Levi stops pacing and leans onto the backrest of the big couch. "Can we cut the bullshit? You tried to run. You did exactly what we asked you not to do. Rule number one. How are we supposed to keep you safe like that?"

"Safe?" I question, meeting his stare and immediately squirming under his gaze, the memory of what happened on the roof still so fresh. "This is your version of keeping me safe? That doesn't even make sense. *YOU KIDNAPPED ME*. I'm not here to hang out and get to know you. You're keeping me here against my will, forcing me to do and witness things that are seriously fucking with my head, and then had the brilliant idea to expose me to your father. I've never been so unsafe in my life."

"You tried to run," Levi repeats, his hard, lethal stare boring into mine.

"Not from you," I argue, holding onto his stare and refusing to break. "I thought there was no way you guys would have survived in there. You were outnumbered, and all I could picture was you three lying in a pool of blood next to Abigail and me being next. I had no choice but to run. It was the only way I could save myself."

Marcus stands. "You honestly thought we would have let that happen to you after everything we've done for you?"

"Okay," I laugh, pressing a hand to my temple as a brutal headache quickly starts to set in. "What aren't you getting? I thought you were as good as dead. How would you have saved me if you were bleeding out on the ground? I had no choice but to try and save myself."

Roman scoffs. "By throwing yourself off the fucking roof into an empty concrete pit below? Sounds like a fucking amazing idea to me."

I shoot a nasty glare toward him. "I didn't know the pool was empty," I throw back at him. "What idiots have an empty concrete pit in their backyard? How was I supposed to know? It was pitch-black out there. I could barely see."

"Here's an idea," Marcus scoffs. "If you can't fucking see what's below you, don't attempt jumping into it."

"Fuck you," I snap, narrowing my hard stare. I can't handle his bad mood right now. So what if I let his brother fuck me on the roof? It's not my fault that he decided to stand there and watch. My body is mine to give to whoever I want, and if he wants to climb out onto the roof to watch, then that's all on him. "You're a little bitch when you're jealous."

"Jealous?" he roars, striding toward me and towering over me with that menacing stare of his. "I don't get fucking jealous."

"Really? You're not standing here, biting your tongue over the fact that Levi fucked me when I told you that I was all yours? That I wouldn't let Roman or Levi touch me, but I shared my body with him. I let him take whatever the fuck he wanted from me and damn it, I plan on doing it again and again. He made my body come alive and the way my pussy squeezed his cock when I came was fucking incredible. You're telling me that doesn't grind on your nerves?"

Marcus' hand slams against the wall beside my head. "If this is your way of begging for forgiveness, you're doing it wrong. When you beg for your life, your knees should bleed."

I raise my brow, pushing off the wall and putting myself right in his way. "Do I strike you as the type to beg for forgiveness to the three men who brought me into a world full of bloodshed and brutal murder?"

Marcus towers over me. "No, but you strike me as the type to know what's good for her."

I narrow my gaze, the anger boiling beneath the surface. "I'll never beg on my knees for you."

"That's fine," he mutters darkly, shoving into me and dropping his head down low so his mouth hovers just above my ear. "I prefer you on your back."

I swallow hard and push him off me, surprised when he actually moves. "Get off me," I snap. "It's the middle of the freaking night. I've just had your father's men drag me out of bed to play the most fucked-up game of *eeny, meeny, miny, moe*, attempted to fly, and then was fucked while hanging off the top of your twisted castle. You said it was time to talk, so let's talk. Otherwise, I'd like to go back to bed and pretend that none of this happened."

Marcus lets out a sigh, narrowing his eyes on me for a moment before finally stepping out of my way and indicating for me to take a seat. "What do you want to know?" Roman questions as Marcus steps around me and heads back toward his couch.

I drop down on the couch and bring my knees up under myself, not sure where to even start. "I want to put a bullet between your father's eyes," I tell them, figuring I don't want to waste time beating around the bush. May as well get it all out on the table.

"Join the club," Levi mutters. "We only let him get away tonight because we still need him."

"Because you'll be overthrowing him soon?"

"Soon enough," he says. "For now, we need him to keep making deals and running the family business. When we're ready and have what we need, we'll play our cards, but only when it counts. We can't afford to fuck it up. So for now, we just have to be patient and endure it."

I nod, surprised to have a full and honest answer out of him. This is usually the part where they give me just enough to keep me from going insane and get up to walk away, only when they each remain exactly where they are, looking at me expectantly, I realize this is really it. They're going to tell me what I want to know but, if I push them too far, I'm just going to end up right back at square one.

"I, umm ... I don't understand why you guys keep trying to protect me. You've made it perfectly clear that I'm just an object taking up space in your home, yet you went to kill that guy in the warehouse and then protected me against your father when he tried to shoot me in the dining room. I just ... why?"

Marcus sighs, leaning forward onto his knees as his gaze drops to the coffee table, realizing that this question is directed at him. "Wish I could tell you," he murmurs, struggling with what to say. "But I honestly don't fucking know. We've had girls here before and I've just let them perish when my father has decided they're not worth it, but not you. You're a fighter. You throw our shit right back at us. You're intriguing. You interest me, and until I can figure out what that means, I won't be allowing him to take your life."

"And if you decide that I'm not as intriguing as you originally thought?"

He shrugs his shoulders. "I guess we'll have to see if that happens."

Levi pushes off the edge of the couch. "This is unfamiliar territory for us," he explains. "Our father offers us girls to keep here as entertainment, and there's only been one that we've gotten close to. She was a dangerous game and it didn't end well for anyone involved. It would be smart for us to keep our distance."

"You mean Felicity?" I question, my gaze hesitantly falling back on Roman's. "You were in love with her, weren't you?"

He watches me for a long moment and no one says a damn word until he finally nods. "I was," he says, the pain radiating out of his eyes and warning me not to push him on the topic. He'll share what he's willing to say and nothing more. "I would have married her. She was carrying my kid, but this here," he continues, pointing out the scar running from the tip of his brow, right through his eyes and all the way down to his cheek bone. "This is what happens when you allow yourself to get too close in our world."

I suck in a breath, reading between the lines. "Your father did that?" I say, the curiosity pulsing through my veins, desperate to know exactly what went down, but it's something I fear that I'll never be privy to.

Roman nods and glances away. "It was either her or me."

Heaviness sinks against my chest, realizing just how much these guys have lost. They're more than just broken souls. They've been tortured and abused for years on end. Hell, the mother was gone and then the love of his life was taken from him. How much more do these guys have to lose? No wonder they are the way that they are. "That's why you guys are so hesitant to get close to me."

Marcus rests back in his seat, propping his feet up on the coffee table. "Everything that we get close to eventually gets taken away. There's no point making attachments because, not only does it put a target on our backs, but it puts one on yours too. If my father's enemies knew that we had you locked up here to enjoy, they wouldn't stop until they'd taken you away, whether that's alive or in pieces."

"Why are you telling me all of this?"

"Because you keep running," Levi says. "I know you think you're better off alone, that you can go back to your shitty apartment and live your life, but you can't. You've been exposed to this world and whether you like it or not, you're now associated as ours. You need to understand the dangers. We can't protect you out there, not like we can from here."

I shake my head, leaning back on the couch. "But I'm not cut out for this world. You slaughter people for sport and don't even blink when someone holds a gun to your head. That's not me. I can't handle it."

"On the contrary," Marcus says. "You proved to us exactly what you're made of when you slid that blade right into Miller's gut. You didn't hesitate. You just went for it even though Roman and I had it under control. You could have backed away at any point."

I clench my jaw and turn to meet his stare, the memories of that night haunting me. "Is that why you gave me that knife? To see if I'd fight back?"

"Well," he grins. "I gave it to you in the hopes that you'd use it to fend off my brothers if their dicks came searching you out. I don't share well." Levi and Roman both scoff, cutting him off, but he rolls his eyes and continues. "You proved to us all on your own that you could handle this world. You were made for it; you just don't know it yet."

"It's inevitable," Roman mutters darkly. "You're going to be just like us."

I laugh. "Okay, now I know you're messed up in the head," I tell them. "I will never be like you guys. I was born with a conscience and know the difference between right and wrong. You guys castrate assholes in old warehouses. I could never do something like that."

"How do you think we started out?" Levi questions. "You have to work up to it. But you'll get there. It's a natural talent."

My eyes widen in horror. "You say that like it's something to be proud of."

He leans forward, holding my stare. "Isn't it?"

I let out a breath, refusing to answer that out of principle as I wrap my arms around my legs, holding myself in a tight ball almost like a coping mechanism. "What am I supposed to do if your father comes back?"

"Trust us," Roman insists. "Just like tonight, you have our backs and we'll have yours."

I shake my head. "I can't fight like that."

"You don't need to," Marcus says. "Run and hide like I told you to. We will find you when it's over. We don't want you scared while you're here."

I laugh, smirking at him from across the room. "You're shitting me, right?" I question. "You guys literally chased me through a dead-end maze with your freaking wolves, you stalked me through dark halls, and tormented me with creepy shit in that dungeon. My fear gets you off."

"True," Levi says. "But have we done any of that shit since you stabbed Miller?" My brows furrow and I shake my head, realizing that he's right. "Exactly," he continues. "You've been rewarded time and time again. You proved yourself worthy, so now, you get to live in peace inside these walls."

"In peace?" I question, my eyes narrowing in suspicion, not trusting his word one bit. "What's that supposed to mean? Something tells me that our ideas of peace vary."

"We'll leave you be," he confirms. "No more tormenting you in the middle of the night. We'll behave, and in return, you'll be a pleasant house guest."

"So, I can come and go as I please?"

"No," Roman says. "You are confined to this castle just as we are. However, you have freedoms within our home. Consider yourself part of the family. We will train you how to better protect yourself, feed and clothe you, but if you try to run from us again, your freedoms will be taken from you and you will not like the consequences. We rarely give second chances, and you are currently on your third."

I swallow hard and nod before turning my gaze to Marcus. "What about your hand?" I ask nervously. "Do you still plan to punish me for that?"

His gaze narrows on mine as he taps his fingers on the armrest of his couch. "That's a good question," he murmurs, deep in thought as his gaze shifts to the dark scar on the top of his hand. "I am undecided on your punishment, but I won't lie, seeing that fire in you when you stabbed me is part of the reason why I'm so intrigued by you. Perhaps there is still a chance that I will let you off the hook."

"Really? Because last time you hung me from a hook, I liked it."

His eyes burn with a raging lust, igniting the fire deep within me, but Levi's tone pulls me out of my trance. "So, we have a deal? You won't run."

I nod. "We do, but I want one thing in return."

"What's that?" Roman questions hesitantly.

I take a breath and slowly let it out, knowing this could blow up in my face. "I want to get to know each of you, and not just the callous, cruel versions of yourselves who slaughter men in warehouses. I want to know who you really are. I want to hang out with you guys, maybe even become friends."

"You want to hang out with us?" Levi questions, completely stumped by my request.

I nod. "Yeah, what's so wrong with that? We're hanging out now and it's not that bad. It might even be nice if we were talking about something other than me developing a wicked case of Stockholm syndrome."

"Okay," Roman finally says. "You can get to know us, but I can guarantee that you're not going to like what you find."

"That's a risk I'm willing to take," I tell him as a wicked grin stretches over my lips. "And here I thought you guys didn't have pets, just weapons."

"Don't you worry," Roman fires back. "We have nothing but time to turn you into our most lethal weapon yet."

Well, shit. I should have seen that one coming.

I stand and adjust my sweatpants. "Are we done here?" I question, glancing down at Marcus and Levi while trying to ignore Roman's narrowed stare.

"What's your rush?" Roman asks, a deceiving sparkle hitting his obsidian eyes. "I thought you wanted to hang out and learn about all the things that my brothers and I like to get up to."

I swallow hard. "I do," I insist, meeting his stare with one of my own. "But I've had your brother pouring out of me for the last twenty minutes after discovering one of the things that he likes to get up into, and I've happily sat here without complaint, but now it's dripping down near my knees. So, if it's alright with you, master, I'd like to go and shower."

He doesn't respond, but assuming everything they've just said to me was true, then I shouldn't have to wait for his approval. I turn on my heel and start stalking toward the entryway of the living room, hating just how dark the rest of the castle is. My hand hooks around the side of the wall and just as I go to fling myself around the corner, Marcus calls out. "Shayne, wait."

I stop and glance back at him, my brows furrowed as I wait to figure out why I'm needed. "I just have one question," he says, making his brothers pause. "How did you get out onto the roof?"

"Oh, umm … Snow White's room right up top. There's a hole in the wall. I had to pull out a few pieces of stone but eventually I was able to squeeze through."

Levi pushes away from the couch and steps toward me, his brows low in confusion as both Roman and Marcus stand too. "Who the fuck is Snow White?"

"You know, the Disney princess," I explain, realizing too late that these guys probably would have been deprived of all Disney movies as kids. "She was poisoned by the old bitch and then she was put in a glass coffin, just like you have that dead woman in upstairs."

Marcus drops his chin and I'm reminded of the fearless man I saw in the warehouse. "What dead woman upstairs?" he questions slowly.

I find myself backing up a step as I look between the two other brothers only to find them as equally confused. "You know, the woman in the glass coffin. Long black hair, looks like she's been rotting in that thing for years. If it weren't for the freezers, she'd probably be a skeleton by now," I watch them cautiously, flicking my gaze between each of them. "You guys really have no idea what I'm talking about, do you?"

"Does this look like the face of a man who knows what the fuck you're talking about?" Levi mutters before pointing toward the massive staircase just outside the living room. "Start walking."

Well, shit. There goes my shower.

TWENTY-SIX

The tension rolling off the three brothers is like nothing I've ever felt before and having them at my back makes me feel sick. They follow me upstairs, twisting through hallways and retracing my steps, but I'm disoriented by the million different paths to take.

"You're full of shit," Levi grunts behind me. "There is no fucking woman in a coffin."

"I swear," I spit back at him, glancing over my shoulder to show him the heated anger swirling in my gaze at being questioned. "I'm just … lost. I wasn't exactly thinking straight when I came running through here. Besides, how don't you know about this? Didn't you just follow me straight out?"

"No," he mutters. "I saw you from the hallway window and had no choice but to break through the bastard. That's reinforced glass. I almost broke my fucking wrists trying to get through it."

My brows furrow and I find myself looking back at him again. "Oh, I uhh … I just figured."

Marcus groans. "Really? Did you pay no attention to the fact that you came back in through a different window?"

"No," I snap. "I was a little preoccupied with the fact that I'd just been fucked on the roof after nearly falling to my death."

The boys mutter behind me and I do my best at trying to ignore them when I finally come to a familiar staircase. I start winding my way up it and the further I go, the more the tension in the room rises. "What?" I question, glancing back and seeing the hard expression in Roman's eyes. "I thought you guys knew everything that was in this place. Have you never been up here before?"

Roman shakes his head. "Never had a need to before. As far as we were concerned, it was all empty."

"So, that little nagging voice inside your head that pulls at your curiosity never once pushed you to come looking up here? Not even a little?"

His gaze narrows and he looks at me as though I'm speaking right out of my ass. *"Little nagging voice inside your head?"* he questions. "Shit, and you think we're the ones who've gone insane. That's not normal, Empress. You need to get that shit checked out."

"Oh sure," I grumble. "Why don't you book an appointment with the doctor? Oh wait. You killed him."

"Fucking hell," Levi mutters under his breath, more than done with the long-ass night we've all had to endure, his tone suggesting that whatever comes out of his mouth next is about to be some kind of verbal smackdown. "Why didn't anyone warn me how fucking hilarious you are?"

I scoff, dragging my gaze back toward the long hallway ahead of me. "Because they're probably too busy laughing at what a joke you are."

A hand curls around the back of my neck and before I get a chance to even gasp, my back is pressed up against the wall. "Watch it," he growls. "My patience is wearing thin."

"Do you need me to help you with that?" I murmur, dropping my tone low and pushing my tits up to press against his wide chest. "I have a few ... tricks that I'm sure could ease your frustrations. All you have to do is say the word and I'll blow your fucking mind."

Marcus grunts behind us, rubbing at the raw skin at the back of his neck. "Unless you want my fucking handprint plastered across your perky ass, I suggest you get on with it. If there's a fucking shrine up in here, then I want to know about it."

I shove Levi off me and am surprised when he steps back without question. I don't think anything more of it and continue down the hallway, a strange hollowness appearing in the pit of my stomach at having to walk into that fucked-up little coffin room again. "I'd hardly call it a shrine," I tell them. "It's more like a creepy tomb."

"I don't give a shit what you want to call it," Roman says. "I need to see it."

I grumble under my breath and I can practically feel them rolling their eyes at my back. Silence falls around us as we keep making our way further up toward the very top of the castle and when I finally come to the very last staircase that leads to the old wooden door, I find myself pausing in the middle of the hallway.

"Is that it?" Marcus asks, stepping in beside me and nodding to the door up ahead.

"Yeah," I murmur, glancing up into his dark eyes. "Please don't make me go in there. It's … it's just fucked up, okay? I don't want to see it again."

Marcus' hand discreetly falls to my waist and he gives it a small squeeze before finally nodding and putting me out of my misery. "It's fine," he tells me. "You can stay out here."

Relief washes through me as he steps past me with his brothers following behind. They walk up the final five steps to the big oak door and leave me alone in the dark hallway. Unease swirls through my gut and without another thought, I find myself racing after them.

Who would have thought that I'd ever find myself racing toward the grim reapers in a dark hallway instead of running in the opposite direction? I guess the evil I know is safer than the evil I don't.

Roman tries the door as I hover back a few steps, not wanting to get too close. After all, I don't know who that woman is, but something tells me that what they're about to see is going to mess with their pretty little heads.

The door jams and he has to shove his hip into it just as I had done, and the moment it swings open with a loud squeal from the old hinges, the three of them pause. I watch as each of their backs stiffen and the tension starts rolling off them. "What the fuck is this?" Levi mutters darkly, taking in the glass coffin in the center of the chilly room.

Roman shakes his head and slowly steps deeper into the room. "I've got no fucking idea," he mutters, his gaze sweeping from left to right before settling on the glass coffin in the center of the room. "This really is fucked up."

I scoff from my firm position at the door. "Out of everything you've put me through and done over the past week, *this* is what you see as fucked up?" I question. "I guess it's nice to know where you draw the line."

Marcus strides right up to the coffin, peering into it but coming up blank as the frost completely covers the glass. "Who do you think it is?" he asks, not showing a shred of hesitation.

Roman shakes his head and I can't help but notice the fear deep within his warm, silky tone. "I have a good idea, but I really hope that I'm wrong."

Marcus glances back at his brothers with his brow raised, waiting for their silent approval to go ahead. When no objections come his way, his hand presses down over the glass and gently wipes the frost away, revealing the woman within.

My eyes go straight to the boys as each of them freeze, the tension I'd felt before, tripling in size. Levi sucks in a pained gasp as Roman clenches his jaw, but Marcus … Marcus looks completely dead inside.

"What?" I breathe, slowly creeping deeper into the room until I'm standing between Roman and Levi, their big shoulders sagged with devastation. "Who is it?"

Levi's fingers brush up against mine and quickly latch onto them as Roman continues to peer into the glass coffin, looking over the dark-haired woman with nothing but dead eyes. "It's our mother," he says factually, his tone firm and final before turning on his heel and stalking out of the room, his grief filling the air around us and constricting my heart in every possible way.

The need to go after him pulses through my veins but my eyes are glued to Marcus and Levi as they continue looking at their long-lost mother. Confusion and heartache swirl in their eyes and my heart breaks for them, and without question, I know that this won't go unpunished.

They will find out who did this to their mother. But what I've come to learn from my short stay at the DeAngelis castle is that the majority of the time, all roads lead straight back to their father.

TWENTY-SEVEN

"No way in hell," I demand, looking back at the three brothers as they stand in the open door of the Escalade staring back at me. "You said we were going out on business. You said nothing about a fucking party."

Levi stares back at me, his brows dipped low. "What's the difference?"

"The difference," I spit, "is that I figured you'd just chain me up in here and I'd hide out until you were done. There's no way in hell that I'm going in there and mingling with all your screwed up friends."

"These people aren't our friends," Marcus says. "They fear us too much."

I roll my eyes and flop back against the leather seat. "Oh, because that makes everything better," I mutter, crossing my arms over my chest. "Besides, I'm hardly dressed for a party. I'm in sweats and an old tank. I'm going to stand out like dog's balls in there."

Levi groans, resisting the urge to just grab me and haul me over his big shoulder. "You're going to stand out like dog's balls whether you are dressed up or not. Now, get your ass moving before I drag you in there by your hair."

I stare him down and as a twisted grin cuts across my face, I give him a sultry wink. "You just can't help yourself can you, big guy? You love a bit of rough hair pulling."

Levi lets out a frustrated groan and forces himself to step away from the open car door before he does something stupid like fuck up our little deal. It's been three days since Giovanni's visit and our talk in the living room, and those three days haven't been so bad. Sure, the guys have struggled to bite their tongues every now and then, but it's not like I've been the perfect house guest either. I argue with them every chance I get but we're all doing our best to make this work. There's a learning curve. Maybe in a perfect world, I would be far away from a life like this one, but I understand why I need to be here. Until Giovanni isn't a threat, this is my only safe place.

That doesn't mean that I can't have a little fun with it though. These guys have forced me into a life that I never wanted for myself, and if I can get under their skin just a little bit while I'm here, then I'm going for it. But I have to be careful. These aren't just the regular assholes I'm used to dealing with at the club. They react differently, they're quicker and have tempers worse than mine. If I push them too far, it could be game over.

Letting out a sigh, I scoot to the edge of the seat, narrowing my gaze on Levi. "How long are we talking? Is it like a quick in and out like Levi? Or are we talking all night like Marcus?"

Marcus laughs as I watch Levi take a few more steps away as he groans low, physically having to distance himself from me just to keep from bending me over and proving just how good he really is. Though he doesn't have to. Both he and Marcus have been slipping into my room over the past few nights, and both of them have more than demonstrated just how skilled they really are. Roman though, he likes his distance, and after what happened to Felicity, I don't blame him.

Roman's jaw clenches, telling me that my fun is over. "Get your ass out of the Escalade *NOW,*" he demands, that all too familiar authority rising in his tone.

Giving him a hard stare but seeing absolutely no wavering in his gaze, I slip out of the Escalade with a huff. "I better not get killed in there because of you guys," I mutter to their backs as they turn and start walking down a long alleyway that runs parallel to one of the many clubs in the heart of the city.

"The only thing that's going to get you killed tonight is the way you keep running your mouth," Marcus throws back at me.

My lips twist into a sneer and he glances back before I get a chance to wipe it from my face. Marcus smirks and pulls back a step, falling in line with me. "You're going to be fine," he says, keeping his voice low so that our conversation remains private. "Just sit still, don't talk to anyone, and stay close. Though, if you wanted to go causing trouble," he adds, his eyes sparkling with a sick excitement, "I wouldn't mind tearing out a few throats."

I give him a blank stare. "You're sick, you know that, right?"

Marcus winks and leans in close. "Do you want to find out just how sick I can be?"

I pull back from him, unsure what he really means by that. Is he talking in the bedroom? Because I really don't think I could push the limits any further with him. Hanging from chains and rubbing my clit with the handle of a knife is about as far as I think I can go.

Seeing my horrified expression, Marcus laughs and presses his hand to the small of my back. "You've got that knife I gave you?"

I shake my head and indicate down my body. "Do I look like I have anywhere to hide a knife on me right now?"

Marcus' intrigued gaze scans over my body, following my subtle curves and lingering on my ass. "You sure as fuck do," he murmurs. "You'd be horrified if you knew all the different places I've had to shove weapons over the years."

My eyes widen as a sharp gasp tears from the back of my throat. "I'm not shoving a fucking knife up my ass."

Roman and Levi stop up ahead and slowly turn to face me, their brows furrowed. "The fuck are you talking about?" Roman questions, his gaze narrowing as it shifts to his younger brother. "This is hardly the time to be talking about what you're going to fuck her with."

"WHAT?" I screech in horror as Marcus just grins, not bothering to set his brother straight. "That is not what we're discussing."

"Right," Levi chuckles, turning his back and continuing down the narrow alleyway. "Don't come crying to me when that blade accidentally tears right through your ass."

I groan, the frustration quickly getting to me. "I AM NOT SHOVING A FUCKING KNIFE UP MY ASS," I shriek just as two bouncers step out from the side of the alleyway, their sharp gazes falling on me with raised brows.

"Fucking hell," I mutter to myself, embarrassment flooding through me.

The bouncers turn their gazes to the DeAngelis brothers, and suddenly those brows aren't so high. Jaws clench as Marcus leaves my side to stand as one with his brothers, and quiet words pass between them. When the bouncers glance at each other with pale faces, their hands fall to the weapons at their hips. Roman shakes his head. "I wouldn't do that if I were you."

The bouncer on the left swallows hard, his gaze flicking back to Roman's as a cold chill sweeps through my body. Those were the very first words Roman said to me after being taken by them. I try to put it to the back of my mind, reminding myself that things have changed for the better since then.

"We don't want any trouble," the bouncer says, cautiously glancing my way and wondering why the fuck a girl like me would be out with guys like this.

"Neither do we," Roman tells him. "So, I suggest that you step aside before we're forced to eliminate the trouble."

The other guy shakes his head, his eyes wide in horror, knowing exactly who it is that he's dealing with. "Please, man. I have a wife and kids at home."

Levi raises his chin, the look on his face like nothing I've ever seen before. "Then walk away," he says. "Otherwise that wife of yours will be calling me daddy."

The guy goes white and without another word, his gaze falls to the ground and he starts walking back up the alleyway as though not a damn thing just happened, leaving all three of the brothers' gazes to fall upon the other bouncer. "What's it going to be?" Marcus questions, knowing just how intimidating the three of them can be when they stand as one.

"Like I said," the guy repeats. "I don't want any trouble."

"Then that's up to you, isn't it?"

The guy cautiously glances back toward the internal door of the club, knowing that if he were to let us pass, he would likely lose his job, but if he didn't he'd likely lose his life. Knowing what's best, he steps aside, dropping his chin as though he failed himself, but I don't see it that way. Tonight he saved himself.

"Smart move," Roman murmurs before looking across at his brothers and nodding. "Let's make this quick. It won't be long until someone recognizes us and calls for backup."

The brothers nod and Roman steps through the back entrance of the club as Levi follows after. Marcus waits for me to move in between them so that I don't fall behind just as the heavy back door slams shut behind us.

We trail through the club and I follow the boys closely, not liking what I'm seeing. This club is different from what I'm used to, and I quickly start to see familiar faces of the men that I usually have to turn away. These are the kind of men who pose threats to others, the kind of men who you don't want creeping up on you in a club, men who you need to watch your drink around. Hell, there are faces here that I recognize from the boys' party at the castle only a few short nights ago, which speaks volumes.

This isn't the kind of place I want to be, and seeing the way people around us are nodding to the brothers in recognition or respect has shivers trailing down my spine. Maybe Marcus was onto something about hiding a knife up my ass. I could use its comfort right about now.

The brothers walk through the club as though they've been here a million times, and as they approach a crowded table, it quickly becomes their own. People scatter away at the mere sight of the brothers and they move in toward the empty table, ushering me in first to keep me seated behind them.

The music is deafening and from the sound of it, the DJ has no idea what he's doing. I'd prefer Levi's incessant drumming a million times over this shit. Waitresses scurry to our table and offer the guys anything they want—drinks, pills, joints, girls. Anything they want, it'll be catered for, simply in the hopes that they don't tear this place to pieces and turn it into a slaughterhouse. Though from the sound of it, I don't think we're going to be here for long.

Marcus happily accepts a drink and a joint and before the girl has even scurried away, he's leaning back in his chair and propping his feet up on the small table between us. "So," he says, looking back at me as he lights his joint and takes a deep drag, blowing the smoke out in perfect rings. "What's your take on a sex tape?"

I raise a brow and give him a blank stare, my eyes glistening with silent laughter. "With Levi? Sure."

His jaw drops just a fraction and for a moment, he looks almost offended. "Take that back," he demands as Levi attempts to keep a straight face while pretending to not give a single fuck about our conversation.

I shake my head. "You can hold the camera if you want, but I'm sure we'd get better results using a tripod."

"Keep talking like that and I'll be forced to show you the real meaning of a tripod."

My brow arches, knowing exactly what he's talking about and I find myself glancing toward Levi, the curiosity swirling deep inside of me. Marcus watches me closely, his eyes narrowing in suspicion, reading me like a damn book. "Keep looking at us like that and we'll do it right fucking now for the whole world to see."

I swallow hard and quickly glance away but as I do, the three brothers stand in unison. My eyes go wide and I watch as four men approach the brothers, each of them with a grim expression across their faces.

They don't want to be here and they sure as fuck don't want to be in their presence. Clearly they aren't finding it as thrilling as I have over the past few days. You know, after I realized that their threats on my life were nothing more than scare tactics.

The four men move in closer, slowing their pace as they approach our table. "Julius," Roman says, nodding toward the guy who stands front and center, the one who looks the least like he's about to shit his pants. "Got our money?"

I lean forward, trying to get a better look at the guy as his name starts ringing bells. He's one of the biggest dealers in the city and was barred from entering the club I worked at years ago. I've never had anything to do with him, but I know girls who've destroyed their lives over the shit he supplies them.

Julius nods to the guy directly on his left who steps forward and offers a black bag to Levi. He takes it and drops the bag on the table in front of me. "Count it," Levi says. "50K."

My eyes bug out of my head and I stare up at him in shock. "50K?"

"Make it quick," he warns. "We don't have all night."

I quickly scurry toward the bag, knowing that they're all just going to stand around awkwardly watching and waiting until I'm done. "She doesn't need to count. It's all there," Julius says, panic lacing his tone. "I counted it myself."

Roman takes a small step to his right, blocking Julius' vision of me. "Then you shouldn't have anything to worry about, should you?"

Julius pipes down and despite the hundreds of bodies crammed into the club, I can still feel the tension rolling off the boys in waves. I quickly get started, flipping through stacks of cash while trying not to focus on the fact that this is more money than I've ever seen in my life.

Fifteen minutes pass before I look up at Roman with a cringe, my stomach sinking, knowing what's bound to come next. "It's short two grand," I tell him.

"You sure?" he questions, his gaze boring into mine, both of us knowing that if I had counted this wrong and his next steps are for nothing, that blood will be on my hands.

"I've gone over it three times," I say, pointing out the stacks of cash on the table and showing how the final stack comes up a lot shorter than the others. "I got 48K every single time. I'm positive. He's cutting you short."

The three brothers turn back to Julius who looks as though he's about to pass out, and before a single word can be said, Roman pulls his gun and shoots him square between the eyes. Gasps are heard all around as witnesses casually look our way, but seeing the DeAngelis brothers deep in business, they turn back and continue with their night as though they didn't see a damn thing.

The three men surrounding the brothers stand straighter, pretending that their boss isn't dead at their feet. "So, which one of you is stepping up?" Roman asks, his gaze shifting over the three men. "I have a shitload more product that needs to be moved and there will be a bonus included for whoever can sell my next batch and make up for what your boss was lacking."

The guy who handed Levi the bag steps forward. "I can do it," he says. "I know all of his contacts."

"Good," Roman says, nodding to Marcus who reaches below the table and pulls out a black briefcase. "Your boss right here? That's your warning. If you fuck this up, you'll be down on that ground beside him. Is that clear?"

"Julius never told me what he was selling or what your prices were.

I just know the buyers."

Roman watches him for a silent moment before Marcus steps in with the briefcase and opens the latches. I can't help but stand and glance between Levi and Roman, getting a good look at what it is they've been up to, and as Roman goes over his expectations, all I can do is gape.

This is the shit I've seen floating around the club. They're Giovanni's pills, only the packaging is different.

A laugh bubbles up my throat and I fall back against my seat, shaking my head in amusement. I thought the guys were here on business for their father, but that's definitely not the case. They're doing their own business by stealing their father's products, slapping on their own branding, and using Giovanni's contacts to make a profit. It's one hell of a risky game, but damn it, it's the best kind of fuck you to their father.

They're not just undercutting him; they're completely screwing him over.

Levi gets bored and drops down beside me. "What's so funny?" he questions, his gaze narrowed as he looks back at the dead body in a pile at their feet.

"They're your father's pills, aren't they? I recognize them from the club. You're not just planning on overthrowing him. You're undercutting his business deals and completely taking over."

Levi laughs as a wicked grin tears across his face. "You're observant," he comments, leaning back and dropping his arm over the back of my seat. "They're his pills. He manufactures them and we steal them right out from under his nose. He makes so much of the shit that he doesn't even notice. We change the branding in his fucking warehouse and have his guys deliver it right to our front door. It's sold within his city and we make 100% of the profits without even lifting a finger."

"You guys are evil masterminds."

Levi shrugs. "Nope, just businessmen who know how to fuck with the system."

"And he has no idea?"

"There are whispers out there of a new supplier, but he's too fucking blind to see what's right in front of his face. Hell, the fucker even asked us to locate this new supplier and deal with it."

"You're kidding?"

"Nope," he says. "When we're ready to overthrow him, we want to have our whole operation already set up. We're not just taking down our father, we're destroying the whole DeAngelis family. When we're done, there will be nothing left but us. We're starting fresh, and without our father keeping us down, we're going to be the most feared, unstoppable names in the whole fucking country, and you're going to be right there to witness the whole damn thing."

I stare at him with wide eyes, the realization of just how big this is sitting on my shoulders as Roman and Marcus finish up their business and send their new dealer on his way. "Is he good?" Levi asks as though he didn't just drop a massive bomb.

Roman shrugs his shoulders and presses his lips into a tight line. "I guess we'll find out," he says, looking back over his shoulder and watching the three men slip away into the crowd. "He's got a week to prove his worth."

I swallow hard as my gaze shifts over the three brothers. They have every little thing planned out. They've prepared for the worst and taken everything into consideration. They really are going to destroy their father. They're going to take him down from the inside, and only when he's lost everything and everyone around him, they're going to tear him to shreds. So much for the simple bullet that I wanted to put through his head. Their plan is much better, at least, it's one that I can finally get on board with.

Roman takes the drink right out of Marcus' hand and throws back every last drop as Marcus gapes at him, more than ready to throw down over those last few drops. "Let's get the fuck out of here," Roman says, cutting him off before he gets a chance to get even. "It's only a matter of time before someone calls in that fucking body."

Levi flies up off the seat beside me and immediately starts stalking back the way we came with Roman falling in behind him. Marcus looks back at me and silently indicates for me to get a fucking move on.

Wanting to get out of here just as much as they do, I step over the fallen body and walk behind Marcus, keeping close as other men leer a little too hard at me.

The crammed bodies clear a path for the brothers and I follow blindly as the smoke from Marcus' joint is blown back, unintentionally smacking me right in the face. I choke on the smell. It's fucking nasty. I've never been one for playing around with shit like that, but I can understand the blissful high.

Levi pushes out through the back door and Roman quickly follows. I step in behind Marcus and just as he disappears out into the dark alleyway beside the club, a big hand comes down over my mouth. I try to scream as the last of Marcus disappears around the corner but the hand blocks my airway.

A hard body presses into my back and just as I see Marcus storm back through the door with Roman and Levi right on his heels, I'm dragged deep into the tightly packed crowd, completely concealed from sight.

I claw at the person behind me, desperate to be freed as I hear gunshots sounding around me. People scream and bodies start racing around the club in complete chaos. Where the fuck are they?

I kick out, desperately fighting for relief as the hand presses down harder. My lungs scream for air and just as I hear one final gunshot, everything goes black.

TWENTY-EIGHT

My body jostles and slams against something hard and my eyes spring open. I gasp for breath, my lungs aching as the realization dawns that I'm in someone's trunk. I slam my hand against the hard surface above me while kicking at the back of the seat. "LET ME OUT," I scream, my eyes filling with tears as panic overwhelms me.

What the fuck is happening? Didn't the brothers get to me in time? FUCK.

Hard bumps in the road send me flying around the trunk, slamming into the roof and hitting my head against the side. There's barely anywhere for me to move. I'm more cramped here than I was inside that ridiculous club.

Shit, I never thought there would come a time that I'd actually be desperate to have the DeAngelis brothers looking for me, but I've never wanted them more. I'm so fucking screwed. Who is this guy? I didn't get to see his face or even know what he wants with me. Is this one of Giovanni's men? Did they follow us to the club? Or is it just one of their many enemies who saw an opportunity and took it?

No, no, no, no, no, no. This can't be happening.

The road is bumpy and it's clear from the sound of the tires hitting potholes and the way my body flies across the trunk when he rounds corners that he's driving at insane speeds, but he'd want to. If the brothers got even a glimpse of him as he was leaving with me, then he's already a dead man.

I scream and pull at exposed wires, kick out the taillights, and beg to be freed until my throat aches, but his only response is to turn up his music, drowning out my cries. I try to peer through the small hole from the taillights and stick my hands through the small hole like I've seen in movies, but there's no point when we're the only car on the road.

No one is coming for me. I'm back to square one and something tells me that I won't be as lucky this time around.

I endure the reckless driving and violent jolts for another thirty minutes before the car comes to a screeching halt on what feels like a dirt road. Dust flies up around the car and I shrink away from my peephole as the guy cuts the engine and gets out of the car.

The door slams and jostles the whole car, but nothing fucks with my head more than the sound of his boots crunching on the dirt road.

He comes closer and closer and my heart races with terror. There's nothing I can do. I can't move to adjust myself in a better position to try and fend him off and I sure as fuck don't have a knife hiding up my ass to slit his throat with. But I felt how effortlessly he dragged me through the club. This guy is strong. He's relentless. And he sure as fuck doesn't give two shits about me.

He stops at the back of the car and my stomach sinks, listening to his hand squeezing the lever for the trunk. It pops open and a dull light floods in, but before I can get a good look at his face or even scream, he reaches in and grabs me.

The man yanks me right out of the trunk and throws me five feet away. My body crashes into the ground with a hard, painful thud as the sheer layer of sweat coating my skin instantly mixes with the dirt. Keeping his eyes on me, he slams the trunk and begins stalking me, loving my fear as I scramble back, desperate to flee into the thick woods round us.

The man grins wide, the darkness in his eyes barely even scratching the surface of what I'm used to, but unlike the brothers, this man has no intention of stopping. There's something familiar about him, but I can't quite place him, too fucking terrified to even begin going through all the faces I've had to memorize over the past week.

"Finally," he mutters to himself, his eyes lowering with a sick excitement.

I scramble back, desperately trying to get my feet under me, but he's coming too fast. "You've got the wrong person. I … I don't even know you. I didn't do anything."

"No?" he grins wide, grabbing hold of me and raising me up high off the dirty ground. "So you weren't the girl who stabbed my baby brother?"

"What?" I rush out, dread sinking heavily into my gut. "Who?"

"DRAVEN MILLER," he roars. "Those fucking DeAngelis brothers slaughtered him like a fucking animal. They took everything from me, and word around here is that you're their new little toy."

He tosses me to the hard, dirty ground and I scramble back again, scurrying to my feet. Without looking over my shoulder, I take off like a fucking rocket, getting only three steps before he kicks my feet out from under me. I slam down to the dirt road, winding myself and struggling to breathe, barely managing to flip myself over just in time to see him coming for me again. "You can't get away from me, sweetheart, not until I've destroyed you just like they did my brother."

He grabs me again, dragging me through the woods as I scream out in agony, the sharp twigs and branches effortlessly slicing through my skin. "LET ME GO," I scream. "I DIDN'T DO ANYTHING."

He just laughs and I feel my whole world sinking away. They're never going to find me out here.

He finally stops and my eyes go wide seeing an old storm cellar and I barely get a chance to process what's going on before he raises the hatch and throws me down the old wooden steps. He follows me down, pulling an old string and lighting up the room as the hatch slams closed above his head with a loud thud.

I scurry away as he continues to descend until my back slams against a porcelain bathtub in the center of the lonely room. "What the fuck is this?" I breathe, watching as Draven's older brother stalks me, my eyes wide.

He stops and steps to the side where a long table spans the width of the room. All sorts of weapons line the table, old and covered in rust, the kind of shit that I'm going to need to get a tetanus shot for if I somehow survive this.

His finger brushes along the table, carefully considering exactly how he's going to do this as he turns his back on me, absolutely positive that I bear no threat to him, and he'd be right. There's no way I'd be able to get up the stairs and open the hatch before he caught me. And apart from the bathtub at my back, there's nothing else in the room.

"Stand," he orders, still casually going through his selections and wrapping his hands around a thick material before testing its resilience.

"Get fucked," I spit, my gaze focused on the way he slowly turns, the material bound around his knuckles.

With a clenched jaw, he narrows his stare in fury. "I'm not going to ask you again. Stand."

I hold my ground, not daring to move as he strides toward me. Then taking a page out of Giovanni's torture handbook, his hand whips out and slaps hard across my face. "STAND," he roars, spit flying from his mouth.

Tears fill my eyes as the sharp sting rocks through the side of my face. This guy is much bigger than Giovanni, and fuck, his hit packs a fuckload more power. Not prepared to put myself through that one again, I grip the edge of the bathtub and shakily get to my feet.

My heart pounds heavily in my chest, the dread sinking into my gut and weighing me down. He nods toward the bathtub, his eyes sparkling with a savage cruelty. "Get in," he purrs.

Tears stain my cheeks as I shake my head. If I get into that bath, it's all over for me. Nothing good could possibly come from it. "They're going to kill you," I warn him. "They won't stop until your heart is sitting on their fucking shelf like a trophy."

His grin only widens. "Oh, believe me, I hope they come," he laughs. "I'm ready for them, but first, I need to entice that rage within them."

He nods to the bathtub again, stepping even closer and sending a shiver right down my spine. "Get in," he repeats, twisting the material around his hands. "Don't try to make this difficult for yourself because, in the end, you're the only one who's going to suffer. Fair warning though, I love a challenge."

Fuck.

Hopelessness washes over me. I've thought of a million different scenarios over the past week of how I was going to die. It's inevitable in this world, but a part of me had hoped that if it were going to happen, it would be by the brothers' hands and done with remorse, regret, and because they simply had no other choice after doing everything they could to try and save me, not this. I don't want to die out in the woods where no one will ever find me.

This isn't how my story is supposed to go.

With no other choice, I slowly climb into the bathtub as my heart shatters into a million pieces. Tears stream down my face and a loud sob tears from the back of my throat as he props himself on the edge of the tub. "That's a good little girl," he tells me, motioning for me to lay back.

I do as instructed and silently cry as he takes my wrist, fearing what he has planned for me that could possibly rival what the DeAngelis brothers did to Draven in that old warehouse. The thick material is strapped tightly around my wrist, burning my skin as he threads the material through a thick loop, binding me to the bathtub.

He steps around the other side before doing the same to my other wrist and I find myself watching him closely, trying to figure out if there's some way to get out of this, but it's clear that this isn't his first rodeo. He pulls the rough material tight, burning my skin as it keeps me down.

"Did you know," he says, pulling an old knife from his pocket before reaching into the bath and slicing the blade right down the length of my leg, tearing open my sweatpants and letting the loose cotton fall into the bottom of the bath. "The human body holds approximately five liters of blood while this tub can hold up to two hundred liters?"

Nerves settle into my gut and I silently watch him as he continues taunting me with his bullshit chatter. The knife is tossed aside and he pulls out more straps of material before tying them tightly around my thighs and arms like some kind of tourniquet. "It doesn't take a genius to know that the human body can replenish its own blood, and that leaves me wondering, just how long it will take to fill this whole tub."

"You really are a fucking idiot, aren't you?" I snap. "And here I thought you actually knew what you were doing."

He gives me a blank stare and I let out a frustrated sigh. "It takes weeks to replenish that kind of blood. I'll be long dead before you could fill this thing halfway. Did you even do your homework before putting this bullshit plan together or do you just lack common sense like your brother?"

A loud roar rattles through the room and I feel it vibrating right through my chest. "Don't you dare talk about him, you little bitch," he growls, dropping to his knees behind my head and pressing the knife to my throat. "Perhaps I'll pass up my experiment and just watch how your blood coats your skin."

I don't say a word, holding my breath in fear of him sticking to his word, but he just laughs. "Ahhhh, you're awfully quiet now," he says, pulling away from me and allowing me the opportunity to suck in a deep breath.

He steps around me, hovering at the side of the tub and looking down at me. "I couldn't believe my luck when I heard the infamous DeAngelis brothers were making an appearance tonight," he muses. "You should have seen what I had planned for them. It was going to be spectacular, but when they dragged you in along with them, I couldn't resist keeping you for myself."

"You're fucking sick. They don't even care about me. I'm just a nobody who got sold to them. You're wasting your time."

He shakes his head. "But I've gone to all this effort," he says. "Drave really would be disappointed if I didn't at least have a little fun with it. Besides, it'd be a shame to waste such a good opportunity."

He drops down to his knees, with a psychotic widening of his eyes. He looks fucking possessed as he stares down at my bare thigh. "So pretty," he murmurs, leaning over the edge of the bathtub. "I wonder how quickly you'll bleed out."

He goes to reach down and touch me and my knee immediately snaps up, crushing his fucking nose as my survival instincts kick in. "FUCK," he roars, falling back as blood spills from his nose. He holds it with one hand as his other comes flying back at me, the sharp blade plunging deep into my thigh. "You're feisty."

A piercing scream tears through the old storm cellar as agony rips through me. He yanks the blade straight back out and I cry out again, tugging at my bound wrists, desperate to hold the wound and ease the burning pain.

Blood pours from my thigh as I wish for certain death, the aching throbbing too much for me to handle. He's only just getting started. There's no fucking way that I can endure this type of pain. I wasn't built for it. I'm not strong enough.

He peers over the edge of the bathtub, his eyes glowing as he watches the blood spill over the wound and pool in the tub beneath me. Taking both of my legs, he presses down on them, keeping me pinned as he brings his knife down in a shallow arc, slicing his blade straight through my skin.

I cry out, squirming beneath his weight to try and kick him off me, but he's too heavy, too strong. More blood pours from my thigh, pooling with the rest of it beneath my ass as the heavy sobs get caught in my throat, making it hard to breathe. He's careful not to nick one of my arteries and something tells me that's all part of his big plan to keep me alive long enough to fill this stupid tub. It'll never work. I'll surely pass out after I lose enough blood and then hopefully, I'll just slip away into nothingness.

He comes at me again, slicing even deeper and moving higher on my thigh before working his way up to my arms. Each cut of his blade gets more aggressive, more forceful and full of anger, making it clear that his sick need for blood is quickly being replaced by the fury of losing his rapist brother, and rather than taking it out on the three brothers who brutally slaughtered him, he's taking it out on me.

I have to fight back. I have to survive this, but how? He's got me trapped and with each passing second, I'm losing precious blood and energy. He comes at me again and I give it everything I've got, determined not to give up without a fight. If he's going to kill me, then it'll be because I physically couldn't keep going. I just need to hold out long enough for the boys to find me and then everything will be right in the world.

The knife slashes down over my collarbone, slicing through my chest and I just can't take it anymore. I pull my legs up, fighting through the deathly ache as I drop my knee over his neck and slam it down to meet the other, more than ready to endure the worst kind of hell if it means choking him out.

His whole body drops like a deadweight under the force of my thighs, his head dropping hard against the edge of the tub, slamming into his temple. The knife clatters on the ground as his body heavily slumps to the dirty floor. He hadn't expected me to be able to fight back and that's on him.

I stare with wide eyes, sharp pants tearing through my lungs. I watch him for a moment, waiting for him to get back up with a furious rage, but he doesn't fucking move.

Is he dead?

My heart races but I'm not willing to wait and find out. My blood is steadily streaming from my body and it'll only be a matter of time before I pass the fuck out. I only have a few precious moments and I need to make every single one of them count.

Clenching my jaw, I focus on my hand and tug hard against the binds. The material is thick and rough but with blood now coating my skin I have just enough room to move my wrists.

I keep working on it, twisting my hands and loosening the bonds bit by bit as my gaze continually flicks back to the lifeless body beside me. Getting one of them loose enough, I fold my thumb into my palm and pull hard, more than prepared to dislocate my thumb if it means getting my hand free.

A pained cry tears out of me as I pull with every last ounce of energy I have, and finally my hand comes free from the material. Adrenaline pulses through my body as I turn all my attention on my other hand, working tirelessly to release it.

I remember the knife that had clattered on the ground beside my attacker and with my free hand, I grip onto the edge of the bathtub and try to pull myself up just enough to reach over and grab it.

My body aches with every little movement and I feel the blood gushing out of my wounds, but I can't give up here. I'm sure this guy isn't dead and if he's just out cold, he'll eventually wake up, and when that happens, I can't be here.

My fingers curl around the handle of the knife and I let out a sharp cry as I try to settle myself back into position so that I can comfortably tear at the remaining fabric. I slip the old blade beneath the material and grind it back and forth, holding onto my tears as the dirty blade leaves shallow cuts along my wrist. I don't dare stop, hacking at the material until it finally comes free.

Painful sobs get caught in my throat as the desperation and panic courses through my veins.

Finally free, I grip onto the edge and pull myself up, leaving a pool of blood in the tub below me. I shakily get to my feet, my weight on my leg easily one of the most excruciating pains I will ever endure.

I keep the knife held tightly in my palm and every last impulse left inside of me tells me to go and stab it right through my attacker's eye, but I only have a little energy left and I refuse to waste it on him. He'll get what's coming his way eventually, and I believe that whole heartedly.

Stumbling out of the bath, I instantly fall to my knees, my body too weak to keep going, but there's no way in hell that I'm dying here tonight.

Tears fill my eyes and I forge ahead, crawling across the dirty ground until I reach the old wooden stairs. A trail of blood is left behind but it's the least of my worries. If I can just get out through that hatch, I'll be able to hide in the woods until the boys find me, and they will find me. *They always find me.*

Reaching up, I grip the flimsy handrail and pull myself up. I only just get my feet beneath me, struggling under my weight, but all that matters is getting to the top.

Groans and pained curses tear from the back of my throat as the determination to survive pulses through my veins. I feel my head spinning as my body grows weaker by the second. I don't have much longer until it's game over. I have to make it to the finish line.

I will not give up.

Clenching my jaw, I make my way up the stairs until my hand is brushing against the old wooden hatch above me. I give it a hard shove and it takes everything I've got to open it enough so that I can slide my body through the small gap. I'm left with no choice but to fall forward onto the hard earth as the hatch comes down on top of me, crushing me from above.

I snake my body through the opening, using my arms to drag me along the dirty ground until I finally pull free. With a raw, pained cry, I pull myself to my feet, and smelling the sweet taste of freedom in the distance, I stumble forward, hoping that I can make it far enough before passing out.

TWENTY-NINE

ROMAN

The Escalade comes to a screeching halt, skidding along the dirt road as Shayne appears in my headlights. My eyes bug out of my head as Marcus' hand snaps out, bracing himself against the dashboard to keep from flying through the fucking windshield.

"Is that …?"

"Fucking hell," Levi mutters from behind me, throwing his car door open and lunging out into the dirt road. Marcus follows as I hastily cut the engine and race after them.

Shayne stands in the middle of the road, her clothes torn and hanging from her blood-soaked body. Tears stain her beautiful cheeks and as she watches us race toward her, she drops to her knees and falls to the ground with heaving sobs.

Levi reaches her just in time, catching her limp body in his arms and scooping her right into his chest. "SHAYNE," he roars, gently shaking her shoulders as her eyes threaten to close. "Shayne, baby. Tell me what happened? Where is he?"

Her body droops in his arms and he looks up at us, his wide eyes petrified that she's not going to make it, but just looking at her now, blood pouring from her wounds, I can tell that she's a fucking fighter. She hasn't come this far and gone through all the shit we've put her through to call it quits now. She's going to be alright, I can feel it, but in order to make that happen, we have to come through for her.

I drop down beside Levi as Marcus hovers over me, his hands balled into tight fists, more than ready to make this fucker pay. "Where is he, Shayne?" I demand. "Open your fucking eyes."

Levi shakes her again, gently rattling her awake and as those gorgeous blue eyes open and I see the extent of her torment, rage pulses through me. "Come on, little one. Tell us where."

She swallows hard and points off into the distance behind me, barely having the energy to hold her own fucking arm up. "There's … there's an old storm cellar," she says, her voice a soft, pained whimper. "A wooden hatch in the ground."

That's all I need to know.

Marcus takes off like a fucking rocket into the dark woods behind us as I fly to my feet and look down at Levi. "Get her to the fucking car and stop the bleeding, otherwise she won't make it. She's lost too much blood."

He doesn't hesitate, holding her tighter as he gets to his feet and takes off back to the Escalade as I race after Marcus, determined to put this fucker down.

Fury rages through my veins as we storm through the overgrown trees, following the trail of blood and drag marks left in the dirt. Fucking amateur, thinking he can steal from us without consequence. There's a reason we're feared all over the world, why men and women scream and run when they see us coming, why we've been labeled the grim reapers.

Nobody takes from me and gets away with their life.

Shayne Mariano is ours, and the sad sack of shit that took her from us will pay with his fucking life. It'll be the sweetest sin.

Lucas Miller was a fool to think that we didn't clock him the second we walked into that club, watching us like he was trying to find the nerve to slit our throats. Like he could ever get that close. What a fucking joke. The moment we slaughtered his younger brother, he was on our radar.

Dealing with him and his lowlife brother is like child's play. Draven Miller didn't stand a chance, and now his big brother is about to meet him in hell.

It's a shame really, with a bit of training, Lucas would have made an excellent pawn. He's the perfect fall guy—already on the FBI's most wanted list, though not anywhere near as high as me or my brothers. I pride myself on being at the top of that list. It's the greatest form of praise.

We knew there was a chance that Lucas would strike within the club, it's part of the reason that I wanted to get my brothers out of there. They may know how to handle themselves beautifully, but they're still only human and a single stray bullet to the head would take them down just as quickly as the next guy. I couldn't risk it. I never would have thought that fucker would be so stupid as to take Shayne from us. The possibility didn't even enter my mind, but seeing the way he's left her now, I can't wait to end his miserable life. I'm going to take the greatest pleasure in this.

He signed his own fucking death certificate the second he set his sights on her, my only concern is that Marcus gets to him first and takes the pleasure right out of my hands.

We find the entrance to the old storm cellar within moments and Marcus shakes his head, scoffing in disappointment. "He didn't even try to hide it," he spits, shaking his head as he scans over the blood staining the top of the hatch and imagining exactly how it got there.

"What did you expect?" I mutter, scanning over the old wooden hatch. "He left his fucking car out in the open, visible from the main road. He's practically begging for us to find him," I add, though knowing it has a little something more to do with the GPS tracker we had inserted into her arm when the doctor was fitting her with birth control.

Hearing Shayne's familiar cry in the distance, Marcus roars in frustration and I narrow my stare on my brother, watching the deep concern flooding his eyes.

He's getting too attached to this girl. I've tried to warn them. Hell, they saw what happened to Felicity, yet both of my brothers insist on making their own mistakes with Shayne. Fucking morons. They'll learn the hard way that when you're a son of the infamous Giovanni DeAngelis, you don't get to have nice things, and you sure as fuck don't get to fall in love.

Wanting to get this over and done with so we can get back to Shayne, Marcus tears the hatch up and my jaw clenches seeing the pool of blood on the stairs that glistens in the dim moonlight.

He fucking did this to her and now he's going to pay.

Marcus takes off down the stairs and I follow him into the dark pit below, shaking my head at the sheer idiocy of this place. Where's the fucking drainage? The secrecy? The challenge? He's an amateur at best, and if he hadn't touched Shayne, this wouldn't even be worth my time.

A white bathtub sits in the center of the room and Marcus' lips twist into a disgusted sneer, taking in the torn material and blood pooled in the bottom of it. She was tortured here like some kind of rabid animal.

"Fucking hell," Marcus mutters, spying the set of legs that peek out from behind it.

I start making my way toward the tub as Marcus slowly scans the rest of the room, walking down the length of a table filled with tools that look as though they've been left and forgotten for years.

I find Lucas motionless behind the tub and let out a heavy sigh. "Damn, I'm almost upset that this is going to be so easy," I say, scanning over his broken nose and the huge bump at his temple with pride. Clearly Shayne is more of a fighter than I had originally thought. Perhaps we can still make something out of her yet.

Grabbing Lucas by the ankle, I drag his heavy body through the pooled blood on the ground and dump his sorry ass in the center of the room where Marcus and I will have uninterrupted space to work our magic.

I'm passed a bottle of water and I don't waste any precious moments pouring it over his worthless head.

Lucas gasps, his eyes widening as consciousness comes back to him. The moment he sees me hovering over him, panic fills his eyes, though I'm not surprised. Fear, panic, and regret are usually the only emotions we get at times like this. We occasionally get the weak bastard who pisses his pants, but I'm thrilled to not have to deal with that tonight.

Lucas immediately starts to scurry away from me and I slam my heavy boot down over his hand, crushing every fucking bone beneath my weight.

His pained cry is like music to my ears, and I can't help the wicked grin that pulls at the corners of my lips. Marcus turns to me, a knife in either hand and a stumped expression on his face. "What's best for a decapitation? Would you go with the sleek, rusty machete or the common serrated knife?"

A laugh bubbles deep in my chest and if it were the right time, I'd even applaud his attention to detail. How else would we stand out from all the others? We didn't earn our title by slacking off with our kills.

I grin down at Lucas, knowing he's more than aware of the

question floating in the air. "Machete is too easy. Too quick. Go with the serrated," I tell my brother while keeping my hard stare on Lucas. "It's a bit messy, but nothing compares to the crunch of bone as you grind through it."

The machete flies carelessly over Marcus' shoulder but, keeping in mind that we need to get back to Shayne before she bleeds out, we get to work.

Marcus steps in and crouches down beside Lucas, that same questioning expression on his face as he spins the rusty serrated blade between his fingers. "The only question is," he says slowly, watching the way that Lucas stares at him in horror, "do we do this face up, or face down?"

I shake my head, the amusement not lost on me. We've done this too many times for him to not know how I prefer it done, but nothing is better than watching the color drain from our victim's face, learning exactly what we plan to do to them.

I slowly walk around him, releasing his crushed hand from below my boot. "Hmmm," I muse. "Face up, and he'll bleed out too quickly. He'll probably be dead before he gets to hear that magical crunch of his spine. Let's go face down. We wouldn't want him to miss out on something so exhilarating."

Lucas sobs, shaking his head. "No, no. Please. I'm sorry. I'll never touch her again. I swear. Please, don't kill me. I don't want to die."

Marcus tilts his head, capturing Lucas' tear-filled eyes. "Tell me, did Shayne beg for her life before you tortured her? How about when you slid your knife through her flesh? Did she scream? Beg for you to stop?"

He doesn't respond, but he doesn't have to. We've put Shayne through enough torment to know exactly how she would have reacted. "You were relentless with her fragile body, and now, we get to repay the favor."

Marcus knots his fingers into Lucas' hair and throws him face down into the dirty blood-stained ground. Without skipping a beat, he slams his heavy boot down between his shoulder blades, keeping him pinned. "This is going to be fun," he murmurs, his tone filled with venom.

Marcus hands me the serrated knife and I crouch down, gripping his hair to keep him still. "Say hi to your brother for me," I mutter, no doubt in my mind that this asshole is going straight to the deepest pits of hell, where I will one day join him.

Lucas cries and Marcus shushes him. "Quiet now," he whispers. "You're going to miss the best part."

And just like that, I hack the blade of the serrated knife across the back of his neck, watching as his flesh is torn to shreds before listening to the beautiful sound of the blade grinding through his spine.

The sickening crunch is all I need to feel the pure satisfaction pulsing through my veins. The moment his head is dangling from my fingers, the serrated knife clatters to the ground and echoes through the room. Marcus and I don't waste any more time on the prick as we turn to leave, determined to get back to Shayne before it's too late.

THIRTY

SHAYNE

A piercing cry tears from my chest as loud, pained sobs get caught in my throat. "Stop," I beg Levi as he draws me in close to his warm chest, holding me so damn tight. "Stop. Please. Just let me go. It hurts too much. I'm not going to make it."

I cry out in pain, the agony too much for me to handle as my head spins. My body is weak and I barely have the energy to fight him off. "This is going to hurt," Levi tells me as Roman and Marcus take off into the dark woods. "We have to get you out of here. There's a suture kit and antiseptic in the back of the Escalade, but I'm going to have to move you."

I shake my head as my eyes go wide, fearing the very thought of being moved right now, but he doesn't give me a chance to argue as his strong arms tighten around me and he takes off at a sprint toward the Escalade.

Blood pours off me in waves, coating his warm skin and making it harder to hold onto me. I cry and groan with the jostling movements but he ignores every last one of them, his only mission to get me to the safety of the car.

"Hang in there, little one," he tells me, my weight doing nothing to hold him back. "I'm gonna make the pain go away."

"Please," I cry into his wide chest as stray leaves and branches whip past our faces. "Just make it stop."

"We're almost there."

He runs past the beat up car that I was brought here in and the fresh memory of being trapped in the trunk darkens my soul. A soft whimper pulls from deep within me but before I get a chance to linger on the thought, Levi is adjusting me in his strong grasp and opening the trunk of the Escalade.

He lays me down as though I was the most precious jewel and instantly climbs in behind me. He tears his shirt over his head and doesn't waste time ripping it into long bandage-like strands. I keep my gaze locked on his tattoos as he starts wrapping them tightly around my wounds, desperate to control the bleeding.

He keeps his focus, not daring to slow his pace and before I know it, my world is going black.

A sharp jostling has my eyes springing open and I wake to find my head cradled in Levi's lap, his hands pressing down to keep me still as Roman straddles my thighs, keeping me pinned. The pain comes rushing back in waves and I scream, thrashing to get him off me.

"Keep her still," Roman grunts to his brother as Marcus hits the gas, sending the Escalade hurtling down the dirt road, hitting every fucking pothole and bump imaginable.

The momentum of the car moving has something rolling into my side and I glance down to find the head of my attacker, his open eyes wide with fear. A terrified shriek tears from deep within me and Levi grunts, grabbing the head and tossing it into the back seat of the car. "Fucking hell," he mutters, clenching his jaw, but the thought is gone the moment Roman adjusts himself on top of me, sending a wave of searing pain shooting through me.

"Let me die," I beg of him, staring up into his deep obsidian eyes, knowing with absolute certainty that a quick death would be a million times better than having to suffer through the horrendous pain of living inside their world.

Roman shakes his head, regret sweeping through him. "You can't die before you even know what it means to live."

"Please," I whisper as Levi hovers over me, his eyes full of terror as he holds me down. "Just put me out of my misery. I can't do this anymore. I'm not going to make it. Just let me die."

Marcus hits a corner, racing toward the highway and far away from my hell as Levi grips my arms just a little bit tighter, demanding that I stay here with them. "We're not going to let you go," he insists, the desperation in his tone filling the car. "You still have so much to discover. I know you've seen the worst parts of what it means to be with us, but you haven't even scratched the surface of the good stuff yet. Just stay with us, you're going to be alright. I'm not going to let you go."

The tears stream heavier, dropping right off the bottom of my jaw and to my chest as Roman tears open a small black bag filled with medical supplies and lets them spill out onto my blood-stained stomach.

I groan with every jostle as Roman rummages through the medical supplies, finding exactly what he needs. "This is going to hurt," he says. "But you're going to be okay. I swear, I won't let you die."

I shake my head, absolutely terrified. "No," I cry. "I don't want it."

"Sorry, Empress," Roman says, grabbing a bottle of something clear and using his teeth to pull off the cork top. "You've got no other fucking choices." And just like that, he pours the liquid over my body and I scream until my lungs give out.

Levi holds me down as I thrash under Roman's weight, the burn almost enough to knock me right out. "STOP," I scream as Roman reaches out and unforgivingly pours more over my arms and chest. "PLEASE STOP."

Roman throws the empty bottle aside. "I don't have anything to numb you with," he warns me, pulling out a suture kit and tearing open a little sterilized packet with his teeth. A small, curved needle appears in his big hands and my eyes go wide.

"No pain, no gain," Levi mutters as Marcus turns onto the highway, the tires of the Escalade screeching below us as the smoothness of the road instantly eases the reckless jostling.

I clench my eyes, too terrified of what comes next. I've never been good with needles. The very thought of it digging into my flesh makes me nauseous, but I have no choice. They're going to hold me down and stitch me back together whether I like it or not.

A searing pain tears through my inner thigh and my eyes spring open. "Keep her still," Roman growls as I desperately try to kick him off me. He digs straight back in again, threading the string through the inside of my thigh and pulling it tight to draw the stray pieces of muscle and flesh back together.

He works quickly and with skill as though he's done it a million times before, but I bet his previous patients weren't such little bitches about it. My jaw clenches as the tears continue down my face and I try my best not to thrash beneath him, knowing one slight fuck up with that needle could cause all kinds of havoc.

I look straight up and meet Levi's hard stare, my eyes pleading for some kind of relief. "Make it stop," I beg, the words getting stuck in my throat.

He shakes his head. "I can't. You'll bleed out."

"Please," I whisper, my hand curling around and gripping onto his strong arm as he holds me down. "Put me out of my misery."

He glances up at his brother who works tirelessly to save my life before dropping his gaze back to mine. "Are you sure?" he questions, concern deep in his dark eyes. I don't respond, but he sees my wild desperation, and without another word, he presses down on the side of my neck. And with just a bit of pressure, darkness consumes me.

THIRTY-ONE

Something drops and the soft clattering has my eyes springing open into the dim light of the castle's living room. All three brothers are hovering around me, and a grim, bored expression lingers on Roman's face. Marcus sends an irritated glare to his younger brother, who looks guilty as shit bending low to pick up his dropped drumstick.

I groan and turn my head to face the backrest of the couch. "Geez, anyone would think that a bunch of serial killers would know a thing or two about being quiet."

Marcus drops down on the end of the couch, carefully pulling my feet on to his lap as the torturous memories of my time in that storm cellar fill my mind, playing on replay. "You saw us in action. Do we really strike you as the type to go in silence?"

I roll my eyes, knowing he has a very good point, but the subtle movement has a deep pounding settling into my skull. "No, you're the type to accidentally drop your gun at the door and alert every fucker in the room, so instead of a simple assassination, it turns into a chaotic shootout."

Marcus laughs, slicing his stare to his younger brother, who rolls his eyes and sinks into the soft couch opposite me. "It happened one time," Levi says, "and it wasn't even my fault. You knocked the fucking gun out of my hand."

I can't help but turn back to face him. "You're kidding right?" I laugh, attempting to reach for the painkillers that have been carelessly tossed onto the low coffee table. "How did you guys earn such an outstanding reputation when you're doing shit like that?"

"Simple," Roman mutters, leaning in and grabbing the painkillers for me. "Make them think it was intentional. We came out with six clean kills that night, stripping an opposition of some of their biggest players. Besides," he adds with a wink that has me gasping for breath. "It was fun."

"Fun?" I sputter, trying to swallow the small pills and choking on the water as it goes down the wrong hole and makes a mess of my black tank, instantly making my body ache with my movement. "That's what you call fun?"

Roman shrugs as a wicked grin stretches over Marcus' face. "Nah," he says, amusement swirling deep in his dark eyes. "That's what I call a Saturday night."

"Fucking hell," I mutter under my breath, trying to adjust myself to see them all better.

"Don't move," Marcus says, gripping on to my feet a little tighter to hold me down, as if I haven't already been traumatized enough by men pinning me down. "You can't risk tearing your stitches. Trust me, that's not something you want to go through a second time if you can avoid it."

I roll my eyes and kick his hand off my feet. The guy has a point, but I'm not about to go and tell him that. "Then help me sit up. I've been laying here for hours."

"You sure?" Levi questions, getting up and slowly creeping toward me. "Moving you is going to hurt."

"Just do it," I tell him. "I can handle it."

"Can you?" he questions, moving in behind me and gripping me under my arms to help drag me up the couch. "From what I remember in the back of the Escalade, you weren't handling it too well then."

"I was tortured in a bathtub and sliced open like a fucking Thanksgiving turkey," I mutter darkly, the reminder weighing heavily on my chest. "It fucking hurt. So if I wanted to scream and bitch at you assholes while you shoved needles deep into my already burning flesh, then I had every damn right. Not to mention, you didn't even give me anything to numb the pain, you just went for it like I was supposed to be enjoying myself. And for the record, I didn't."

"Wait," Roman cuts in, stepping right into my line of sight. "You're pissed at us for saving your life?"

I huff and cross my arms over my chest, groaning with the movement. "No," I mutter with a heavy sigh. "Seeing your Escalade pulling up in front of me was the happiest moment of my life. I've never felt such an overwhelming rush of relief and gratefulness before. What I'm pissed about is being in that situation in the first place. If you guys hadn't felt the need to castrate his brother, then none of this would have happened."

"Woahhhhh," Roman says, holding up his hands to cut me off. "You're the one who started shit with him during our party. You're the one who shoved a fucking knife into his gut. This is your war, Empress. You're just lucky that we were there to finish it."

"LUCKY?" I shriek, shoving my hands under me to try and force myself up a little higher. "What about last night would you call lucky? Look at me," I demand, waving my hand over the multiple shallow cuts covering my body. "I look like I've just been sliced and diced by a fucking maniac. Oh wait. I WAS!"

Marcus watches me, his lingering gaze full of curiosity as he slowly narrows his eyes. "What's this really about?" he questions. "There's something more. You knew that we moved against Draven to protect you, and you even looked fucking thrilled when I ended his life. You were okay with it, so what else is going on?"

I glance away, my jaw clenched as my chest constricts with a dull ache that I don't fully understand. "Can't a girl just be angry that she spent a night bleeding out in a tub?"

Roman shakes his head and moves in closer. "You have every right to be fucked up over that, but Marcus is right. Something else is on your mind."

I can't help but meet his haunted stare, and as I see the real concern deep within his dark eyes, a lump begins forming in my throat. I let out a sigh and drop my gaze to the glass of water on the coffee table, watching as the condensation slowly trails down the slim glass and leaves a ring on the expensive wood. "You said that you would teach me how to protect myself," I murmur, my voice so low that I don't even know if they can hear me properly.

Marcus' hands flinch on my ankle and he holds on a little tighter as Roman lets out a heavy breath. "We did say that," he admits. "But that was only a few days ago. Whether we had started training you or not, you wouldn't have been strong enough yet to fend him off."

"You don't know that," I rush out, tears filling my eyes. "You could have taught me the basics. Or at least taught me how to get him off me long enough to have called out to you in the club. It didn't need to go that far. You could have saved me before it was too late."

"We didn't save you," Levi says, sitting on the edge of the coffee table to meet my hard, pained stare. "You saved yourself. You're so much stronger than you give yourself credit for. You broke that motherfucker's nose and knocked him out cold. You got yourself out of that bathtub and through the hatch when other people would have given up. All we did was mend you up at the end."

"Don't act like I didn't see his fucking head rolling around in the back before you knocked me out."

"Well," Marcus grins, a sick sparkle hitting his eyes. "We couldn't exactly let him go unpunished."

"You cut his fucking head off."

Marcus laughs. "Give credit where it's due," he says. "We didn't just cut it off, we hacked at it with a serrated knife. It was pure brilliance. No, it was a masterpiece. A work of art."

My stomach churns. "Ugh, you're going to make me throw up."

Marcus gently pushes my feet off his lap and stands. "Then my work here is done."

Without another word, he walks out of the living room, and before getting too far, a low whistle echoes behind him and two big wolves go bounding through the room. My eyes widen in surprise. I hadn't even noticed they were in here.

Roman watches the wolves bound after Marcus before glancing back at me. "We good?" he asks.

I raise a brow. "Are you forgetting that you kidnapped me and practically painted the target on my back for your father? Not to mention all the other shit you've put me through since being here. In what world would we ever be good?"

He rolls his eyes. "It's not like we tied you down in a bathtub."

"How's that any different to stalking me through a maze and letting me think I was going to die?"

"Because we never intended you any harm. You were always safe with us; you just didn't know it. We just like watching the fear in your eyes, whereas he had every intention of ending your life. We are not him. So I'll ask you again. Are we good?"

I let out a heavy huff and clench my jaw. "Make me a morphine smoothie and I might just consider letting you off the hook."

Roman holds my stare and, judging by the gruff expression on his stunningly wicked face, I'd dare suggest that he's struggling to hold his tongue. The seconds tick by and I refuse to break his stare until he finally gives in and turns toward the big entryway of the living room.

"Hey," I call after him before he can get too far away. Roman turns back, his obsidian gaze narrowed on mine as he waits impatiently. "I, umm … thank you. I know I kinda gave you guys a hard time, but whether I want to admit it or not, you saved my life. You didn't have to go down into that storm cellar, but you did. I would have always feared that he'd come back for me. If you guys hadn't … you know," I say, drawing my thumb across the front of my throat. "I never would have been able to sleep at night. I'm just … I'm glad it's over."

Roman watches me a moment longer, his hard stare slowly softening as silence fills the room, then he simply nods and tears his addictive gaze away. He strides out of the room as though he couldn't get out of here fast enough and I find myself glancing back at Levi. "What's his problem? He looks like someone just lit a fire under his ass."

"Believe it or not," he chuckles, leaning back onto the coffee table and getting comfortable. "I think you're probably the first person to ever thank him for saving their life."

"No shit?" I mutter, my brow arching with disbelief. "What about you and Marcus? Out of all the fucked-up situations you've been in, you've never once been backed into a corner and had to rely on your brother to save you?"

He shakes his head. "Shit like that doesn't happen to us. We only ever go into a situation where we know we can win. We don't foolishly risk our lives."

"What about with your father?" I question. "You don't think he's ever taken the brunt of his abuse to keep his attention off you two?"

Levi's brows furrow and he quickly sinks into a deep silence. "I guess," he says after a long pause, his eyes on me yet focused somewhere far away. "It's possible, but he wouldn't. We're all more than capable of handling his shit."

I shake my head. "I know you're more than capable. You've proven that time and time again, but I think you're wrong. I think Roman does more for you than you will ever know."

"What makes you say that?"

I shrug my shoulders and look toward the entryway that Roman had just disappeared through. "I don't know," I murmur. "Just a feeling."

I scoot back down on the couch, feeling the painkillers starting to do their thing, though I really hope Roman can come through with that morphine smoothie. The pain is manageable, but if there's some way that I can forget about it all together, then I'm down. Perhaps a morphine smoothie isn't really what I need, maybe I should be hitting up Marcus for something a little ... stronger.

I glance back to Levi to find his curious stare on me. "What?" I ask slowly, watching as his stare lingers with an odd sense of pride. I narrow my gaze on him, unsure why nerves are bubbling through my system.

He shakes his head softly, letting out a gentle breath. "Nothing," he mutters. "You're just … kinda blowing me away."

My face twists in confusion. "Huh?"

Levi laughs and sits up a little straighter on the coffee table. "You're different," he tells me. "You're a fighter and not at all what I'm used to seeing around here. The girls our father drops on our doorstep give up. They don't push back and they sure as fuck don't have the balls to be out here making demands. But look at you. You've somehow turned this place into your home. You have Roman fetching you drugs and Marcus making a fool of himself. Fuck, little one. You got me to fuck you on the roof despite my better judgment."

I scoff. "Don't act like you weren't into it."

"I said no such thing," he throws back. "I was down, but did I think it was fucking risky? Hell yeah."

I meet his stare and push up onto my elbow. "What are you trying to say?"

He shrugs his shoulders, his gaze becoming soft and full of wonder. "You're surprising me. We followed you for months before making our move. We thought in that short time that we'd learned everything there was to know, but I've never felt so lost. We thought we were getting a broken girl with absolutely no will to push back, but that's not who you are at all. You're thriving here. You're going to make strides in this world that no other has before."

"Okay," I laugh. "Are you sure you didn't hijack some of my painkillers?"

Levi rolls his eyes, desperately fighting the grin that threatens to tear across my face. "What I'm trying to say is that you confuse me.

You're like a puzzle that I can't quite figure out."

"How so?" I question, my brows dropping low.

He narrows his gaze, watching me closely. "Because that girl that I watched for so long was broken beyond repair. You were struggling and in a constant state of exhaustion. You only ever spoke to the old bat who lived down the hall and never treated yourself to shit. You worked more hours than anyone has the right to work, and for what? Your apartment was trash."

I clench my jaw, glancing away as the shame of my real life quickly catches up to me, but Levi isn't about to let me get away with it that easily. "What was going on, Shayne? We saw that eviction notice on your fridge."

I let out a heavy sigh and fight back the tears that well in my eyes. "My father happened."

Levi doesn't say a word, just sits and watches me through a narrowed gaze. Though something tells me that he's more than ready to sit here all day until I finally give him a glimpse into the real me. I slowly push myself up, painfully aware of my skin pulling around the stitches. Levi reaches out and helps me sit up, and I let out a grateful sigh.

"My father is a piece of shit," I tell him. "I spent my whole childhood locking myself in my closet just to keep away from him. He was an angry drunk and would spend his nights gambling every cent we had. He liked horses, but poker machines were his weakness. By ten years old, I was fishing through dumpsters just to eat, and thinking about it now, it was a miracle that I even had a roof over my head. I was able to convince my local grocer to let me help stack shelves for a little bit of cash and I would hold on to that so tightly. It was only a few extra dollars here and there, but it was my greatest lifeline."

I let out a breath, distantly noticing the way Roman and Marcus discreetly appear in the entryway with the two massive wolves at their side. I keep my gaze locked on Levi's, knowing that if I dare look away, I won't ever get the words out. "That job was everything to me," I continue. "It gave me purpose and allowed me time away from home. When my father realized that I'd been hiding money from him, that's when the real abuse started. I was only eleven when he first hit me. He would throw me down the stairs and ransack my room. I quit my job just so there wasn't any more money for him to find. I thought that he'd back off, but he just assumed I was hiding it somewhere else. That went on for years and I toughed it out until the day I turned eighteen. I moved out of there so fast and never looked back. I had to sleep on the streets for nearly two weeks before I could find somewhere to live, but that first taste of freedom made it all so worth it."

Roman steps into the room, my morphine in his hands. "That's why your first response is to run," he comments, moving in beside Levi with the big wolves following behind. One of them jumps up onto the couch, right where Marcus had been sitting earlier, and drops down until its head is resting just by my thigh.

I can't help but reach over and scratch between his ears, loving the way that the big wolf pushes against me for more. "I thought that I would never see him again, but he tracked me down and took everything I had. I ran and ran again but tracking me down became an obsession. The last time I saw him was six months ago. He broke into my home and took every last cent that I had."

I let out a heavy breath, the heartache that I've suffered through over the past six months coming back to haunt me as the boys eagerly listen, trying to figure out the pieces of the puzzle that they weren't able to work out from simply watching over me for three months. "He ransacked everything that I'd worked for until I was left with nothing, and the worst part is that he truly believes that he's entitled to everything that I have. I was planning on taking a break. I'd saved up nearly five grand so that I could actually spoil myself, maybe take a few weeks off from working at the club, go somewhere nice, maybe a resort or somewhere that I could just lie on the beach for days on end. Instead, I ended up with crippling debt, working double shifts, open to close nearly every night. I would work myself to exhaustion and fall asleep on the fucking bar."

I keep my gaze focused on the big wolf, terrified of showing them just how broken I really am. "The same day I got that eviction notice, I'd nearly lost my job. Then to top it all off, I got kidnapped by the freaking grim reapers, courtesy of my deadbeat father. As long as I live, he's always going to come for me. My only saving grace is that while I'm here, he won't be stupid enough to try anything."

"Well," Marcus says, moving in beside his brothers as a haunting darkness flashes in his eyes. "For argument's sake, let's hope he is."

I let out a deep breath and flop back against the couch, cringing as the sudden movement has pain rocking right through my chest. "How soon until the pain goes away?" I question, feeling my head starting to go a little woozy. "Because if you guys decide to do something stupid again, I'm going to need to hightail it out of here. If I could at least outrun you long enough to hide out in the woods, that'd be great."

Roman narrows his gaze, thrusting the box of morphine toward me. "You're not funny."

"Oh really?" I mutter, raising a brow. "Because I think I'm fucking hilarious."

"Yeah, that's clear," he throws back at me. "Now hurry up and take your morphine. It was peaceful before when you were knocked out cold."

A wicked grin stretches across my face. "Ooooh, look who's funny now."

Roman groans and huffs as he turns on his heel and stalks back out of the room. "You're impossible," he growls, not looking back as he disappears around the corner.

I can't help but laugh and as I meet Marcus' amused smirk, I bite down on my lip to keep from cackling like a little schoolgirl. "Are you ever going to ease up on him?" he questions. "Eventually you're going to make him break, and when you do, it won't be pretty."

I shake my head, having too much fun with it. "Now, why the hell would I do something stupid like that when getting under his skin is my favorite part of the day? Besides, isn't the whole positive vibes and feeling good shit supposed to help the healing process?"

Levi lets out a heavy sigh and glances toward his brother. "Not gonna lie," he mutters, his dark eyes glistening with silent laughter. "She has a good point. We're all about the healing process."

Marcus nods slowly, deep in thought. "That we are," he says, running his fingers over the stubble on his sharp jaw as his gaze shifts back to mine. "You leave us no choice. We simply have to get on board and help you get under Roman's skin every possible chance we can."

THIRTY-TWO

My foggy reflection stares back at me through the full length mirror of my private bathroom. I might have forgotten to turn on the fan before stepping into one of my favorite scalding showers, but I can't say that I'm disappointed. It's only been a few days since the bathtub incident, and while I'm fine to get up and slowly walk around, looking at the physical mess he made of my body devastates me. I'm covered from head to toe in angry red cuts, each of them held together with surgical string as my body tirelessly works to fuse itself back together.

Looking at myself breaks my heart, but every day has gotten a little easier. I just hate that these scars are never going to go away.

While the memories might fade and become easier to deal with, every time I glance down at my body, I will be hit with a reminder of what he did to me.

Averting my eyes from the mirror, I wrap my towel around my body and start brushing out my hair. It's been hard to shower over the last few days, but I've given it a good try. Every movement seemed to pull at my stitches, so all I've been able to do is stand under the hot stream of water, but not today. Today I was able to really wash the dirt out of my hair and scrub the remaining dried blood off my body. I feel like a whole new woman, but that doesn't mean that the dreams will magically stop.

Every time I close my eyes, I see him. I feel his hand pressing down over my mouth, making it impossible to scream. I see the darkness trapping me inside the trunk of his car, the rough ground as I was thrown down ... the lone bathtub in the center of the cellar.

It'll never stop.

I've woken up screaming every night. Marcus sat with me the first night as I just laid and stared at the ceiling. Roman and Levi took shifts the second night, and as the third night crept in, they shoved sleeping pills down my throat. I slept sixteen dreamless hours and I'm not going to lie, I feel a million times better, but what about tomorrow night? What about a week from now? I've never quite feared being alone in the dark like I do now.

I don't know what I would have done if the boys hadn't found me.

Letting out a sigh, I quickly blow dry my hair and put on just a touch of makeup, lining my eyes and adding a bit of mascara to make them pop. I step out of my bathroom and slowly get dressed, unable to figure out how the hell the guys talked me into this.

Dinner at their father's mansion.

A bullet through the head sounds more enticing than this, but apparently it's a monthly business meeting that the boys are required to attend. I would have preferred that they leave me locked up in their big-ass castle, but Marcus quickly pointed out that leaving me here alone is only going to send me into a raging panic attack the moment they step out of the castle.

I hate that he's always right. All of them are always right, and what's worse is that they like to point it out. It's like a constant reminder that I have no idea how to navigate this messed-up world.

My backless gown is gorgeous and I feel like a fucking fraud in it, even more so as I step into the black, red-bottom heels that match. The long gown skims along the ground as the sleeves come right down to my wrists, somehow covering every last scar on my body. Whichever brother picked this out went to a lot of effort to get it right. The dress has a high slit that comes right up to the top of my thigh, but it somehow covers the massive stab wound and manages to keep my horrific injuries concealed.

Glancing at the time, I let out a breath. I really don't want to do this. I don't feel strong enough to be taking a trip out, especially somewhere that I'm going to have to constantly be on guard and watch my back. I'm still weak from the blood loss and can barely go a few hours without needing to dose up on painkillers, so tonight is bound to be interesting.

I make my way down the stairs and I'm not surprised to find the three brothers waiting at the bottom, each of them in a jaw-dropping suit that would have any girl falling to her knees. The last time I saw them look so good was my second night here when they insisted on the world's weirdest dinner party. Things were different then, and I didn't get the chance to admire the merchandise, but now, I'm as shameless as they come.

Their suits are sculpted to their bodies and fit perfectly, showing off their wide, strong shoulders as their tattoos peek out at the base of their necks. They look terrifyingly delicious, exactly what any girl should expect of a man born into the mafia.

Marcus looks up at me, appreciation in his eyes as his gaze sails down the length of my body, stopping at the high slit at the top of my thigh. "Mmmm," he murmurs, a rawness to his tone. "We can still make a mafia wife out of you after all."

I pause halfway down the steps, my eyes going wide as my heart kicks into action. "What did you just say?"

"Nothing," he laughs as Levi smirks, a silent message passing between them. "Hurry up and get your ass down here so we can leave. Trust me, you don't want to be the one running late to one of Father's business meetings. After all, it's not a good look to have his sons disrespecting his rules in front of his business associates."

"Wait," I breathe, my gaze flicking between the three brothers. "There's going to be other people like him there? No one said anything about other people. I thought it was just going to be us and maybe his wife."

Roman scoffs. "There's no one quite like him, but no, the men who he usually deals with and their wives will be there. It's usually a big pissing contest to remind everyone who's boss. You can expect at least three men to lose their lives and then you'll feel like shit watching their wives wailing in grief, but then it'll all be over and we can get you back home."

"You say that like it isn't a big deal," I comment, clutching the railing as I make my way down the rest of the stairs."

"Because it's not," Levi explains, meeting me at the bottom and taking my elbow. "Once you've sat through it so many times, it becomes repetitive and boring. You'll see. You have nothing to worry about."

My gaze drops to the ground as the boys lead me right out the front door, and for a moment, it almost feels wrong. I don't think I've ever seen this door open and close the whole time that I've been here. Though Roman is forced to enter a unique code supplied by his father.

We walk down the massive entrance stairs and Levi grips my arm tighter to keep me from falling. A black SUV is parked out front, and as I step up to the door, I can't help but look back at the massive castle. It's the first time that I'm truly seeing the front of it up close and personal. It truly is an incredible sight, creepy but incredible. The gargoyles really are the cherry on top, acting as a final warning to anyone who dares get this far that they should turn and run before it's too late.

The guys don't let me appreciate their home for long as they usher me into the black SUV, and before I know it, Roman is hitting the gas, sending us sailing down the long driveway toward the most fucked-up business meeting that I'll ever sit through.

We drive for nearly an hour and I find myself sitting in silence, deep in thought about the night of the attack. So many things just don't make sense, like how did Lucas Miller know we were going to be at that club, and how the hell did the boys find me that quickly? I was certain that I'd be hiding out in those bushes for days before they found me. Even then, I probably would have bled out.

Roman veers into the driveway of a massive mansion and pulls to a stop outside the impressive iron gates. He rolls down the driver's side window and enters a code into a small keypad, only as the gates begin to roll open, I find the question falling from my lips. "How did you guys find me so quickly that night?"

Silence fills the car and I watch as their sharp gazes flick to one another, each of them studiously ignoring me, but their silence speaks volumes. As Roman hits the gas again, sending us flying down the long driveway, an enraged gasp tears from deep inside my chest. "YOU ASSHOLES PUT A TRACKING DEVICE IN ME?"

All three men focus their heavy stares straight out the windshield as we continue down the long driveway, doing everything they can to avoid my questioning gaze.

I grip the knife from my thigh and lean forward, curling my arm around the seat and pressing the blade to the base of Roman's throat. The fucker doesn't even blink as his brothers watch on in amusement, looking at me like a lion cub trying to roar, but all they hear is a pathetic little squeal.

"Answer me," I growl, hating how this position pulls at the stitches in my arm.

Roman sighs and glances at Marcus beside him. "Really? You're not going to do anything about this?"

He shrugs his shoulder and rests back into his seat as Roman approaches the wide circle at the top of the impressive driveway. "Looks like you have everything under control."

I can't help the smirk that sails across my lips. Marcus and Levi have stuck by their word and have backed down at every opportunity over the last few days, allowing me to fly free as I've gotten under Roman's skin time and time again. It's been amazing, but my smile doesn't last for long, realizing that both Marcus and Levi were more than likely in on this stupid little tracking device as well.

Roman brings the SUV to a stop outside his father's massive entryway and meets my stare through the rearview mirror. "What did you expect?" he questions. "You were gifted to us as property and we knew there was a good chance you would try to escape. Believe it or not, you're not the first who has tried to run. It was in our best interest to insert a GPS locator, and you know it. Had we not done that, it would have taken days to find you in those woods, and you know just as well as we do, you would have bled out before we got to you. So bitch at me all you like, but that tracking device is what saved your life."

I glare at him through the mirror, hating just how right he is, but my stubborn nature will always win out when it comes to Roman DeAngelis. "I want it out."

"Go ahead," he says. "Do it now. Slice that knife deep inside your arm and tear it out."

My jaw clenches as he holds my stare, knowing damn well that the thought of this knife pressing against my skin will send me into a horrendous panic attack, but he doesn't relent. "What's the matter?" he pushes, curling his hand around mine and forcing the blade away from his throat. "Would you prefer that I do it for you? Hold you down and press the sharp edge into your creamy skin?"

Fear pulses through my veins and I open my hand, letting the knife fall into his lap. "STOP," I scream, tears brutally filling my eyes. "STOP IT."

He releases his hold on me and as though nothing happened, he reaches for the door handle and pushes out of the car. "Let's get this over and done with."

Both Levi and Marcus follow his lead, and before I know it, Levi is already there, opening the door and offering me his hand.

I let out a deep breath, trying to gain control of my wild emotions as I take it gingerly and allow him to help me out of the SUV. Roman and Marcus walk ahead of us and I find myself hiding behind Levi's big shoulder as he leads me up the stairs of the grand entrance. The boys don't stop to knock at the door, just simply let themselves into the house that I'm sure they probably grew up in.

Conversation fills the lobby, yet there is no one in sight, so I take the small opportunity to look around. We've barely even walked a few steps, but I can already see just how expensive this home must have been. It's fit for a king with high ceilings and gold trim on nearly every surface.

A massive grand staircase sits in the center of the room leading up to another wide-open space. My body itches to go and explore, but I won't dare leave the brothers' sides on a night like this. Separating from them in this house would be a mistake that I'm sure would cost me my life.

Giovanni DeAngelis already has a target painted on my back and I don't intend to find out what would happen if he were to get me alone.

"You're late," comes a chilling tone from the entryway of a huge dining hall.

Giovanni stands before us, staring down his three sons as his new wife stands at his side, looking as though she actually wants to be there. Levi's hand flinches on my back, and I can't help but remember the last time they met with their father. Shock collars were forced around their throats and they were tortured for information about the night we went into the old industrial area. It ended with one hell of a deadly brawl that made Giovanni cut and run with the few guards he could make it out with.

It's also the night I fucked Levi on the roof and found their dead mother rotting away in a glass coffin.

I can only imagine how tonight is going to go. It was a bold move for Giovanni to have his sons here tonight, though he couldn't possibly know that after all these years, they've finally found their mother.

"Precisely," Marcus mutters as Roman's hands ball into tight fists at his side, though I can't possibly begin to figure out which of the many haunting memories or reasons would have him reacting like this. There are just too many, and while my gut is telling me it's because of the Snow White mom thing, my head is telling me that it's something different entirely.

I feel a sharp gaze lingering on my body and I risk glancing up to find Ariana's hungry stare on me, a promise in her eyes to collect on the favor she claims that she's owed, but fuck her. Now knowing who she is and what threat she could hold over me, I won't be going anywhere near her.

Giovanni huffs at his sons before boldly turning his back and striding into his busy dining hall. Men and women fill the room in gowns and suits that are worth more than I made in a year.

Marcus discreetly steps into my other side as we make our way around the room and I do what I can to walk normally and act as though every step I take isn't killing me inside. I try to commit every face to memory, knowing that these are likely the men and women the brothers will one day lead. Assuming we're still alive by then.

Levi leads me straight to the long table, pulling out a seat for me as the people watch on around us. Lingering stares capture my attention and I force myself not to look. I'm nothing more than property in this room, and I can guarantee that the other men here sure as hell haven't brought their midnight entertainment along.

Marcus and Levi drop down in the seats on either side of me, watching the people around them with trained gazes as Roman sits directly opposite, a bored expression resting on his face.

Their father looks on with a narrowed gaze, shifting over all four of us in disapproval. I can guarantee that tonight's invitation didn't extend to me, but if he was surprised to see me, he didn't let it show. Though, I have a feeling that stepping out of line in front of their father's business associates isn't exactly something new to them. Giovanni would be prepared for the worst where his sons are concerned, which more than likely explains why the room is littered with security.

Arrogant, loud chatter fills the room as men drain their glasses filled with scotch and whiskey. Women stand at their sides, pretending to be interested in their husband's conversations as their gazes linger on the other men in the room, wondering which one they should try and seduce later in the night.

Ariana drops down beside Roman with a sultry smile resting along her lips, her seat immediately next to the head of the table. I let out a nervous groan. A part of me had hoped that Giovanni would be sitting way at the opposite end of the massive table, but with Ariana right here next to Roman, my chances are dwindling.

Ariana looks at me and I can't help but stare right back as I watch her hand disappear under the table to rest on Roman's thigh. She laughs as Roman's expression hardens, and while it's obvious that they have something going on, it's clear in Roman's hard glare that he's not interested in pushing those particular boundaries tonight.

He pushes her hand away and a thrill travels through my veins. I have no right to feel jealous of their strange little relationship, yet here we are.

Ariana falters at Roman's rejection, causing a soft chuckle to pull at the back of my throat. Her hard stare instantly shoots back to mine, and her eyes narrow in suspicion. As Giovanni moves into the space at the head of the table, she wipes the irritation off her face, looking up at him adoringly with both of her hands visible on the table.

"Let us take our seats," Giovanni announces over the noise of the room, instantly gaining everyone's attention as the chatter falls away to a distant hum. "Dinner is ready."

THIRTY-THREE

What the ever-loving fuck have I got myself involved in? Giovanni sits and within mere seconds, the men and their wives are filling each of the seats around us as though they have some kind of assigned seating. Their asses barely touch the chairs before waiters in penguin suits come pouring out of a side entrance with plates of food piled high on trays.

The waiters begin serving dinner with Giovanni and his wife, moving on to his sons before handing out meals to the other guests. I stare cautiously at the plate of roast chicken and vegetables in front of me, wondering if it's safe to eat. After all, the boys warned me that people tend to lose their lives during these events. When you're an enemy of the boss, I suppose anything could happen.

Conversation turns into hushed chatter as people speak to only those who sit around them, almost as though exceptional table manners is a requirement of sitting within Giovanni's presence. Not wanting to draw attention to myself, I do everything I can to appear small. I eat small bites and only sip my water every now and then. My head is kept down at all times and I ignore the leers coming from Ariana across the table.

"It seems you've managed to get your girl under control," Giovanni says to his sons, making my head snap up, fearing that he's referring to me, but who else could he be talking about?

I raise a brow. This must be some kind of compliment to his sons, but as Roman's gaze narrows on his father and the two boys tense on either side of me, I realize that it's anything but. I swivel my gaze toward Giovanni to find his hard stare on me.

I swallow hard but when no one responds to his comment, I find myself raising my chin. "Excuse me?" I question, keeping my tone low so as to not draw attention my way.

Giovanni rests back in his seat, using his napkin to wipe his mouth before carelessly tossing it down on the table. "I'm not going to lie, the impression you left me with on our last two meetings was less than acceptable. You looked ratty and broken, but it appears that my sons have wised up and pulled you in line. Perhaps you have learned from your mistakes," he says, his tone darkening, "unlike your father."

My brows dip low as my hands ball into tight fists beneath the table. A chill sweeps down my spine and I suck in a deep breath, forcing myself to remain seated. "What's that supposed to mean?" I snap, instantly regretting my tone as he leans forward, his hard stare becoming hostile and full of disdain. Levi's hand slips onto my lap, clutching my fists and forcing them free, a silent message telling me to calm the fuck down before this goes somewhere I'm not prepared to go.

Giovanni glances toward his sons' hostile stares and laughs, probably assuming that he has us right where he wants us, or in the very least, assuming that I give a shit about my father. Giovanni stands and leans his big hands onto the table, his thick, gold chain clanging against the wood as his stare bores into mine. "How does it feel to be so worthless to your father?" he questions. "My sons are pieces of shit, and yet I wouldn't give them up for anything."

I scoff, unable to reel it in this time. "You wouldn't give them up only because they're too valuable to you, not because you have any fatherly affection toward them."

He shrugs his shoulders. "I raised my sons in my image and they are exactly what I need them to be."

"Soldiers."

"Correct," he says. "You, on the other hand, are just as worthless as your father. Imagine selling your child to a man like me and then coming back for more. Little does he know that you barely even cover his original debt, let alone his new one. I wonder what else he will give up. Tell me, Miss Mariano, do you have more siblings that we don't yet know about?"

My jaw clenches at his arrogance and just the thought of my fist sailing across the table and slamming into his stupid face has something settling within me. "If I did, I sure as hell wouldn't tell you."

"Careful," he warns me, his gaze narrowing dangerously. "You wouldn't want to find out what happens to little girls who destroy my dinner parties. Watch your mouth. I'm feeling lenient tonight. This is your only warning."

I swallow hard, not prepared to push my luck any further as I divert my stare back to my plate. I nibble at my food but my appetite is completely gone. This night has been impossible. I don't know what to do, what to say, what not to say, and how the hell to even breathe without causing issues.

Conversation fills the massive dining hall and I find myself trying to distract myself by listening in. The couple just down from us are complaining about their three daughters and will be shipping them off to a boarding school, while the two men sitting just down from Roman are discussing real estate.

I let out a sigh, having hoped that at least one person in this room would have been discussing something interesting enough to hold my attention. Not able to continue torturing myself by shoving food down my throat, I push my plate away and find myself glancing up at Roman. His heavy stare is on me but his mind is clearly far away, deep in thought.

My brows furrow as I watch him in return, but he soon comes back to reality, his eyes softening just a bit. Ariana glances up at Roman with her big, fuck-me eyes, and seeing that I have his attention, she turns her ferocious stare on me. Her eyes narrow, and as I glance back at her, she's left with no choice but to force a smile as jealousy courses violently through her veins.

She leans toward her husband, resting her fingers along his wrist. "Please excuse me," she murmurs, keeping her tone low. "I need to use the restroom."

Giovanni nods and she rises from her seat before cutting her sharp glare across to me. "Shayne, dear. Won't you accompany me to the bathroom? What better chance for us to get to know one another? After all, it seems as though you might be around for a little while."

My heart stops as both Levi and Marcus clutch on to me from under the table. Roman's eyes harden while his body remains relaxed, all three of them determined not to show just how much her simple request disturbs them, but what choice do I have? Denying her will only throw suspicion my way.

I simply nod and rise from my seat. "Of course."

Ariana beams as though she's just won something and I slowly walk around the long table, my heart thundering as I'm forced to pass closely by Giovanni's back, way too close for liking. The three brothers watch my every step while trying to appear relaxed, but I see the rage burning in their eyes. They have no good reason to get up and follow me, and certainly no reason to trust Ariana.

The moment I break free from the table, Ariana steps into me, scooping my arm into hers and holding me close. "How wonderful," she beams at me, putting on a show. "You and I are going to be best friends."

We walk out of the dining hall, and the second we round the

corner, her fake smile fades away and the nerves settle deep into my stomach. We only get a few steps down the hall before she pulls me into a coat closet that's bigger than my apartment bedroom.

Ariana walks around me, her gaze shifting over my body. "Remove your dress," she demands, her tone expecting no complaints.

I scoff, raising my brow and stepping away from her while slowly turning, keeping her in sight at all times. "Like hell I'm about to strip down for you again."

Her eyes widen, looking at me as though I just kicked her puppy. "You know the deal, Shayne," she purrs, quickly recovering. "When we met, I did you a favor and now it is time for me to collect. I have been patiently waiting all night, but time is quickly wearing thin."

A grin tears across my face, and for a moment, she thinks she's got me exactly where she wants me. I step into her and she raises her chin, her eyes becoming hooded with desire. "You want me on my knees?" I murmur. "You want to feel my tongue working your clit as my fingers massage deep inside you? You want me to make you feel alive?"

"That was the deal," she whispers, gripping the material of her gown and beginning to scrunch it up between her fingers, showing off her long, toned legs.

I lean into her and roll my tongue over my bottom lip, watching the way she becomes mesmerized by the subtle movement. I lower my voice, my tone barely a whisper. "I will never get on my knees for you," I tell her. "You're nothing to me, just a whore who forced herself onto me during a party. I don't owe you anything."

"Excuse me?" she demands, pulling back from me as a wicked grin cuts across my face. "You knew the deal. I made myself clear. I don't give out favors for nothing."

"Except that you did," I tell her, stepping with her as she moves away. "I was alone and scared at that party. I was thrown into a world that I didn't understand and didn't know how to navigate. I was under the impression that those three brothers were looking for any excuse to end my life, so when you pressed up to Roman and demanded that you taste my pussy, I had no choice but to sit there and take it. Was it good? Yes. Did I make the most of it? Yes. But did I ask for it? Hell fucking no."

I pull back, walking back toward the door of the coat closet before glancing back at her shocked face. "You gave yourself willingly, so that's on you. I don't owe you for something that you forced on me," I tell her. "But if you're really that desperate to get fucked, perhaps you should spread your knees for your husband. I'm not even a little bit interested in getting involved in your bullshit games."

I pull the door open and go to step out when she races after me and shoves her hand against the door, forcing it closed. "Don't you see?" she questions. "You and I have to stick together. We're the same."

I laugh in her face. "You and I are nothing alike," I tell her. "You whore yourself out at parties and allowed yourself to be married off to a man like Giovanni DeAngelis. You're a dead man walking. What do you think is going to happen when he finds out that you attend all their parties and fuck everything with a pulse? Hell, it's pretty damn clear that you've been fucking his sons as well."

"You think I wanted this?" she screeches. "I was forced into this life just like you were. I allowed myself to get too close to Roman and Giovanni took me away to use as leverage over him."

"What?" I demand, my face scrunching up in confusion. "What are you talking about?"

Ariana lets out a frustrated sigh. "Do you not know anything?" she spits. "Roman and I were together in high school. He was everything to me. The only person who ever truly understood me, and while our relationship was toxic and dangerous, he always stood by me. Roman is my whole fucking world, and at one point, I was his too."

I suck in a gasp, my eyes going wide as I take it all in. She was his girlfriend in high school, probably the first girl he ever really cared for, and still to this day, they are close, despite everything that's gone down. But I guess that explains why she looks at him as though the sun shines out of his ass. So why the hell didn't he do anything about it? He just let his father take her away and then marry her to rub it in his face. "How the hell did you end up married to Giovanni?"

"Because that's just what Giovanni does," she says, not really giving me the answer I want to know. "When he sees the boys getting too close to someone, he finds a way to destroy it, just like he did to me. We were only sixteen when he took me away from Roman. He did the same to Felicity, only she wasn't so lucky as to get away with her life, and now you. What do you think is going to happen now that he's watched you sitting at his dining table, doting on his sons and giving them hope for a brighter future? I know you might think you're strong enough to change the system, but you're a nobody, just like me. I'm not the only dead man walking."

I let out a shaky breath, her words rocking me right to my core, but all I can do is stare back at her as she continues. "I fuck because it's all I've got. It's the only way that I can stab Giovanni in the back and it just happens that his sons love both a good fuck and screwing over their father. Fucking is a win-win situation for me, and if that makes me a whore, then so be it. But you, you might as well be fucking those boys right on the goddamn table. We're both playing a dangerous game, but you're the one rubbing it in his face."

Without another word, Ariana pushes past me and pulls the door open. She walks straight out without even a glance back at me as she leaves me standing here, my heart racing with fear.

It's a pattern. Giovanni has taken every girl that the boys have gotten close to. He took Roman's high school girlfriend and then killed Felicity right in front of their faces. If they were to get close to me like that … fuck. No wonder Roman has been keeping his distance and insisting his brothers do as well, though I can guarantee that's to save their heartbreak. He probably doesn't care all that much about my life.

If I were smart, I'd keep them at arm's length and be the perfect little house slave. I should move back down to the torture chamber and keep myself far away from them. Though, if they really cared for me, they'd let me go and send me somewhere their father would never find me.

My heart races with the fear of what's to come, and if I were anywhere but here, I'd hide out in this closet all night long, but the thought of being left alone in the DeAngelis mansion has me breaking out into a cold sweat.

I scurry out of the closet and make my way back to the dining hall, and despite it only being a few steps away, I can't help but watch my back, the nerves quickly getting the best of me. The dining hall looks just as I left it, people talking among themselves while waiters scurry around, desperate to make the night perfect for their boss, but the boys look anything but comfortable.

They speak quietly with their father, but they're all too aware that Ariana returned without me. All three of them glance my way as I hover near the entrance, relief settling over their ruggedly handsome faces as I make my way back to the table.

Keeping my gaze down and not drawing attention to myself, I drop back into my seat and shrug off the boys' touch as they attempt to take my hand under the table. Marcus looks at me with a concerned and suspicious stare but I immediately drop my gaze, determined not to give Giovanni another reason to want me dead.

"Why haven't you found this guy yet?" Giovanni says, continuing whatever conversation they were having before I came waltzing back in here like my life was hanging in the balance.

Oh wait. It is.

Roman shakes his head. "The dealer's gone quiet," he says, speaking to his father like he wasn't attempting to slaughter him only a few nights ago. "We don't know any more than you do."

Giovanni's hand comes slamming down so hard on the table that I feel the vibration traveling right through me, shaking the stray cutlery. "THAT'S NOT GOOD ENOUGH," he roars. "This asshole is undercutting me, stealing my customers right out from under my nose. It's bad for business. I NEED A FUCKING NAME."

I clench my jaw, forcing myself not to laugh in his goddamn face as the conversation I'd had with Levi in the club comes rushing back. The suppliers and dealers undercutting him are his own sons and I am so here for it. Hell, they're not just undercutting him, they're stealing his product as well. I don't know much about mafia business deals, but as far as screwing someone over goes, this one pretty much takes the cake.

Levi groans and leans back in his chair. "How do you expect us to get you a name when we're locked up? Give us some room to move and I'm sure we'll have a name for you by the end of the week. Hell, we might even take the motherfucker out for you."

Giovanni stares down his son, rage burning in his eyes, but he knows he's right. The boys have no hope of catching a guy if they're stuck in their castle. Not that there's anybody to actually catch, but something tells me that the boys have ways around their father.

"Fine," Giovanni finally says, making the men around him glance our way in concern. "You get free rein until the week is out and if you can't complete your mission before then, you will suffer the consequences."

"In that case," Roman says standing, his sharp stare slicing toward his father as a terrifying darkness sweeps through his eyes. "We better get going. We wouldn't want to miss our deadline."

Without another word, Levi and Marcus stand on either side of me, Marcus twisting his fingers around my elbow and pulling me up with him. Roman turns and stalks out of the room as the three of us follow along, dead silence in the room behind me.

I can't help but glance back, looking over the nervous faces of the guests who remain behind. "Are you sure?" I hear one man question Giovanni. "The last time your sons had free rein over the city …"

"There will be no repeats of last time," Giovanni snaps, his voice bouncing off the walls behind us as his gaze falls back on mine. "They know the consequences for stepping out of line. They wouldn't dare risk that again."

Marcus grips me tighter, practically dragging me out of the dining hall as he takes long strides to keep up with Roman. Not a word passes between us until we've flown down the impressive grand entrance and are pulling the doors of the SUV closed behind us.

The engine roars to life, and as Roman hits the gas, his hard stare meets mine through the rearview mirror. "What the hell did Ariana want?"

My brow arches. "That's not what's important," I rush out. "What the hell happened last time you assholes had free rein over the city? And why didn't you interrogate your father about your mom?"

"It wasn't the right time to ask about her, not during a business meeting. We need to be able to corner him first, and nothing happened last time we had free rein," Marcus explains. "It was just a simple misunderstanding. It's in the past. What did Ariana want?"

"Why is it important?" I question, glancing across at Levi. "She wanted me to get her off but I told her to get fucked." I let out a groan and glance back at Roman. "Why the hell didn't you tell me that she was your high school girlfriend? What the hell is going on here? Daddy

Dearest takes your girlfriend and then kills Felicity. Am I next?"

"Of course you're fucking next," he spits, tearing through the front gates, barely patient enough to wait for them to open the whole way. "Why do you think I've been so adamant that my brothers keep their dirty hands off you? He is going to use you against us. It's only a matter of time."

"But you're not going to let that happen, right?" I demand, glancing between them. "You were just a kid when he took Ariana from you. You can't let him take me like that."

Roman clenches his jaw as an uncomfortable silence fills the car and I realize that if it came down to it, they'd let me go. To them, the only thing that matters is sticking to their plans to overthrow the whole DeAngelis family. If Giovanni happens to get to me first, then that's my own bad luck.

"It's not going to happen," Marcus finally says. "Not yet at least. We still have time, and if we keep you off his radar, then it should be alright."

"You're full of shit."

"Well what would you like me to say?" he throws back at me, frustration swirling deep in his eyes. "He'll probably tear out your throat if you look at him the wrong way? For fuck's sake, babe. I'm trying to make this easier for you."

I let out a heavy sigh. "I should have fucked his wife when I had the chance."

Levi laughs before quickly smothering the grin that stretched across his face. The mood in the SUV immediately eases and I roll my eyes, glancing out the window as the world zooms past us. "Why are we rushing? You have all week to find this person who doesn't even exist. Why can't you just make up some random dealer and tell him that you killed him?"

"Why make one up when we can throw someone else under the bus?" Marcus says. "But that's not the reason we're rushing." My brows furrow as he glances back at me, his eyes sparkling with a sick excitement. A shiver travels down my spine. "We have a surprise for you, and if we don't get there soon, it might just be too late."

THIRTY-FOUR

Roman drives the SUV right around the back of the castle before pulling into what looks like an old parking garage. My brows furrow. "What in the ever-loving psycho bullshit is this?" I question as he slows his pace, heading down a steep ramp that puts us right below the old castle, only nothing about this looks old. It's probably one of the only parts of the castle that looks like a big gust of wind isn't going to tear it down. "I thought my torture chamber was underground."

"It is," Roman says, his headlights hitting the cold concrete walls and lighting our way down. "But this is even further underground."

"No shit," I breathe, scooting to the center seat to see better out the front windshield, my thigh pressing right up against Levi's. "What do you have down here?"

Marcus grins and looks back at me, his eyes sparkling dangerously. "All sorts of things, but only one that you need to know about."

I roll my eyes, already exhausted from the bullshit business dinner I just sat through. It's only been a few days since the attack. I'm tired and sore. I'd give anything to climb straight back in bed and pop a few more pills. I really don't have the patience for his twisted games tonight. "What's going on, Marcus?"

"Come on," he laughs. "Do you really think I'm going to ruin the surprise like that? You'll have to wait and see."

I groan and flop back into my seat, immediately regretting it as the pain shoots through my body. "Fuck, I can't do this right now. Just take me back up to the castle. I need some painkillers, a hot shower, and my bed. Can't we do this tomorrow?"

Roman just keeps driving, ignoring my pleas to turn back. "No painkillers," he says. "You're going to want a clear head for this."

"For what?" I ask, the nerves slowly seeping into my body the further down we go. The ramp winds deeper below ground and the further we go, the darker and creepier it gets. "How much further is it? This place is giving me the creeps."

"Really?" Marcus questions, glancing back at me, disappointment in his eyes. "This is my favorite place in the whole world. I thought you'd love it."

"Just how much were you guys messed up as kids?"

"You're not ready for an honest answer to that question," Levi says as Roman hits the bottom of the ramp and drives out into a wide-open space. He brings the SUV to a stop near the far wall and the three boys climb out.

I bail out of the SUV and watch as Roman strides toward the wall. He grabs a lever and pushes it up, and one by one, big overhanging lights flood through the dark room. "Welcome to our playground," Roman says with pride.

I stare in shock, my mouth hanging open as I take in the massive space. It's like a big concrete box with reinforced walls holding up the castle above it. Cells line either side of the creepy playground and as I scan over them, I count at least fifteen on either side.

There are private rooms complete with drainage systems and hoses to wash away evidence while heavy chains and hooks hang from the roof. "What the fuck is this?" I breathe, shivers rushing through my body and sending a cold sweat over my skin. "Is this some kind of slaughterhouse?"

"Majority of the time," Marcus says, that same wicked darkness flooding his gaze. "Though when it's not in use, it can hold some pretty epic parties."

I shake my head, not even remotely interested in an explanation. "Can we just ... do what you brought me down here to do?"

Roman nods and starts walking, heading toward the left side of the room to the line of wide cells. I follow behind him with Marcus and Levi stepping in behind me. "Does your father know about this?"

Levi sighs. "Unfortunately. It was supposed to be our little secret, but now he has his henchmen using our facilities and fucking up our tools. Fucking amateurs."

"Can't you stop them from coming in?"

"We did at first," Roman says. "But that didn't go down so well with Daddy Dearest. It's just easier this way, but we keep them on their toes. They're just as terrified to come here as the people they drag along with them. It's like a potluck. Which one of them will lose their lives?"

I swallow hard, crossing my arms over my chest. "You didn't go to many potlucks growing up, did you?"

Marcus glances my way, his brows furrowed as he tries to make sense of my comment, but his blank expression has an amused smile spreading across my face.

I look away as Roman comes to a stop in front of a wide cell that's as big as my old living room. "Here we are," he says, looking back at me and patiently waiting for me to catch up. I keep my gaze down, too afraid to look up and see what's inside the cell as I step into his side. "Consider this a peace offering for what happened with Lucas Miller."

Intrigue has my head slowly rising and my gaze settling on the man inside the cell. He dangles from heavy chains wearing nothing but a pair of stained underwear. Blood pools on the ground beneath him and slowly runs to the small drain at the back of the room.

He looks completely defeated, knowing without a doubt that he will never see the light of day again. My stomach churns as I take him in, regret settling deep inside my gut, but as he raises his head and his familiar blue eyes rest on mine, my heart constricts, aching with what to do.

Maxwell Mariano. My deadbeat father.

I stumble back a step, the very sight of him like a punch right to the gut. "What the hell is this?" I demand, unable to look away from my father as a slow smile spreads over his face.

"A peace offering," Marcus says, confusion lacing his tone. "What's the matter? I thought this is what you wanted? It's a gift."

"I …" I shake my head, horror sweeping through me. "You want me to kill him? My father?"

"You said you suffered years of abuse at his hands," Levi says. "You were made to eat out of dumpsters and fear for your life everyday living with him. He stole from you time and time again, and you just want to stand here and gape at him?"

My father laughs and spits a mouthful of blood onto the stained concrete. "She's too weak. She'll never do it."

Rage pours through me and I reach for the back of Roman's pants, gripping his gun and tearing it free. I point it right at my father's chest, the anger swirling through me like a wild tornado. "I'm only weak because you made me that way," I seethe. "I spent years running from you, funding your bullshit addictions while fearing that one day you would do something stupid like sell me to settle your debts, and look where we are now. I'm the one with these assholes standing at my back, not you."

Fear flashes in his eyes before he shrugs it off. "Doesn't matter who you've got standing at your back, sweetheart. You'll never pull the trigger. You don't got it in ya."

Tears well in my eyes as I fight the urge to do something I know will come back to haunt me. I fight between right and wrong, strength and weakness, honor and disgrace.

A lump forms in the back of my throat, making it nearly impossible to breathe. "You're a worthless piece of shit," I spit. "If I don't kill you now, Giovanni sure as hell will."

"You don't know shit about Giovanni."

"Really now?" I laugh. "I just spent the night at his mansion, sitting around his dinner table, listening to his plans on how he will destroy you. I was never in your life, so how the hell does selling me to his family pay your debt? All you've done for me is introduce me to three men who will shamelessly stand by my side as I tear you down. So, tell me, how have you spent your night?"

My father clenches his jaw and I step forward, not prepared to hear another word that comes out of his mouth. Giovanni was right, he is worthless, and as long as he lives, he will continue to come for me. He will destroy me until I have nothing more to give, and that will be on me for how I allow tonight to play out.

But he's also right, I don't have it in me to kill a man, whether it's my father or someone else. Maybe if I stay with the DeAngelis brothers long enough, that might change, but I'm not there yet. The thought of someone's blood being on my hands cripples me with fear.

My fingers curl around the latch of the cell and I pull it wide, grateful for the boys remaining behind as I stride into the cell. My father watches my every step, and as I move toward him, repulsion swirls heavily in my gut. "I might be weak," I tell him, "I might not be able to take a kill shot, but I can sure as hell make your life a living hell, just as you've done to mine."

His eyes widen and—*BANG*.

The bullet pierces right through his kneecap and a wave of satisfaction washes through me. I feel elated, on cloud fucking nine. Screw the painkillers and morphine smoothie, I'm fucking good.

My father's screams echo through the underground playhouse and just like that, I finally get it. I turn to the boys and smile as my father bleeds behind me. "The acoustics in here are incredible."

Marcus grins. "Like I said, we can still make a mafia wife out of you yet."

I roll my eyes and stride out of the cell before handing the gun straight back to Roman. He takes it without question as his eyes linger on mine, checking to see what part of my soul that just cost me. "I'm not like you guys," I tell them. "I cannot simply kill a man without losing myself in the process, and I can't stand here and ask you to do it on my behalf because that blood will still be on my hands."

I glance over at Levi and Marcus to make sure they're listening as intently as their older brother. "You're not to kill him under any circumstances. I forbid you to. I want to see him fear for his life the way he's done to me. I want him watching over his shoulder everywhere he goes. I want him to contemplate taking his own pathetic life every single night out of fear of his debts catching up to him. So tonight, you will not kill my father. You will throw him out with the wolves and he will fight for his life, and if he happens to die in the process, then that's on him. If he happens to live, then we will spend the rest of our lives haunting him like he fucking deserves."

And just like that, I walk away, hoping to God that I never have to see this man again.

THIRTY-FIVE

Leaning over the bathroom sink, I let my head hang limply. Did I really just shoot my father and leave him to the fucking wolves? Who the hell am I? I don't even recognize myself anymore, but one thing is for sure, when I saw him, I didn't run.

Every day the thought enters my mind; what would I do if I ever saw him again? And every time, I've told myself that I would pack up my shit and run as far as I could to escape his abuse. But, I didn't. I looked him in the fucking eye and proved once and for all who the weak one of the family really is.

Tonight I faced my fears and I feel more alive than ever before, but what did it just cost my soul?

Had I hung around and spoke with the boys about it, I'm sure they would have told me that there's no such thing as a soul. They wouldn't believe in that shit, and maybe that's the outlook I need to have on life in order to survive in their world. Sooner or later, I'm going to be faced with a situation that will destroy what's left of me, and my guilty conscience is going to be my downfall.

I let out a heavy sigh and splash water over my face, but my mind just can't settle. The image of my father dragging himself through the thick woods surrounding the castle won't leave my head, blood spilling from his knee as the wolves capture his scent. There's no way he could survive that.

There's no doubt in my mind that he will die tonight, and if he does … fuck. I don't want to think about that either. But what worse could he do to me? I've already been sold to the most dangerous man in the country and gifted to his psychopathic sons. Though, I'm not going to lie, the more time I spend with them, the more I'm starting to feel right at home here. Except for the creepy torture basement and dungeon shit they've got going on. Not to mention, the whole locked up vibe really isn't meshing well with my free spirit.

Turning off the faucet, I turn and make my way out of the bathroom, flipping off the light as I pass. Marcus sits on the end of my bed and I pause, leaning against the frame of the bathroom door, the exhaustion already getting to me.

His eyes are filled with something I can't quite make out, but what I can tell is that it's deep. I shake my head, glancing away from his heavy gaze. "Did you leave him to the wolves?"

"Yeah," he says, tilting his head in that creepy way I've become so immune to as his eyes darken with something sinister. "Something like that."

A chill runs down my spine and I quickly realize that I don't want to know what their version of leaving him to the wolves really means. "Okay," I say, shaking my head, seeing him watching me with concern, having only just finished washing the blood splatter off my body and throwing my destroyed dress into the hamper. The thought of talking it through makes me want to hurl. "It's over. I don't want to talk about it."

Marcus stands and slowly walks toward me, hovering over me and making it impossible to look anywhere but right into his dark, seductive eyes. "I don't want to talk," he tells me, his low tone vibrating right through my chest. "I want to make you feel."

My brow arches as heat swirls deep in the pit of my stomach. His hand falls to my bare waist as I stand before him in nothing but a cropped tank and black Brazilian panties. "I don't know," I murmur, desperately wanting what he can offer, but knowing that my body simply can't keep up with him, not tonight at least. "I need to rest. I'm sore and woozy. I think I need another hit of morphine and sleep."

He shakes his head, a wicked grin pulling at his lips. "I've got something better for you."

My brows furrow as Marcus' hand falls to mine and he gently pulls me across my room. I follow blindly, trusting him with my body despite my better judgment. His fingers are skilled far beyond anything I could ever comprehend and could take my life within seconds, yet when he touches me, I know that he will never hurt me. At least not at this very moment. When it comes down to it, if it were a choice between me or one of his brothers, it would be my life ending that night.

He leads me to the edge of my bed and turns me so that the front of my thighs are gently brushing up against the soft mattress. He steps in behind me, his fingers sailing over my skin, moving down until they're hooked into the edges of my panties.

Marcus draws them down my legs, being careful not to allow the flimsy lace to touch any of my stitches. They fall to my feet and I step out of them before gently kicking them under the bed. His hand immediately presses back to my waist as I lean against his wide chest, his wicked scent overwhelming my senses in the best way.

Wetness floods between my legs, and despite the exhaustion weighing me down, I know that I won't be able to resist anything that he's willing to give me.

His other hand curves around my waist and slips under the hem of my tank, sailing up my body until his fingers are skimming over my nipple. He gently pinches it and I suck in a breath, pressing my back harder against his chest.

I slowly raise my arms and he doesn't hesitate, pulling my tank over my head. He does it with ease, not catching on a single stitch, unlike me who just spent over five minutes trying to get the bastard on.

Marcus presses against my back, pushing my torso down. My hands shoot out and catch myself against my mattress as Marcus' hand skims over my ass. "Have you ever tried E?" he questions, making me peer back over my shoulder to watch the way his darkened gaze sweeps over my exposed ass.

My brows furrow, having absolutely no idea where he's going with this. "I mean, I tried it in high school but it's not like I really knew what I was doing."

He nods and glances toward the bedside table where a small packet of white pills sits right in the center beside a mess of powder, telling me exactly what he's been doing in here while waiting for me to finish in the bathroom.

I feel his fingers between my legs, mixing with my arousal and dragging it up toward my ass. "Spread them wider," he tells me, the desire and nerves pooling deep in my gut as I try to figure out what the hell is about to happen.

"What are you doing?" I breathe as his fingers come back to my pussy and slowly push inside, making my eyes roll as a soft groan slips from between my lips.

"Making you feel," he tells me. "Do you trust me?"

I shake my head, looking back over my shoulder and meeting his heated stare. "Hell no."

His returning grin is everything I need, and damn it, the sparkle in his eye tells me that he knows I'm lying. Only unlike any other man, this one right here loves it when I lie to him. "Good," he mutters, pushing deeper into my pussy and slowly massaging my walls, making me feel something real for the first time in days.

He slowly pulls his fingers out of me and a soft cry escapes my lips as he drags his fingers up past my ass before he completely releases me.

Curiosity gets the best of me and I watch as he dips his glistening fingers into the white powder and meets my eyes. Nerves begin to take over as I start to figure out exactly what he plans on doing with that powder, and damn, if someone told me I'd be doing this a few weeks ago, I would have laughed in their face. But, I'm not going to lie, the thrill is exciting me like never before. I've never done anything like this and I don't know how my body is going to react to the drug, but I've never been so down.

Not once does he take his eyes off mine as he reaches down and presses his fingers against my hole, slowly pushing them deep inside. A breathy gasp slips from between my lips and I push back against him, the pressure just right.

His fingers move gently within me before he slowly pulls them out and curls his other arm back around my waist. He pulls me up until I'm standing and turns me to face him. "The high hits faster this way," he tells me. "Give it a minute, and I promise, everything bad is going to slip away and all you'll be left with is the high of feeling my touch all over your body."

Well damn.

His hands roam over my skin, leaving a trail of goosebumps in their wake and I moan, already slipping into the effects of his touch against my body. Though, something tells me that has absolutely nothing to do with the E he just inserted into my ass.

Marcus leans into me, his lips pressing down over my collarbone as he pushes against my waist, forcing me back a step until the backs of my knees are pressing against the bed. He keeps going, stepping with me until I drop down on the edge of the mattress, my hand slipping under his shirt and feeling the warmth of his toned body beneath.

He drops to his knees while pushing mine apart and my eyes roll, the anticipation already getting the best of me. Marcus meets my eyes, the intoxicating smirk playing on his lips telling me that he might be even more excited about this than I am.

"Lean back," he tells me, that deep tone hitting me in all the right places. "I don't want you to do anything. Just feel."

Well, damn. What's a girl to do?

I lean back onto my elbows and I can't resist dropping my head back too. The sweetest sensation ripples across my skin as his lips roam over my body, his fingers touching me in all the right places as he slowly makes his way down south.

My eyes grow heavy just as his lips close over my clit, and the moment I feel his warm tongue working its magic, a sense of euphoria pulses through my veins. "Oh my God," I breathe, knowing without a doubt that the white powder has made its way into my bloodstream and is making me feel more alive than ever before.

My body becomes heavy as I allow my eyes to close and consume me with darkness. Marcus works my clit and I groan low as my back arches, desperately needing to feel him all over me, but I don't dare ask him to move because what he's doing down there is nothing short of magic.

I feel his smile against my pussy and in the same moment, his thick fingers push up into my throbbing cunt, instantly easing the burning ache deep inside of me. "Fuck, Marcus," I breathe, not willing to ruin this moment by screaming out.

I've never been so fucking relaxed in my life. I feel as though I can do anything, like I'm floating above the clouds, the only thing keeping me grounded is the devil between my legs. It's like the perfect mix of heaven and hell. Good versus evil. Right versus oh so damn wrong.

Peering down at Marcus, I watch as his tongue moves over my clit before his mouth closes around it and sucks hard. My whole body shudders with overwhelming pleasure and I groan, even more so when he curls his fingers inside of me and finds that one spot that has my head falling back all over again.

"Holy shit," I breathe, my chest rising and falling with rapid movements, euphoria filling me like never before. I've never experienced Marcus like this. He's usually the hard and fast type, the *chain me to a fucking hook and suspend me while he slams into me* type. He likes to see his fingers bruised on my hips in the morning, but this softer side of him is something else entirely, and I won't ever get enough of it.

My pussy clenches and I reach down, knotting my fingers into his hair and holding on for the ride. It's incredible, breath-taking, and relentless in all the best ways. He doesn't dare stop and I cry out, desperate for a sweet, sweet release.

I feel so fucking alive. So relaxed and aware. It's as though I can feel the power of my blood pulsing through my veins, strengthening me and making me feel like I can do anything. Is this what it's really like? Ecstasy has such a bad name, surely it couldn't be this good? Or perhaps this is all Marcus.

Damn. Whatever it is, I'm so down for it.

Marcus flicks his tongue over my clit one more time and it's all

I need to throw me over the edge. My pussy clenches hard around his thick fingers before turning me into a spasming mess. My world detonates and I see stars behind my eyes. "Oh, fuck, Marcus. Yes."

He doesn't stop, letting me ride out my high on his fingers as his tongue continues curling against my clit. He sucks a little harder and I cry out, the intensity almost too much for me to handle.

Once I come down from my high, Marcus releases my clit from between his skilled lips and stands, a proud as fuck smirk playing on his lips. "How are you feeling?" he questions, his warm eyes hooded with desire, and sending a wave of need pulsing through me.

My tongue rolls over my bottom lip and I don't doubt that he sees the hunger in my eyes. "Like I could go all night," I murmur, my voice low and full of seduction.

His eyes bore into mine and they only get darker as he reaches for his belt buckle and tears it from his pants in one easy flick of his wrist. "That's exactly what I wanted to hear."

I bite down on my lip, the excitement growing deep inside of me as I watch him shrug out of his shirt, showing off his impressive tattoos. A soft gasp slips from between my lips. I'd forgotten about the girl he has marked across his ribs with the diamond dimple.

I can't help but reach out and run my fingers along his warm skin, watching the way he sucks in a breath, not used to such a personal touch. I glance up and meet his heated stare. "Who is she?" I question.

He shakes his head. "You don't want to do this right now."

"I do," I insist.

He watches me for a short moment before his hand comes down

over mine on his ribs. "That's Flick," he tells me. "She was my best friend and meant the world to me. She was in love with Roman, but there's no denying that she felt something for me and Levi as well. It wasn't the same though, she belonged to him."

A pang of jealousy flashes through me and I'm left wondering if he would ever care for me like that. My finger brushes over the small diamond piercing. "She had dimples."

"Yeah," he grins, his eyes brightening with the overwhelming fondness that he had for her. "She was fucking gorgeous."

Marcus comes down over me, curling his arm around my waist and effortlessly scooting me up the bed. My head comes down on the pillow as his eyes linger on mine. "You don't feel for me what you felt for her."

He shakes his head, the raw honesty darkening something deep in my soul. "No, I don't," he says, momentarily killing me inside. "What I feel for you is something different, something more that I haven't quite figured out yet."

His lips come down on mine and I sink into his touch, barely getting a chance to make sense of the admission that just came falling from between his sweet lips. It's the first time that one of the brothers has kissed me and it has a world of emotion swirling through my chest. My arms raise and curl around his neck as his tongue slips inside my mouth, letting me taste my lingering arousal.

I moan into him as he reaches down around me and takes my thigh before pulling it up over his hip so he can do whatever the fuck he wants down there without hurting me.

His lips drop to my neck and my head tips back, the pure elation filling my veins like nothing I've ever experienced before. His touch is magical and his kiss is everything. I find myself holding on just a little bit tighter, terrified that if I were to let go, this feeling of euphoria would slip away with him.

"Marcus?" I breathe.

"Mmmm?" he murmurs against my sensitive skin.

"That night in the industrial area when you castrated Draven Miller …"

"What about it?" he rumbles, caution filling his tone.

I knot my fingers into his hair, forcing his head up to meet my hooded stare. "When I first got here, you would refer to me as *mine* to your brothers, like I was some kind of property. But that night in that old warehouse when you were talking to Draven, you said *'Do you know what happens to a man who spits filthy words at my girl.'* It was different, Marcus. *My girl* isn't property, that's something more … something real."

His stare narrows, but doesn't harden like I expect. "That was nearly two weeks ago, Shayne. You've been holding onto that question for that long?"

My gaze drops away as embarrassment filters through me. "Forget I said anything. I'm probably just reading into something that isn't there."

"Oh, it's fucking there, babe," he says. "But don't be fooled. Being my girl isn't going to be the same as being with some ordinary dickhead that you meet in the club. Living in my world is nothing like trying to survive it. Can you cut it?"

I swallow hard, knowing exactly what he's trying to ask me—am I strong enough to not only survive with him, but to thrive and fucking love it. I nod, "Yeah," I tell him, a small smile pulling at the corners of my lips. "Just say the word and I'll fucking blow you all away."

Marcus' lips drop straight back to mine and within moments, he reaches down between us and guides his thick cock inside me, pushing further and further, taking his sweet time until he's completely seated inside of me.

My head tips back as a deep groan tears through me. He's too good, too fucking much. He's like the devil who sits upon your shoulder, promising you all the wicked deliciousness that you could possibly handle. Only, he gives more and watches with delight as your system overloads with satisfaction, pushing you until you explode.

It's everything.

He starts moving, soft and gentle while pushing deep and overwhelming me with pleasure. In and out with skilled precision as his fingers touch, brush, and pinch, sending waves of electricity pulsing through my veins and making me feel like the only girl in the world.

"Fucking hell," he mutters, his gaze shifting over my pebbled nipples. "So fucking responsive."

"That's all you," I tell him, biting down on my lip. "I've never been like this with anyone, never felt my body burning with life, not until I experienced what it truly meant to be with a real man."

Fuck Tarzan back in my trash can. Nothing will ever compare to this.

Marcus' hand drops to my thigh as he starts to pick up his pace. This isn't his usual style and it shows by the determination on his face. He's used to hard and fast, but this soft side isn't just surprising me, it's rocking right through his system and pushing him to the edge, threatening to throw him right into the pits below, and he fucking loves it.

His fingers tighten on my thigh and my back arches off the mattress, pressing my tits up against his chest. "Fuck, Marcus. I'm going to come."

He slams deep inside of me, forcing a gasp from between my lips. "Not fucking yet, you're not," he says through a clenched jaw as my thigh hitches higher over his hip and somehow forces him deeper.

I groan, that familiar burning building stronger and stronger within me. My nails dig into his back and the rumble that vibrates through his chest nearly kills me. He's everything. How could I possibly consider running away from this place when I can be treated like a fucking queen right here in my bed?

His thrusts get faster, his jaw clenching tighter as his hand drops from my thigh to my ass and grabs one hell of a handful. He squeezes and I throw my head back again, every nerve in my body on fire.

My pussy clenches around him and I know deep in my soul that I can't possibly hold on much longer. "Marcus," I breathe, the desperation filling my tone. "I can't … I need to come."

He grunts and adjusts his hold on me, slipping his hand between our bodies until his skilled fingers are pressing down over my clit. He rubs tight little circles, bringing me closer and closer. "FUCK," I pant, my chest rising and falling with rapid movements.

I dig my nails in harder and his eyes roll with pleasure. "Come now," he demands. "I want to feel your tight little pussy squeezing me."

His words are my undoing and I come hard, my orgasm exploding through me, curling my toes and forcing my eyes shut. I clench them tight as the walls of my pussy turn into a quivering mess, shattering and convulsing wildly.

"Aw, fuck. That's it," Marcus groans just as I feel his hot cum shooting deep inside of me. He doesn't dare stop moving, letting me ride out my high as my orgasm continues to overwhelm me.

I curl my arms around him and pull myself up until my lips are pressed right against his. He kisses me deeply, lowering both our bodies back to the mattress as we come down from our high together, and only then does he roll to the side, pulling out of me and dropping onto the sheets beside me.

Marcus pulls me into his arms and holds me beside him, my chest constricting with this odd new need to be close to him. I drop my head to his chest, listening to the sweet sound of his heart beating within, fearing that the moment he gets up and walks out the door, this will all be gone.

THIRTY-SIX

Unease settles into my stomach and my eyes pop open, taking in the darkness that swirls around my bedroom. It was well past two in the morning when Marcus fell asleep beside me, but I've spent the last few hours staring at the darkened ceiling, watching as the moonlight slowly trails across my bedroom.

I haven't been able to sleep. Maybe it's the aftereffects of the drugs or perhaps it's this weird vibe Marcus and I have got going on. I don't understand it. It's as though someone flipped a switch inside of him and suddenly that hard exterior faded away, leaving me with the raw and honest version of himself, the one that doesn't hold anything back. Hell, he made comments about becoming a mafia wife last night and that sentence hasn't left my head since.

I am no mafia wife. I'd be shot within the first few hours. I consider myself to be more of a mafia boss. I don't take orders from anyone, nor do I give in. At least I try to be that strong. In reality, I'm a scared little bitch who runs from everything. But, I feel that changing. I feel myself evolving, and if I stay here long enough, nothing will be able to hold me down, not even the three men who stormed through my apartment in the middle of the night.

I drop my head away from the moonlight, glancing across my room as Marcus sleeps soundly beside me, only as I do, a dark shadow cuts across my vision.

I suck in a gasp, my eyes going wide. The shadow disappears and I sit up, my gaze shifting around the room. I blink rapidly, rubbing at my eyes and searching for the shadow, but there's nothing there.

I must be seeing things, but I was so sure. It felt so real.

My heart races and the unease in my stomach only gets worse, more defined, telling me that something isn't right. My hand falls to Marcus' chest and as my fingers start to dig into his skin to wake him, the shadow steps out in front of me. "I wouldn't do that if I were you."

A soft, feminine whisper flows through my bedroom as the shadow steps forward into the moonlight. A dark hood covers her face, flowing down into a long, floor-length cloak, but I see long strands of dirty blonde hair peeking out from underneath. Her head remains down, concealing her eyes. "Who are you?" I rush out, shrinking back toward Marcus, more than ready to scream this place down if that's what it takes.

"You're a fool, Shayne Mariano," she tells me. "A blind fool."

"How do you know who I am?"

Her hand slips inside her cloak and my eyes widen in fear as she pulls a gun. "You're going to run," she says. "You're going to run and never come back here. There's a car in the driveway with money and a passport in the glovebox. The door is unlocked. Get out of here before they do to you what they did to me."

"Excuse me?" I breathe, trying to peer beneath her hood. "Who are you? What who did? Their father? Giovanni?"

"Now," she demands. "I will not ask again. Go before it's too late. You don't have time."

I shake my head, not trusting this woman one bit. "No, I'm safer here," I tell her, knowing deep in my gut that the only place I will ever find freedom is within the walls of this old castle. My gaze flicks to her gun, terrified of what she might do with it, but I'm standing my ground. This is my new home. No one could protect me from their father like they can. "The boys will protect me."

She steps closer, her gun raising toward my head. "But who will protect you from them?"

I swallow hard, my hands shaking in my lap.

"Stand," she demands, her tone so low that I barely hear it.

The authority in her tone has me cautiously getting to my feet and as I do, I get a small glimpse of the woman hidden beneath the cloak. Her face is scarred and dirty and her lifeless blue eyes look as though she's ready to turn the gun on herself. "Who are you?" I question again.

"Last warning," she spits. "They're not yours. Go now, or you'll leave me no choice but to make you run."

They're not yours.

Who the fuck is this?

I shake my head, the determination pulsing wickedly through my veins. "No. I'm not going anywhere," I demand. "You don't scare me. You're just a bitch in a cloak. There's nothing you can do to me that they haven't already done."

"Have it your way," she says before turning the gun on Marcus as he lays peacefully in my bed. "You leave me no choice."

I dive toward her. "NOOOOOOO," I scream, Marcus' eyes snapping open and looking right at me.

BANG!

The bullet plunges deep into his chest as I body check the girl into the ground and tear the gun right out of her goddamn hands. Marcus groans and I find myself flying up from the floor, scrambling across the bed to get to him. His eyes are wide and blood pours from the bullet hole in his chest. "MARCUS," I cry, tears filling my eyes as I drop the gun to the bed and try to press down on his chest.

His eyes grow heavy, the blood pooling over my fingers as Levi comes barging into the room. "WHAT DID YOU DO?" he roars, gaping at his brother in horror.

I look up, violently shaking my head. "No, I …" my eyes flash around the room but the hooded girl is nowhere to be seen. "It wasn't me. I didn't. I …"

"MOVE," he roars, barging into the room and scrambling to get to his brother. He grabs me by the arm and throws me across the room before shoving his hands down hard on his brother's chest. "DON'T YOU FUCKING DIE ON ME, MARC."

Panic sets in and I find myself creeping back toward the door.

He thinks I did it.

He thinks I'm responsible for killing his brother.

If Marcus dies, I'm fucking dead. They won't stop to ask questions or give me the benefit of the doubt. I'm their number one enemy.

The woman's words circle my head as I continue backing up, my eyes wide and my heart racing. *'Go now, or you'll leave me no choice but to make you run.'* She knew exactly what she was doing.

My back slams against the frame of my bedroom door and as my eyes focus on Marcus and see his life slipping away, I know that without a doubt, my days are limited.

I have to run.

Levi's gaze snaps up and seeing that decision in my eyes, fury tears through him. He reaches for the gun in a flash of lightning and I don't dare look back. I race from the room just as another bullet plunges deep into the doorframe, right where I'd been standing only a moment ago.

My feet slam against the old floors, racing through the fucking castle like a bat out of hell. I hit the stairs in no time, fumbling down them as the fear rockets through my body. My heart thunders in my chest, beating faster than ever before.

I have to get the fuck out of here.

I reach the lobby and race toward the massive front door, feeling the stitches in my legs pulling and splitting apart. She said the door was open.

"WHERE THE FUCK IS SHE?" I hear Roman's furious roar tearing through the castle, telling me that he's seen exactly what Levi has, and unlike Levi, his hands aren't buried deep inside his brother's chest.

"SHE'S RUNNING."

FUCK.

Fuck. Fuck. Fuck. Fuck.

I'm dead.

My clammy hands grip onto the door handle and I tear it open as I hear Roman bounding through the castle, flying over handrails like a fucking ninja and dropping down levels with ease as he tears after me.

I break out into the cold night, the chilly breeze slamming upon my skin like a wicked assault as rain pours down around me, but I push through it, skipping down the grand entrance steps two at a time. I can barely see shit and it's not lost on me that both my father and the wolves should be out here somewhere.

I see the car in the distance but Roman is quickly gaining on me. I have to reach it before he reaches me. It's my only hope.

Hitting the bottom of the stairs, I run toward the car with rain pelting down against my face, hearing Roman breaking through the door at the top. "STOP," he roars, seeing my perfect getaway. "I WILL HUNT YOU DOWN FOR THIS."

No. No, no, no, no.

Grabbing hold of the car door, I tear it open and throw myself into the driver's seat. More than aware that this thing could be traced, just like the fucking tracker in my arm, but I have to try. I'll tear that thing out of my arm with my teeth if that's what it takes.

The key rests in the ignition and my nerves become recklessly wild in the bottom of my gut as I turn the key and kick over the engine. It takes precious seconds that I don't have, and as I release the brake and put the car into drive, I glance into my rearview mirror to find Roman barreling after me, the stairs long behind him.

"FUCK."

I hit the gas and take off like a fucking raging lunatic. The tires screech on the wet pavement and I quickly lose control as the back tires skid out to the side. Roman stops behind me and just when I think I've made the perfect getaway, I glance into my rearview mirror one last time and watch with horror as Roman pulls a gun.

Laying onto the gas, the car jolts forward and I struggle to maintain control. "No, please. NO," I cry, my eyes filled with unshed tears.

BANG!

A loud *pop* echoes through the night as Roman's bullet pierces through my back tire. The car skids and quickly breaks into an uncontrollable spin before hitting the edge of the driveway and launching into the sky.

I scream out, my hands slamming against the door to try and brace myself as it flips once, twice then three times before finally coming to a smoking stop on the manicured grass.

Blood pours from my head as a horrendous pain tears through my stomach. My vision blurs and black spots threaten to blind me but my fight isn't over yet. I blink, my head spinning as I glance down to the thick shard of glass protruding from my stomach.

"No," I cry, blinking into the dark and quickly realizing that the whole fucking car is crushed around me, upside down and leaving me absolutely no escape. My hand presses against my stomach, trying to hold the shard of glass still as my elbow slams against the broken window beside me, clearing a path.

Grabbing hold of the window frame, I pull myself out of the wreckage and scramble out onto the grass, sharp cries of pain tearing from deep in my throat. The car headlights shine back toward the castle as I hear the distant sound of a wolf's loud howl.

Roman stands in the light, the gun hanging loosely at his side as he slowly stalks toward me, his eyes silently telling me that I am out of chances. I scurry back on the grass, the protruding glass making it nearly impossible to move away as blood pours from my stomach. "No," I cry, violently shaking my head as he approaches the wrecked car. "I didn't do it. It wasn't me."

Step by step, my life quickly fades out of my reach.

His expression hardens, betrayal thick in his eyes as I pull back just a little bit more, the rain pouring down around me and washing the blood down the side of my face. "Please," I beg. "It wasn't me."

One final step and he stands above me, and with fire burning in his eyes, he raises the gun.

"ROMAN. NO."

BANG!

PSYCHOS

THANKS FOR READING

If you enjoyed reading this book as much as I enjoyed writing it, please consider leaving an Amazon review to let me know.
https://www.amazon.com/dp/B099QHCBPC

STALK ME

Facebook Page
www.facebook.com/SheridanAnneAuthor
Facebook Reader Group
www.facebook.com/SheridansBookishBabes
Instagram
www.instagram.com/Sheridan.Anne.Author

OTHER SERIES

www.amazon.com/Sheridan-Anne/e/B079TLXN6K

YOUNG ADULT / NEW ADULT DARK ROMANCE

The Broken Hill High Series | Haven Falls | Broken Hill Boys | Aston Creek High | Rejects Paradise | Boys of Winter | Depraved Sinners

NEW ADULT SPORTS ROMANCE

Kings of Denver | Denver Royalty | Rebels Advocate

CONTEMPORARY ROMANCE (standalones)

Play With Fire | Until Autumn (Happily Eva Alpha World)

URBAN FANTASY - PEN NAME: CASSIDY SUMMERS

Slayer Academy

Printed in Great Britain
by Amazon